ANCIENT VAMPIRE DEATH CULTS AND OTHER ANNOYANCES

VAMPIRE INNOCENT

BOOK TWELVE

MATTHEW S. COX

DIVISION ZERO PRESS

CONTENTS

TRACERS

Weird has become my new ordinary, and it's usually pretty fun—except when little balls of fiery death are whizzing past my head.

Know what's pretty cool? Vampire reflexes seemingly slowing down time to the point bullets look like laser bolts straight out of *Star Wars*. Know what's considerably *less* cool? Watching those glowing bullets creep through a cloud of floating white bits from the headrest of the car seat I'm presently occupying. Fortunately, the vampires chasing us aren't terribly good at shooting. The orange streak passing two inches from my ear had to be luck. Bet they're using a PlayStation controller instead of a keyboard and mouse.

Trust me, Sierra and I have gotten into long debates about it. Mouse wins, no contest.

Also in the car with me is Holden Marston, several bullets, and a giant pile of unanswered questions, plus whatever this odd fluffy lump on the floor by my foot is. Probably a bit of stuffing from the back seat. Oh, and some weird-ass giant vase thing my new associate decided we *had* to steal.

Who's Holden?

A bullet clanks into the door on my side.

He's a co-worker, basically. There's nothing between us other than smoke and bits of foam.

So, umm, both good and bad are going on at the moment. In the good column: this isn't my car, so any damage it suffers won't get me in trouble with the 'rents. Also, Arthur Wolent didn't sound too fond of the vampires chasing us, so it's also unlikely we'll get in trouble with him for stealing the thing in the back seat. Item three in the 'good' column is no bullets have hit me yet. The car is, alas, down several windows, a few big chunks of seat foam, and the driver side mirror.

In the bad column, the weird vase in the back seat is giving off some seriously dark vibes. I don't mean vibes in a hippie or pothead sense. The thing is legit radiating evil. It kinda reminds me of a worse version of my Uncle Hank. They're both full of hatred and malice but stuck sitting wherever someone puts them, largely powerless to act on their contempt for the world at large. Also under 'bad,' I'm pretending to adult by wearing a skirt suit, hose, and heels. Makes me feel like a twelve-year-old playing dress up. Also, if I ever get my hands on a time machine, the first thing I'm going to do is find whoever came up with the idea to put a stick on the heel of women's shoes and stab them with one.

Tires shriek as we swing around a hard left turn, running a red light and nearly mowing down two people. The ass end of the Caddy swings wide, dragging us to the side and costing us a little speed. A dull *thump* in the back makes me picture the giant vase attempting to break out and run away.

"Careful!" I shout. "You almost ran two people over!"

"It's fine," says Holden, calm as anything. "They're hipsters. No one would notice."

I glare at him.

A bullet pings off the roof close to me. More people outside scream. It's nothing short of astounding we don't have half the police in Seattle following us already. Good thing—for them. So weird. It's almost as if the cops know when vampires are doing stuff and stay away. Wouldn't surprise me if the local elders have influence over the police and mortal government, but getting them to ignore a car chase with gunfire downtown is a bit much.

"What?" Holden looks at me, all innocence. "Did you hear about the one hipster who tried to sue a place for using his photo without permission in a satirical thing that said all hipsters look alike, and it turned out not to even be his picture?"

"They're still people, Holden. You can't randomly run them over."

The side mirror on my door explodes from a bullet strike.

"Gah!" I jump like my kid brother snuck up on me and popped a paper bag. "Why are they shooting at us?"

Holden accelerates, weaving around slower cars and going into the oncoming lane. "Because it's difficult to use claws in the middle of a car chase when you're not in the same car as the vampire you want to hurt."

We screech back into our lane and whip around a right turn. My ability to fly is the only reason I don't end up in Holden's lap. Maybe I should put my seatbelt on. Nah. If we crash, getting flung out the window is preferable to being trapped inside a burning wreck. It's way easier to heal broken bones than cremation.

As soon as the G forces relax, I stare at him. "You know what I meant."

"Honestly…" Holden shrugs. "I'm not sure what you meant."

This guy. I swear.

I've only known him for like an hour, and the urge to slap him is almost irresistible. Yes, he's that annoying. At least he hasn't treated me like a child. He's merely sarcastic, relatively callous about the lives of mortals, and it's entirely his fault I'm stuck in the middle of a car chase.

"We're out in public. They could hit someone."

He says, "hold on" as calmly as if asking if I want cream in my coffee, then drives up onto the sidewalk, skirting around a bunch of cars stopped for a red light and cutting the corner to make a turn. We hit three people. A woman slides off the hood into the road on the left. Two guys smash the windshield before bouncing up over the roof and rolling off the trunk.

Thankfully, we aren't going too fast and all three people get right back up.

Once he straightens out on the road again, Holden checks the center mirror. "Fairly sure the ones chasing us aren't terribly concerned if they hit bystanders."

"Neither are you."

He sighs. "We weren't even doing twenty miles an hour. Hardly the same as being shot."

"A car chase is bad enough, but shooting? It's going to get the police involved, which is only going to be an enormous pain in the butt for everyone. Besides, bullets don't really work on vampires too well."

A streak of orange zips between us. The center mirror explodes.

I duck down in my seat. "Unless they hit us in the head. Ugh, when you said 'a chance of mild disagreement,' I expected an argument. Maybe shouting. Possibly a fistfight. Not this *Last Action Hero* BS."

Holden stomps on the gas to beat a yellow light. "When in the history of bad people doing bad things has anyone ever stopped because someone asked nicely? Did you honestly think they were going to leave the area because we asked?"

Grr.

The car chasing us—*not* a Cadillac, by the way—rams us from behind. My face bounces off the glove compartment. Wow, genuine leather. Nice. Yeah, there's no way a giant Caddy is going to outrun or outmaneuver a... whatever they're driving. It's some kind of muscle car, but not an antique. Like a boxy Camaro or a Charger or something, one of those new cars trying to look like an old car. Smaller, faster, more agile. I'm not sure what the hell Holden's plans are. Unless they run out of gas before we do, this luxury land boat isn't going to be able to get away.

From the sound of the engine, we're going way over the speed limit.

"Please tell me you're not doing 110 in downtown Seattle."

"I'm not." Holden smiles at me. "We're doing 120 in downtown Everett."

"Oh, that's so much better." I climb back up into the seat. If we hit something, I want to fly out the windshield. Better yet, if I see a collision coming, I'm launching myself out the window *before* the crash. "At least they stopped shooting at us."

Holden points a thumb back over his shoulder. "Because they're shooting at the police."

I bite my lip. In another world where girls like me remained blissfully unaware of vampires, imps, demons, and all the other craziness now part of my life, seeing cops show up while I'm stuck in a car being shot at would have been awesome. Now? I feel bad because the cops are going to get hurt trying to interfere in something they have no business getting involved with. As my dad would say, they're a party of level one characters trying to kill a beholder.

Sure, mortals *can* be a threat to vampires, but it takes preparation, equipment, and a bunch of luck.

Looks like he's gotten us onto a highway, probably 529. We're stuck on a two-lane bridge crossing the Snohomish River. The red Camaro is like twenty car-lengths behind us, unable to get closer due to slower traffic. Two vampires hang out the windows, firing handguns at several police cruisers behind them. Okay, I've played *Grand Theft Auto*. Looks like we're about on level two wanted. Won't be long before the cops have a helicopter coming after us. This crap needs to de-escalate like *right now* before anyone dies. Problem being, I have no idea how to do it. Can't exactly jump out of the car and fly into a claw fight with dozens of witnesses and police dash cameras capturing it all. Video of me streaking out of the medical examiner's building caused enough problems. I really need to thank the gods of cameras for making all security video footage so damn blurry. Ever notice how every time there's a 'paranormal activity caught on video' posted to YouTube, the resolution is crap? Wonder if it's on purpose. Also, a flying leap onto their car would almost certainly end with me taking a bullet in the forehead. Won't kill me directly, but it's a semantic point. I doubt those vampires are going to leave my body alone long enough to heal.

Squealing tires and the *whump* of metal against metal make me look back again.

Multiple bystander vehicles spin out like bumper cars on ice. My guess is, the vampires chasing us shot out a few tires, creating a roadblock to trap the police. Headlights flash sideways from a small car in a spin. Horns blare. The Camaro, Mustang, or whatever it is, swerves around a yellow rental truck then rushes up behind us, gaining ground easily.

Holden floors it, but this Caddy isn't built for hard acceleration or racing. With no other options, he uses bystander vehicles for cover, weaving back and forth from lane to lane. It seems to be working as the other vamps aren't shooting at us. Doubtful they care about hitting innocent people. They're probably low on ammo and don't want to waste whatever they have left.

We zoom over Smith Island, another little bridge, then onto a short strip of land where Route 529 goes under an overpass. The vampires chasing us try to get up on our side far enough to attempt the thing cops do to throw a car off the road. Think it's called a pit maneuver. Holden sees it coming, swerving to block them. Back and forth we go, 'car jousting' as the Camaro alternates from left to right. We bump a few times whenever Holden blocks them from getting in position to shove us into a spin. Our car jousting takes a pause at a bend in the road. We slide across lanes, drifting a curve.

An oncoming motorcycle forces Holden to veer even farther into the wrong lane, allowing the sports car to get around us on the right a split second after we clear the overpass. Poor dude on the bike is going to need clean underwear for sure. The red car rams us, starting a fishtail, but Holden corrects, skidding onto the left side of a fork that brings us up onto an elevated highway. The vampires overshoot, continuing on 529... at least until they slam on the brakes.

I think we're on Route 5 now.

We race over another bridge, heading for downtown Tulalip.

"Ack. No!" I yell. "Don't go back into a populated area!"

"Not planning to."

Holden cuts off a small delivery truck to take the first off ramp after the bridge, followed by a strikingly illegal left turn. It's the sort of maneuver where a cop wouldn't simply give you a ticket, he'd question your intelligence while doing so. Holden didn't even slow down to look. Vampire reflexes make up for a lot of shortcuts, but they can only do so much. If an oncoming car had been there, smack. We get lucky, not suffering a T-bone. We also get unlucky as the red car reappears behind us seconds later.

We get unluckier: I smell burning plastic. Oh, and smoke is starting to fill the back of the car. This is not good.

The road here is wider than the bridges. Two lanes in each direction, plus a giant turning lane between them. Holden's all over it. Painted lines are for lesser mortals, apparently. Not sure if the weird vase in the backseat is a passenger or an abductee. Damn thing feels like it's alive and watching us, probably cursing us out in ancient Sumerian. Or Slavic. Dunno. It kinda has an old-world vibe. Giant, antique vases are supposed to give off a faint purple glow, right? Totally normal. Nothing to worry about at all. Merely some angry spirit light.

On the positive side, we are avoiding the populated area of Tulalip, heading out toward the reservation. I think at this point Holden is trying to reach a spot without spectators so we can have a proper vampire fight. Society really needs to bring back swords as fashion accessories. Silly me, I thought it might be inappropriate to carry a katana into what sounded like an official political meeting. Hmm. This area looks pretty free of spectators and we haven't stopped. Maybe he's going somewhere specific he hasn't bothered to tell me about.

The dudes chasing us resume trying to ram us off the road. I grab the door in one hand, the dashboard in the other, so the constant swerving doesn't throw me around as much. Some manner of church blurs by on our left side. Lots of trees around here. Good, means less chance a bystander is going to end up dead. Where'd the cops go? Did they give up?

I'm about to ask Holden why the heck we haven't tried to call Wolent for help when a sudden, alarming sense of doom pulls my attention to the rear. Dread subconsciously makes me amp myself, turning reality into slow motion *Matrix* style. The guys obligingly shot out the back window some time ago, so the smoke from the burning back seat cushion is being sucked out and not blinding us. An orange streak comes from the passenger-side window of the red Camaro, disappearing out of sight beneath our trunk. The rear end of the Cadillac inflates somewhat slower than one of those automatic rubber life rafts, only with a *lot* more fire involved.

They shot the damn gas tank.

The instant my brain processes the sight of a growing fireball, two ideas hit me at once. First, I thought cars turning into fiery plumes was movie BS. Oh, wait. They're using tracer bullets. Yeah, those don't play nice with gasoline.

My second idea is, I should probably get the hell out of the car before the expanding bloom of fire reaches me.

2

DELICATE NEGOTIATIONS

So, yeah. I'm in an exploding car.

How'd I get here? Let me back up a bit.

They say life imitates art. Or is it art imitates life? Maybe both. Everyone's imitating everyone. Whatever. Point is, you know that movie *Pulp Fiction*? Two guys work for a crime boss and get sent to do some questionable things? Yeah. Hi. I'm Sarah Wright and my vampire boss sent me to do something questionable. This is why I look like a kid trying on her mother's work clothes. Officially representing the boss, so I had to dress the part.

Arthur Wolent, the de-facto 'boss' of vampires in the Seattle area, at least the 'civilized' ones, sent Holden and me on what should have been a simple, diplomatic errand. Okay, perhaps less than diplomatic, but a car chase ending in a fiery explosion hadn't been on my list of 'ways this can possibly go wrong.' The whole scene felt like something straight out of a movie. Two 'problem solvers' going to a disused bar to meet some people—vampires—causing trouble for the boss.

In all fairness, we hadn't been planning to start a fight.

According to Wolent, a group of vampires who'd been exiled from Portland holed up in a small, derelict bar downtown. The place had been closed for years, definitely not open to the public.

This crew simply broke in and squatted. Not surprising. Vampires tend to help themselves to real estate rather often. Paying rent is for mortals, after all. Even elders or vamps who prefer the nicer things in unlife find ways around actually paying for their homes. They don't 'squat' per se, but use mental influence to secure legal ownership of property without money changing hands. I found out kinda recently Aurélie isn't paying for her massive penthouse. The management company running the building has records showing she's prepaid for thirty years or so, but can't locate the funds.

This is how rich vampires stay rich. They never use the money they collect. Granted, it's pretty much the same thing wealthy mortals do, only they use byzantine legal loopholes and teams of attack lawyers instead of mind powers.

Our mission sounded simple. Go to said disued bar, meet the vampires, determine what they planned to do in Seattle, and if we didn't like their answer, tell them to leave. Wolent couldn't verify the exact reasons the exiles got the boot from Portland. Inter-city cooperation among different vampire factions isn't the most seamless creature. I'd like to say Seattle is more organized in terms of undead political structure. The feel I got from Portland is basically an anarchist-slash-gang 'tribal council' situation. They don't have an Arthur Wolent, meaning a single guy everyone defers to as being in charge. There, it's more a collection of faction leaders forming a tribunal.

My mom has certain unfavorable opinions about the efficacy of committees. She's more or less right. Wolent's request for information is probably still sitting on a desk somewhere ignored on infinite 'when we get around to it' hold.

You'd think these leaders might do something logical like organize around bloodlines or something? Nope. It's total chaos as far as I can tell. No rhyme or reason. Just some elder decides they want power, so they grab up some followers and party on. Not like the Academics and the Old Guard and the Furies are all distinct groups. In all fairness, they don't do that in Seattle either, but we also don't have two dozen separate clans and a tribunal council of leaders. We have a few cliques pretending to respect one leader.

I guess vampires really *are* like the government. If something makes too much sense, they obviously can't do it that way and look for something more pleasantly convoluted.

I'M SITTING IN THE PASSENGER SEAT OF A NICE BLACK CADILLAC.

This guy, Holden Marston, is driving. He's a vampire, Old Guard, part of Wolent's group. Technically, I am part of Wolent's group, too. Okay, no 'technically' about it. I'm officially active in local politics to a point. I've had my debutante ball, my undead coming out party, talked to rulers in London, and I've even carried out a bombing. It's a lot for a girl to get done in a year.

All the vampires who pay attention to such things recognize me as being 'one of his.' It's somewhere between being a staffer in a political campaign office and a low-level associate of an organized crime boss. If you ask my dad, the only true difference between politicians and organized crime is the law. One side makes the law do whatever they want, the other ignores the law to do whatever they want. Otherwise, they're pretty much identical. Everyone's merely trying to get rich and have power.

Vampires, generally, obey mortal laws about as well as cats. Do felines care it's illegal to jaywalk? Okay, to be fair, most vampires merely disregard laws. We don't stare into your eyes *as* we break the law and mock you for having rules. We're not *entirely* cats.

Go ahead. Declare something illegal. Vampires will do it anyway and make you forget seeing it. Expecting mortal laws to stop us from doing something is about as asinine as expecting a 'gun free zone' sign on a bank is going to make a robber change his mind, or switch to a knife. Some crazy vampires—like me—still obey (mostly) the law. For one thing, it's ingrained in my being. I grew up as Follows Rules Girl and it hasn't been too long since my Transference. For another thing, keeping my head down makes it easier to blend in.

One major thing vampires want to do is stay hidden, blend in pretending to be mortal. Individually, mortals are no match for us, even newbies like me. However, if knowledge of vampires went mainstream, there's no way we could survive all of humanity trying to kill us.

People aren't known for welcoming the strange and unusual. Anything they don't understand, they try to destroy. Take magic, for example. According to what my sister Sophia learned from the mystics, all that King Arthur stuff, Merlin, and so forth really happened. However, humanity tolerated magic nervously only for a few hundred years before becoming terrified and going collectively rage-crazy and trying to wipe them out. So, the mages went into hiding, pretending magic didn't exist.

A scary high number of people can't tolerate the idea of girls loving girls or boys loving boys. No way are they going to tolerate vampires... who *are* a threat to them. And phew. A vampire girl loving a vampire girl would *really* make them freak out. Ideally, we need to keep society around the world believing we are creatures of myth. Running around flagrantly breaking mortal laws is the exact opposite way to go about being inconspicuous. It's just easier to behave. Or pretend to behave. I'm the lame kid who's still afraid of getting in trouble, as pathetic as a twenty-one-year-old living in their own apartment still going to bed at 10:00 p.m. because their parents gave them a bedtime right up until eighteen and they don't want to disappoint Mom and Dad.

No, I'm not *that* pathetic. I have no bedtime.

Okay, technically a lie. But, my bedtime is enforced by the sun, not parents.

Anyway, Wolent is concerned about a group of exiles being in Seattle. If they did something bad enough to get them kicked out of *Portland*, it's probably not a good idea to allow them to stay around here. No slam against Portland by the way, just saying things are way more lax there. And weird. I've heard some vampires even walk around 'fangs out' and no one cares. People think it's cosplay. Guess when your city is known for some guy who dresses up like Darth

Vader and plays bagpipes on a unicycle, something as mundane as vampires barely gets a raised eyebrow.

My first thought is to suggest the exiles head down to Ventura, California. As far as vampiredom goes, it's completely lawless there. I'm sure the PIBs hate the place. Yes, the government has agents whose sole job is making sure the people remain unaware of the existence of everything paranormal.

So anyway, Holden... don't know much about him. He appears to be around thirty, but doesn't act like a millennial. Dude doesn't look anything like Leo DiCaprio except for the blond hair, but he reminds me of Jack from *Titanic*. Same mannerisms, speech patterns, and so on. Guessing he turned vampire in the early 1900s. 'Holden' is also kind of a dated name. Don't see many guys running around these days named Holden. Probably because it's easy to make fun of. Any kid going to school these days would hate the name. And his hair is tragically basic. Total millennial mess.

I'd seen him before at the soirees, but never met or spoke to him. Sure, I've 'gone official' but I'm still trying to exist as normally as possible for the time being. I never considered myself shy or socially awkward—my friend Michelle would disagree—but anyone seeing me at these vampire parties would assume me shy. According to 'Chelle, both Ashley and I are introverts. Not sure what makes her think so. Ashley's like the most friendly, bubbly person I know. So what if she won't walk up to total strangers and start talking? If someone approaches her, she has no problem chatterboxing away. She simply doesn't initiate social contact with people she doesn't know. In fact, I think she's *more* outgoing than I am.

Okay, maybe 'shy' is closer to accurate than I let on. Whatever.

The most shocking thing about Holden thus far is he hasn't once made a comment about my age or given me a dismissive smirk. It's odd. Even the friendlier vampires in Wolent's periphery tend to make condescending remarks about me being adorable. To be fair, the 'treating me like a child' thing kind of waned after I firebombed a nest of hostile vampires in Astoria. Guess it earned me a little respect.

Holden spends most of the ride to the abandoned bar telling me what he knows of the exiles and discussing what Wolent shared in our briefing. Supposedly, the vampires in question got the boot for carelessness, leaving bodies around, kill-feeding, and generally being a danger to vampires in general due to attracting attention. Stories about a deranged serial killer who thinks they're a vampire stalking the Portland area are making the rounds on the news. Chances are, it's going to end in one of three ways: fade out of public awareness, some poor guy is going to be framed for it and paraded around on the news to make the story go away as resolved, or some random dead body is going to be the killer 'dead in a shootout with police.'

Might not even be vampires who do it, rather the Persons In Black. It makes sense to me why vampires would work hard to keep the reality of our existence a secret, but I have no explanation for why mortals do. Unless the whole department is controlled by a vampire? Hmm. Who knows?

Holden idly taps his fingers on the wheel while waiting for a traffic light. "There is a good chance this will turn into a mild disagreement requiring delicate negotiations."

"Are you being literal or doing the Dalton thing?" I ask.

"The 'Dalton thing'?" Holden glances at me.

"If he told me to expect a 'mild disagreement,' I'd plan for fireballs, toads raining from the sky, wailing, gnashing of teeth, and so forth."

Holden chuckles. "Ahh yes. Something of that nature, though hopefully without the frogs. Shouldn't worry too much. These vampires left Portland when asked to. I doubt angering Mr. Wolent is of interest to them."

"Hope so."

"Even if they decline, our job tonight is not to physically throw them out. We merely bring word of their refusal back."

"Sounds easy."

"You'll find most things are."

I chuckle. "Right up until they aren't. And 'easy' hasn't exactly been my fortune lately."

A few minutes after the signal goes green for us, we arrive at the former bar. The building is mostly grey on the outside, windows boarded up. It's sandwiched between a record store—unsurprisingly also shut down—and a furniture-refurbishing place, which still appears to be in operation, but closed now. No surprise there, considering it's almost midnight. 'Commercial space for lease' signs are all over the bar, the record store, and the next place to the left. I can't tell what it used to be other than a retail store of some kind. Doesn't look like any of the three properties have been occupied for years.

Holden pulls over into a conveniently empty spot right outside the place. Gee. Can't imagine why no one would want to park in front of two abandoned properties at this hour.

Seattle, as cities go, is pretty nice. We still have crime, but unlike, say, New York City, a nice Caddy is still going to be here when we exit the building. I hop out, cheating by using my ability to fly to manage high heels. They're not like extreme stilettos or anything, merely 'normal' heels. My dumb ass wanted to look more professional-slash-serious, so I borrowed one of my mom's old pairs she doesn't use anymore. The only pair in the house belonging to me are kitten heels. I already look like a high school freshman. No need making it more pronounced. Alas, it would've made sense for me to get used to walking in 'real' heels before using them for a job. Oh, well. I can fly. Which means faking it is easy.

Seriously… how does any woman *like* these things? Ugh.

I feel like an ostrich on ice skates wearing a harness connected to helium balloons to stay upright.

At least I don't *look* as ungainly as it feels. No mirrors around to check myself in. Holden would definitely have said something otherwise, or laughed. Definitely come off more like baby lawyer on her first day than a female version of Vincent from *Pulp Fiction*, Agent Scully, or even a nameless background detective from *Law & Order*. I am going to intimidate exactly no one. Kinda strange Wolent sent me on this job, but maybe he's doing it in hopes my presence keeps the meeting from turning into a bloodbath. Slight chance he's hoping for the reverse. I did, after all, incinerate a nest of kill-feeders in Ventura. Well, *help* incinerate. The Peters brothers brought the flare gun.

Or, more likely, he doesn't view these exiles as a serious threat and it's a job for the new girl.

Holden leads the way across the sidewalk to the door. Not sure what made him try the knob, but to both of our surprise, the door opens. We step into a somewhat cramped room. A bar takes up about half the wall on the left near the front. Square, freestanding tables and chairs fill the majority of the floor space except for an area around a smaller-than-average pool table in the back by a hallway labeled 'restrooms.' Sports crap is all over, mostly Seahawks logos. Everything is covered in dust. The place smells of damp wood, seawater, and stale beer.

Two men seated at one of the tables near the inner end of the bar glance over at us, as excited as if we're the guy who went out to grab food coming back. Can't tell how old either guy is... somewhere between twenty and forty. One's dressed like a backup singer for a Cure cover band. He's gone full Goth. White face paint, puffy black hair, black trench coat. Far too many spikes and purposeless chains. The cops would write him a ticket for excessive metal accessorizing. His buddy's long ponytail makes him look like Paul Revere fell through a time hole into an Aeropostale outlet.

My brain almost shuts down when I realize what's on the table between them... Warhammer 40k minis and dice. Kinda cool and unexpected. Dad convinced us to try playing it once. Sam and Sophia liked the detail in the rules. Sierra moaned the whole time about it being tedious. Took forever to finish the scenario. However, vampires have nothing but time on their hands and this building doesn't appear to have working electricity, so no video games. If not for the chance these two might be kill-feeders, I'd respect them as fellow geeks.

Small, painted figurines hold my attention for only a moment before something... else grabs it. Two tables behind them, a plain white bed sheet conceals a large cylinder roughly the size of a fireplace log. Eerie, but faint, purple light shines out from under a fold in the linen, stretching shadows over an unreadable word carved into the table surface. I'd ask if they bought a giant blacklight to host rave parties here, but electronic devices don't generally give off a tangible sense of malice—though my mother has a few stories about her old Blackberry. Whatever the thing under the sheet is, it's staring at me like a cat I just gave a bath to.

"Sorry, place is closed," says the goth dude.

Holden takes another step. "We're here on business."

The guys appear to realize we're vampires at roughly the same time. Upon processing we're not mortals—and thus, not self-delivering food—their smiles fade to annoyed smirks. Goth Dude's body language goes full 'ugh' like a pair of Jehovah Witnesses cornered him and asked if he had a few minutes to talk. 'Paul Revere' radiates more of a 'here we go again' attitude.

"I'm Holden Marston. This is my associate, Sarah. We are here on behalf of Arthur Wolent. Shall I assume you know of him, or would you rather I explain?"

'Paul Revere' closes his eyes, emits a silent pained sigh, then looks at us. "We are aware of him. However, we had not realized he has decided to embrace the silliness of the Old World."

"I am unsure to what you refer," says Holden.

Goth Dude shifts his 'can we kill this guy' stare off Holden to check me out. It's not a comfortable look, but I'll suffer it if it keeps us from having to get into a fight. Wait, no… he's not leering at me. That's confusion. Grr. I bet he's trying to figure out if I'm old enough to leer at. Okay, so not a total creep.

"Announcing arrivals?" 'Paul Revere' raises both eyebrows. "My name is Albert Pemberton, and my associate is Robert Bryson. I assume by virtue of your being a proxy in Mr. Wolent's stead, this satisfies the requirement."

Holden smiles, taking another casual step closer. "Oh, no. There is no need to formally present yourself. This is not Europe. We are here simply to ascertain your intentions for being in the Seattle area. Mr. Wolent is aware of the circumstances surrounding your departure from Portland and wishes to avoid similar disruptions here."

"I'm afraid you have been misinformed." Albert drops a pair of six-sided dice on the table among the figurines and walks over to us. "The reasons for us leaving Portland are entirely political. Certain groups with… issues are no doubt spreading exaggerated stories."

Up close, this guy looks as pale as Robert. Hmm. When we walked in, I figured the 'goth dude' had white face paint on, but don't smell any. My high school had a small goth clique. I never noticed a cosmetic aroma from them, but I also didn't have a nose sharp enough to track human scents at the time. Any beer stink soaked into the floor and tables should be weakened enough from age not to conceal fresh face paint. No, these two are both as white as chalk.

Such paleness isn't too unusual for vampires, but it stands out in vampire society the same way going outside naked does to mortals. Aurélie gets away with it—being pure white, not public nudity— because she dresses like she's from sixteenth century France. Well, she *is* from sixteenth century France, but I mean she still wears the costumes. Nobles back then painted themselves white, so it fits her outfit. Except for Innocents and Shadows, vampires can force their bodies to take on a more lifelike coloration. Innocents don't have to, and Shadows can't. They also happen to be grey rather than white. Point being, 'warming up' is considered as customary to vampires before going out as it is to put on clothes.

Then again, we did barge in on these guys. This is the vampire equivalent of rural cops storming into a house and catching a guy watching TV in his underwear. I shouldn't infer too much by them not bothering to force themselves to appear lifelike when they're hanging out at 'home'. Goth Dude—Robert—probably leaves himself pale on purpose for style. Still, these guys are giving off an odd vibe. Or maybe it's coming from the thing under the sheet.

"What manner of political reasons?" Holden tilts his head. It's not a confused tilt. It's a scheming sort of tilt. "How did you manage to get the council to all agree on not wanting you in their city?"

"The usual petty drivel." Robert, evidently unable to figure me out, peels his gaze off me to stare once more at Holden. "What else would it be? You know how they are."

Holden bows his head. "Yes, I know how they are. Twenty-two different groups, no more than six ever able to come to a consensus on any particular topic. I find it implausible or alarming to suggest they *all* managed to agree you two needed to leave Portland?"

Robert and Albert look at each other. I swear a pulse of hostility wafts from the object under the sheet.

An explosion goes off next to me.

Or at least, it sounds like an explosion. One second, Holden's merely standing there. The next, his right arm is extended holding a gun. Robert and Albert reel backward simultaneously, each man shot once in the forehead. My vampire reflexes kick in—hey, better late than not at all. Both exiles crumple toward the ground in slow motion while Holden hurries over to the sheet-covered table. Looks normal to me, but he's moving so fast a few of the Warhammer figurines fall over from the breeze. He grabs the cylinder, wrapping it in the linen, and rushes straight for the door behind us, passing the two guys before they're done falling.

Stunned at the sudden, unprovoked violence, and clueless as to why he's running, I end up standing there like a gawking fool watching the two guys sink to the floor. A relative three seconds after Holden's outside, a door beside the back hall opens. Four corpse-pale men dressed somewhat like a motorcycle gang run into the room.

Crap.

I'd complain about high heels again, but they don't matter. I'm flying, maybe forgetting to move my legs to make it look like I'm running. Who cares? Four-on-one never ends well for the one, especially when she's small, not a master at hand-to-hand combat, and left her sword at home. I cruise out the door. Holden's already driving away. He's opened the window on my side at least. Not difficult for me to accelerate faster than a Cadillac. I swing my legs up, swerve in the window, and land in the passenger seat.

The vampires spill out of the bar. Two try chasing our Caddy on foot. Given we're in downtown Seattle traffic and they're vampires, it's not as unreasonable as it sounds. However, it is after midnight and there aren't too many other cars on the road in this area, allowing us to break the speed limit. I stick my head out the window to look back at the two sprinters falling behind. Three blocks away by the bar, one of the two not chasing us on foot straight up GTA's a dude out of a red sports car, grabbing him by the chest and yeeting him across the road before jumping in behind the wheel.

"Shit! They stole a car."

Holden squeezes the wheel tighter.

"Can I ask you something?"

"Sure."

I stare at him. "WTF?"

"Pardon?"

"Argh. What the hell did you shoot them for? And why does the *thing* in the back seat feel like it's alive?"

The red sports car slows to pick up the two guys still trying to catch us on foot. Dammit. I never signed up for a car chase. So much for a professional meeting. If I'd have known the night would turn into this, I wouldn't have bothered wearing nice clothes. Probably would've brought my sword along, too... and some car chase music. Dad would insist. Oh, and I'd have put on a headband. We're only going a bit over the speed limit. Not sure it counts as a car chase yet, but the vampires do seem to be following us.

"Sorry for assuming, but you're fairly new, yes?" asks Holden.

"Yeah. About a year."

"Anyone mention Oblivare yet?"

I blink. "Oh-bli-var-ay? Guessing it's not a new boy band or a line of Italian purses."

He snorts, trying to suppress a laugh. "No. They're a nihilistic bloodline. It makes sense to me now why they got kicked out of Portland. Took me a moment to realize what they are."

Whoa. I whistle. "These Oblivare are bad enough to get the entire council to agree on something?"

"Yes." He nods.

A gunshot goes off behind us. Oh, wonderful. Not merely a car chase. An *extra spicy* car chase.

Holden accelerates. "They want to destroy society. Ours as well as mortals."

"Uhh. So, they're morons."

"Not as much so as you are thinking. They don't want to destroy vampires and people, just society as a construct." He slams on the brakes, skidding us into a right turn.

Someone in a light green Prius lays on their horn—until the Oblivare resume shooting at us.

I grab the roof handle to keep myself in the seat. Crap. Total mistake to wear heels and a skirt tonight. "Society. So, what? They want anarchy?"

"Not exactly. They think mortals should be barely advanced past the point of using fire to cook and live in tiny villages, constantly in fear of vampires coming out of the wilds to feast on them. They also believe vampires should exist in small roving independent packs like wolves. No large communities or governments or leaders on either side. Whether or not it's true, they believe the world used to be that way thousands of years ago, and they want to go back to it."

"Wow. Okay, still crazy." I glance into the back seat. "So, what's that thing?"

"A reliquary."

"Isn't that like a eulogy?"

"You're thinking of requiem." Holden chuckles, grunts, then yanks the wheel to the side, throwing us around a left turn.

The move is so abrupt, I kiss the passenger side window. Two bystander cars smash into each other trying to avoid us... but the Oblivare overshoot the turn and slam on their brakes, the wail of screeching tires echoing over horns.

"Oh, okay. Reliquary..."

"Basically, a soul jar," says Holden. "Oblivare don't invoke the Transference the same way as other vampires. They claim never to have been human."

I look around at relatively quiet streets. No sign of a red sports car. "Those guys looked pretty human to me. Well, except for being obviously dead white."

"The bodies were human. They pour Oblivare souls from the reliquary into a corpse."

"Whoa." I gawk at him. "Doesn't that make a *Sefil*?"

"No, you're thinking blood. *Sefil* are the result of a standard Transference done too long after death."

"Yeah. I know that." I exhale hard. "Nothing good ever comes from messing with a jar of ghosts. Ask me how I know."

"Later. We have a problem." Holden points backward.

I twist around to look behind us. The red car gains on us, weaving around people who have the temerity to drive at or under the speed limit.

"They're back."

"Yes. I noticed. The vase might contain a hundred potential Oblivare or perhaps only two. I'm sure they're rather interested in getting it back."

"Holden... there's no way you're going to lose them in this Caddy. It's a beautiful car, but it's not going to outrun a... whatever they have. Let's ditch it and fly."

He groans. "I wish. Can't fly. Go ahead if you want. Won't ask you to stay."

"Grr." I squeeze my fingers into the plush seat, watching the sports car creep closer and closer. Two guys lean out the windows, pointing guns at us. "They're gonna shoot!"

Holden swerves into the oncoming lane to get around a pack of cars stopped at a red light, threads the proverbial eye of the needle between two SUVs on the crossing street, and stomps the gas once we're back in the clear. Good thing I'm dead already or I'd have had a heart attack.

"Why did you grab the stupid thing instead of just smashing it?" I yell.

"Breaking it only lets them out. The Oblivare would eventually collect them again. We need to bring it to Eidolon so he can destroy them."

Whoa. Sounds impressive. I blink. "Who or what is Eidolon?"

"He's the oldest Shadow in the Pacific Northwest." Holden lifts his right hand off the wheel for a moment to wave around in a random gesture. "He knows all sorts of weird mystical stuff people don't believe in anymore. Even most vampires think the stuff is nonsense. It's not his real name, though. No one knows it."

"So, you're saying no woman named their son 'Eidolon'?" I fake roll my eyes. "Wow, never imagined."

He laughs.

The back window explodes into tiny crystals as a barrage of gunfire goes off behind us. Orange light smears go by outside, bouncing off the street ahead of us. Some vanish, some spiral into the air.

"Okay, that's weird. Kinda pretty, but weird."

"Tracer bullets." Holden stomps the brakes so we don't drive into the window of a Starbucks on a turn. "I believe they are attempting to light us on fire."

I gawk at him. This guy is unbelievable.

3

PEAR-SHAPED

Anyway, so I've ended up playing chicken with a fireball in a gradually exploding Cadillac.

Shame, too. It's a nice car. Or was. Well, not 'was' yet. It's presently in the rather expedited process of transitioning between past and present tense in regard to being nice. I must be absolutely terrified in order for my reflexes to have amped up enough to perceive an expanding fireball in such slow motion. It's gotta be like a hundredth of a second and it feels like ten.

As Dalton would say, tonight's meeting went pear-shaped. No idea what the heck being pear-shaped has to do with failure, but the British are odd. Maybe he'd say tonight went tits-up. He likes that phrase, too. It also means something went quite wrong.

So, right. I have a serious problem at the moment. No time to think.

My primitive lizard brain takes over, and I'm not going to argue. Its desire is to move directly away from the fireball as fast as possible. This involves launching myself out of the windshield. Smashing my skull into automotive glass is a lot more comfortable than burning. In fact, it hurts less than the time Sierra pranked me by sneaking Justin Bieber onto my iPod. Not the boy, his music. Sophia might be able to put the actual boy in my iPod now using magic, but I hope she doesn't try. Besides, demons are Sam's thing. Also, our lives are crazy enough without our family being sued by a giant record label.

Wonder how they'd explain it to the public? Would they put the iPod on stage so the trapped Bieber could sing out of it?

Bleh.

The instant I clear the windshield, I veer straight up. Next thing I know, I'm hanging in midair above the road, looking down at a flaming wreck in the trees. Lots of forest to the northwest. There's a small residential area a short distance farther southwest of where the Caddy went into the woods. Oh, my shoes are gone and nylon has bunched around my knees. Feet are slightly sore. The shoes probably fell off. Guess the fireball came close enough to melt my stocking soles. Eep.

Tire screech redirects my attention straight down. The red Camaro slides to a stop, jumping up onto a little bit of sidewalk at the edge of the road. Our Caddy narrowly missed a utility pole and trenched a path into a thick mass of underbrush and pine trees. It's still on its wheels—the whole 'exploding gas tank makes cars flip over' thing definitely *is* Hollywood nonsense—and is rapidly becoming engulfed in fire.

Groaning in the scrub draws my gaze to Holden dragging himself away from the wreckage—or trying to. I think he's pinned under the back tire. Yeah, most vampires could make themselves strong enough to move a car, but he's also on fire. Probably taking all his concentration to resist the burning. Gah. Acrid fumes make my eyes water so bad I have to flinch away. Car fires stink. Good thing I'm already dead or breathing this stuff would probably give me cancer.

Four Oblivare exit the Camaro, still holding guns, and stalk toward the Caddy. Somehow, they haven't noticed me up here. Sure, I'm like 200 feet in the air, but how could they have not seen me flying? Oh, wait. The fireball was pretty bright. It's not fun to go from near total darkness to blind. Yes, a flashlight *can* buy a few seconds in a vampire attack. Gotta be a good one, though. Not a convenience store single-AA battery cheapo. Get one of those ridiculous internet flashlights capable of setting paper on fire from across a room and anyone could be a vampire hunter. Seriously though, even an unexpected police Maglite will blind us for a good thirty seconds. Enough time to run and hide.

Damn. I'd really rather get the hell out of here, but I can't leave Holden to die. I pantomime tying on a red headband, take a deep, unnecessary breath, and foolishly decide to dive-bomb the Oblivare in the back of their group, taking advantage of the element of surprise.

By the way, it's not on the periodic table.

Silly me, I didn't bring a weapon of any kind, so I improvise with what I have: my fist. Being 200 feet in the air lets me gather a bit of speed, which goes into my best attempt at a WWE elbow-drop... kinda. I'm not using my elbow. Looks kinda the same, though. Oh, also, what I'm doing is not fake.

The guy's skull crunches under my knuckles. Blood streams from both ears. Pretty sure his eyeballs shoot out of his face. Feels like I've mashed my hand through a solid chocolate bowl into a mass of warm pudding. The rest of his body cushions my impact against the ground. I probably only broke two fingers on my right hand from hitting his skull. Pain can wait a moment.

Gotta love adrenaline.

I'm already pushing all I can into speed and strength, giving me a few relative seconds before the three remaining Oblivare react to the splat behind them. Sure, all vampires can speed themselves up, but it takes about a second or so, leaving a tiny window where even other vampires appear slow when they're not expecting a fight. This is how Holden got the drop on Albert and Robert. And, he's crazy fast. Like, the fastest I've ever seen. Maybe he came from the Old West, a former gunslinger.

The other three are all starting to turn. Since the dude I flattened was obligingly carrying a handgun, I grab it, aim, and shoot the next nearest guy in the back of the head. An orange light smear flies from my gun and disappears into the dude's head above his left ear. Flames burp out of the hole.

Oh, they definitely have tracer bullets. Not good. Well, not good if I get hit by one.

The instant unconsciousness of a bullet having an argument with his brain turns a rapid twist into a pirouetting fall. I have no real urge to find out what it feels like to be shot with a burning bullet. Also, I'm not exactly the most experienced when it comes to using guns. My panic-fueled attempt to shoot the other two biker dudes before they shoot me results in four misses—and my gun locks open, out of ammo.

Made them flinch, though.

This is the moment—standing here unarmed in front of two vampires holding handguns—where I have a tiny bit of self-doubt and wonder if maybe I should have tried talking to these guys first instead of going straight to an aerial hammer fist. Like, 'hey, sorry, my associate is off his meds. Take your reliquary back, we'll go this way, you go that way.' It's pointless to think about it now since I kinda started something in motion here.

Funny how time seems to hang sometimes. The three of us seem to stand there staring at each other long enough for me to feel like a dumbass and think about random stuff like what Sierra learned in her sword class. Conventional wisdom says an attacker using a knife can cover twenty-one feet and strike before a person can draw and fire a gun. I'm only like ten feet away, but they already have guns out. I also don't have a knife, rather claws. Still counts. Anyone in the know would be more afraid of my claws than a simple knife.

Also, no time to debate my odds. As Yoda would say, there is no try, there is only stab.

Okay, he didn't really say that; I'm ad-libbing here.

Claws out, I launch myself forward.

The biker dudes both get off a shot each before I'm on them. Luckily, they didn't expect me to literally fly at them. No idea where the bullets went other than they didn't end up inside me. I grab the arm of the dude on the left, shoving the gun away. The other guy hesitates, not wanting to pump a red-hot nugget of burny death into his buddy. Damn, this would be so much easier if I had a sword on me. Dammit! Why does society have to frown on the routine carry of long blades?

Dude swings me into the air, trying to throw me off his gun arm. Flight is a huge help. I stay put, causing him to inadvertently smash me into his friend. The shock of impact is enough to break my grip on his forearm, but I don't go away easy. The dull *thump* of a handgun hitting the ground confirms my weaponized fingernails shredded all the tendons in his wrist. Every finger on his right hand is gonna be useless for a few days.

He howls in pain, staggering to one side, clutching the bleeding slashes.

The other guy stumbles forward from the force of me hitting him like a human club. I drop to the ground on my side. He wheels around, aiming down at my face—so I kick his arm away an instant before the gunshot goes off, putting a bullet into his friend's left foot. A tiny jet of fire rises up from the hole in his boot. Between his 'oh shit, sorry' expression and the other guy's cartoony yowl of pain, I almost laugh. If not for Holden's distant wails of agony, I probably would have.

Burning boot guy dances around in a circle, stomping.

I spring up and bite the dude in front of me on the wrist. The pain of vampire fangs causes his hand to reflexively open, dropping the gun. I don't have a chance to grab for it before burning boot dude shows me his claws—at least the ones on his left hand, which still work. Straight down my back. Ouch to the power of twenty. Worse than having burning oil dumped on me. Not quite as painful as being tied to a chair and forced to stay at a KISS concert. Unfortunately for his friend, such pain makes me clench my jaw. The little bone in his arm shatters in my teeth.

This, predictably, upsets the guy.

He grabs the back of my neck. Hell no. I rake claws at his gut, mostly in hopes he backs off before breaking my spine. Blood sprays over my head, but it works—he lets go and jumps back. Smoking boot dude catches me across the chest, slashing from my left shoulder to the base of my ribs on the other side.

I don't care how big, bad, and tough a vampire you are. Claws freakin' *sting*.

Screaming happens.

At least I'm not the only one. I'm screaming in pain. The dude whose hand I almost bit off is screaming in pain. Holden is screaming in pain. We're like a choir from a *Hellraiser* movie. Smoky boot swipes at me a few more times, trying to literally rip my face off. I manage to duck and dart around, avoiding the worst of it. He only lands a few superficial slices to my back and sides before opportunity knocks and he's wide open for a flight-assisted kick.

Sure, I'm presently barefoot, but hammering a heel bone into an eye socket at vampiric levels of strength is still *quite* effective. The whole front of the dude's face smashes inward like a hard-boiled egg dropped on tile floor. I spin out of the maneuver to hover in a standing pose a few inches off the ground, staring at bit-hand guy.

Like a scene straight out of a Tarantino-directed neo western movie, we both eye the dropped guns in the flattened path of vegetation between the road and the burning Caddy. Screw it. I dive at the one nearest me. He might not have the power of flight but he fakes it pretty well. As much as I'd love to claim victory and sound all cool, dude legit gets to the gun faster than me and fires first. He is, however, using his left hand and the tracer round makes it *way* obvious he missed.

I miss as well.

We both fire a second shot at the same time. He misses again, though I felt the warmth go past my right ear. My second shot hits him directly under the nose; the back of his head blows out. Roughly a two-inch wide section of teeth from his upper jaw are now inside his brain. Ooh... that hurts just looking at it.

The gun falls from his limp hand. He teeters over backward and lands in the dirt.

Whew. Holy crap. I'm alive. We won.

Holden moans in agony.

Okay, perhaps 'winning' here is relative.

Hey, it's kinda cold.

I peer down—at my bare chest. Scraps of my blazer, shirt, and bra are all over the ground. From neck to waist, I look like a hamburger covered in fake grill marks, only they're red lines.

Sigh.

"Dammit!" I stomp. "Again? Seriously?"

It's tits-up, luv, not tits-out, says Dalton's voice in my mind. *You okay?*

Mostly. Sore, but they're all shallow slices. Worst ones are down the middle of my back.

Aye. That's where ya lost your kit.

What kit?

Kit means clothes.

Brits are weird.

He laughs.

Hey, have you ever heard of Oblivare?

Aye. Nasty lot. About as close to true monsters as vampires get. The heck are they doing here?

Beats me. Should I be worried?

Nah. They're a little more potent than vampires made the usual way, but nothing to stain your knickers over. According to rumor, they 'ave a bunch of drawbacks of the mystical kind. More vulnerable to that sort of thing. Somethin' to do with their souls not properly belonging to their body or some such bollocks. Ya believe in that?

My kid sister has a teleporting kitten with occasionally glowing eyes. Let's just say my mind is a lot more open than it used to be.

Grumbling, I rest my hands on my hips and frown at the carnage around me. Yeah, possibly good info to know magical stuff works well on them. It doesn't help me much. No way am I going to involve Sophia in vampire politics. Self-defense is one thing, but dragging her into a mess? No way.

And grr. I really need to start packing a spare shirt in my purse… which I left at Wolent's place.

The night keeps on getting better.

4

A SMIDGE BEYOND BACTINE

L ooking around doesn't improve my mood.

Between gunfire, claws, and head-smashing, all the Oblivare's shirts are bloody messes, on fire, or shredded. Both Oblivare I shot are burning. Smoking boot guy managed to extinguish his foot, but I tore his shirt to ribbons. The one I dive-bombed has brains and blood all over his T-shirt. Some might think a blood-soaked shirt is better than going topless, but either one is going to make people get in my way and require memory alteration. If both options are gonna demand mind powers, I'd just as soon *not* touch some other vampire's blood and brains.

During the fight, Holden appears to have freed himself from the now-fully-engulfed Cadillac. He's dragged himself a relatively safe distance away up the channel of flattened bushes. Poor guy is somewhere between Deadpool and Freddy Kreuger. Most of his clothes are gone as well as all of his hair. A few smoking scraps remain of fabric. Tougher materials like his belt, underarm holster, and dress shoes survived; however, they're kinda embedded in his skin like mushrooms on pizza—at least, where he still has skin and the muscle isn't exposed.

Okay, I'm not feeling so bad about some claw scratches. Got off easy, only losing my shirt.

He pushes himself over onto his back, gives a wheeze, then shudders. Holden no longer even appears to be human at all. He's legit turned into some kind of medieval ghoul.

I crouch near him. "Please tell me burns aren't permanent..."

"They're not... just hurt for a while." He grimaces—I think. There really isn't enough skin left on his face to read any expression. "I'll be back to normal in a month."

"Uhh, how the heck did you get messed up so bad? Weren't you fast enough to get out?"

"Yeah." He wheezes. "But the car ran me over after I jumped. Dragged me along. I can't fly."

"Sorry..."

He shakes his head, making the same squishy-crunchy sound as biting into fried chicken. The crispy kind. "Don't be. I'm glad you got out. You probably wouldn't have survived this. Do me a favor..."

"I don't have any Bactine in my purse. Don't think they make a bottle big enough for this."

"Stop making me want to laugh." He points a twisted ghoul-claw hand behind me. "Toss those sons of bitches on the fire."

"Umm... I don't feel right deciding to kill them permanently."

Holden stares at me. A slight twitch suggests he might be trying to blink in astonishment. Alas, he no longer has eyelids. "I just watched you rip them apart like a wildcat, but you don't want to kill them?"

I gesture at them. "They'll all get back up. This is kinda like playing paintball with better special effects and more pain."

"You aren't deciding to kill them. I am. If you told Wolent they're Oblivare, he'd order you to destroy them." Holden spits to the side. "Political reasons my ass."

If my opinion matters, says Dalton's voice in my thoughts, *you should do it. They are in no way human. Merely stolen bodies full of dark forces. All the vampire stories where we're portrayed as mindless savage monsters are from this lot.*

Dalton's endorsement means way more than Holden's say-so.

"Okay. Fine… fine…" I trudge over and grab shot-foot guy. "Where'd the reliquary go? I don't see it anywhere."

"Probably in the car," rasps Holden.

I stare at the inferno. "Yeah, well. It's gonna stay there until that fire is out."

"Wolent's people can get it from the police later. Not a problem." Holden grunts, trying to sit up, but is in too much pain to do so. "Dammit. Hurry up and toss them on the fire. We need to leave the area before the cops show up."

Distant sirens tell me we've got maybe two minutes to get out of here.

Within seconds of me tossing the first guy onto the burning car, bright purple energy briefly appears around the corpse and blows away on the wind. Not too long ago, I witnessed a vampire die permanent death right in front of me thanks to the sun. No weird purple energy. My remaining doubts as to the legitimacy of this Oblivare soul jar thing evaporate along with the energy.

Claws help me pick up the three remaining 'unconscious' Oblivare. One after the next, I chuck them onto the Cadillac bonfire. Heat from getting close enough to throw them dries the blood on my chest into a sticky mess. Ugh. Claw wounds sting bad enough when fresh. The shower or bath I foresee in my imminent future is going to hurt.

After collecting every recognizable piece of my jacket and shirt, I rush back to Holden, scoop him up in my arms, and fly. No, the clothing isn't even close to wearable—except the sleeves—I don't want the police finding women's clothing and no body to match. Having to mind control a whole bunch of cops after they do some forensics magic to trace the clothes to me is a pain in the ass I'd rather avoid. Maybe I'm giving forensics too much credit, but it's still better to cover my tracks. Hopefully, Mom's old high heels in the car will burn beyond recognition. Drat. I should get her a replacement pair.

Cars and trucks awash in brilliant flashing lights converge on the crash site. Police vehicles, fire crews, and at least two ambulances roll up. Little late for EMTs, but I suppose they'll be on hand in case someone gets hurt cleaning up our mess.

Sigh.

I'm not sure if I should worry more that standing around topless doesn't feel like a big deal, or killing four guys, evil vampires though they may be, bothers me about the same. Either one should be problematic, or at least make me feel awkward. Does this mean I'm changing or merely adapting to the demands of a new reality? Also, cradling a severely burned ghoul against my bare chest is a totally normal thing everyone does, right?

Is killing a vampire permanently considered homicide or some other -icide? Bleh. Whatever.

I need to get home before my parents start worrying.

5

EVERYTHING WILL BE HANDLED

F lying while carrying a man is *not* fun.

Like six months ago, I flew while Ashley hung on my back. She's my size, noticeably smaller than a dude, and her weight made it impossible to maintain any dignity during landing. Holden might not be the biggest guy, but lugging him across the sky is exhausting. Also makes me feel like an overweight songbird struggling to stay aloft.

In an effort to avoid face-planting the pavement in front of Wolent's manor house, I decide to try a new approach. Instead of swooping down to land on my feet like any other time, I stop all forward motion and hover 150 feet or so in the air, then descend straight down like an elevator. See? This is the benefit of taking calculus. Landing in the normal fashion fails to consider the forward momentum imparted to the body in my arms (or on my back), which would push past my center of gravity, thus resulting in the aforementioned faceplant. By stalling all forward momentum in the air, I avoid looking like a drunken figure skater trying a triple backflip.

"What the...?" mutters Aziz.

Wolent's big security guy has one of the most boring jobs in the world. He spends almost every night standing on the front porch watching the grounds. As far as I know, he doesn't go anywhere unless ordered to. Hope the guy gets a night off here and there. However, he's a damn effective deterrent. The man is simply massive. One of the reasons he likely contents himself to stay on the property is his size. His proportions are legit inhuman. People don't have arms the size of an average man's waist. Some of the other vamps call him the Moroccan Hulk. The name works. As far as I know, he actually *is* from Morocco originally.

Despite his ridiculous bulk and menacing appearance, he's generally soft-spoken and sweet.

Everyone is super polite to him, too. Any man as big as him would intimidate people, but he also happens to be a Beast. No one wants to be the reason he goes off on a rage-fueled frenzy, but they wouldn't be. Furies are the vampires who experience abnormal fits of anger at the smallest things. Beasts just go off sometimes without reason. Doesn't matter how much someone annoys them, they're not going to explode until that timer reaches zero.

Though, Aziz did tell me how he manages the problem: meat.

Go figure. Vampires with a strong affinity to animals can also consume raw meat. Maybe they *have* to and the uncontrollable rage comes from them not realizing it and only drinking blood? Who knows?

Anyway, he steps out from under the porch, staring up at me as I sink down to the courtyard in front of the manor house like some kind of Valkyrie maiden bringing a fallen warrior back home. I'm quite a bit shorter and skinnier than them, and I don't have wings, but it's gotta look similar.

Take a bunch of yarn strands and krazy-glue them in a crisscross pattern to your bare chest. Let it all dry, then rip all the yarn strands off at once. If you do that, you'll understand what it feels like when Aziz takes Holden from me and his burnt body peels the semidry blood sludge from the claw gouges. It hurts so much, flashes of light dance in front of me.

I may even black out on my feet for a moment. Seems like Holden vanished into thin air and Aziz is in front of me offering his black jacket. Seriously, like six of me could fit inside this thing. Well, I say 'offering,' but he's not waiting for me to accept it, already in the process of wrapping it around me. Another security guy carries Holden into the house.

"Are you okay, Miss Wright?" asks Aziz.

"Mostly." I snug the giant blazer around myself. "Thanks."

He nods, grinning. "You are most welcome."

"Sorry. I'm all bloody." I fuss at the big jacket. "Gonna stain this."

"No worries, Miss Wright. I have a whole closet full of them." He walks me to the door. "Mr. Wolent is waiting to talk to you."

Ugh. Great. This giant blazer doesn't make me feel any less awkward about a meeting with the boss while topless and bloody. I'm sure he's seen far worse, but it's going to take me quite a few more years before becoming so jaded it won't feel like doing something inappropriate to walk into his office looking like I just survived an air raid on a small village in Baghdad. It's like disrespectful, embarrassing, rude, whatever, all rolled into one unpleasant emotion.

Still, I'm being asked to meet him and he obviously knows the state I'm in. Ugh, whatever. Follows Rules Girl is too chicken to protest. I stand around in the giant foyer for a while, trying not to drip blood on the fancy marble floor tiles or blush too hard. Clicking coming down the curved staircase in the next room announces the arrival of Vanessa Prentice. Usually, when I see her, it's at one of the routine soirees and Aurélie is standing next to me. There's a teeny bit of jealousy there, about ninety-five percent coming from Vanessa's side. Sparks always fly between them. Jennifer Ruiz, too, but she's not as openly jealous as Vanessa.

They both tend to treat me like the poor orphan waif some high society woman decided to adopt and 'scrub up' into being presentable. Wait, no... not quite. It's not *derisive* condescension. They don't object to me being there. It's merely condescension with a bit of aww.

At the moment, however, Vanessa shocks me. Her demeanor is entirely normal. No cattiness, no pity, nothing more than a bit of a 'wow, you had a rough night' eyebrow lift. Not sure how genuine she's being, but I'm too tired to question.

"Come, dear." Vanessa stops at the bottom of the stairs, waving for me to follow her. "You can clean up and change before explaining what happened."

I walk over. "Thanks."

Vanessa nods once, then leads me up to the second floor, down a long, lavish hallway to a bathroom bigger than my bedroom. "You don't need to rush, but try not to take all night."

"Okay. Appreciate it. Thank you."

The tall, voluptuous redhead gives me the most genuine smile ever to appear on her face in my presence, then walks off. She's clearly not jealous of me. Also, I couldn't care less. Looks aren't forev—wait.

For us, they are.

SOAKING IN A BATHTUB WORTH MORE THAN MOM'S GMC YUKON IS A strange experience.

The claw marks are still way too tender to enjoy the bath, so there's no point trying to get comfortable. Pain slows down the process of cleaning up, but I manage to wash off the dirt, shredded bits of vegetation, and blood, then dry off in a reasonable amount of time. The 'change of clothes' part turns out to be a red dress Vanessa left hanging on the inside of the bathroom door. It's probably hers, or at least made for a woman a little bigger than me. Not sure if she chose red to hide blood or because her closet is full of red dresses.

By now, I've stopped bleeding even though some of the slashes *look* open. The dress hides most of them, except for a few right below my neck. The upper portion of the back is bare, but my hair is long and thick enough to cover the scratches. Yeah, I'm going to be staying inside for a few days or wearing turtlenecks.

She didn't bother leaving shoes, but I don't care. I'm so used to Mom's rule about no shoes in the house, it feels completely normal not wearing any while inside. I head downstairs to Wolent's study-slash-office. He's there, along with Vanessa and—ugh—Stefano Bianchi. Seeing him makes me tense up, but he's not sneering, rather giving me more of an 'oh, you' look. He's clearly not happy to see me, but active disdain appears to be turned off for now.

"Sorry for the delay. Got ripped up a bit." I ease the door closed behind me and approach the big green chairs facing the desk.

"Understandable." Wolent smiles, gesturing at them. "Please, sit and tell us what happened. Holden was not in any condition to speak."

I sit. "How is he?"

"He will recover... eventually." Wolent grimaces.

"We went to the bar where the exiles were supposed to be and found them there..." I proceed to explain everything important. Don't really need to go into detail about them having Warhammer figurines. "... so, I'm assuming the strange purple light when they burned must be proof of them being Oblivare."

Stefano, who sat through my story stone-faced, shifts to an expression of worried annoyance.

"The reliquary remained in the car?" Wolent raises one eyebrow.

I nod. "Yes. No way could any vampire have possibly gotten to it. The fire burned too intense. I had to toss the Oblivare from like twenty feet away not to burn myself."

"Understood. Good job, Sarah." Wolent smiles.

"Oblivare... here?" Stefano cuts his gaze to the boss. "This is not good."

Wolent pats the armrest of his chair. "Ahh, Stefano. What would I do without you here to point out the obvious?"

Vanessa suppresses a laugh.

Amazingly, Stefano smiles.

"You sound surprised." I squeeze my hands into fists, forcing myself not to fuss at the itchy scratches.

Wolent nods once. "The Oblivare generally dislike North America and prefer to remain in Europe."

Heh. I chuckle. "Yeah, we're kinda destroying society well enough on our own without their help."

Stefano puffs air to the side, a little roll of the eyes conveying agreement. He's a hardcore traditionalist, so he definitely thinks society is in flames. I imagine if any vampire existed as opposite as possible to the goals of the Oblivare, it would be him... and Paolo Cabrini. Of course, those two would bring back royal courts and a harsh division between nobility and commoners. Old school 'society' so to speak. They're also not too big on women being much more than accessories a man wears on his arm, but at least he's stopped saying crap like that out loud.

"Indeed." Wolent chuckles in a 'sad but true' manner.

"Should we be worried about them?" I ask.

"I wouldn't," mutters Vanessa. "Those cretins have spent the last few thousand years trying to drag us back ten thousand years, and still haven't managed to organize anything more destructive than a drunken Viking raid on a small fishing village."

The men laugh.

"Ms. Prentice is correct." Wolent leans back. "Their beliefs create their greatest flaw. They despise large groups, organization, anything even remotely resembling a system of leadership. It is unlikely there are more in the area, but we shouldn't disregard the possibility. You saw six?"

"Yes. Holden shot the two we spoke with, then the four chased us. Four are dead, but the two in the bar might still be there. Holden only shot them in the head. They're going to recover unless you send people to clean up."

He steeples his fingertips, mulling. "You need worry no more about the issue. I'm proud of you. Handled things quite well tonight, given the unexpected nature of what happened."

"Thank you, Mr. Wolent."

"I can tell you're looking forward to relaxing at home." He gestures at me in a 'be my guest' manner. "Fly safe."

"Thanks." I stand and nod in gratitude to Vanessa. "I'll get this back to you as soon as I can."

"Keep it, dear. I have dozens." She winks.

"Are you sure? It looks expensive."

Vanessa waves dismissively. "It's not as pricey as you think. Don't feel guilty. However, I'd hope you don't wear it to your next fight. It *is* too expensive to shred."

"No problem. Not planning to dress fancy for my next near-death experience." I face Stefano and offer a shallow but respectful bow of farewell. "Mr. Bianchi."

He nods once at me. Wow. Okay, not gonna argue. The man no longer seems to despise me. There's definitely no like there, but at least the hate's gone. He's not going to change too much of his opinion about me until I'm no longer living among mortals. Whatever. I can wait.

I head out, grab my purse from the foyer—so glad I decided to leave it here before getting in the car with Holden—and exit via the front door. After a brief 'thanks again and see ya' hug for Aziz, I'm in the air.

Wolent said not to worry.

Yeah, right. We killed four Oblivare, stole their reliquary, and two who saw me up close are still out there. I'm gonna be looking over my shoulder for at least a month. Good thing school's almost done for the year. Feel *much* safer having a hellhound nearby.

Seriously, my life is weird.

6

THE TOME OF F-SOMETHING

S ophia didn't feel out of place at all in the mystic's library.

Sure, she sat on a chair too big for her in a room decorated like it belonged in the 1400s while wearing a Sailor Moon T-shirt and a frilly, multilayered pink skirt. The room smelled of dry papers, candle wax, and an unrecognizable milieu of blended arcane herbs. Klepto curled up asleep around a candlestick on the table beside the book, a fuzzy grey donut with ears. Her small MP3 player —loaded with anime soundtracks—also didn't fit the scenery. Nor did the purple flip-flops on the floor beneath the chair. Good chance foam shoes didn't exist in the days of King Arthur. She half expected to see a bunch of knights here, except for one significant problem: a *rectangular*, not round, table.

A second significant problem responsible for the lack of knights involved the modern era. Knights simply didn't exist in large enough numbers anymore to congregate around randomly placed round tables.

She pondered making some out of illusions but didn't want to startle any of the mystics. They had, after all, been gracious enough to welcome her here twice a month to help her learn. Not that she'd ever say so, but Sophia felt they ought to help since they happened to be responsible for her magic being usable. According to them, she'd always had untapped—inaccessible—potential. Due to the circumstances of the world, the gift following along her family line remained sealed in a mental vault, out of reach.

Today's reading involved theories of magic and how the majority of the Earth's population not believing magic really existed had a genuine effect on it. The book claimed magic had more power and became easier to perform when no one could see it except the person using it. Exceptions, of course, for other people who firmly believed magic worked. A spellcasting event big enough to be seen by everyone in an entire city would undoubtedly fail, as their collective disbelief would negate the energy. Further exceptions could happen if the effect of the magic covered a large area but worked in a way as to not be visible. If no one observed unusual phenomena, their resultant disbelief energy wouldn't be triggered and tamp down the arcane forces.

The book didn't read like something intended for an eleven-year-old, but Sophia had little difficulty keeping up. She tended to read novels aimed at teenagers or adults—as long as her parents approved the content.

Speaking of parents, Darren Anderson had evidently made a decent enough impression on Dad for him to trust leaving her here for the afternoon and running some Saturday errands. Much the same way he drove her to dance class sometimes or Sam to Taekwondo, he occasionally brought her to see the mystics. He stayed the whole four hours the first time, watching the lessons and chatting with Darren, Callum, and Landon.

She'd briefly met the fourth member of the lodge, a woman named Anastasia Grant. Between her mild English accent and hairstyle, she reminded Sophia of the 'pleasant but demanding' nanny an aristocratic couple living in a remote castle might hire to watch their two kids. The woman also happened to be the one who cast the spell to yank Sophia's soul out of her body and borrow it to search the house for Coralie's mummified remains. Anastasia gave off a sense of unease around her, probably expecting revenge of some form.

However, the other mystics already explained Sophia's ghostly self would have gone back where it belonged once the spell ended.

As long as no wandering random bad thing did something to her first.

Once she finished reading the stuff about collective consciousness having an effect on magic, she slipped out of the big chair, stepped into her flip-flops, and headed across the library. Klepto teleported onto her shoulder, clinging like a furry version of a parrot perched atop a pirate. Mr. Anderson asked her to go to the 'fire room' once she finished reading. This likely meant they intended to have her attempt using elemental magic. In the days of King Arthur, people like Merlin could summon actual fireballs and throw them or even call lightning down from the clouds. Since she'd thus far surprised them by learning magic so rapidly, the mystics wanted to see if Sophia could come close to doing anything so obvious.

Fireballs sounded neat, but Sophia didn't like the idea of hurting anyone. However, Sam told her about Mel—another demon he'd made friends with—and how she destroyed a bad vampire in an instant using fire. As long as she could consider bad vampires to be 'not people,' she might be able to set aside her guilt.

Midway along the library wall on the left, nestled between a pair of ceiling-high shelves, a large book sat on a pedestal inside a wood-framed glass case. Curious, Sophia rounded past the end of another long table—it remained a mystery why a lodge of mystics with only four members needed a library big enough for fifty people—and approached the case.

She'd obviously seen the book in the background during previous visits, but it hadn't piqued her curiosity. Also, today had been the first time the mystics left her alone here to read on her own. Something about this book felt special. It looked rather old, dusty but not too worn. Intricate gold inlay on a forest green cover contained no titles or words, merely a decorative pattern. It had to be at least six inches of gild-edged pages, and probably two feet tall. Despite it being a book, and rather obviously neither alive nor able to speak, she picked up a distinct sense it didn't particularly care if she read it or not.

Sophia had never been 'yeah, whatevered' by a book before, so she continued staring at it.

"Mew," said Klepto, the kitten's mouth at her left ear.

"Yeah, I know. I feel it, too." She gingerly brushed her fingers down the glass wall of the case.

Darren Anderson poked his head in the library door, spotted her, then rushed over while grimacing in an 'I best get there before the child breaks something' way. For no reason they had yet explained, the mystics adored wearing clothing from the late 1800s. Every time she came here, she felt like she strayed onto the set of yet another Sherlock Holmes re-imagining.

"Finished reading?" Darren sidled up on her right.

"Yes." She clasped her hands behind her back and smiled up at him. "What is this?"

"It is, umm." He grasped the lapels of his old-timey coat. "The Tome of F Knowledge."

Sophia raised one eyebrow. "F knowledge? Like... all about the letter F?"

He chuckled. "No. We're not entirely sure if it's forbidden, forgotten, frivolous, fanciful, or something else like... oh, freakish. Damnable water stain on the records ruined the ink."

"Doesn't it say the title inside?" Sophia pointed at the case.

"I imagine it might, but we haven't yet seen any reason to disturb it."

"Disturb it?" Sophia blinked. "It's alive?"

Darren pulled at the sad little goatee he'd been trying to grow. "Not alive, no. Certain magical tomes can be used as devices in which to seal powerful energies. It might be harmless, or it might be like a box of fleas that go everywhere once you open the lid."

"Hmm." She leaned as close as she could to the case without letting her nose touch glass. "It can't be the Tome of Forgotten knowledge, because it's in a book. As soon as you read it, it won't be forgotten knowledge."

"Whatever is in there, it's highly advanced." Darren nodded to the side in a 'come on, let's be off' manner.

"Couldn't help but overhear," said Callum out of nowhere, making Darren jump and grab his chest.

Callum Bailey strolled out from behind a freestanding floor-to-ceiling bookshelf a short distance to the right. He wore a shimmery blue outfit sporting a ruffled collar. Totally looked like he belonged in a Renaissance painting, though he'd pulled his longish blond hair back into a style reminiscent of Colonial America.

Sophia glanced from Darren to Callum and back to the book. *Great. Sherlock Holmes and Vampire Lestat.* It baffled her why the mystics—except for Anastasia—liked dressing up in historical clothes. They, unlike vampires, couldn't possibly have been alive long ago.

"You startled me." Darren gave his coat a sharp tug of annoyance.

"Letting the book rattle you again?" asked Callum in an amused tone. "He believes it is dangerous. Legend says a mystic can use the tome to discover the answer to whatever is on their mind when they open it. Within reason, of course. I doubt it will provide an answer to questions like 'why are we here' or esoteric philosophy."

"Hrmph." Darren shook his head. "It is undoubtedly a repository of information associated to rituals of a decidedly unpleasant nature. Those rumors it contains answers to whatever one wishes to read about are fancy, nothing more. A trick to lure the unwary into temptation."

Sophia continued sensing indifference from the book. Didn't seem dangerous, evil, or even scary. "Let me guess… it's a monkey's paw?"

"Not as far as we know." Callum flicked a bit of lint from his sleeve. "We don't know much, though. My dear associate here refuses to open it."

"With good reason." Darren folded his arms.

"Really? No monkey paw? No horrible payment for whatever knowledge the book gives?" Sophia peered through her reflection at the innocent-seeming book. "So why is it locked in a case?"

Callum laughed. "To prevent anyone from stealing it. Or to ensure it doesn't steal itself."

Darren sighed.

"Steals itself?" asked Sophia.

"There are records indicating the book often changed location, apparently of its own accord... but always back to its preferred shelf." Callum grinned as if teasing Darren with spooky stories. "Perhaps old man Crowley grew tired of people borrowing and not returning it, so he gave it an enchantment."

"Pff." Darren sighed louder. "You and I both know full well Crowley couldn't have enchanted a light bulb to work when connected to electricity. I dare not mention where his interests lay in the company of our guest."

Uh oh. Must be bad. Sophia cringed.

"Also, we haven't figured out how to make it work." Callum nudged Darren.

"Umm, it's a book. They're not difficult to operate." Sophia put on an innocent face. "Can I look at it?"

Darren winced. "Perhaps in time. You are not near advanced enough for this tome."

She lifted her arms and let them drop at her sides. "Oh, come on. No one spends this much time talking about an object unless it's going to be pivotally important later on."

The men blinked at her.

"I'm *definitely* going to end up reading this book at some point. Might as well skip the delay." She smiled.

Darren laughed. "You may be right, but it shall not be this day. We've only two hours left for you to test the waters of elemental magic before your father returns to collect you."

"Ugh. Okay." Sophia turned away from the case and followed the men out of the library.

At the door, she peered back at the giant book. With the library lights off, the Tome of F Knowledge appeared to be shrouded in a faint golden glow.

Hope I don't forget about it when it's important.

7

THE MAGIC OF PEACHES & CREAM

Completely underwater on a Saturday night.

Kinda sounds like the name of a concept album from one of those strange early Eighties bands Dad listens to, like the Talking Heads. Classic Hollywood loved to show vampires resting in coffins for some reason. The reality is closer to a tub full of opaque whitish-orange water. Not sure how many other vampires like to take hour-long soaks, but it can't only be me. Full immersion solves a few minor nuisances. It keeps me warm all over and offers privacy in the event of a sibling invasion. My family also happened to get amazingly lucky by finding a house where the main bathtub is long enough so I don't get stuck having to decide if my head, knees, or feet end up out of the water. Granted, most normal people leave their face above water intentionally. Breathing is important to mortals, after all.

Having another vampire go full Jackson Pollack on my chest and back with claws leaves me so tender I can't wear a shirt comfortably. Even air blowing across the wounds is unpleasant, but fabric rubbing it? Ack. Thankfully, whatever they put in these P&C bath bombs is amazing. Not only does it make my skin silky smooth, it eases the sting from tainted undead claws. Got a feeling Bed Bath and Beyond isn't going to use 'soothes vampire wounds' in their marketing campaign.

My thoughts go to weird places while I float here, hoping for the stinging to stop.

I forget who mentioned it, but at one of the soirees, someone told me 'back in the day' female vampires didn't usually get involved in public violence. My daydreams play out a scenario of some woman vampire in a gown worthy of Aurélie getting into a claw fight, but the instant one of the hostile vamps shreds her dress, exposing her chest, all the men scream and avert their eyes as if they'd witnessed Medusa. You know, being gentlemen of the day and all.

The reason lady vampires didn't fight back then is boobs gave them an unfair advantage.

It's difficult to laugh underwater. Yeah, I know it's silly and not at all true. If vampires got to the point they went claws out, it's really unlikely they'd care much about decorum and avert their eyes from the bosom of the lady they tried to tear to pieces. Like, murdering her is just fine, but oh noes, don't look at the bare skin. In those days, showing a little too much *ankle* could get a lady called unkind things in whispers.

Pretty infuriating how men always blame us for their lack of willpower. As if all women have magical powers of charm men are helpless to resist. Okay, so I *do* happen to have charm powers mortal men *can't* resist, but that's not the point. Hmm. Maybe some guy a thousand years ago survived an encounter with a lady vampire and figured out what happened… so *all* women in his mind became devils.

Bleh. Whatever.

I'm not out to change the world, only get these stupid slash marks to stop burning.

Back to daydreams. Now I'm picturing a sarcastic lady vampire in the 1800s not giving a crap what anyone thinks of her, going out to kick ass, and spending a week rattling around her lavish manor house in her birthday suit because she's been torn up. Can't bear the pain of touching fabric and she has no F's to give who sees her parading around.

Of course, I don't have a large manor house, or servants. I *do* have parents and siblings, so that's a big no on sitting around shirtless for a week. I ended up borrowing one of Mom's super-soft bathrobes. She didn't mind me using it and the plush material made the idea of moving simply unpleasant rather than dreadful. Can't wait for these rips to finish closing. It's damn annoying, but one of those things to deal with.

Live by the claw, die by the claw as they say. Or, 'if you're gonna play with claws, expect to be scratched'. I can't help but laugh at both phrases since I first heard them from Ashley, and she was talking about having cats, not being a vampire.

Also, my wounds are taking longer than usual to heal. Aurélie thinks it's due to Oblivare having much darker, more malignant energy. So yeah, it sucked. Even after a week, I still have a cross-hatch pattern of thin red lines all over my chest. The constant stinging pain and itching are bothersome, like getting trapped behind a slow walker in a narrow aisle at Target or having a four-year-old kid sister who just got a toy karaoke machine for her birthday.

On a more pleasant note, it seems being chained to a tree during sunrise had an effect on my ability to resist sunlight. Dad compared it to someone trying to build up a tolerance to spicy food by eating a Carolina Reaper pepper whole when they're only barely able to handle jalapeños. And no, there's no way in hell I'm touching a reaper pepper. Spicy chicken nuggets burned like a medieval inquisition torture involving a red-hot iron being poked somewhere red-hot irons do *not* belong. While I don't know which type of pepper the Brass Tap uses in their hot sauce, I am almost certain it's *not* a reaper. Probably habanero, but still. I'm not going through that again. I'd rather get into another claw fight.

As far as the sun goes, my earlier theory about my resistance to it counting as a 'power' or skill appears to be correct. Being forced to endure exposure to sunrise basically exploited my vampiric survival instinct to smash down the mental barrier created by my fear of the sun. Wanting to avoid painful daylight whenever possible didn't make it easy to practice tolerating it. Mom compared it to how a little kid is afraid to jump in a pool… until they get pushed in, then realize it's not as scary as they thought.

So, yeah, I've somewhat renegotiated my contract terms with the ball of fiery ouch.

Not a drastic shift, but it's noticeable. My butt still isn't going to be anywhere near California beaches in July, unless it's at night. Gloomy days no longer bother me at all. The formerly nuclear Seattle 'nice' weather that kept me locked up in my basement room is now 'annoying.' I can tolerate direct sunlight from a clear sky—at least in the Pacific Northwest—for a little under an hour before it starts to hurt. One could say I've given up smoking. Combustion would probably still happen if I pushed it too far, like going to Nevada or standing too close to Ashley in a bikini on a sunny day. I'd crack a joke about her being so white she looks like a vampire, but legit vampires *have* mistaken her for undead by paleness alone.

I thought about attempting a normal school schedule next semester instead of night school, but sun resistance hasn't affected my sleep and wake times. Even though it's possible for me to put up with daylight more easily, my butt still refuses to become conscious any earlier than around 2:30 p.m. So much for day classes. Not happening. College in general is not particularly beneficial to me. I'm doing it mostly for two reasons. One, I spent the past four years of high school expecting to go to college, and two, my parents *really* wanted me to go. Getting past my expectations isn't too difficult, but I don't want to disappoint Mom and Dad. Becoming immortal *really* made me aware how precious little time we have together.

Anyway, living in Seattle has moved a big notch closer to normal for me. I'm still totally offline when in contact with daylight, but it has to be really bright to reach the point of uncomfortable. Granted, resisting sunlight drains power fast, forcing me to feed every day or every two days if I go out in it.

In other Earth-shattering news, Sam's turning ten next week on the nineteenth of June. Speaking of my little brother, his demons have kept kinda quiet. Blix, of course, has become a permanent part of the household. He's cool around the parents, allowing them to see him and even lending a hand sometimes with chores, hobbies, or fixing stuff. I had to laugh the other week when Blix chased Dad away from the kitchen sink. My father insisted he could fix the disposer, but the imp agreed with Mom.

As for his other demons, Olmaz, the hellhound, and the succubus he nicknamed Mel, they've been pretty much out of sight. The dog is still basically living in our backyard. He's invisible, so he doesn't bother anyone. Never thought I'd think this, but having a demonic dog around makes me feel safer. If Robert or Albert somehow managed to find where I live and showed up for revenge, they'd have a *really* bad night. Hopefully, if they realized we destroyed their four friends, they aren't in any great hurry to come after me. Even if *I'm* not scary, they'd worry about retaliation from Wolent. Guess 'becoming official' ended up being beneficial to me after all.

My brother doesn't even know why or how the hellhound showed up. His best theory is he simply wanted a dog but didn't bother asking the 'rents since we all knew Mom would say no. Not sure why she's so against pets. Suppose I could find out. Nah. Can't break my promise about mind-reading my family. Besides, it's not important. Sophia's got a kitten—sorta. And Sam's got the hellhound, plus two frogs.

It's a good thing the bigger ones aren't obvious. I'm sure Mom wouldn't appreciate Sam inviting demons over. His friends Daryl and Jordan are close enough. No, they're okay kids. Just... boys that age are deafeningly loud engines of destruction. Another good thing: my brother hasn't sprouted any additional body parts. It's fairly safe to assume at this point Olmaz didn't turn him into a half-demon or something weird. Amazingly, the 'rents handled his wings in stride. Mom's stride in this particular case involved a large glass of wine, but she handled it. As Dad said, kids are eventually supposed to spread their wings.

Mom didn't appreciate the pun.

What made the difference is the wings aren't like permanently part of him. Once we put it in D&D terms—a spell that summons them temporarily—Dad understood and all became cool.

So, yeah. Peaches and Cream is my world at the moment.

My stomach growls.

Damn. Figures. Great timing. Another irritating part of recovering from claw wounds is how I'll get hungry out of the blue at strange times. It's kinda like being pregnant, only without the accompanying random urges to kill. Healing hunger is harder to put off than ordinary hunger, but right now? It can wait a little while.

Don't wanna waste the bath bomb.

8

EVEN VAMPIRES GET HANGRY

F igure an hour and twenty is enough to get my money's worth out of the bath bomb.

It appears to have helped. Wrapping myself in a towel doesn't feel like I'm rubbing alcohol-soaked sandpaper over my skin. It's been a week. About damn time for it to heal. Know what was *not* fun? Sitting in class wearing a long-sleeved, high-necked top and feeling like I'd wrapped my torso in barbed wire. Twice, I came close to compelling the teacher to think I'd stayed all night and going home. Alas, Follows Rules Girl chickened out.

Once downstairs in my bedroom, I trade the damp towel for a pair of jean shorts and a loose-fitting long-sleeved Seahawks shirt. Sports aren't really my thing, but the accessories are comfortable. Yeah, I know. Why wear a long-sleeved shirt with shorts. Looks kinda strange, but whatever. Going for comfort, not warmth. Besides, it's June.

Out of laziness—not wanting to take the few seconds to cross the house and grab shoes from the cubby at the front door—I skip them and go out the patio door. Won't be staying out long, only enough to find someone to eat. If I keep my internal machinery happy, maybe the claw marks will disappear faster.

Note to self: don't let an Oblivare scratch you again.

Easier said than done. If I'm aware of having to deal with them, bringing a sword should give me enough reach to stay away from diseased fingernails. Well, not technically 'diseased,' but it's a lot easier to say than 'claws tainted by vile inhuman necromantic energies no one truly understands.' The problem here, though, is it's pretty unlikely any remaining Oblivare in the area are going to call ahead to schedule a fight. If I ever again meet them, it'll be either Wolent sending us in to clean up or being on the receiving end of an ambush.

Can't exactly carry a katana with me everywhere I go. People might start thinking I'm strange.

Or a weeaboo. Honestly, I'm not one of those *ooh katana!* people. It happened to be handy when I needed it, and, well, its former owner has no further need of it. A falchion, saber, or cutlass would fit my style better, but *real* versions of those swords are much more difficult to come by. The ones they sell at renaissance festivals tend to be for show, and largely blunt.

Use what you have, as they say.

Suppose I could ask Dad where he got the sword he gave Sierra for Christmas. It's as real as a sword can get these days. Dalton called it an 'arming sword.' Medium sized, straight, two-edged, the sort of weapon knights tended to carry as a backup in case they lost their longsword or broadsword.

Anyway, not an issue. Maybe I *should* bring the katana with me, but it creates certain problems of the attention-gathering kind. A girl walking around carrying a sword is kinda memorable. Existence as a vampire is all about blending in and not standing out. Besides, I can run. Only reason I didn't haul ass after the crash is not wanting to be responsible for Holden's destruction. Yeah, those four would have destroyed him. Dwelling on the truth of it has helped me set aside my guilt for perma-killing four vampires. Helps they're not 'really' vampires, but some other dark AF thing pretending to be a vampire.

This girl can kill monsters just fine. They're like the stevia of creatures—guilt free.

My shirt flutters from the breeze on the flight from Cottage Lake to Seattle. It's nice living near a major city, especially a port town. No shortage of strange faces. Feeding works much better when the person I bite is one who's never seen me before and never will again. Picked up a tip from Amy, one of the local Lost Ones. She suggested cruising around the wharf districts and areas frequented by sailors in town only long enough for their boats to transfer cargo and refuel. If I can take a meal from someone who doesn't even live in this state, even better.

A few minutes after leaving home, I'm cruising over Georgetown, a little east of the Duwamish Waterway. It's a bit late for restaurant traffic, but there should be some bars still open. Odd. Tonight's fairly quiet out. Not much traffic, either pedestrian or car. City at night can be as beautiful as undisturbed land sometimes. I'm sure it's been said before, but flying is effing awesome. No one really understands why some vampires can and some can't. It's more common in certain bloodlines, but not guaranteed for anyone. Really feel sorry for any vampire who can't fly. Then again, they can't miss what they don't know.

Inhuman hissing and a man's panicked screaming floats up from the direction of a giant yard of parked semi-trailers and railroad cars. It's not an ordinary sort of sound one generally hears in downtown Seattle after midnight unless the Seahawks lost a big game. Curious, I drift toward it, scanning the area below. Doesn't take me long to spot the source: two men running down a channel between rows of cargo containers. A flashlight beam wobbles rapidly across the pavement from the lead guy. He's carrying it, but making no attempt to use it— simply running in total panic.

It's fairly obvious why... the guy chasing him has sprouted claws, bared his fangs, and his eyes are glowing red.

Ugh. Newbies. Seriously.

Still, something more than idiocy is going on. Vampire eyes glow for two main reasons—well, three. The first two are kinda related. If we get extremely pissed off, they light up. We can also *make* them glow as an intimidation thing. Extreme anger just kinda does it whether we want to or not. Second reason, and more concerning, is when we're freaking out. Eye-glow freakouts are generally situations where we've lost our mind for one reason or another: starvation, sudden exposure to bright sunlight, or watching someone order two Big Macs with a super-size fries and a *diet* coke.

I dive after them, swooping in low behind the vampire. Hard to tell under his wild mop of black hair, but he seems kinda young. He's young in the other way, too. It's hard to describe the sense, as it's not one any mortal has. Vampires as old as Wolent and Stefano radiate a certain vibe, a silent conveyance of power that puts me on eggshells in their presence. This guy has the exact opposite feel. He's radiating anti-dread. Watching him freak out chasing this security guard is almost funny. Ever see a skinny sixth-grader threaten to kick the ass of a high school senior? Same way everyone looks at the little kid, I'm looking at this guy. Also, a bit of 'hey, are you okay' in there too, but it's probably due to me being a softie.

Neither of them notice me. Baby vampire is focused on his prey, and said prey is pretty damn focused on staying alive. The almost Tasmanian Devil frenzy going on is an obvious clue someone's not in his right mind. It is kinda funny watching him stumble-run after the mortal, clawing at the air, hissing, growling, and nearly tripping over his own legs.

The security guard, however, is totally not finding the situation amusing.

Biggest initial problem to deal with: this newbie vampire is gonna kill this man.

This is how I *always* get into trouble. Try to help someone and it ends up biting me in the ass. Maybe reframing it to helping vampires in general rather than one specific security guard will give my butt some Kevlar plates. Hopefully, this nonsense isn't appearing on any CCTV cameras anywhere. Okay, Sarah, time to do something before we run out of ground. The row of stacked-up cargo boxes only goes so far.

I lunge forward and shove Baby Vamp—doo doo doo—sideways. He face-plants a metal cargo box, sending a rolling, hollow *boom* over the whole yard. The sudden loud noise makes the security guard shriek. He screams again when I grab his shoulder and spin him around, but it trails off to a bewildered stare. Poor guy had been expecting a monster, not innocent li'l me.

Without giving him time to say a word, I dive into his thoughts and compel him to forget being chased around the shipping yard. We got lucky. He'd been so terrified, he hadn't been able to grab his radio to call for help. Don't even need to create a memory of chasing a homeless person out of the yard so he can tell the other guards he had a false alarm. It's easier to change reasons than remove a traumatic event entirely, so dude thinks he had a stray black bear coming after him.

He gets an instruction to go back to the office, use the bathroom, and resume his night as if nothing supernatural happened. Baby Vamp leaps at us while I'm finishing up the memory overwrite. I flick my right arm out and catch the guy by the neck, holding him back as he tries to shred the security guard. Flailing claws wave back and forth inches from the guy's shirt. He's gone full feral—or is as dumb as a brick—and keeps up the futile scrabbling for the ten or so seconds it takes me to send Security Man on his way.

As soon as he walks off, I throw Baby Vamp against the nearest cargo container. Not trying to hurt him, merely give him enough of a whack to hopefully snap him out of his crazed mental state. He crashes against the sky-blue painted metal with a subdued *whump*— guess this one's full. The guy bounces off it and rushes at me, a momentary flicker of confusion in his eyes. Yeah, he's probably realizing I'm a vampire too and thus not food, but his brain's not really present.

I catch the guy, shove-walking him backward until his shoulders touch the cargo box. Gotta look pretty silly for me to manhandle a guy a full head taller than me, but he's skinny, too. He struggles, unable to go anywhere despite his height advantage. Feels like I'm holding down a possessed ventriloquist dummy. This poor guy is weaker than one of Uncle Hank's political arguments. In fact, Sam could probably overpower him. I don't mean it as an exaggeration.

My almost-ten-year-old brother is legit as strong or stronger than him. Baby Vamp here has to be starved for blood.

"Hey. Wake up. Get a grip."

He keeps trying to push me away.

After a few seconds of us being nose to nose, it hits me I know this guy. At least, he looks super familiar. I'm damn sure I've seen him somewhere, but can't think of where. His clothes are relatively normal, if a bit on the nicer side. My confusion lasts a while, not an immediate problem as I'm kinda stuck here holding him down. When he finally emits an annoyed groan, his voice makes my memory click. This is Brady Welch. The paleness seeming normal threw me off. I didn't meet him at some vampire event. I knew him *before* he became a vampire. He's familiar because we were in the same class all four years of high school. Brady used to be seriously into the goth thing, to the point he wore white face paint and black lipstick to school.

Didn't recognize him right away because we didn't exactly hang out. He had his clique; I had my non-clique. You know, the smallish group of high schoolers who don't fit any of the stereotypes and simply exist. Popular kids probably lumped me in with the nerds or oddballs, but not so much so they picked on me.

Anyway, what the hell?

"Brady?" I ask.

He shows zero recognition, simply keeps trying to get away from me. Some portion of his brain stem is still operating because he hasn't tried to bite me. There's a trace of processing going on, enough to make him realize biting me won't result in feeding.

"What happened to you?" I pat him on the face a few times while keeping him pinned against the cargo box. "You're like days old, aren't you?"

Brady grunts, still attempting to shove me away.

Grr. This stinks. He might be seriously new, but I'm not old enough to read his thoughts. Something like a hundred-year age gap is needed before a vampire can see into another vampire's head. As far as I know, it's not possible for us to mind-control each other no matter how ancient we get. Works for me. Kinda reassuring to know I'll never be the victim of a compulsion.

Hmm. What do I do with him? Can't leave or he'll go maul someone and make a big hard-to-hide spectacle of it. He might even get himself destroyed. There's clearly no talking to him at the moment.

Son of a... whoever gave the Transference to him obviously abandoned him right after. Probably didn't even explain what happened. Bet he's got no idea he has to drink blood, and this is him experiencing the aftereffects of starvation. Okay, we might not have been friends, but I definitely didn't have a problem with the kid. Kinda pisses me off some jackass randomly turned him, maybe as a joke, for being a goth. Well, former Goth. At the moment, except for the hair, he's a male model for an LL Bean catalog.

Obviously, he needs blood. But... he's most certainly going to kill anyone he bites. In his state of mind, he won't be able to stop feeding before he takes too much. Problem is, I can't hold him back *and* go find a blood donor.

I pin Brady to the cargo box by one hand around his neck and pull my phone out.

"Hey, Siri. Call Glim."

"Calling Glim..."

It rings four times before silence, which is normal for him. He never says anything when he answers a phone until he knows who's on the other end.

"It's me. Do you have a couple minutes? Found a new guy who's a little out of his mind, and I could really use a little help wrangling him."

"Hello, Sarah," says Glim. "All right. I'll be there soon."

9

MOSTLY PAINLESS

B rady keeps fighting me like an android unaware of its surroundings.

He's not even really looking at me, almost as if his brain can't process the reason why he's unable to roam off in search of food. Even though I'm expecting Glim to arrive at any minute, when he finally steps out from between two cargo boxes amid a whorl of black fog, I jump. It amuses him to lightly startle people. Shame he can't do it too often. Any mortal who sees him would scream and either faint or sprint away.

Shadows are, as they say, not 'aesthetically pleasing.' Grey skin, bald, pointy ears, yellow eyes, extremely obvious non-retractable fangs... yeah. His appearance never bothered me. Horror movies have never been my thing. By all expectations, I *should* have taken one look at him and screamed or cringed away... but I saw the guy he really is inside. Yeah, sappy as hell, I know. But it's what happened.

"Hmm." Glim leans close, examining Brady. "You know him."

Not a question.

"Sort of. We went to the same high school. Never really talked. I saw him like every day for four years... except like summer and stuff."

"Would explain the weakness of the connection."

Whoa. I raise both eyebrows. "What kind of connection? We're connected?"

Glim flashes a toothy smile. "Spend enough time in someone's presence, a connection develops, even if you do not interact. Your energies are familiar with each other."

"I didn't turn him."

"Of course not. The link between the two of you is nowhere near strong enough for such a bond. He's quite new."

"Yeah. Got that feeling. He's starved, isn't he?"

Glim takes his left arm. "Yes."

I let go of his shirt and grab his other arm. "He can't feed while he's like this or he's gonna kill someone."

"We will need to bring him somewhere he can be contained while we find some blood for him."

Ack. Can't bring Brady back home. In his condition, he'd be way too dangerous to my parents and the Littles. Though… it might be more a matter of protecting Brady from my siblings. Maybe I could ask the hellhound to sit on him. Nah. "Umm, any idea where we can take him?"

"Yes. Follow." Glim floats upward.

Between the two of us, we carry Brady while flying north and east of the railroad-truck interchange. Glim leads us a few blocks deeper into the industrial district. We land behind a possibly abandoned small warehouse or factory in a lot packed wall-to-fence with junk, mostly parts from large machines. Maybe truck engines or factory stuff. I don't recognize any of it. Even a few random old toilets lay tossed around. An overwhelming stink of heavy fuel oil mixes with the ocean smell all over this part of Seattle.

If not for already being dead, I'd be afraid of growing an extra toe standing barefoot on this dirt. This is like the kind of place you always see EPA dudes in full clean suits raiding. Glim drags Brady over to the building and breaks the door open. We enter a large room containing various giant machines, most of which are covered under plastic tarps. Yeah, definitely abandoned. Or at least closed down for a while. It's not a ruin, but we are in no danger of being disturbed here. The fragrances of dust and metal add to the ambiance. Every breath tastes as though I'm licking dirty steel covered in motor grease.

Glim keeps dragging Brady across the former factory, so I help. He appears to be heading for a spot in the back where a metal mesh wall forms a security cage around three empty shelves. Someone has already cleared out whatever high-value items used to be kept in there. A broken padlock lays on the floor not far from the door. Glim shoves Brady into the security cage and closes it. I grab the busted padlock. It will never lock again, but simply hanging the metal U in the latch is enough to keep the cage closed.

Most vampires, with sufficient motivation, could break out of here. Brady has neither the strength to bust the door open nor the mental faculties to remove the busted padlock. He merely flings himself at the closest part of the mesh and bangs on it.

"Wow, he's pretty far gone," I whisper.

"Seen worse." Glim winks. "It's quite a bit scarier when it happens to an elder. Would you rather keep an eye on him while I go find a donor, or shall I watch him while you go hunting?"

I fidget. Sure, feeding has become pretty casual, but it isn't entirely free of guilt. Doesn't bother me much really, but abduction is a little bit too far, even knowing we practice catch and release. Honestly, the only apprehension I feel about feeding nowadays is dreading bumping into creeps or sickos. There are some minds out there too frightening to look into.

"Go for it. I'll stay with him if you don't mind."

Glim smiles as if he expected me to say that, then vanishes in a whorl of inky black vapors.

Can't tell if he jumped into the shadow realm or simply made an illusion, then stopped allowing me to see him. Yeah, Shadows get some really cool abilities. As much as they give up in looks, they deserve to get *something* out of the deal.

I stand by the door of the security cage attempting to talk to

Brady. We existed in two entirely different orbits back then. Listen to me saying 'back then' as if talking about a time more than one year ago. Okay, to be fair, it's five years ago. High school lasted four years and we've only been graduated one. Five years to a nineteen-year-old is a significant portion of our lives. So yeah, being a freshman *does* kinda feel like a long time ago. Add to it how much has changed for me since then.

Because we had no common interests and didn't even talk to each other, I'm stuck trying to reminisce about goofy things teachers did or a few things students did so crazy everyone from the jocks to the nerds to the delinquents all talked about it. Some guys from the senior class two years ahead of us broke into the school at night in April and spread mass quantities of spray lubricant—like what people cook with —all over the floors. Most of the kids found it hilarious to watch everyone flailing around, unable to stay upright, clinging to locker doors and so on. The faculty didn't appreciate the prank. Rumor had it the principal even wanted to press breaking and entering charges, but they couldn't figure out the specific students involved. Apparently, none of the security cameras had been on that night.

I'm sure it was a total coincidence this kid everyone called Sparks stopped being picked on the next day. Poor guy was eighteen, two years older than me, but looked more like twelve. Probably the smartest kid in the whole school. Total nerd—and AV geek. Yeah, the football guys going from throwing him in trash cans three times a week to defending him overnight had nothing whatsoever to do with the mysterious shutdown of the school's security system.

Brady agrees. At least I think his partially coherent enraged moan —tinged with highly confused desperation—means he thinks the same thing. Either that or he's trying to read *Battlefield Earth*. Nah, he's out of his head. Simply a well-timed animalistic noise randomly lining up with my words. Trying to talk to him seems futile, but I keep rambling. Nothing appears to get through to him until Glim reappears behind me, holding up a late-thirties guy in a frumpy business suit. He's got the man's arm across his shoulder as if helping a drunken friend go home. The mortal's staring off into the ninth dimension, obviously under the influence of a mental fog.

Glim pulls a small pack of red Solo cups from one pocket of his olive drab trench coat, slices it open using a fingernail, and plucks one out. After stuffing the package back in the pocket, he punctures the man's arm with a fang, and begins to let blood dribble into the cup. The instant the man's skin breaks, Brady launches himself at the cage wall in a renewed frenzy. Loud metal rattles echo over the entire building. It's creepy watching him act like a starving dog smelling steak. No trace of humanity at all in his eyes or behavior.

I never got the chance to feed yet. Smelling the blood—buffalo wings for some bizarre reason—makes me even hungrier. A twinge of pain echoes the lines of my healing claw marks. Yeah, I know. Relax. I'm gonna eat soon. This blood isn't for me.

Once the cup nears fullness, Glim seals the wound in the man's arm. He hands me the cup, which is icky warm to the touch, and moves to the security cage. "I'll hold him back. You feed him. Once he tastes it, he should calm down a bit."

I nod.

Glim opens the door, catches Brady when he tries to charge at me, and gets him in a reverse bear hug.

"You want this?" I hold up the cup. "It's yours. Just relax."

Brady squirms. He couldn't throw me off. No way is he getting out of Glim's hold. The closer I get, the less frantic his flailing becomes. Gingerly, I raise the cup toward his face. He strains to lean forward. There's a damn good reason people don't feed infants using open cups. If Brady flails at the wrong moment, we'll have blood all over the place. Fortunately, his lizard brain appears to understand what's going on here.

A few seconds after blood touches his lips, he stops fighting Glim and stands there. By the time half the blood is down, his eyes have stopped glowing and he reaches up to grasp the red plastic cup. At a nod from Glim, I let Brady have it and take a step back.

Glim releases him.

Brady drains the remainder of the blood, then holds the cup in the air over his mouth, catching drops until they stop falling.

"So, umm... Brady Welch?" I ask.

"Wow, yeah." He blinks at me. "How do you know my name? And whoa. Where am I?"

"Lucky guess. You're in a random place we found to keep you safe. Kinda lost your mind for a bit there. So, how'd you end up starving?"

Brady looks down into the cup. "Blood."

"Uhh, yeah." I fold my arms. "Are you unaware of what's happened to you?"

"No... I sorta." Brady grinds the heels of his hands into his eye sockets. "Woke up in a basement somewhere. A note next to me said some wild shit about being 'elevated' above mortals, and what I always wanted was mine now. Said I needed to feed on blood. Didn't want to believe it. Sounds so crazy."

I exhale. Okay, this is kinda weird. "It does sound crazy, but it isn't. I didn't believe it at first, either. But it's pretty cool once you get used to it."

Brady averts his gaze from the cup as if horrified by it. "I don't want to hurt people... or be a vampire. I... can't do it."

"Bit late for regrets, kid," says Glim.

Startled, Brady spins to look behind him. At the sight of a Shadow, he jumps back. "Gah!"

I grab him by the collar of his Abercrombie & Fitch sweater and pull him close. "Knock it off. He's here to help you, not be ridiculed."

"Chill." Brady holds his hands up. "I'd have yelled like that from anyone sneaking up behind me." He glances at Glim again, unable to conceal a mild wince. "Do we all end up looking like that?"

"No," I say, annoyed. "We're not all lucky enough to have their amazing powers."

Glim chuckles. "You don't have to lay it on so thick. And I did sneak up on him."

"Sorry. Just pisses me off when people can't see past the outside." I let go of Brady. "He's a Shadow. Guess you don't know about different bloodlines yet. You probably also don't know which one you are."

"I'd wager Scion." Glim leans in to sniff him, purely to be unsettling... probably.

"The heck does that mean?" asks Brady in an uneasy voice. "You were in my class. I remember seeing you. Or at least you kinda look like someone I remember. Did you have a slightly older sister?"

"Hah. No. It's me. The change made me look a little younger. So, gave up the goth thing? Crombie isn't exactly gloomy."

Brady again casts a despondent glance at the floor. "Nah. After graduation, I got into it with the parents. Didn't want to go to college right away. My dad gave me one year to straighten up or I'd have to move out."

"Straighten up? Did you get into some nasty stuff?" I ask.

Glim walks over to the still-dazed man in the suit. "I shall return momentarily."

They vanish in a black whorl.

"Whoa." Brady stares at the empty floor. "Did that freaky dude just disappear?"

"Yes, and please don't call him freaky. It's beyond obvious he looks like he looks. There is no need to mention it. The outside does not match the inside."

Brady tosses the cup aside. "Nothing nasty at all. Just a little weed. Dad meant my friends, my 'band that will never go anywhere', the makeup, black clothes... he wanted *this*." He gestures at his A&F outfit.

"And you don't?"

"I wanted to be myself... not some clone of my dad. Kinda stupid. My parents were basically willing to let me stay there for a whole year and try to get somewhere with the band on the condition if it failed, I 'went normal' and picked a college."

Can't say I'm qualified to comment either way. Spent my whole life as the normal girl, so I'm unable to imagine what it would be like to have my parents tell me to change. Then again, you don't really see actual adults going around in goth makeup too often... unless you're in Portland or at a Cure concert. Can't think of any time I went somewhere and saw a thirty-plus person working a 'real' job in white face paint and black lipstick. However, Brady's parents did support him for a whole year, giving him a chance to get the band off the ground. Can't really call them unreasonable.

"Wow. Umm. I wanted to go to college. Had plans to attend USC. Got accepted and everything."

He looks up at me. "Why didn't you?"

I extend my fangs. "California sun."

"Oh."

"So, how'd the band do?"

Brady barks a sad laugh. "Nothing. Played a few gigs. Sent out tons of demo tapes. Not one call. We got so desperate we even tried to get on *Idol*, but they ignored us too. Guess my dad was right. Life kinda sucks. I haven't seen any of my friends outside the band since after graduation, and even they've stopped showing up. Everyone's either working or at school, or both. Here I am just laying around the house like a total slacker."

"Yeah, I know the feeling. Both my friends are usually working or in school. We really don't have any time to hang out."

"Huh? Hang out? Your friends? But you're a vampire." He points at me.

"Yeah, it's… complicated."

Brady studies me for a long minute. "Hey, you're the girl who got stabbed. I remember the Facebook page."

"The Facebook page?" I raise both eyebrows. "What page?"

"Justice for Sarah… trying to raise money to find the killer." He scratches at his shoulder. A feral glint flashes across his face, but he's not eyeing me like a steak dinner. Probably still quite hungry and at the edge of losing control again. "Then they said the cops messed up and you weren't dead. Was it really a mistake?"

"Heh, no." I chuckle, shaking my head. "I almost died. Scott stabbed me right in the heart. Only reason I still exist is a vampire happened to be stalking me that night, intending to feed on me as soon as he could get me alone. He kinda mistook me for a kid, felt bad watching my murder happen, and turned me so I didn't die."

"Wow…"

"Yeah. So, I might as well go over the basics since you are clueless." I explain the basics of how to mind-fog and feed from people. "... as easy as wanting them to forget seeing you. It's difficult to explain in words, but as soon as you make eye contact with someone, it will feel as second-nature as breathing."

Brady holds his hands up in a 'back off' gesture. "Hang on. I don't want to bite anyone. It's wrong."

"Uhh, you were a big-time goth in school. You guys basically pretended to be vampires. That one kid you always hung out with even wore fake fangs. Now that you *are* one, you don't want to be?"

Brady offers a helpless shrug and a humorless laugh. "Lame, right? Just an act. We never wanted to hurt anyone. Not too sure about the others, but I was never obsessed with death or dark crap. Just, uhh, liked the music."

"Cool. Look, you are obviously still hungry. I haven't fed yet tonight. Let's go grab a bite."

"But I don't want to hurt anyone."

"Listen to me. Blood isn't like an addiction we can beat by simply not having it. It's going to drive you legit crazy if you don't feed. If I didn't randomly feel hungry tonight and go out for food, and randomly pick this area to hunt in, you would've mauled some security guard."

He shakes his head. "No way. I'd never hurt anyone."

Glim reappears in a cloud of black non-smoke between us. Brady jumps so bad he nearly falls over. To be fair, I jump, too.

"Everything all right here?" Glim fails to hide a smile for having startled us.

"Yeah." I grab Brady's arm. "Still need something to eat myself, and he's not done being hungry yet. Went way too long without feeding."

Brady tries to tug his arm back. "I don't want to hurt anyone. Why would you think I'd go out with you and randomly attack some stranger?"

"You *will* hurt someone if you're out of your mind with hunger." I stare into his eyes. "You damn near killed a security guard tonight. Doesn't matter what you 'want,' your subconscious isn't quite the same as it used to be. Starving it won't work. If you don't want to hurt anyone, you *need* to take blood when you're rational. C'mon."

Brady looks down. "This is so wrong. How do you just *bite* people?"

I tug him toward the door. "Chill out. Trust me. They don't feel a thing."

10

NO ONE SUSPECTS THE CUTE GIRL

Alas, Brady can't fly.

He didn't even know the possibility of vampires flying existed. Can't even tell him he might grow into it. Any vampire who is lucky enough to have the ability can do it within hours of being turned. It's as subconscious as breathing. In fact, without even knowing vampires existed at all—or I'd become one— my sheer revulsion at falling into a puddle of brackish water propelled me airborne. There's not much difference between refusing to fall and flying. Some vampires simply 'refuse to fall' really well.

"Flight is a fairly rare ability among Scions," says Glim.

Brady looks over at him, then at a group of people walking past us on the sidewalk. Once they're out of earshot, he asks, "Not to offend, but why didn't any of them even look at you?"

"Because they didn't see me." Glim smiles.

I'm used to him, so I recognize his smile. Some people mistake a Shadow trying to smile for a sneer or a sarcastic baring of teeth.

Brady leans away. "Sorry."

"He's smiling." I nudge him.

"What the heck is a Scion?" mutters Brady.

"A relatively recent bloodline. They first started appearing in the early 1980s." Glim sidesteps an oblivious mortal walking in the opposite direction. "If the Old Guard is 'dad,' the Scions are the spoiled trust fund kids too enamored with computers, cars, electronics, and other toys to care about the old ways. Why fly when you can get a sports car? And so on."

"Oh. You sure I'm one of those?"

"Mostly." Glim smiles again—this time Brady doesn't flinch.

We have a brief discussion regarding how all vampires can sense other vampires. Some, like Shadows, can occasionally discern bloodline. Glim says they 'smell different.' His nose is clearly sharper than mine. All I smell on Brady is 'worn the same outfit for a week' plus a serious lack of self-esteem. The poor guy's head must be spinning. He's acting kinda out of it and slow. Probably a cocktail of denial, shock, and WTF. I'm hardly one to judge him. My first few weeks of being a vampire came with a heaping dose of maudlin navel-gazing, too. In hindsight, I hadn't gone emo and missed the sun or daytime. Vampirism took my fears and anxieties over transitioning from childhood to adulthood and made them ten times worse. Kinda like twisting my ankle when I'm already entertaining the monthly visitor. Holy shit, am I happy to be free of that. Why the hell do some girls celebrate their first periods? It ought to be more of a funeral than a party. Like, hey, here's this phantom monster who is gonna sneak up on you randomly once a month for the next several decades and beat you over the head with your uterus until you scream.

So damn happy to be a vampire.

Upon reaching a fairly secluded area, we focus on task. Since we're in the industrial district, convenience brings us to a pair of overnight security guards roaming a massive parking lot on Harbor Island in a little white pickup truck.

Glim and I walk Brady through the process of applying the mind fog, then feed.

This security guy's blood also tastes like buffalo wings. Must be a craving. It's almost tempting to eat some real ones, but the consequences are *not* worth it. Maybe if I got mild ones... still, not easy to find wings at almost three in the morning.

As usual, I give the men a compulsion to go have a cookie and orange juice. After we finish feeding and send the security guys on their way, Brady's expression looks like we forced him to punt kittens into a wood chipper.

"You okay?" I ask.

"Feels so wrong to do that to people." He sighs, grabs his head in both hands, and sinks into a squat.

Wow, dude. I think he's trying not to cry.

"You'll get used to it." I squeeze his shoulder. "Bugged me at first, too. Really, if you do it right, they don't remember anything and suffer no lasting effects. Don't feed from the same person twice in six months. Also, you can smell it if they're already low on blood. Kill-feeding is bad. It's like the vampire version of turning into a heroin addict."

He lets his hands fall away from his head, gawking up at me. "You get high?"

"In a manner of speaking." Glim tilts his hand in a so-so gesture. "It's a rush of power. The crash afterward is pretty heavy. It doesn't give you a 'high' like drugs with hallucinations, euphoria, or altered states of consciousness. Mostly increased strength, speed, and energy for a few hours."

"Oh." Brady nods. "Don't want that. Hell, I barely want to bite people at all. Just curious."

"Most vampires don't like kill-feeders." I smile.

"No kidding?"

I exhale. "It's not really a compassion thing. Is for me, but others simply don't want the attention it brings. Too many weird deaths in an area attracts vampire hunters. And yes, they exist."

Brady stands, stuffs his hands in his pockets and stares at me for a long minute, giving off no readable expression. "Wow, Sarah. You totally don't look like a vampire."

"Thanks."

"I mean, you're like some character from one of those silly movies. The little innocent girl who turns into a piranha-faced carnivorous monster, eats someone whole, then goes back to looking harmless."

"Umm. Relax." I poke him. "There's nothing evil about feeding as long as you don't take too much. It's better than being a bear or wolf and having to kill what we eat. Really, the worst thing a responsible vampire does to someone is cost them five to ten minutes of their life they can't remember."

He gazes up. "How do you deal with never seeing the sun again?"

Glim chuckles.

I bite my lip. His emotional state seems brittle. Might not be the best idea to say 'oh yeah, I can tolerate the sun in small doses just fine.'

"I mean…" Brady hangs his head. "I'm dead. Only nineteen. My parents have no idea where I am. How the heck is anyone supposed to just accept this? I don't know if I can handle being trapped in the dark for the rest of my life. I already miss green grass, blue sky, daytime…"

Glim rolls his eyes.

"It's fine," I whisper to him. "Brady's been practicing for this role for years. The whole melodrama thing is nothing new."

Brady stares at me. "The goth lifestyle is nowhere near the same as being a literal monster."

"Oh, come on. This is awesome." I spin around, arms out. "We're never going to get old or sick. You don't need to worry about going to school or getting a job."

Brady kicks at the pavement. "Ironic, right? You used to be like the straight girl. Total norm. Now you're into vampires and the ex-goth is the lame-ass."

I shrug. "Death has a weird way of changing a person."

"Right." He exhales. "So, what am I supposed to do now? Do you have like a place where you live or hang out?"

"Yeah. It's kinda complicated though. It would be a major project to add another vampire to my living arrangements." I pull my phone out. "You have a phone?"

"No. I'm dead, remember? My parents don't know it yet. Phone's at the house. If I use it, they'll know."

"Okay. We can get you a new one soon. Let me make a few calls and see if I can find someone willing to mentor you, or at least let you crash with them."

"Yeah, great. Thanks." Brady glances off, clearly 'thrilled.'

I don't get the sense he's annoyed he can't stay with me. He's falling back to his goth attitude. Everything sucks, life is a constant slow death, happiness is an illusion, and so on. Great. This is going to be a project.

M<small>Y</small> L<small>OST</small> O<small>NE</small> <small>FRIENDS OFFER TO LOOK AFTER</small> B<small>RADY</small> <small>FOR A LITTLE</small> while and show him the ropes.

Since it appears I've got the situation handled, Glim leaves me to it and goes off to resume doing whatever he'd been doing before I called. He stays long enough for me to give him a big hug and thank him profusely for his help.

Amy, Luke, and Dante are presently living in a basement apartment under a high-rise building on 3rd Ave, two blocks away from Antioch University. The space had probably been intended for a live in superintendent or maintenance worker. Whether or not they displaced said worker or the building management decided not to use it, who knows. It's not the biggest space, already a tad cramped with three people, but they've got an open sofa Brady can sleep on. The place is vampire-proofed. It only had two small half-height casement windows, both of which are blacked out courtesy of spray paint.

I sneak away to the bathroom to rinse the industrial grime off my feet. Rather do it before going anywhere near home. Last thing I need would be to track some crazy chemical into the house and have Blix grow a second head, or one of the Littles get sick. I'd worry about Klepto, but no one is sure if she's a real kitten. At least, in terms of being vulnerable to sickness. Otherwise, she's pretty normal as kittens go if you ignore her habit of teleporting, stealing objects randomly, and having an almost human-like ability to understand spoken English.

Upon my return from cleaning up, I walk into a conversation about vampire generalities. The guys are a weird combination for sure. Amy had been a fairly innocent unworldly blonde twentysomething when she became a vampire in the late Eighties. Wardrobe and attitude wise tonight, she's invoking Joan Jett—leather jacket and jeans. Something about Dante makes him feel like he belongs in a Vietnam war movie, or a film about a veteran struggling to cope with civilian life after returning from the war in the seventies. Only thing missing to complete the Sixties look is the giant round afro. Can't put my finger on what's giving off the vibe. Maybe it's the Grateful Dead T-shirt. Luke's a total long-haired hippie type somewhere between a younger Willie Nelson and Axl Rose before he turned into *Throw Momma from the Train*. I'm not entirely convinced Luke is aware the Sixties ended. Then again, my dad is stuck in the Eighties, so who am I to criticize?

Yanno, if my father ever ended up turning into a vampire, he'd totally be like Max from *Lost Boys*. Outwardly, he'd seem to be this complete milquetoast, ordinary dude.

As much as I want to go home and do a little studying for end-of-semester exams, it feels a bit rude to bail so fast after dropping Brady off here, like I'm dumping him on them and running. Upon my return from the bathroom, he's in the midst of explaining to the guys how he has no idea who gave him the Transference. His last mortal memory is going out to buy soda and chips at around 10:00 p.m., then waking up in a basement clutching a note.

"You think someone's gone a bit loopy?" asks Dante. "Randomly turning people?"

"Maybe." Amy leans back into the sofa, her leather jacket creaking. "I've heard of some who select someone for the Transference, do it, and watch the new vampire from afar for a few days to see how they handle it before committing to a sire-progeny relationship."

"What, like a test?" asks Brady.

"Either that or amusement, man." Luke laughs. "Closest thing we have to reality TV. Turn some dude and set them loose, see what happens. Like watchin' baby sea turtles try to make it across the beach to the water and betting on which ones swim and which ones the seagulls get."

Amy also laughs.

"Ugh." Brady leans forward, raking his hands at his hair. "My year of grace period is basically over. Dad started nagging me about a decision."

"What were you gonna do, hon?" Amy leans forward, elbows on her knees.

He gives her an odd stare. Probably confused why a girl who looks only a year or so older than him is calling him 'hon.' Takes a while to get used to age as a vampire. She's really like fifty, older than my parents by a few years.

"Umm. Look at my outfit. What choice did I have? My parents were willing to pay for school. All I had to do was turn into the mass-produced society-ready clone they wanted." Brady flicks at his fluffy, black mop. "Got into a little argument over my hair. Dad wanted me to cut it, to look 'respectable.' I was probably going to cave in and do it."

"Aww man, no way." Luke, whose hair is down almost to his waist, shakes his head. "Hate that conservative bullcrap. You gotta do you, man. Ain't no law says a dude's gotta have short hair. That's some bull."

"Too late now." Brady continuously flicks a finger at his pants, making a soft swish-swish noise. "Maybe I should at least call them or go see them one last time. Last time we talked, we argued. Feels wrong to just leave them never knowing what happened to me."

"Probably better not to." Dante gestures at me. "Less you wanna wind up like her."

Brady twists to look in my direction. "What do you mean like her?"

"Sarah went back to her mortal family." Amy gives a wistful sigh. "It's sad and adorable, but it's turned into a hairy mess."

"It's not *that* bad." I roll my eyes.

"Not that bad?" Amy raises both eyebrows. "Like a third of the city's society vamps think you're a risk for doing it and want to kill your family. Only reason they're not is you have the creepy doll queen ready to go all Wednesday Addams on anyone who messes with them."

"You're overstating it." I lean on the sofa. "They wouldn't simply attack my family. They'd tell me to leave and probably—just to be assholes—force *me* to be the one who makes them forget I exist."

Dante and Amy cringe simultaneously.

"Still, though." Luke winks at me. "You have all sorts of issues... and your 'society' vampires all think of you as a baby."

"Hah." Grinning, I hold my head high. "It's all part of my master plan to make everyone underestimate me."

The guys laugh.

Brady stares. "You seriously went home to your parents?"

"Yeah." I topple over the sofa back and land seated between Amy and Dante. "It's a loooong story..."

NOT FOR CHILDREN UNDER TWELVE

Baggy pajama pants and a loose T-shirt didn't make for the best sword-fighting attire, but Sierra settled.

Trying to sneak a few minutes of practice in her room before bed demanded certain sacrifices. Wary of her bare feet discovering another Lego or some equally horrific trap lurking in the carpet, Sierra went through the motions of practice strikes. She left the scabbard on for safety reasons, even if it threw off the balance. Unlike Sam's friends, she didn't love having a sword because it looked cool—like something out of a D&D game—and felt no need to show it off or play with the blade out. Her desire to have a sword came entirely from the want to defend herself and her family if need be.

She slashed the sheathed sword at the air, went up on one foot, spun, then stabbed at an imaginary vampire behind her.

Sometimes, Sierra wondered if she'd traded one fear for another. Ever since around second grade when an active shooter drill at school fooled her into thinking it really happened, she'd lived in a near-constant state of dread. It kind of annoyed her how Sophia, by all accounts a giant chicken, showed such little reaction to the idea they might not come home from school one day. She probably thought the adults overreacted and 'most people are way too nice' to do something so horrible.

Sierra didn't feel too much shame since only Sarah knew the true extent of her fear. Outwardly, she refused to show it as much as she could. Throwing up from anxiety a few times on the way to school over the years, she easily blamed away on 'not feeling well.'

Before all the vampire stuff happened, her worries had already started to change from some random stranger showing up at school to kill all the kids to the shooter *being* one of the kids. That's what the news showed, and it sorta made sense, as much as something so horrible could. Crazy adults would target a school full of *little* kids to maximize tragedy. The news never mentioned a grown-up attacking a high school. Even in sixth grade, she already watched her classmates, looking for signs they might be the one to snap sometime. Ironically, keeping distance, not talking much, and randomly staring at people all the time made her seem like the crazy kid.

Not talking to her parents about it had probably been a mistake. *Still* not talking to her parents about it definitely was a mistake... but she couldn't quite make herself admit to being such a wimp for the past six years. It made zero sense how she'd gradually isolated herself emotionally from her parents and siblings. The only reason she could think of was wanting to lessen the pain they'd feel if she ended up dead at school.

After Sarah almost died, she couldn't keep acting rude and abrasive to hold her family at arm's length. Her big sis hadn't been the most awesome of siblings before. Sierra always adored her older sister as the perfect balance between old enough to be a protector and young enough not to feel like Mom. But, Sarah—being an ordinary teenager—had friends of her own and stuff she wanted to do. She usually made excuses to avoid hanging out with her younger siblings. Even if it hadn't been from malice or anger, it still bothered Sierra. Her pride got in the way of admitting how much she truly felt. Sophia had no such qualms and openly clung to Sarah, crying if ignored. Watching Sarah act annoyed by Sophia's overt neediness further pushed Sierra away from showing any outward signs showing how she felt about her big sis neglecting her.

But everything changed when the family almost shattered.

Generally, Sierra loved the new normal. Not only had her family come together in a way totally unbelievable to imagine a year ago, her nightmare fuel changed. She still kinda worried about someone showing up at school with a gun, but bad vampires or other as-yet-unseen paranormal monsters scared her more.

She also didn't have any credibility left in terms of being, as Dad would say, a 'hardass.'

Sarah saw her hiding under the shelf in the warehouse, crying and shaking as bad as Sophia having a nightmare. No more secrets. Sarah hadn't told anyone about it, either. Rather than leave her terrified about blackmail or mortified, it opened a door. She could talk openly about her fears to at least one person now and not fear ridicule. Kinda silly to think about keeping secrets from a vampire anyway, but she trusted her big sister's promise not to eavesdrop on thoughts.

Dad once used the idea of 'building confidence' as a reason to take taekwondo classes. At the time, Sierra smirked at him. However, he'd been right, even if her increased confidence came from sword skill instead. It helped she cheated more than a little by asking Dalton to essentially 'upload' some of his knowledge into her head.

Vampire blood tasted absolutely horrible, but again, small sacrifices.

Surprisingly, Sierra didn't feel any jealousy toward Sophia for having magic nor Sam for collecting demons, but couldn't bear the thought Sophia might be the one protecting her someday. Her younger sister had always been the receiver of protection. Learning how to fight plus the boost from vampire blood kept everything normal. Sierra protected Sophia, just like in the D&D games Dad ran. Warriors stopped monsters from eating the mage.

Sierra's arm twitched.

She stopped, reset her stance, and repeated the sword motion.

Her other arm twitched, and a weird cramp gripped her side. It didn't *hurt* so much as felt unpleasant. Figuring she might've pulled a muscle or something, she decided to stop for the night and go to sleep. After stashing the sword under the bed, Sierra headed to the bathroom to brush her teeth and use the toilet.

An odd sensation scratched at her stomach as she crossed the hallway, like a bunch of mice with teeny claws clinging to her skin. She lifted her shirt to look. No wounds, but her body seemed a bit too gaunt. Like every other Wright in the house, she'd always been rail thin. Now, however, she felt *too* skinny. Worried, she let the shirt drop back over her belly and hurried into the bathroom to the sink.

Staring at herself in the mirror didn't help.

Her face looked gaunt, cheeks sunken. Dark shadows under her eyes gave her an almost ghoulish visage. She half expected to see her canine teeth extending into fangs like Sarah's. Fortunately, they didn't. The more she stared at herself, the more she became aware of a deep-seated craving making all the nerves in her limbs tingle. Not quite hunger in a literal sense, but she definitely wanted *something*.

No, not 'something.'

Blood.

Specifically, vampire blood.

"Uh, oh." She nibbled on her lip. "Shit. Not good."

Sierra looked down at her hands. They didn't shake—much. Could be from fear as much as her body demanding power. Her mind raced. What to do? Obviously, continuing to rely on vampire blood to boost her strength and speed couldn't continue. Sarah worried about side effects. Dalton didn't believe anything bad would happen, but he'd also been talking about problems like ending up mind-controlled or a brainless servitor to a vampire. He never mentioned withdrawal. Continuing to have vampire blood might not do bad things to her, but *stopping* kinda felt like it would.

Two tiny fangs extended into view below her upper lip.

Sierra gawked at herself in the mirror for a second before jumping away with a gasp, clamping her hands over her mouth. It took her a second to stop shaking and realize her tongue didn't bump into any abnormally pointy teeth. Hesitantly, she leaned close to the mirror again and opened her mouth.

Normal teeth.

I'm seeing crap.

Sierra shoved a hand up under her shirt, pressing against her chest. Heartbeat normal. *Fast* normal, but she still had a heartbeat.

Am I having a nightmare when I'm still awake?

She scurried out of the bathroom and veered left into Sophia's room. Her little sister stretched out in bed, surrounded by a small army of stuffed animals. Light from her Kindle made her face seem whiter than normal, her lemon blonde hair aglow. A puffy pink nightgown concealed the shape of her scrawny frame, making her look like a cloth doll with a plastic head and hands.

"Soph!" Sierra rushed over to the bed. "Do I look weird to you?"

"You always do," deadpanned Sophia without looking up from her e-book.

Sierra grabbed her arm. "I'm serious. My face is like changing and…" She pulled her shirt up to show off her stomach. "I'm deflating."

"Huh?" Sophia glanced at her.

"It's the vampire blood," whispered Sierra. "I think it's starting to wear off and I'm like going a little nuts wanting more. When I checked myself in the mirror, it's like watching Sare sleep."

Sophia shook her head. "You look normal."

"I don't have fangs, do I?"

"No. Stop." Sophia poked her. "You aren't turning undead."

Sierra paced for a moment, then crouched and lifted one side of the bed a few inches.

"What are you doing?" Sophia grabbed a tumbling stuffed unicorn before it fell to the floor.

"Testing." Sierra set the bed down and stood. "Still have some left. But it's gonna wear off, soon. Am I shaking?"

Sophia watched her for a moment. "Maybe a little, but you're probably scared."

"I am not." Sierra folded her arms, bit her lip, then looked down. "Okay, maybe a little."

"It's probably dangerous for you to keep drinking vampire blood."

Sophia lifted her blankets aside so she could scoot over and sit on the edge of the mattress. "We're too young for coffee. Vampire blood's gotta be worse. If they sold it at stores, people would need to be twenty-one to buy it, like beer."

Sierra sat on the bed beside her sister, swiping her feet back and forth over the carpet. "Feels like I'm super close to Sarah now. When we're in the same room, I like know how she feels. Even know what she's gonna say a second before she says it."

"Mew!" Klepto crawled out from under the blankets and walked into Sierra's lap.

"Yeah." Sophia skritched the kitten's head. "You have a blood link or something to her."

"Uh huh." Sierra pet the kitten, not sure what to say. Nothing sounded like a good idea. If she stopped asking Sarah for a sip of blood here and there, she'd go back to being an ordinary twelve-year-old. It wouldn't make her magically forget how to use a sword, but she'd be too weak and slow to have any chance against a bad vampire. If she kept taking blood, other bad stuff might happen to her. A cop came to her classroom last year to do a presentation about drugs. She remembered him talking about withdrawal. The longer she stayed on vampire blood, the worse it would be to stop. What if it got to a point where she *couldn't*? Would she go crazy for it?

As soon as she started shivering, Sophia put an arm around her back.

"What's wrong?"

"Scared."

"I don't like seeing you scared. You're the brave one. I'm the chicken."

Sierra chuckled.

"Don't worry. You look fine. It's all in your head." Sophia yawned. "Don't have'ta be scared of turning into a vampire overnight. Doesn't work that way."

"I'm not worried."

Sophia's 'gimme a break' expression almost made her laugh.

Klepto peered up at her. "Mew."

Even the kitten noticed.

If she admitted to being afraid, Sophia might not feel better whenever she tried to protect her from stuff... but Sarah said everyone, even superheroes, got scared sometimes. Sierra let out a long, slow breath.

"I'm not scared of what might happen to me. I don't wanna be too weak to stop bad vampires from hurting you or Sam... or Mom and Dad." She squeezed her toes into the carpet. "I hate not being able to do anything but hide."

Sophia nodded. "I don't want anything to happen to you. You are kinda shaking. I think you should stop having vampire blood before it messes with you too much."

"I have to. Not gonna let bad vamps, or any of the other weird stuff, hurt us. Don't care what it does to me."

"Hey." Sophia squeezed her hand. "I got an idea."

"Uh oh." Sierra snickered. "What's going to end up covered in pudding this time?"

"Nothing. Not gonna summon a faerie." Sophia tapped a finger to her chin. "Maybe I can try to enchant you so you're strong and fast without needing vampire blood."

Sierra stared at her for a long minute. "Oh, that couldn't possibly go wrong in any way."

"Hah."

"Seriously. You tried to fix that one kid's clothes and almost destroyed the school."

"I know, but... I'm not gonna do anything right now. Need to research." Sophia held up one hand. "I promise I won't use any magic unless I'm totes convinced it's safe."

"Mew," chirped Klepto, sounding happy.

Sierra tilted her head. "So... you're not going to do anything."

Sophia stuck out her tongue.

"Well..." Sierra looked down at her hands. Even if Sophia didn't notice, she saw the trembling. It didn't come from fear. Her body slid downhill toward normality and did *not* like it. She needed the surge of power, the confidence it gave her. Every charge of vampiric blood made her feel like she played *Call of Duty* for real. Stronger, faster, tougher than everyone around her.

Crap. I'm an addict. She had to stop now before it became impossible to do. If she could hide her fear of being shot at school from everyone for so long, she could keep a lid on her craving, too. Her sister had twice paused time in a small area. Pulling off a mild enchantment had to be possible, if unlikely. Most things Soph tried to do magically went haywire. The only time her magic worked right is if she happened to be terrified, desperate—as when Mom almost told her to get rid of Klepto—or angry.

Her mousy little sister had a weird look in her eyes. A look she'd never seen before. It almost seemed as if Sophia had decided to do whatever it took to protect *her.* The role reversal embarrassed, amused, and—she begrudgingly accepted—comforted her. Sarah's almost death could have torn the family apart, but it had the reverse effect. They'd become tight.

I gotta stop trying to do everything myself. We help each other.

"Well, what?" Sophia blinked.

"Umm. Okay." Sierra put an arm around her. "If you think it's safe. Let's try it."

12

THE OLD WAYS

Intro calculus had to be my weirdest class this semester.

While I've never really adored math, I'm also not one of those people who despises it. Math doesn't even count as a 'necessary evil' to me. It's not evil, merely tedious. Calculus does things with math the Universe never intended—sort of like those ghouls who put bacon on ice cream. Wait, no. *That* is pure evil.

It's 9:27 p.m. on Wednesday, June 13th. Why isn't that a series of horror movies? No one really likes the middle of the week. The *Wednesday the Thirteenth* films. They could have an undead monster crawl out of a lake and just do tedious stuff to make the day last forever. Or maybe they'd have an undead camel asking everyone what day it is and brutally murdering everyone who didn't answer correctly. Okay, yeah, makes sense why no one made those movies. Anyway, I'm sitting in my last calculus class for the semester, listening to Dr. Mercer ramble about the reasons students who aren't going into science or technical fields might want to consider taking on additional math classes. Only she could consume eighteen minutes to say 'mental aerobics help you stay sharp and think about everything, not only math.'

This is also most likely my last calculus class in general. There's no reason for an English major to take such heavy math. Yeah, I've decided to swap majors. Going into computer programming only because it's what my dad does plus the idea it would let me 'work from home' isn't the greatest reason. No newbie programmer gets a work-at-home job. I hadn't been worried about a job forcing me into the office, confident vampire mind control would guarantee me work-from-home permission. Of course, it would be just as easy to add myself to the payroll of some giant corporation as a 'consultant' and collect a modest salary without having to actually do anything. Yeah, it's scummy and basically stealing, which is why it didn't occur to me as a serious option. Whether or not I'm going to end up needing income at some point, going into a field should involve me being interested in it. Programming is cool and all, but it's not my passion.

My problem boils down to me not really having a passion. Sophia already wants to go into cosmetics as a career. Not a beautician, though. She wants to work on movie sets doing makeup for film actors, maybe even special effects type stuff. Hate to say it, but by the time she's grown up, there probably won't be too many studios left using practical effects. Heck, computer graphics are getting scary good. They might not even use real actors anymore by the time she's out of college—or whatever sort of school one goes to in order to learn how to do movie makeup. Everything will be on computers. Granted, she could go into computer art. Sierra wants to make video games. She's also one of those people who consider math evil. Dad is eagerly awaiting the wail of existential anguish when Sierra realizes making video games is *all* math.

Sam's like me. He's never expressed anything close to an interest in any particular career.

Guess I count as moderately lazy and unmotivated. Is it normal for a kid in high school to already know exactly what they want to do for the rest of their lives, or is that considered weird? What kind of society are we living in where everyone's forced to slot themselves into a career path as early as possible? Ninety-eight percent of us bust our butts to make two percent rich. Of course, *not* entering the rat race isn't an option for ordinary people. The world doesn't offer too many paths for anyone refusing to play the game. Become homeless or go out into the wilderness and try to live off the land, which is basically the same thing in different surroundings. 'Homeless' people live in cities. 'Survivalists' live in the woods. Neither has a debit card or takes routine showers.

Sigh. I'm too fond of modern amenities to abandon civilization. Hard to get a Wi-Fi signal deep in the forest. Plus, squirrels don't open Starbucks franchises, so getting coffee would be a pain in the ass. Vampirism, weird as it is to say, feels like the Universe sensed my conundrum and sent me an express ticket out of the rat race.

Awesome.

I'm also not particularly passionate about literature, but an English degree kinda works since nothing else really calls out. I do like reading. Can do it anywhere, and the employability of whatever degree I get is entirely irrelevant to me. Honestly, there aren't too many majors *less* useful for getting a good job than English unless you count stuff like anthropology or generic liberal arts. Not condoning the perception, just saying. Society doesn't reward people for pursuing their passions. It benefits those who do what consumerism demands.

Anyway, for the first time all semester, Dr. Mercer ends her class on schedule without being under the effect of mind powers. The woman is not a fast speaker. Her class routinely ran ten to twenty minutes past time. Well, considering today's session consisted mostly of her going over the final test scores and being here to answer questions and provide academic guidance, that we *still* didn't officially end until 9:28 p.m. probably counts as going long. Calc took place on Wednesday and Friday, but the school's closed on Friday, making tonight the final session.

I'm glad to be finished, but oddly, I kinda miss Dr. Mercer already. As annoying as her slow delivery could be, she's like a character from a television series you start off finding irritating, but by the time the season's over, you love them.

So, yeah. I've got philosophy and sociology tomorrow night and then I'm done for summer. It's almost more astounding to think I've got one year of college under my belt than one year of being a vampire. Mostly a year, anyway. Friday, June 22, 2017 had been my last day as a mortal, so I'm technically ten days shy of being a vampire for a full year.

Wow, time flies when you're plummeting head first down a kaleidoscopic tunnel of psychedelic craziness.

Thankfully, my life appears to be stabilizing as much as it can. No part of my future is even close to what I'd spent the previous eighteen years thinking it would be, but I'm making this work. Even Stefano has backed off his overt contempt. Not sure if he respects me for doing what had to be done or if he's afraid I might visit him with a giant firebomb in the middle of the day. Innocents are not a 'powerful' bloodline, but we don't need to be strong during the day when other vampires can't do anything. Meh. I doubt he's afraid of me. Not only is he old enough to read my mind and know I have no interest in causing trouble for him, if he truly feared me, I'd be gone by now. Yeah, I'm afraid of him. But not like terrified afraid. It's more like respect. He's an elder. I'm no more 'scared' of him than a low-level D&D character is 'scared' of a level-twenty monster. If the barbarian pokes the dragon with a stick, the barbarian deserves whatever happens to her.

At least he's an Old Guard, not a Fury or Beast, so I don't have to worry about a sudden fit of rage.

Year one of college is basically over. Guess I will finish after all. Might take me five years instead of four due to night class scheduling. Whatever. Not like I'm in a rush to jump into the workaday world. I take my time meandering along the sidewalk in a group of other students, all heading toward the parking garage at the corner. It's dark now, but the sun's doing its thing early again, preventing me from flying to class. Gotta bring the car home.

No sooner does my sneaker hit the sidewalk after crossing the street than a woman comes out of nowhere at my side and clamps an arm around me. I say 'clamping' because I kinda feel like a prize in one of those grabby claw games. She's as strong as a forklift, and 'escorting' me past the parking garage entrance.

Conventional wisdom says not to let aggressive strangers take you anywhere isolated. This fact of life for young women generally assumes several things being true. One, the aggressive stranger's a guy. Two, bystanders will be of some assistance. Three, screaming and or making noise will dissuade the attacker into running. Four, the person grabbing you is not an old vampire.

None of this is true for me now.

I'm being—sorta—abducted by a woman, who's clearly a vampire, and old enough for me to sense as being old. Any mortals trying to 'help' me are only going to end up dead or maimed, and the best result of me screaming would be for everyone to ignore me. Worst result of me screaming is some poor guy runs over to help me and ends up wearing his intestines as a necktie.

"We have to talk," says the woman, her tone confident.

She's got a mild accent, too. Can't place it. Maybe Russian, Slavic, or some flavor of Eastern European. It's not pronounced enough to be recognizable. Maybe she's one of those people who thinks all vampires should do a crappy Dracula impression but decided to dial it back a bit not to sound so campy. Then again, I wouldn't know Russian from Polish from Turkish hearing it spoken. She's taller than me by a good margin, her chin's even with the top of my head. Long, straight black hair, black clothes, chalk white skin, black lipstick. She's basically a gothed-out version of Xena. It takes serious commitment to wear heeled thigh-high boots and a pleated leather skirt outside of a comic con—or an adult club. Tim Burton meets Roman Imperial Army here.

Her accent doesn't lend any malice to her words. For example, hearing the phrase 'we have to talk' when a guy with a strong Italian accent drags you off means something entirely different than say someone who looks like Ashley says it. Either that or I've seen too many movies. Not sure what to make of a *Boris and Natasha* version of 'we have to talk.' Pretty sure she's not going to ask me if I have a spare tampon she can have.

Also, I really hate it when girls ask to 'borrow' a tampon. Like, no, hon. You keep it. Don't want it back.

She's already got a heck of a grip on me. I'm not happy about it, but in the interest of not wanting any innocent bystanders hurt, I let her lead. This amazon would probably pick me up and carry me otherwise. Once the initial shock of having a strange elder yoink me out of pedestrian traffic fades, I look her over.

The woman looks a little bit younger than Xena and, other than having long black hair and a sexed-up version of fantasy leather armor on, bears no resemblance whatsoever to Lucy Lawless. Guessing mid-twenties when she became undead. Dark blue eyes and snow-white cheeks turn her into a life-sized version of a creepy doll no one would want to be alone in a dark house with. No obvious weapons, but her black fingernails are awfully long and certainly not as fake as a normal person might assume.

"Are they filming another *Underworld* movie around here or did you not notice the Nineties are over?"

She narrows her eyes at me.

"Seriously. Too much makeup." Yeah, I know she's not wearing face paint, but playing innocent might make the difference between me spending the next two weeks soaking in peaches & cream again or being able to walk.

"I'm not wearing makeup." She guides me downhill along Pine Street, past the parking garage. We hook a right on Boylston Ave and cross to the opposite side, going by a Capital Loans place and an Enterprise rent-a-car.

"Your lips are naturally black?" I ask.

She sighs. "Fine. I'm wearing lipstick. The rest is natural."

We pass a tall grey and blue building marked 'Heath Printers.' Huh, wow. There's a coincidence. Wonder if the professor is related to whoever owns it. The woman drags me into a small, rectangular parking lot behind the printing place, surrounded on all but one side by three-story buildings. Balconies on the building straight ahead at the back of the lot tell me it's an apartment building. She pins me to the less-than-clean wall of the printing company.

"You kids have it rough these days," says the woman.

"Umm, are you planning to kick my ass?"

"Not yet."

"Whew. Okay. I have no idea who you are."

"Call me Ladonna."

I nod once. Yeah, sure. If that's her real name, I'm Catherine the Great. Hey, for all I know, this woman might actually *be* Catherine the Great. Nah, she's totally a Freja or Olga or something along those lines. Looking right at her, my opinion of her accent changes. Thinking Swedish or Norwegian… maybe Finnish. I'd bet money her last name starts with a J and ends with 'sen' like Jansen. Maybe a -berg or -borg. She's going way overboard with the goth look. Oh, wow. Is she the one who turned Brady?

"Hi, I'm Sarah. Is, umm, Brady yours? You here to tell me to stay away from him and let him learn to fly on his own or something?"

Ladonna regards me, no emotion on her face.

"Okay, maybe not. What did you mean we have it rough?"

"I awoke during the Civil War to vast fields of blood everywhere. We were free to prey where and whenever we wanted."

"I'm not religious."

She laughs.

Hah. Direct hit. Finally got one past her wall.

"Wrong kind of prey, or were you making a joke on purpose?"

"Sorry. Joke. Should I take you threatening me more seriously?"

Ladonna quirks an eyebrow. "I'm not threatening you… yet."

"You're dragging me off with a grip like a forklift. Figured a verbal threat would come soon if I missed the implied one."

She gives this wicked little smile. I've never been a good liar, and the handicap extends to body language. Ladonna undoubtedly knows I'm afraid of her. Nothing personal, all elders have that effect on me.

"Where is the reliquary?"

Aww, shit. She's Oblivare… and if she's as old as she feels, she's already seen into my thoughts and knows what I did. A spike of dread sends a wave of heat washing over my face down to my chest. Feels like Follows Rules Girl got tricked into shoplifting and ran out the door straight into two cops. Never mind I'd been ordered to burn the four Oblivare. Also never mind the probable truth destroying them *had* been the right thing to do in terms of the greater good for both mortals and vampires.

"No idea. The car was burning too hot to go near last time I saw it. We left the reliquary in the car. If it didn't shatter from the fire, the cops have it."

Ladonna frowns.

"So, umm... is it true you guys were never human? Sorry, I'm new. You know, kids and questions."

She brushes the back of her hand across my cheek. "The cute act is not going to work on me."

"Okay. But to be fair, the destroy all civilization act doesn't work for me." Channeling a bit of Sierra, I find a nugget of irrational bravery and stare the woman in the eye. "Really, why would you want to? What did vampires do for fun before video games and television? Weren't you bored?"

"We are alphas, child. Humans belong hiding in their pathetic little huts, huddled together in the dark, not knowing if they'll see the sunrise." She flashes an eerily warm smile, like a twisted Rachel Ray sharing a recipe for roast infant. "They have been allowed to breed out of control. There are too many of them. Earth cannot handle the strain. Vampires are a necessary darkness. Your kind are not true vampires, merely aberrations, an accident. A meal who should not have survived escaped. They eventually became sire to all the false vampires. It happened so long ago, not even my kind knows how this mortal got away from us. Your kind has potential despite your inherent weakness, but they refuse to claim their proper place as masters of the night."

I'd lean away, but the cold bricks at my back are a bit on the solid side. "Umm, nah. Dominant power fantasies aren't my thing. Love the black leather on you, though. Looks awesome."

"You will surrender the reliquary."

"Seriously." I raise my hands. "I don't have it. We left it in the car. Cadillacs burn really hot when the fire is engulfing an urn of ancient evil."

Ladonna folds her arms, tapping one foot. "The reliquary would not affect the flames."

Aha! She didn't dispute the evil part.

Her eyes narrow. Damn. Well, figured she could read my mind, or at least see my surface thoughts. That means she obviously knows I'm not lying about abandoning the bottle of vampire mix in a car fire.

"Can I ask you something?"

"Hmm?" She quirks an eyebrow.

"You mentioned being turned during the Civil War, but you sound European. If it's true about the Oblivare not having human souls, wouldn't that mean you aren't the woman whose body you inhabit?"

"For such a young one, you are quite perceptive. A few of my brethren made the journey to America to enjoy the Civil War."

"Enjoy?" I blink.

She laughs. "To us it was an open buffet. Food everywhere for the taking. Dinner and a show so to speak. My brethren found this body you see before you, dead to a stray bullet in a field, and thought her a suitable vessel to free me from the oubliette."

Oh, hmm. So, the odd accent must be from her Oblivare soul.

"Finland," mutters Ladonna. "Spend enough time in a place, the accent creeps in."

"Oh, neat. You kinda look like the front woman for a symphonic metal band."

She stares at me. "The world these mortals cling to will drown in blood. Be sure you are on the correct side when the new order arises."

I tilt my head. "Star Wars? Wait, no… they had the 'First' order. Hope your vampire apocalypse has a better screenwriter."

Ladonna sighs, shakes her head, and walks off, muttering, "Kids."

Whoa. I let my head lean back until it rests against the wall, then stand there shaking from nerves. The clicking of Ladonna's boots on the sidewalk grows distant. My heart races kinda like a velociraptor charged out of the bushes, cornered me, then only sniffed me a few times before walking away. I'm genuinely shocked she didn't break me in half for revenge over burning those four dudes. Wait… purple glowing stuff wafted off the bodies. Holden said something about smashing the reliquary would only allow the Oblivare to collect the souls again. Duh. No wonder she's not angry with me. We didn't destroy anything except some already dead bodies. Those vampires are pure energy.

And wow. 'Mortals will drown in blood.' Vigo the Carpathian's daughter is trying a *little* too hard.

13

DOUBLE DIGITS

W ell, I survived a year of college—and a dark elder.
Wolent didn't sound too worried when I called to tell him about meeting Ladonna. It's also unlikely he'd allow me to hear him sounding worried even if he had been. No idea how 'a little more powerful than normal vampires' translates to elders in regard to Oblivare.

I stayed after class on Thursday to pick Professor Heath's brain about them. Suppose it should reassure me he'd only heard of them in passing and has never met one face to face. As far as he thinks, they're a fringe group of weirdos kind of like PETA. Don't think Oblivare are going to sit in cages on street corners while screaming at passersby, though.

He did spend about an hour sharing his opinion on Ladonna's claim the Oblivare were the 'original' vampires and the rest of us happened by accident. In short, he called it rubbish. His actual word. I don't use 'rubbish,' like ever. Vampires have had as much luck understanding where they came from as mortals, meaning none. When I brought up the obvious problem of vampirism being parasitic in nature, requiring a vampire to exist before a vampire could exist, he explained the most well-accepted theory.

Ritual magic.

The story goes something like a group of powerful mystics who didn't want the minor triviality of a natural lifespan getting in the way of their search for knowledge attempted to make themselves immortal. The end result of their effort to 'magic' themselves into living forever turned them into the first vampires. Some theories even claim the different bloodlines are the result of each member of the original society. Like one dude who detested being around people, kept to himself, and was willing to sacrifice anything for power started the Shadows. Another who wrapped his entire life around science started the Academics, and so on. Not sure I buy that. Scions, for example, didn't exist until the Eighties. I can maybe believe some of the bloodlines exist because of the originals—assuming the whole 'sect of mystics' story is truth—but most of them probably evolved. Maybe some died off.

Obviously, demons exist. Professor Heath thinks the Oblivare are, in fact, a form of demon lacking a physical body. Bear in mind, people have a bad habit of calling supernatural entities they don't understand 'demons' without caring how accurate the word is. If you ask the average religious person—the true believers, not the get rich quick guys—demons are unabashedly evil.

Blix and the hellhound prove that wrong. This also reinforces my belief all dogs are good boys. Even demonic dogs.

Olmaz, I don't know well enough to say. He's probably not evil. He *could* have pushed Sam off the cliff and watched him try to swim in lava, but he didn't. Unless he's got some long-game style elaborate plot to use my little brother as an agent of discord in the mortal world, an 'evil' being would totally have tortured or killed two small boys. Mel, the succubus, seemed reasonably nice.

Where am I going here? My point is, the blanket statement of all demons being evil is false. Unless, of course, the ones my brother talks to aren't true demons, which brings me back to disputing the use of the word 'demon' to describe the Oblivare. Sure, they're energy beings from another plane. Doesn't make them demons.

Whatever.

Oblivare also aren't responsible for vampires. Professor Heath thinks—and I agree—they have delusions of their own grandiosity. Since their consciousness has never been human, it's easy for them to think of people as herd animals for the taking. I'd initially been kinda shocked Ladonna didn't rip me apart. Chances are, she didn't because the Oblivare want to destroy society as a construct, not every person or vampire they run into. Even if they *did* want to kill everything, it would be also hypocritical of someone from a 'bloodline' seeking to destroy everyone else to be upset at me for destroying some vampires.

I had nothing she needed, so Ladonna left me in peace.

Fair bet she also regarded me as a harmless kid who couldn't possibly be a threat to her. Is it weird an ostensibly evil inhuman vampire has more integrity than some humans?

So, anyway, first semester is over. Nothing happened as far as I am aware in regard to the Oblivare or the reliquary. Wherever it is, Wolent and his people are handling it without my involvement. Works for me. I'm the new girl. I shouldn't be involved in anything too important. Keeping to myself and my family is still my greatest desire. The more they leave me out of, the happier we are.

It's Tuesday, June 19ᵗʰ. Halfway into my first full week of not having classes, also Sam's birthday. I took advantage of summer freedom the past two nights to hang out with Ashley and Michelle. Tonight—assuming no one opens an interdimensional rift in our living room—I'll be on a date, then going back to Hunter's place.

A few minutes after I wake up, someone drops a dead deer down the stairs from the kitchen to the basement. Just kidding, it's Sam. It would be easier to determine the origin of vampires than understand how such a scrawny boy can make so much damn noise on stairs. Hunter did not spend the night in my room, so there's no need for me to panic and race to throw something on before the boy gets to the door. I'm already wearing a long T-shirt. In the TMI column, Ashley told me she usually sleeps naked when at home. Not really the sort of thing one needs to know about their best friend. In the *Way* TMI column, she mentioned her mother does, too. Apparently, according to some internet article, it's healthier. Not exactly a concern for me now. Okay, I've done it sometimes, but only when Hunter slept over.

Unless the two days I spent in a morgue cooler count as 'sleeping.'

Sam pokes his head in, sees me sitting up looking at him, then smiles. "Hey."

"Hey, yourself. How's it feel to be in double digits?"

"Same as yesterday." He steps in, eases the door closed, and walks over. "I'm excited for the party and stuff."

"Cool. You smell like people. You guys went out already?"

"Yeah. We hit the mall. Party moved back here." Sam looks at the door as if to make sure no one followed him downstairs. "Can you do us a little favor?"

I shrug. "Probably. As long as it doesn't involve inflicting grievous bodily harm, having to watch anything containing the Kardashians, shock therapy, or breaking another ethereal containment vessel."

"Nope. Promise." He smiles. "Can you please do something to Daryl and Jordan's heads so Blix doesn't have to hide all day? I feel bad he can't have fun because my friends can't know he exists. I want him to be part of it, but it would be really crappy of me not to invite the guys over, too."

Seeing him torn between two separate worlds he can't mix is kinda painful. Next time any traditionalist vampire gives me grief about risking secrecy by living at home, I'm going to introduce them to Sam. How many boys his age could keep this stuff secret from their friends for even one week?

I pull him into a hug. "Sure, kiddo. Yeah, I think I can give them a compulsion to ignore everything supernatural they see for a day. Might cause them to go derpy sometimes, but they won't remember seeing Blix, or anything he does."

He hugs me. "You're the best! Blix is gonna stay invisible, just wants to be in the party with us."

"Give me a few minutes to change, okay?"

"Sure." Sam darts to the door. "Gonna bring them down here to see your katana."

I throw on a shirt and shorts after crawling out of bed. My brother's two friends have known him since kindergarten. They're as tight as preadolescent boys can be, which is a few degrees less than combat veterans or anyone who's gone to Walmart with a friend on Black Friday and escaped with all their limbs attached. Despite the craziness in our lives, Daryl and Jordan have mostly avoided it— except for one time a group of vampires abducted them. Giving the boys a command to ignore unusual things tonight will block short-term memory, preventing any information from ever migrating into long-term memory. Since I won't need to touch their long-term memory, there shouldn't be any risk of breaking the erasure of being caught in a vampire free-for-all at an old factory.

Sam returns in a few minutes, his friends in tow. Jordan's a few months younger than Sam. He's blond like Hunter's kid brother Ronan, but not as skinny. Little dude kinda resembles a mini-Thor. Daryl's the oldest and biggest. Wouldn't call the kid overweight, but he's probably two of Ronan. Then again, Hunter's little brother is *small.* Every class group has a runt. Ro is definitely going to be the smallest in his class all the way through high school.

Speaking of Ronan, he hovers in the doorway watching. No need to play with his memories. He's fully aware of the supernatural stuff. Between his spending so much time hanging out over here with Sam and being the little brother of my boyfriend, we figured it inevitable he'd see stuff and way too much work to keep him ignorant of it. And, crap. It also occurs to me that Daryl and Jordan have already seen my sword. In fact, I took it from one of the vampires who abducted them. Slight chance, but it's possible seeing it might put a crack in the memory erasure. Probably not since Dalton did the bulk of the thought surgery. He's had a lot more practice than me.

"Hey, Sare." Daryl saunters over to me, his thumbs hooked in his jean pockets.

He's so unimpressed with the world, it's kinda cute. Ten going on thirty. He's also the only one of the boys with short hair, so brown it's almost black. Even Sam's letting his go... nearly to his shoulders already.

"Hi." Jordan waves. "Is it true you have a sword that's killed someone?"

"Well... maybe. It's really old. Authentic Japanese katana. Sam thinks it might have killed someone, but if it did, it was a really long time ago." I lean toward Daryl and stare into his eyes. Maybe I'm stretching truth, but we are talking about normal mortals here. *I* haven't used my katana to kill anyone alive. Slicing up vampires is not 'killing people.' We're already dead. Can't speak for the dude I took it from. Maybe *he* killed a mortal using it, but no angry ghosts are following me around, so it's probably safe to say it's been a while since this blade has killed a mortal.

I give Daryl a mental compulsion to dismiss anything inexplicably supernatural he sees today. Jordan gets the same. Once done, I insert a memory of checking out my sword, but change it from a white-and-silver handle to black-and-red. Don't want to accidentally unlock memories. These kids watched me use the katana to lop the head off a vampire. They probably also saw it stuck into me. Pity I can't make myself forget that.

Hopefully, tweaking a couple of kids' memories is going to be the most outlandish thing to happen today.

———————————

SAM'S SECOND PHASE PARTY IS REASONABLY NORMAL AS BIRTHDAY parties for ten-year-old boys go.

One problem with summer birthdays is not getting to bring cupcakes to school. Sam's never complained about it, though. He's too old for inviting random kids to a party simply for being in the same class. He's also not too worried about trying to be everyone's friend. My li'l bro is definitely in the 'better a small number of good friends than a large number of people who sometimes remember who you are' group. Before I woke up, the parents took the boys to the mall for the 'first phase' party. Whether 'tis nobler in the mind to trust Sierra and Sophia to be home alone or suffer the slings and arrows of cramming six tweens in one GMC Yukon, who can say.

The house hadn't been sucked into a wormhole by the time they returned.

Honestly, if ever kids existed who could be trusted home without parental supervision existed, it would be my sisters. Sierra might be willing to misbehave, but she's generally glued to the PlayStation. Even if she did something against the rules, it wouldn't be dangerous like playing with fire or drinking. Before, I'd have said Sophia is the perfect, harmless angel. She would still never misbehave on purpose, but *now* she might try to do something innocent with magic and end up causing a catastrophe. To be fair, having Mom or Dad home wouldn't make any difference if her magic got out of control, so, I can't fault them for trusting her. The only real reason to be nervous about leaving the girls home alone is outside forces. E.g. a man breaking into the house. However, we have a hellhound. And a Blix. Not that an imp is a dire threat to anyone's life, but it's hard to chase frightened tweens when your clothing comes to life and attacks you.

Sam's presents include a PlayStation game (*Jedi Fallen Order*), a couple toys from franchises I don't recognize—making me feel old— as well as some Dad classics: Transformers and GI Joe. The boys run around being generally loud and having fun for a while. Due to 'birthday,' the other kids are having dinner here—pizza—then cake. Blix pretty much acts like another one of the kids, not really doing anything obnoxiously supernatural, beyond being an imp. The mental compulsion avoids only a handful of awkward explanations whenever he bumps an object over or crashes into Daryl while they race around the backyard trying to kill each other using a Nerf football. Blix recovered the ball a few times when it left the boundary of our backyard, momentarily derping the boys as their brains rejected the sight of a self-propelled football. Jordan also ran face-first into the invisible hellhound. Thanks to my mental poke, he thinks he hit the fence. Fortunately, he only suffered a mild bruise. The nosebleed stopped in a few minutes.

Like a pair of cats laying low when guests come over, my sisters have been hiding out upstairs all day.

However, they come down for pizza and cake.

Sophia gives Daryl a weird look. Not too surprising. He did, after all, tie her to a tree in the backyard last summer. Granted, he'd been possessed at the time. Sierra seems a little off. More subdued than usual. Looking down a lot. Fidgety. Ever since I gave her some blood at the warehouse so we could fight those jackasses, her mood has radiated off her as obviously as mind-reading. It's a weaker version of the link I have to Dalton. Unless they go halfway around the globe or deep underground, a sire essentially has access to the mind of any vampire they've given the Transference to. It's the one situation where we can read another vampire's thoughts without having to be a century older. Can't implant compulsions or erase memories, merely see what's going on and carry on telepathic conversations. None of that's going on between me and Sierra. She is *not* a vampire.

But, the blood link—stronger due to us being actual family—tells me she's scared-slash-worried. We've gone a whole month (roughly) without anyone trying to kill us, so she probably thinks we're about due for a crapstorm. Ugh. I also get the feeling she wants to ask me for another taste of blood, but is hesitating. Glad she is. I mean, it was pretty freaky to see her zooming around fighting vampires. Risking whatever potential side effects come with thralling my sister is far better than the alternative of her getting killed. Neither Dalton nor Aurélie mentioned *bad* side effects. As in, giving her blood won't hurt her or end up turning her into a mindless servant. Aurélie said it can likely slow down aging if she has regular feedings, but she'd never heard of anyone turning a child into a thrall before. Hollywood likes to do the thing where if a person who's been existing as a thrall for decades is deprived of their master's blood, they suddenly age into a pile of dust. Doesn't work that way. A thrall cut off from the supply simply resumes aging normally, though depending on how long they've been 'on vampire blood,' they might feel so weak and lethargic they can barely move for a long time.

Sierra had a good reason to ask me to boost her when she did. I bet she's trying not to make a habit of asking frivolously. Good chance the next time the Forces of Evil ™ show up at our front door, she's going to appear at my side like a hungry baby bird. Yeah, now there's a mental image I really could do without. She doesn't look *too* freaked out, depressed, or worried, so I decide to respect her space. If anything bothered her enough, she'd tell me.

I have a slice of pizza not to seem weird, then lurk by the wall in the dining room. Putting pizza down in front of four tween boys is about as gory as throwing a whole cow in a river of piranha. Blix kills half a pie on his own. No idea where he put it since he's a little smaller than an adult housecat. Finally, Mom brings the cake in. The kids cheer. Cake's not on the table for a full two seconds before all ten candle flames turn red and stretch upward into jets of fire, sizzling like firecrackers about to explode. Daryl and Jordan don't react, but everyone else—including Sam—leans back from it, wide-eyed.

Blix lands on the table, pumping his spindly little arms in the air, cheering.

Some of the new toys—especially the plastic GI Joe airplane—begin flying around in circles. Ronan and Sam cheer along with Blix. My sisters laugh. Daryl and Jordan clap, oblivious to the weird stuff, and urge my brother to make a wish.

Not sure Sam *could* blow those candles out at the moment.

However, as soon as he tries to blow them out, the bizarrely intense flames vanish. Each candle fizzles up a sparkling stream of smoke, lets off a miniature fireworks display—gotta be an illusion as I do not smell explosives—then quiets.

Mom cuts the cake, distributes slices to the kids, then walks over to stand with me and Dad at the side of the room, handing us each a small paper plate. Dad, on my left, grins at the spectacle like he's gone back to being ten.

"I don't know how it's happened." Mom gives her cake an 'oh screw it' look before digging in. "But it feels like we're living inside one of your crazy Eighties movies."

"Yeah." Dad keeps grinning.

We stand there eating cake, watching random objects fly around, a

GI Joe guy fight a Transformer on the table, and half the 'happy birthday Sam' signs I hung up last night come to life as if animated into cartoons.

"This is like *Gremlins* crossed with *The Gate*." Mom shakes her head, then stuffs a hunk of cake in her mouth.

"I know, and it's awesome," whispers Dad.

Mom peers toward the kitchen. "No hellhound?"

"He's asleep." I wag my eyebrows. "Ate a whole office of telemarketers. Kinda overdid it."

Dad whistles.

My mother gasps, nearly dropping her cake.

"Relax, Mom. He didn't hurt anyone." Mmm. Lemon cake. Nom. Guess who ignores calories? *This* girl.

"At least he didn't hurt anyone considered a living being," mutters Dad.

"Telemarketers?" Mom gives him side eye.

"Debatable," mutters Dad.

"Jonathan." Mom sighs.

"You remember what the boy said, right?" Dad smiles. "Hellhounds feast on misery and suffering. Not flesh."

"Oh. Right." Mom exhales out her nose. "Not enough wine in the world."

She is mostly kidding, making fun of the mom-wine stereotype. She does use the occasional unsmall glass to cope with a bad day, but I've never seen her drunk. "Don't worry, Mom. Worst he'd do is make them drowsy or give them mild medical conditions." I wink. "Besides, I'm kidding. No idea what he's been eating. Probably only has to go smell Niedermeyer's house once a month and he's gonna put on weight."

Dad snickers.

Mom almost chokes trying to laugh, coughs once, then slices off another bit of cake on her fork. "I'm not sure how to handle this. Life's becoming so bizarre. Almost as strange as my first job right after I passed the bar. Night traffic court. All the weird ones come out after dark."

"Maybe you should make time for a hobby?" Dad nudges her. "You wanted to try painting a few years ago."

Mom blinks. "In *this* family? Painting? Hah. My hobby ought to be something like tarot reading or channeling spirits."

I pretend to shiver. "Mom, if you start singing *Day-O* in a man's voice, I'm going back to bed."

Dad chuckles. "Sarah, don't give Blix any ideas."

14

OF COURSE IT WOULD HAPPEN

Sophia buckled the seat belt and swished her feet back and forth, proud of herself.

Mom backed the Yukon out of its parking spot by the dance studio. No one, not even her mother, noticed Sophia change out of her leotard into a dress. She'd waited for the perfect moment, when most of the girls—plus the two boys in her dance class—rushed for the door. The magic hadn't been extreme, not involving conjuration or apportation of objects over long distances. She'd brought the dress along and used magic to trade the garment in her hands for the leotard she wore, which appeared in her hand, neatly folded. She'd broken Callum's advice, but she considered it practice.

According to Callum, people shouldn't use magic for any task they could do normally if at all possible. Changing clothes hardly required magical intervention. However, she wanted to practice doing something minor in a way no one noticed. Simultaneously obvious and subtle. The sort of thing people called a 'glitch in the matrix.' A person noticing she'd gone from a dance leotard to a dress in an instant would doubt themselves, say they'd imagined it because obviously what they witnessed couldn't possibly happen. They'd go on with their lives and not question anything.

If Mom noticed, she hadn't said anything. Considering Mom *always* said something, Sophia believed her mother missed it or perhaps saw, but dismissed it as being tired and seeing things.

Darren Anderson's favorite saying went something like 'the greatest feats of magic are often the smallest'. He referred to how giant explosions come from small sparks. The best spells did something minor resulting in ordinary events snowballing in a desired manner. For example, a tiny fire spell no more potent than to light a candle igniting a cache of explosives to destroy an entire building. Did magic destroy the building or not? Obviously, such a practice didn't lend itself to every situation and took a great deal of planning. He claimed some of the greatest (or most nefarious) moments in history happened as the result of tiny spells. Alas, many of the events he referred to hadn't been recorded anywhere, as they occurred during the 'lost period,' referring to the time around Camelot, Atlantis, and so on. All real, but deleted from the collective human consciousness.

Except for Sam's birthday party yesterday when the house had been too loud for her to think straight, she'd spent the past week trying to work out a way to help Sierra. Her sister *definitely* appeared to be suffering from the absence of vampire blood. It hadn't gotten to the point Mom or Dad noticed it. Sarah hadn't even said anything. Mostly, Sierra acted like she had a mild cold. Little lethargic, little surly. No sniffles, coughing, fever, or such. If anything, she had a reverse fever, her head somewhat colder than normal to the touch.

There had to be a way to essentially 'enchant' Sierra to accomplish something similar to what she gained by drinking a sip of vampire's blood. No need to go crazy. Sierra only needed to be able to survive vampire attacks, not throw cars across the street. Any prodigy mystic capable of localized time suppression ought to be able to safely make a kid a touch stronger and faster.

Safely being the most important word.

She considered the times her magic worked perfectly, rare as they'd been. In all but one case, she'd been trying to protect her family. The outlier, when she rewound time to redo a botched conversation path with Mom regarding Klepto, had also been a moment of high emotion. Step one in getting anything she did for Sierra to work needed to be grounded in a strong emotional anchor based on wanting to protect her sister.

Easy. She totally did.

Sophia only had to concentrate on her enchantment being vital and necessary for keeping Sierra alive and safe. Again, shouldn't be too difficult. The hard part would be figuring out how to shape intention and desire to do exactly what she hoped to do. No more accidental pseudo-faerie summonings. No more accidentally launching her clothes into space. Attempting to remove a sauce stain from her dress using magic had been an embarrassing mistake. Fortunately, she'd been in the school bathroom at the time. Her magic failed to differentiate between contamination and fabric, consequently getting rid of the whole dress. Klepto bailed her out by teleporting in with a replacement from home. Having a long-distance mind link to her kitten familiar rocked.

Lesson learned. Leave stain removal to washing machines, not magic. As Callum said, use spells only for stuff she couldn't do otherwise. Making Sierra stronger and faster—to a point she could survive vampires trying to kill her—couldn't be done without magic… or whatever Cold War Russia did to its female athletes, but she had neither the time nor the steroids. Sierra needed to feel safe right away, not after years of intense training.

"Sweetie?" asked Mom.

"Huh?" Sophia blinked and looked over at her.

"Did you not hear me ask if you wanted to stop by Starbucks?"

"Oh. It's a little late for coffee, isn't it?"

"I'm going to be up late working."

Sophia cringed. "Sure. I'll get cocoa or something." *I'm gonna be up late studying.*

A CUP OF VANILLA CHAI SAT ON THE RUG BESIDE SOPHIA.

She lay on her stomach, rereading all the notes and ideas she'd jotted down over the past week. Practical testing earlier in the day took the form of attempting to speed up the local squirrels. Initial tests showed promise, despite one momentarily hairless—and highly surprised—test subject. Squirrel four ended up so fast he appeared to teleport around for a few minutes until the magic wore off. Another shot off like a bullet and crashed through Mr. Niedermeyer's window. She'd hastily thrown a spell to repair the broken glass, fast enough the old man couldn't tell which window he heard break. Poor guy spent hours walking around the outside of his house, then nearly fainted from shock when a squirrel darted out the door as he went back inside.

Sophia rolled over and sat up, cradling the mostly empty Starbucks cup to her face, inhaling the yummy smell. *Before I do anything to Sierra, I have to make sure it's safe.* Asking the mystics for advice wouldn't help. They'd totally try to convince her not to do it and never even try to think it over. Expecting them to advise her against continuing should have been enough to put an end to the project. However, they admittedly did not understand everything about her magic, being mostly ritualists. She also didn't want to tell them about it due to secrecy. Any explanation for *why* she wanted to do it would lead back to vampires. Sure, they already knew about Sarah, but no need to keep talking about it all the time.

Sarah made it quite clear the security of their whole family depended on keeping stuff secret.

I don't have to keep vampires secret from vampires.

"Pff." She sputtered at the cup of vanilla chai. "I don't really know any. And they don't understand magic. Sarah found one vampire mystic, but they had to blow him up."

Of course, the man had been the one responsible for sending 'zombies' after the family, so he probably deserved to be blown up. Maybe Dalton knew someone who understood mystics and wouldn't break the secrets.

Sophia blinked, felt stupid for a second, then bonked her head into the chai cup a few times. She already knew a mystic who—while not a vampire—she could talk to about anything and not break secrecy: Coralie. Even better, the ghostly oracle would know if doing something to Sierra would go wrong in a severe way.

She hasn't shown up to warn me yet, so maybe it won't be dangerous.

"Miss Coralie? Can I talk to you, please?"

Sophia sat cross-legged in the middle of her room, sipping the last of her chai and gazing around for any sign of an answer. She'd spoken to Coralie a few times before, but hadn't yet called for her when she hadn't already been in the room. The ghost probably wouldn't show up at all if she didn't feel like talking. Then again, she might not be able to listen everywhere for anyone trying to get her attention.

Once she ran out of chai perhaps ten minutes later, Sophia fidgeted at the cup. She didn't want to be rude or bother the spirit, but if anyone could give her solid advice as to whether or not her plan should be abandoned, it would be Coralie Hall. The woman had been a mystic in life, now an oracle. The Universe sometimes had a wicked sense of irony. It gave her the gift of seeing the future, but took away her ability to share anything she learned with pretty much everyone— by killing her.

The temperature in Sophia's bedroom dropped about ten degrees.

A year ago, such an event would've made her scream and run. Now, she smiled.

"Thank you!" said Sophia in a half whisper.

Coralie manifested a step inside the door, still wearing the same old timey dress. She looked like some antique photograph from the early 1800s brought to life. "Hello, dear. Good of you to call. I'd been feeling a little lonely tonight anyway and wanted someone to converse with."

"Sure." Sophia stood, not wanting to be rude. "You're welcome to stay all night, at least until I have to go to bed."

The spirit smiled, glided across the room and sat in her desk chair. "What is it you wanted to ask about? We may as well handle the important things first, then see where our words decide to roam."

Sophia hopped on her bed and explained the situation regarding Sierra.

"Hmm." Coralie's body flickered. She stared off into space, flickered again, then shifted her gaze back to Sophia. "I do not see anything dreadful occurring, certainly not as much as will occur if your sister continues to consume vampiric blood."

"Eep!" Sophia clutched a fat plush unicorn to her chest, half hiding her face behind its rainbow mane. "It's going to hurt her?"

"Indirectly."

She squeezed the unicorn even tighter. "How?"

"You must understand what I sometimes see is similar to a pattern of light cast by a complex chandelier in the sun. It is as true as anything may be in a moment, but a slight breeze unmakes it. In a state of stillness, events will come to pass as they have played out in my vision. Even in the time it takes me to explain, something small may occur and rearrange everything."

"Okay."

"If she continues down the path she is on with nothing changing, the combination of her craving and her fear will overwhelm her reason. Sarah will become concerned, try to refuse her. Sierra seeks out another who makes her a thrall, and likely a vampire before another three years pass."

Sophia squirmed. *Bad, but not as bad as getting killed.* "What is she afraid of?"

"That, you will need to ask her. I see potential events, not into the hearts of the living."

"Okay. One more question. Can I do what I'm hoping to do so she doesn't have to go nuts?"

Coralie regarded her for a moment before dusting at her left sleeve. "Your magic is unusually strong for someone so young. Wild, though. Once you learn to control it, there is much within your grasp."

Sophia nodded once. "Hope I can figure it out before Sierra does something stupid."

"Let me give you one more piece of advice." Coralie floated up out of the chair and settled on the bed next to her. "Magic is like a serpent we are forced to seize by the tail. Sometimes, it tolerates us.

Sometimes, it whips around and bites. There is never a time when a person does not risk the forces they attempt to control lashing out at them. Magic also feeds on our emotion, desire, and essence."

Sophia swallowed. "Essence? Like it eats our souls?"

"No, child." Coralie gave a soft chuckle. "The essence of who a person is affects how they interact with magic. The advice I want to give you is this: act in a pure manner. My husband and I sought power and… look what became of me."

"Oh." Sophia bowed her head against the plush unicorn. "I want to protect Sierra."

"As you should. That is a pure motive. If you can resist the temptation to use your ability for greed, pride, vengeance, or other ignoble endeavors, it shall serve you well. You are so innocent now, but young. This world is an unkind place to those who fail to shroud their hearts in steel."

"That's just as bad, though. It's like hurting yourself before the world can do it. I don't wanna give up and stop feeling. Better to cry it out and keep trying."

"Spoken like one who has never truly cried."

Sophia lifted her face out of the rainbow mane. "I thought Sarah died for a couple days. I've never been so sad. If you stop yourself from feeling so you never get hurt, you also never have happy stuff."

"Oh, you sweet dear." Coralie attempted to kiss her atop the head, making a cold spot. "I fear you will cry far more than you expect, but the tears will be pure."

Umm… "Is that a prediction or pessimism?"

Coralie chuckled. "The difference between pessimism and realism is shaped by one's experience. A pessimist expects the worst will happen because they believe themselves unlucky. A realist expects the worst will happen because they have lived it."

Sophia lay in bed, staring at the ceiling.

Talking with Coralie for a couple hours about ordinary nonsense had been fun, if mildly frustrating. While it made her feel like a character in some kind of Jane Austen book—mostly due to Coralie's attire and habit of talking about things she experienced while alive— she couldn't work on helping Sierra and chat at the same time. She didn't mind, though. The spirit had already helped a great deal. She now knew what she hoped to do *could* work... she only needed to figure out how to control the spell properly.

She also required a teacher she could talk to and not break secrecy. A teacher capable of understanding magic. Someone who could answer any question she had. Or perhaps some*thing* capable of answering her questions.

The Tome of F.

Wide eyed, Sophia lurched to sit up, displacing a few plush animals.

Klepto, curled up on top of her chest, slipped down into her lap. "Mew?"

She picked the kitten up, raised her to eye level, and touched noses. "Can you borrow the book?"

"Mew," chirped Klepto before vanishing into a brief flicker of purple light.

This is either going to be amazing or horrible.

Thirty-ish seconds later, the kitten reappeared, her teeth clamped onto the giant book, which plopped onto the bed beside Sophia. Seeing such a small kitten 'carry' such a huge book made her giggle.

Coralie reappeared.

"Uh oh," whispered Sophia. "Is someone going to die if I open this book?"

"No, dear. I'm merely curious. The Aurora Aurea have not been able to get anything out of it thus far."

"How come?"

The spirit nonchalantly paced about. "A combination of their lacking sufficient power as well as skepticism. You have two advantages they do not. Power, and you are a child."

Sophia blinked, then cringed. "Is my magic going to get weaker when I grow up?"

"Only if you allow it to."

"Why would I do something silly like that?"

Coralie laughed. "All children believe in magic. Few adults do. By skepticism, I meant you have nothing holding you back from believing magic works. You trust, wholly and completely, in a wondrous world most adults are no longer capable of believing can exist. Darren, Callum, and Landon grew up before they ever saw proof magic exists. They see and act in small ways. Their doubt anything larger is even possible limits them to small things. You, on the other hand, believe in unicorns."

Sophia grinned. "I'm not as bad as Sarah's friend Ashley. The girl has a serious unicorn addiction. It might be time for an intervention. And yes, I am well aware I'm presently surrounded by a stuffed animal army, including six unicorns."

Coralie covered her mouth to mute another laugh.

"Besides," whispered Sophia, "Brownies are real. So are leprechauns. Unicorns have to be. Just because we haven't seen something doesn't prove it's not out there."

"I am going to make another prediction." Coralie raised an eyebrow, her expression one of complete seriousness.

Sophia bit her lip.

"You are not planning to go to sleep right away."

"Guilty," muttered Sophia. "It's summer, and it's not even ten yet. Also, I have to return this book before they notice it's gone."

Coralie nodded. "A good plan."

She hopped out of bed lugging the ponderous book. It practically dragged her to the floor. *Hmm. Let's not be dumb this time.* Even if it turned out not to be needed, Sophia created a protection circle from crayons, paintbrushes, glitter, and two sheets' worth of star stickers. The mystics would laugh at her, but she already suspected ritual materials didn't *truly* matter in most cases as much as the intention behind them. Sure, some herbs, minerals, and crystals had genuine properties, but a girl didn't need $250 worth of mandrake root or moonsilver to do what a handful of strategically arranged crayons could handle. The preparations had power because she gave them power, not because they grew on the underside of a rock somewhere in Ireland being nibbled at by goats in the light of the full moon.

Once satisfied she'd properly shielded herself from any potential entities bursting out of the giant book, she moved it to the center of the circle and put her hand on the cover. Still, the tome gave off a noticeable air of indifference, seemingly unconcerned whether or not she bothered it or went away.

Sophia concentrated on her question. *How can I protect Sierra from becoming dependent on vampire blood, and maybe enchant her so she doesn't need it?* After fixing the idea in mind, she pulled the cover open.

Blank pages.

She looked at the old, yellowed paper. Oddly, it didn't surprise her to find the book blank.

"You're not really empty. You've got too much information even for this many pages, so you can't show it all at once." She traced her fingers down one page. "How can I help Sierra? How can I control my magic?"

Dark brown lettering faded into view. Fancy illustrated capitals festooned in faeries and flowers started each paragraph, no two written in the same size lettering. The text had a handwritten quality to it and even gave off the scent of fresh ink.

"Whoa." Sierra stared in awe.

"See?" Coralie stood tall, proud. "Do what you need to. I shall go distract the mystics so they do not notice the book missing. Be sure and return it when you are done."

"Yes. I was going to." Sophia nodded. "Absolutely."

Coralie vanished.

Sophia knelt on the carpet in front of the book, extending one hand to summon a small magical light in her palm. Enough to read by, but not so bright Mom or Dad would see it leaking out under her bedroom door and come check on her.

The fancy writing described the process of creating a manner of potion, infused by magic and her intention. Several paragraphs detailed the exact ways in which she needed to envision the effect of the spell operating. The remainder described how to prepare the concoction as well as the most important, and some not so important but still necessary, ingredients. It also went on to describe the safest way to deliver the enchantment to Sierra, which surprisingly involved *not* drinking the potion but soaking in it.

"A grey acanthia mushroom nourished in spirit water, a silver ring saturated in mystical energy, and dirt trodden upon by fey." Sophia cringed. "Oh, wow. I don't think Safeway's gonna have this stuff."

A page turned. More text appeared. Sophia read as fast as the letters faded into view. All three items could be found in the same place. She drew in a surprised, happy breath. Alas, the place was Salem, specifically an old, abandoned house formerly occupied by a coven of mystics, now abandoned and rotting. Her happiness crashed to the floor.

Ugh! Salem? That's on the other side of the country. Mom's not going to want to drive me there.

The facing page explained she could find the mushroom growing in the basement, adequately nourished by water dripping from the ceiling. Such an amount of paranormal energy suffused the structure, the rain became spirit water by the time the leak reached the basement. A focusing ring adequate for her purposes could be found in a bureau on the second floor, and fey had once danced upon the dirt in the garden beneath the rose bushes.

She sighed silently out her nostrils. So close, but so impossibly far away. No way would her parents take her across the country to Massachusetts so she could do some 'magic stuff' on Sierra. Well, Dad probably would... but Mom would freak and tell him no. Sarah might be willing to help if properly warned what would happen to Sierra if she kept drinking vampire blood for power. But, Sarah might also simply command Sierra to stop wanting it and go back to being an ordinary kid sister. She'd totally use mind control on them, too, if she thought it necessary to keep the Littles safe. While it would stop Sierra from doing stupid things, it would *not* keep her safe if bad guys showed up on their own.

"Salem isn't as far away as London." Sophia closed her eyes. *I need to protect my sister. She isn't supposed to turn into a vampire or get hurt. I have to help her.* "How can I open gates like the London mystics did and not have a giant void octopus smack me in the face?"

The pages fluttered up as if in a breeze, rapidly turning from right to left before settling. More text wrote itself in.

"Ooh!" She leaned close to the book.

Time to read.

15

STRANDED ON A WOODEN BOAT

Reality has several immutable constants: death, taxes, and whenever something unpleasant occurs, the aristocracy tends to gather in secret and figure out how to save themselves at the expense of everyone else.

While not every vampire is financially wealthy, we're basically sectioned off from mortals in an aristocracy of sorts. It's not quite the same as the French elite gathering in fancy manors to gripe about peasants. However, if mortals found out about us, I'm sure metaphorical guillotines would follow soon.

Anyway, bad stuff is happening, so it's time for a party.

Tonight's soiree didn't come out of nowhere on an hour's notice. I had a whole day's warning. Or night's warning to be technical. Starting to wonder if there's something wrong with me since it doesn't bother me anymore to get all dressed up in period costume. Aurélie always gives me this mildly disapproving look whenever I think of her clothing as 'period costumes' even though I'm not making fun of them. Are we presently in the 1600s? No, then they're period costumes.

I suppose these elaborate gowns are a lot more comfortable when breathing is an option, not a requirement.

Aurélie's limo brings us to the usual hotel. It's not her limo per se. She hires a car service whenever she needs to go somewhere publicly, which isn't often. Riding in a car this big makes me feel like we're on the way to a funeral or a wedding. Makes no sense to me why anyone would want to do this all the time. She thinks of it like the modern equivalent of a fancy six-horse carriage. It boggles my mind because it's not like she can go out into the world and soak up fame. The big car driving a couple blocks across the city before dropping us off in front of a hotel isn't playing to any crowd or media, merely a handful of vampires who might be close enough to see us.

Dressing up and getting a limo is a lot of effort for only a small audience, but it's kinda fun. Coming to these gatherings isn't too nerve-wracking for me anymore. Sure, being in a room with elders is going to put any vampire on edge, but at least the two elders who used to want me destroyed have relaxed from contempt to distrust. It's not so much they don't trust me. They think I'm being reckless and risking all of vampiredom to exposure by living at home with my family. Little do they know the existence of undead is only one of many secrets we need to keep.

We exit the limo in front of the hotel. The strangest feeling someone's staring at me makes me look behind us, across the roof of the car. No one stands out as suspicious. No humans anyway. I spot an impressively large blackbird perched on a streetlamp across from the hotel. This is either a hallucination caused by all the research I did into Edgar Allen Poe for my class project recently, or that crow is seriously lost. Something about it feels a touch off. Hmm. Beast vampires can supposedly see through animals as well as talk to them. Haven't witnessed it happen yet, though I suspect Garret Adler spied on me via Sam's pet frogs when we'd been camping by the caverns he lived in. Before I can ask Aurélie what she thinks of the bird, it flies off.

Hmm. Strange but hardly panic-worthy. Just because I'm a vampire, one of my sisters can use magic, my brother collects demons, and we have a hellhound in the backyard doesn't mean everything is supernatural or after me. Sometimes a large raven is simply a large raven.

Aurélie heads up the stairs, so I follow her into the hotel, across the lobby, and down a hall toward the convention room where the soiree is happening. Two dozen or so younger vampires hang out in clusters littered around from the entrance to the double doors at the end. When I say 'younger,' I mean younger than the usual attendees. They're all much older than me vampire wise and don't usually show up at every gathering. The number of vampires in the Seattle area younger than me are countable on one hand. Probably one finger— Brady. Must be something serious going on if they've emailed everyone to show up.

The two of us are the only ones who look like we're chronologically challenged. Aurélie's big on the whole 'fashionably late' thing. I'm sporting a crushed green velvet dress with a decadently low neckline and puffy sleeves. Mind you, I'm talking 1600s decadent. I've got the tiniest hint of cleavage visible. The yellow gown from last month made me look like Belle from Beauty and the Beast. Tonight, I feel like I should be fanning myself and fretting over someone named James being killed on the battlefield before he can return to me. Modern women complain—rightly so—about the discomfort of mammograms. These women have never worn an authentic bone corset. I've never been so happy before to have my father's genes. Can't imagine a girl like Bree Swanson trying to squeeze her chest into this thing. The dress would push them up into her face. She'd look like a Honda Civic with both front airbags deployed.

So, yeah. Vampires who don't usually attend these gatherings give us WTF looks. Everyone else is used to our unusual fashion statements. Aurélie heads into the convention hall and proceeds to do the required rounds. Like a dutiful little protégé, I follow and exchange pleasantries. It's a weird dance of old-timey customs, high-society, and the modern world. Doesn't truly feel genuine nor does it feel like we're putting on a theater play.

The room fills as the clock nears midnight, many more in attendance tonight than I'd ever seen before. Still no sign of Dalton or my Lost One friends. Aurélie generally ignores anyone who isn't a regular attendee, so it only takes us about forty minutes to make a show of social politeness before she installs herself in a conversation cluster with Wolent, Vanessa Prentice, Jennifer Ruiz, Henry Arnold, Ashton James, Stefano, and Paolo.

As catty as Jennifer, Vanessa, and Aurélie can get, they do seem to enjoy hanging out together. Huh. Maybe it's all show and they really don't care as much about who's the prettiest as they want people to think.

Weird thing is, other vampires are no longer content to ignore me. Not sure if it's from going official, proving myself by blowing up the crypt in Astoria, or simply being around long enough for everyone to stop assuming me to be Aurélie's toy she'll bore of in a month. A handful of relatively young (undead for less than four decades) vampires drift over to start up a conversation with me. My days of standing around like a piece of room decoration are, apparently, over. They're mostly curious about the 'living at home' situation. No need to share the lengths to which my family's personal weirdness has extended, but other than leaving out Sophia's magic and Sam's otherworldly friends, I'm more or less honest with them. I couldn't hide giving Sierra some blood to improve the odds of her remaining alive, so she is 'officially' my thrall for the time being. There's no small bit of disdain at the idea of enthralling a twelve-year-old, but it's tempered by the extremity of the situation. Not like it happened for my personal amusement or being irresponsible when Sierra asked simply to mess around and play super hero. They all relax when I explain my intention to let the thralldom lapse.

One of the vamps who decided to talk to me tonight, Chantal Emerson, a twentyish blonde with a runway model body and giant French waif eyes, starts going on about her time as a thrall. One of Stefano's associates, Devon Lachlan, found her at a—wow surprise—fashion show and 'claimed' her. It's not as creepy as it sounds. Some fashion models use cocaine or other drugs to stay skinny. Chantal took vampire blood instead. Started at seventeen, got the Transference at twenty-one, but she still looks seventeen. A mature seventeen, but according to her, she stopped aging as soon as she tasted vampire blood. Back to the not creepy part. Her former patron and later sire 'collected' her like Aurélie collects porcelain dolls. He thought her beautiful and wanted to preserve her as is. Yeah, okay, that is creepy, but it wasn't an older guy lusting after a young girl situation. He neither touched her nor treated her like property. According to her, he enjoyed long conversations and was quite a bit lonely.

It's a common Hollywoodism to wrap vampires up in sexiness. And while many are dripping with lust and many more still enjoy sex, there's a surprising number who don't. You know, being dead and all. Her sire is one such vampire who lost all carnal interest when his heart stopped beating.

Anyway, Chantal cautions me to wean Sierra off the blood as soon as I can. In her case, after four years, she began fiending for it 'worse than a heroin addict' as she puts it. It hadn't been Devon's intent to give her the Transference at all, since thralldom can go on for centuries. She tells us he planned to 'let her go' if she ever bored of their arrangement and asked to leave. However, to spare her from the maddening addiction, he brought her fully into undeath.

This tells me two things. One, Devon didn't expect her to become addicted to the blood, and two, she did. Sounds like it's possible but based on the individual—a psychological addiction more than chemical. My read on her is she'd been a motivated rising star in the media world willing to do whatever it took to stay young, beautiful, and successful. Such a personality certainly had an effect. Sierra is about as opposite as is possible to be. She'd happily spend the rest of her life in our living room playing video games, doesn't give a rat's ass about fashion, and couldn't care less what anyone thought of her looks.

I still don't want to run the risk of her becoming addicted, going insane, or suffering some other supernatural calamity. Maybe I should take comfort in her not asking me for more blood yet. The connection we had immediately upon her drinking from me has faded to almost gone. I'm sure it means she's back to normal, as in, no supernatural strength or speed.

Hmm. She did seem a bit twitchy, but it could have come from ordinary nervousness. If she knew she'd gone back to being a normal kid, she might be on edge, worrying about another vampire attack or something along those lines. I take some comfort knowing if she'd become addicted, she'd be begging me already for another 'hit.'

Despite being part of Stefano's crowd, Chantal doesn't sound particularly concerned about me living at home. The group gathered around me chuckles at my description of how the 'rents have coped with everything. For example, Mom yelling at me over compelling people to buy Girl Scout Cookies like I'd forgotten to take out the trash.

I'm in the midst of stressing how my whole family is committed to maintaining secrecy when Wolent clears his throat. Aurélie lets off a pulse of charm to draw everyone's attention to herself. She happens to be standing right next to Wolent, which results in all the vampires in attendance at the soiree looking at him.

The din of people talking fades to silence—except for one of the 'snacks' singing Chili Peppers' 'Under the Bridge' off key. Dude is baked. Another mortal here for refreshment purposes is so drunk he can't even stand. Yeah, this is the vampire society version of putting out pot brownies and beer for the guests.

A thirtyish vampire in a sharp black suit hurries over and silences the vocalist. Using mental command; he didn't kill the stoner.

"I don't mean to cast a pall over the pleasantries tonight..." Wolent looks over the sea of faces watching him. "There is, however, a situation as of late with the potential to make life difficult on all of us. Some of you may already be aware, but for those who are not, at least half a dozen new vampires have cropped up over the past two weeks."

Most vampires in the room emit a collective gasp. The ones who don't scowl as if they already knew about it.

Wolent, clearly annoyed, continues glancing around while doing this weird 'I just bit a lemon' grimace like he's trying to pull off an impression of Robert DeNiro playing Arthur Wolent. The men don't look or sound anything alike, but he's got the body language and speech cadence down.

No one's sat me down and given me 'the talk' yet. Well, Dad did, but I'm not referring to that talk. I mean the vampire version. It's still kind of a birds and bees thing to be fair. Neither Dalton nor Aurélie thus far thought it necessary to warn me against making baby vampires. Admittedly, my existence caught some of them off guard. Vampires don't have to get permission or anything to make another vampire. Maybe in some super hardcore areas of Europe where they have a legitimate political structure and the ruler's a control freak, but generally, not. However, I get the feeling from Wolent's tone he's not fond of the newbies.

"I do not believe anyone in this room is the responsible party." Wolent turns in place, scanning everyone around him. "Someone is risking us all by creating too many too fast without proper mentoring. We managed to keep a rather flagrant sighting off the local news, but it's only a matter of time before some random person with a cell phone sends video to the internet."

Oh, I see. He's not upset about new vampires in general, merely careless idiots not hiding themselves.

"You worry too much, Arthur," says Eleanor St. Ives in her best unconcerned scientist voice. "This concern will burn itself out soon enough."

Wolent side-eyes her. "Possibly, but none of us should be willing to gamble it does so before the wrong kind of evidence ends up on the national news. Everyone in this room should look for the source of these new progeny."

"You're giving an order then?" asks Paolo Cabrini in a bored tone, swirling blood around a martini glass.

"Don't think of it as an order." Wolent clears the distance to him in three steps and pats him on the arm. "If we are all in a wood boat and someone's kid starts playing with matches, it's in everyone's best interest to take the damned matches away from the brat."

I'd sigh, but this corset isn't letting much air in. Dammit. We just got over one crisis, now this? Though, an idiot is much less scary than an entire group of vampires trying to take over Seattle by force.

"That is all. If no one else has anything to say we all need to hear..." Wolent nods once, then waves in a 'resume' gesture.

Everyone goes back to talking and socializing.

I spend the next almost-hour listening to the small group around me discuss various topics from investments to the bar they live under to clothes and such. Every so often, one of them will ask me about the nest in Astoria or want to clarify some weird rumor they heard about me. No, I really am nineteen. I'm not some thousand-year-old spy sent from Europe who looks like a teenager. No, I didn't turn my entire family into vampires. No, I am not Aurélie's lover, and so on. They tease me a bit for going to college but it comes off as good-natured rather than mean—and leads into this guy Jacob telling us how he spent the first two years post-Transference clinging to his job as a car dealer. His boss kept wanting to fire him for being late every day—gee, wonder why—but everyone he spoke with always bought the car—again, gee, wonder why—so they let him stay. He only disappeared when his suspiciously perfect sales attracted a police investigation.

Me getting people to buy some cookies doesn't seem so bad in comparison.

Eventually, the soiree is over and I'm back in the car beside Aurélie. She's thrilled to see me in high spirits and having been 'part of' the goings on rather than a bit of furniture taking up space until it ended. You know how they have those commentary shows after some sports games where a bunch of guys sit around dissecting every little thing about how the players sportsballed the sportsball? Yeah, we kinda do the same thing in regard to the social event. Gawd. When did I become a gossiping hen? Is it a side effect of wearing such old timey clothes? Makes me think there's no such thing as electricity or television and the only entertainment is talking about other people? Or, am I still 'in character?'

My relationship with Aurélie is really strange. I don't know how to explain it. When we get back to her place, our conversation continues even as I change out of the elaborate gown into my normal shirt and jeans. I don't bat an eyelash at being momentarily naked in front of her, having a conversation as casual as anything. She does, after all, insist on me wearing entirely period-accurate garments. No modern undies allowed. The strange part is, I'd feel super awkward changing in front of my actual mother, or anyone else except Hunter. For the longest time, I never understood how fashion models could all change out in the open, naked in front of each other like no big deal.

Granted, I wondered this before being stranded outside sans clothing for a full day.

Still, though. It has to be like some kind of 'professional' thing. There's nothing even close to a romantic mood between us. She's kinda maternal, kinda sisterly, kinda bossy. I don't mean 'bossy' the way men refer to a woman who isn't subservient. I mean she feels like my employer, my boss, in a way. We're just some bizarre combination of family, friends, siblings, co-workers, and conspiring members of a secret society who can talk to each other about anything we can't share anywhere else. In short, she's my faerie deathmother.

Once I'm back in my clothes, we head to the living room to relax.

"Wolent seemed pretty upset about new vampires. Is that normal? For him to be upset over newbies?"

Aurélie tilts her hand in a so-so gesture. "'E is most concerned at someone creating many new vampires so quickly and not teaching them the basics. They do not keep themselves secret. Also, it is against tradition to pass the gift to so many so fast. The Transference is meant to be a matter of deep consideration."

"Or an act of desperation?" I smile cheesily.

"True." She winks. "While there are some among us who frown on any new vampire who 'as not been groomed for the change, your circumstances are not the same as some reckless fool turning everyone 'e or she feeds from and leaving them to their own devices."

I tap a foot on air. "I'd wonder if it might be unintentional, but it's pretty difficult to accidentally cut yourself and make sure the person drinks your blood while wanting to pass it along."

She gasps into a giggle as if Klepto just did something adorable on the sofa beside me.

Yeah, it's really impossible to accidentally produce a full vampire. Scraps are another matter. Those sometimes happen accidentally during a kill feeding. Even if this idiot vampire rolls a critical fumble and bites his tongue off while trying to feed, he or she would still have to desire to pass vampirism on. Merely leaking blood into the mortal you're feeding from won't do it.

Unless, as my father sometimes says, 'something entirely unexpected and f'd up happened.'

"Arthur is right to be concerned." Aurélie examines her nails, muttering to herself in French for a few seconds before looking back at me. "It is true they will cause problems. Feeding issues, risk of detection. Bad business for all of us. I fear it may be even a more serious problem as none of the new progeny 'ave any memory of what 'appened to them."

"Gee. Sounds familiar." I fake roll my eyes. "It took me hours to remember anything from the day it happened. Is it normal to not remember, or does it only happen if the death is sudden, violent, and unexpected?"

"Loss of memory is normal, but it returns relatively soon if the sire remains with their progeny when they awake. The one doing this is abandoning them right away. It could take months before we are able to find him."

I fidget. This isn't exactly a 'the city is on fire' type problem. More like littering. Can't really say it doesn't affect me, because it does. If some clueless new vampire ends up on television news, it will set off an epic tornado of political feces among the vampire community. The PIBs will lose their minds. No matter what type of disinformation campaign tries to discredit it, hunters will swarm the area. I doubt many of them are as reasonable as Damarco. Most see vampires and want to destroy us, not caring what sort of person we are. They only see monsters.

"What's going to happen to the newbies?" I dig my toes into the carpet. Not sure what it is, but it's amazingly plush and soft. Probably ridiculously expensive.

"It depends on how many the source makes. If they are stopped soon, perhaps nothing unless they refuse to follow the rules." Aurélie gives a sad sigh. "If too many new vampires are made, we will 'ave no choice but to order them to leave the area or be destroyed."

"I understand. How many are there so far?"

"Seven we are aware of. All young men about your age."

Eep. "All of them? That can't be a coincidence."

Aurélie offers a slight nod. "Indeed. We thought the same. Per'aps this source vampire is, what is the word they... psychopath?"

It's tempting to say Sybarite, thinking of Petra, but I don't. Aurélie snickers anyway, picking up my thoughts. Most Sybarite are legit artists. I've only met one who twisted their all-consuming drive into something close to being a serial killer. And ack! There could be some crazy vampire out there preying specifically on young guys—and Hunter is right in the target range. The only thing keeping me from irrational panic is knowing he won't have much reason to go into Seattle until next semester starts. The odds of him ending up a victim of this guy—or woman—are honestly pretty low, but then again, this is my crazy vamped up life we're talking about.

Nah, probably not. Honestly, my boyfriend being turned into a vampire could end up being a good thing. It's nothing I'd ever actively pursue, but it would hardly be the end of the world. Worst part would be feeling guilty he could never have kids or an ordinary life—but being with me has already done that to him. He's so into me, it would come off as creepy if not for my ability to read minds and see it's honest love and not psycho stalker obsession. The boy doesn't care what shape his life takes on as long as he gets to spend it with me.

Aurélie gives me that 'you really ought to consider it—or leaving him' look she usually does whenever she catches me thinking about Hunter. We've discussed it before. She thinks I'm being 'tragic' by letting him stay mortal, grow old, and die. It's not like he asked and I'm refusing. If he asked, it would probably take him about fifteen minutes to talk me into it. Not sure I'd be able to bring myself to do it, though. Not only would it be too difficult to essentially kill the man I love, being his sire and lover goes way too far into creepy territory. Yeah, I know it happens all the time—both in reality and in vampire fiction—but I can't help but feel icky about it.

Ugh. If this weirdo out there does pick Hunter, they might be helping us both.

But I still hope he doesn't.

Yeah, contradiction. That's my name. A vampire who loves being a vampire but gets too sad at the idea of her boyfriend not being alive anymore to share the gift with him.

Aurélie giggles at me again.

16

SCHRÖDINGER'S COP

Didn't leave Aurélie's place until well after two in the morning.

Not a complaint. It's weird to say, but I never imagined simply hanging out and talking could be so entertaining. No electronics involved. Straight up 'partying like it's 1699' as Weird Al said. Maybe it's the immortality. Not having a time limit to my existence could explain my tolerance for not trying to cram every minute of wakefulness as full of as much distracting stimuli as possible. Something tells me the psychological community won't take 'vampirism' seriously as a cure for the negative mental effects caused by the saturation of technology in our society.

Two in the morning ended up being a bit late to go to Hunter's, so I went home, checked on Sierra—who slept peacefully and didn't show any signs of paranormal problems—then spent the rest of the night playing video games in my room. Talk about slam-shifting without a clutch. From an almost 'medieval court' soiree to feeling like a pair of pre-electrical-revolution women passing time together straight to a video game marathon. It's like how my Dad has Enya, Rush, Metallica, Celtic folk music, and heavier metal in his playlist. One second, there's peaceful flute music, then all hell breaks loose.

I slip over to Hunter's house the next afternoon almost as soon as I wake up. He's surprised to see me out during the day when it isn't even raining. Their house is still basically a construction project. It's this freakin' huge two-and-a-half story beast with a wraparound porch, but two-thirds of it would be considered uninhabitable by anyone with First World sensibilities or a passing knowledge of structural engineering. Hunter's asshat of a father intended to fix the place up and 'flip' it for a profit. Sure, after I compelled him to take off and never return, there's no way he's going to finish. 'Course, he bought the house when Hunter was like three and hadn't fixed even one room yet. Safe to assume he'd never have gotten around to it, anyway.

Hunter, however, has decided to help his Mom out by attempting some repairs. He picked up a bunch of books from Home Depot or whatever and is teaching himself how to replace drywall, re-do floors, and re-tile bathrooms. The heavy-duty structural stuff (like collapsing floors and holes in the roof) is going to take more than some DIY books, though. His mother's new job pays much better than her last one. She ought to be able to afford real contractors to do the heavy lifting in another year or so.

We spend all afternoon to dinnertime ripping out moldy drywall in a bedroom on the second floor. The house is basically two 'normal' houses stuck together. It used to be a four-family home, each story divided into two separate apartments with their own kitchens and bathrooms. His dad renovated the side they live in into a two-story single-family home, but the 'empty' part of the house is still two separate apartments. If they ever fix it up enough to pass inspection, his mother might rent them out for some extra income.

Hunter appears to enjoy the work. We joke back and forth about him starting a contracting business. Think he's contemplating it as a backup plan if anything forces him to stop pursuing a degree. He'd likely need to work for an established contractor to learn for a few years before having any real chance of making a go of working for himself. He's kinda in my boat, not sure what he wants to study. So far, he's taking a generic liberal arts curriculum. The only thing he knows for certain about his future is he doesn't want to go into education. His mother used to be a teacher. She lost her job a little over two years ago to some kind of cutbacks. When I met Hunter, she'd been jumping from one minimum-wage thing to another while using all her free time to find a better job... at least when she hadn't been hiding from the father. Hunter's Dad didn't like her working at all. Yeah, he's a real jerk. She liked teaching, but it doesn't pay enough to support two sons and a house on her own. I helped her get an office job.

By the time my phone rings a little after six, Hunter's thinking about civil engineering or whatever degree program will help him get into the Forestry Service. One thing Washington State has plenty of is forests, and he likes the outdoors. Another thing making me hesitate at the idea of his becoming a vampire—he won't be able to be a ranger.

My phone rings.

There aren't many people I'd allow to interrupt my Hunter time by phone. I don't recognize the caller ID, so I ignore it. Alas, it begins ringing right away again. Telemarketers don't call back right away if you decline their call. Worried it might be Ashley or Michelle stranded post-car-accident on the side of the road using a borrowed phone, I answer.

"Hello?"

"Miss Wright?" asks a fairly ordinary sounding man. Uh oh. He's kinda got cop voice.

"Yes?"

"I'm calling on behalf of Mr. Wolent. Your assistance would be appreciated with a minor matter."

Oh, crap. I clench my fist and make a 'grr not now' face at Hunter. "I'm kinda in the middle of something at the moment. How important is this?"

"Fairly. The window of opportunity is small. Do you recall picking up an antique vase for your uncle?"

Blink. Say what? Is this some kind of Bourne Identity code phrase nonsense? "Umm... the frog perched on the steeple in the rain?"

"Mr. Wolent is unconcerned with the minor damage to the car that occurred during the ride."

Ack! "Oh, *that* vase. Yeah, I remember."

"Excellent. Mr. Wolent would appreciate it if you could pick the vase up from the storage facility before dark. Preferably soon."

I cross the room and bonk my head against Hunter's back a few times. "Okay. Yeah. That sounds important. I'll be there as soon as I can. Where am I going and who am I looking for?"

"Parking garage downtown. Second Ave and Union Street. Fourth floor. There'll be a cop there. Ask him what time it is and say a crow stole your phone."

Wow. Okay. They really *are* using spy code stuff. Kinda cool, if a bit lame. "Got it."

"Bring the vase to the manor once you pick it up."

"Can do."

"Great. Mr. Wolent sends along his thanks. He likely won't be awake or available when you arrive. No need to lurk around waiting for him."

"Cool. On the way."

I hang up.

Hunter wipes sweat and drywall dust from his forehead. "Another mysterious phone call?"

"You know." I shrug. "Stuff no one wants to talk about on cell phones. Even if the stuff about the NSA listening to everything is conspiracy nonsense, they don't want to take the risk it isn't."

"What crazy mess are you stuck in now?" He grins. "Anything I can help with?"

"Just picking up a package and taking it somewhere. You don't have to stop working. It's not even going to take me an hour, most of it driving."

"Not flying? Oh, duh. Still daylight." He glances at the window. "Must be something valuable or dangerous if they're asking you to move it during the day."

I lean against him. "Ugh. Thanks for making me nervous."

"Sorry." He kisses me.

"Mmm." I return the kiss. "You're right, though. Only reason they'd ask me to do it now is daylight. Probably worried about the Oblivare trying to steal it back. Weird though."

"Weirder than a jar of souls?"

Oops. Yeah, I told him all about the chase and crash. Maybe I shouldn't share *everything* with him, but he's easy to talk to. "Sun's out. So, the man who just called me is most likely a mortal thrall, or someone paid well enough to keep secrets. I'm supposed to meet a cop, who *has* to be another thrall since he's obviously taken the reliquary out of the police impound or evidence locker or whatever they call the place where stuff found in burning cars goes."

"It's weird for them to have enthralled cops?"

"No." I chuckle. "From what I hear, they have agents pretty much everywhere. The weird part is why are they asking *me* to go get it and not having the cop take it to the manor? Wolent has mortals working for him, both employees as well as thralls. Some are both."

Hunter kisses me again. "The Universe saw us being happy together and had to do something about it."

I squeeze him, thinking about the serial-vampire-maker out there. "Don't say that too loud."

"You sound worried."

"If I say 'nah, it's nothing,' you're going to be dead by tomorrow." I chuckle. "Got a vamp out there randomly turning guys your age into vampires and abandoning them."

"Oh. Hardly the worst thing a creep could do to me."

Yeah, don't have the time nor the desire for *this* conversation again. "Right. There's gotta be a reason. Maybe it's dangerous for humans to be near the reliquary, or maybe they can't have the cop go anywhere near Wolent's house. Just in case, you stay here well out of reach of ancient evil. I'll be back as soon as I can."

"All right. Looking forward to tonight."

"You and me both." I grab two fistfuls of his shirt and pull him closer, kissing him while fantasizing about what we'll be doing to each other later. Ack. Better stop or it'll be dark before I ever go out the door.

I HAVE TO BE THE ONLY TEEN IN WASHINGTON STATE—HECK, AMERICA —who thinks of driving as annoying.

Any normal person my age would be thrilled to have a car they could use whenever they needed, even if it is ancient as cars go. Dad's old Sentra won't win any beauty contests, but it runs. Traveling long distances during daylight hours requires the car, mostly because I don't own a bike anymore and walking would take so long I might as well wait for dark and fly. Problem being, the whole point of this assignment is finishing it before dark.

Naturally, the emphasis on daylight makes me think Wolent knows of Oblivare in the area who really want their soul jar back. I wouldn't put it past someone like St. Ives to try to take it, too. Her motivations might not be sinister, but no movie involving a mad scientist ever depicted an experiment going properly. Even if she merely wants to study this thing, the end result is going to suck. Or, maybe I have her figured wrong and even she isn't reckless enough to toy with the energies contained within the reliquary.

Whatever, I'm not being paid to think here. Just drive a package from point A to point B. I'm not being paid at all, really. Only a phrase.

The parking garage is fairly close to the water, roughly four blocks east from the Seattle Aquarium. This means I have to drive into Downtown Seattle. Irritating, but it could be worse. I don't live in LA, Atlanta, New York City, or anywhere in New Jersey. I think Dad said something about Los Angeles traffic being listed as one of the top twenty causes of mental breakdowns in the country on some study. No idea if he'd been joking.

Anyway, it takes me about forty minutes to drive from Hunter's house to downtown Seattle and the parking garage in question. I hang a left off Second Ave into the garage. Powder blue quarter-walls on each of the levels of an otherwise concrete-grey building make it look like a giant late-Eighties era IBM computer case. Hmm. I probably shouldn't get a job as an architectural critic.

On the fourth level, I spot a cop sitting in his car, which he's parked in a non-spot, one of those areas intended for official vehicles or maintenance workers. There are no other cop cars in sight, so I'm hoping he's my contact. I pull the Sentra into an available spot far enough away not to be overly conspicuous, then walk over to the police car.

The cop gets out when I'm about twenty feet away. He's on the taller end of average height, probably Native American, and giving me a 'you gotta be kidding' sort of expression. Far as I can tell from here, he appears to be an ordinary Seattle Police officer. Can't sense if he's a thrall or not due to being offline, so I try my best to act casual.

"Excuse me, officer. Do you know what time it is? A stupid crow flew off with my iPhone."

Officer Trujillo—according to his name badge—chuckles. "They always come up with the weirdest lines. Are you seriously who I think you are?"

"Depends on who you think I am."

"A friend of a mutual friend. Little young to have, umm, loyalty in your blood?"

"Yeah. I'm who you think I am. Also, not quite as young as I look."

The cop laughs, heading for the trunk. "Yeah, that"—he wags his eyebrows at me—"energy drink sure is good for keeping the wrinkles away."

Wow. I honestly don't know how legit spies put up with all the oblique references and subtle hints. The guy seems nice enough, but two minutes of this weird banter is already making me want to scream. "Sure is. So, you found granny's lost vase?"

"Yep. Right here in the trunk." He pats it. "One sec, let me get it open."

"Probably shouldn't open it."

"I mean the trunk." Officer Trujillo pulls a key fob out of his pocket.

He looks at it for a little too long. These things aren't exactly Space Shuttle console complicated. Two, maybe three buttons tops, all

SCHRÖDINGER'S COP | 139

labeled with pictures so obvious even a flat-earther could figure out which button unlocked the doors and which one opened the trunk.

Finally, he pushes a button and the trunk pops open. The instant a gap exists between trunk lid and car, a sheet of faintly glowing violet smoke escapes, rushing into his chest.

Uh oh. Not good. Think I just figured out why Wolent wanted *me* to pick this thing up and not a thrall. I have questions though. Like: how'd the cop get it here in the first place? I don't, however, have time to find the answer.

Officer Trujillo looks up from the key fob and stares at me, his pupils glowing like purple laser pointers. Gonna go ahead and assume this isn't normal, and I'm probably not looking at Officer Trujillo anymore. At least, not mentally. His smile's gone, too. The *whump* of him slamming the trunk shut again makes me jump.

"Your interference will no longer be tolerated," says the cop in a voice three octaves too deep to be human.

"Nice effect." I take a step back. "Totally sounds demonic."

The cop looks down at himself, notices he has a gun on his hip, and reaches for it.

"Shit."

I run straight out of my flip-flops, hauling ass for the nearest gap between cars. Being shot is never fun, but it sucks extra hard when it can actually kill me. It would be cool to say I pull some kind of Sarah Connor judgement day thing and hit the deck like a soldier. Alas, reality is more like I'm in the first movie where she's a clueless waitress. I might even be screaming, hard to say.

Only thought on my mind is putting as much metal and concrete between me and a bullet as possible.

Parking garages make guns sound like howitzers. A Land Rover side window explodes on my left, pelting me in a rain of tiny glass bits. A few nuggets probably end up embedded in my soles, but I don't feel them yet. Too much panic. The only thing saving my ass at the moment is whatever soul decided to body-jack the cop might be so old he's never used a modern firearm. He obviously—*bang*—knows what a gun is. Aiming it, however, he's not terribly good at.

A clank far too close on my right announces another miss. The cop decides to chase me. Oh, wonderful. This guy would kick my ass bad enough already, but he's also a thrall. Wait... daytime. I think thralls lose their strength in the sun just like I do. Okay, so my only problem is the normal degree of beating a guy his size would inflict on a girl my size when neither one of us had supernatural powers. News flash: this does not end well for me.

Officer Trujillo is fast for a mortal. Tall... long legs.

Every time I reach a lane between rows of parked cars, I zig-zag two or three spaces left or right. Can't simply run away in a straight line or he's going to shoot me in the back. There's not much deep thought going on in my head beyond 'run for your life' until I reach the wall at the end of the floor. The stairwell door gives me an idea: underground levels. Two entrances on Second Ave led into the garage. The closer one went up, the other down. There's definitely a basement. I'm dead if I run outside. My only chance is finding darkness.

I sprint out from between two cars across a traffic lane, heading for the door. My hand makes contact with the knob the same instant the cop crashes into me from behind. Stars dance in my vision. Breathing is merely a hobby, so being squished into the wall doesn't leave me stunned, gawping for air. He bounces away, giving me the chance to go for the door again. I get it open a few inches, but he yanks me back and flings me around, pinning me to the wall by a hand around my throat.

His piercing, glowing purple eyes give off zero sense of humanity. None of my bones have broken, and the grip around my neck isn't crushing my spine. The guy's no stronger than he should be as an ordinary mortal. Unfortunately, he's plenty strong enough to do whatever he wants to me. At the moment, what he wants to do is strangle me. This is *not* what they mean by 'choking under pressure.'

I'm not sure what it is about human nature. We are often driven to do futile things despite knowing full well they'll never work. Like, try to return a coffee maker someone at the office gave you for Christmas a year ago at Walmart without a receipt, separate the last two shopping carts in the stall from each other, or submit an insurance claim hoping the premiums won't go up.

Or, as I'm doing now, try to peel this dude's grip away. Ack. Is this how mortals feel when I grab and throw them around? Can't even budge this guy. Sad thing is, he's clearly not supernaturally strong. I'm a wimp during the day. Same old me from before the Transference. Maybe even a little weaker. Dunno what effect death had on my muscles when the vampire stuff is offline.

Oh, wait. It might be worth smoking myself a little to get away. I can back off my sun resistance to let a little strength out. It's kind of like the whole 'redirect all power to shields' thing they use in every science fiction movie. I could divert some to 'weapons,' only question being how big a hole doing so is going to put in my hull. For now, he's only trying to strangle me.

Wait... he's starting to realize I'm not passing out. Gun's coming up for my face.

Crap.

Offline or not, I'm still a vampire. Subconscious survival instinct is serious. The world turns red for an instant. Next thing I know, Officer Trujillo's in the air, my foot's in his crotch, and I feel like I've been dipped in boiling water. A haze of smoke surrounds me. He scrambles upright as soon as he hits the ground, in complete disregard to being kicked in the balls so hard I lifted him off his feet. Crap. I shouldn't have made a *Terminator* reference before. He looks too much like one; I'm freaking myself out.

Also, ouch.

The sun still stings when I turn my back on it.

I dart out of the smoke cloud and hit the stairs. A few bullets cause explosions of shattered cinder block around me. Once I'm through the doorway, he gives up shooting and resumes chasing. Never in my life have I run away from cops before. They talk about the long arm of the law, not usually the long legs of the law. Bad guys must *hate* this dude when he's out doing normal cop stuff and not busy being possessed by ancient quasi-vampiric energy. I can't even outrun him going down stairs. Even having a one-story lead, he's practically on top of me in seconds.

Luck is with me.

The cop doesn't tackle me until I reach the very bottom of the stairwell at the B2 level. Sure, I kiss concrete floor with like 200-some pounds of cop on my back, but we're underground. Red light flashes briefly on the grey in front of my face, reflecting the glow in my eyes. He wraps his left arm around my chest, trying to hold me down while putting the gun to the side of my head.

I grab the wrist of his gun arm, push the weapon away, and fly/levitate straight up like the woman in *Ghostbusters*… only I'm face down and don't have a bed under me. It's trivial to fling the guy off my back, rotate upright, and toss *him* into the wall. He's clearly not in his right mind. No need to hurt him. It's tempting to give him a bonk since he scared the freakin' hell out of me. Haven't been so frightened since the half second between seeing the knife in Scott's hand and losing consciousness.

Not this guy's fault.

He's obviously still alive. I can smell him. Hear his heart beating—and he's standing next to me.

I glance left. A transparent version of Officer Trujillo watches the goings-on in complete bewilderment. Mind you, I'm still holding Officer Trujillo against the wall.

"Uhh, out in the open is probably not the best place to be…" I look around at the underground parking deck. Reasonably full of cars. Some voices echo, but the people aren't close enough to see us past all the vehicles and partitions.

Like fifty feet away on my left, there's an 'employees only' door. Perfect. Gotta get out of view of random passersby. I drag the struggling cop with me and jog to the door. Seems someone else who didn't count as an employee and wanted to go in there had a similar idea before me. The door's already busted to the point it can't lock. The ghost of Officer Trujillo follows me as I drag his mortal remains into a back hallway. PVC and metal pipes cover the left wall. A couple people who work for the parking place peer out at us from a door on the right, looks like a small office. They get a hard mental stab of 'forget me.' Takes me a second to do and leaves them in Derpville for about a minute.

A grey steel door at the end of the hall leads to a small generator room. This will work. I overpower the cop, shoving him to the ground before swiping the handcuffs from his belt and using them to secure him hugging the generator frame, so there's no way he can reach anything on his belt.

Not sure what to do with the gun. Leaving it near him is a bad idea. Taking it is a bad idea.

The ghost stares at me while his body emits a rapid, pulsing demonic growl in time with yanking on his arms in an effort to snap the cuffs. Wow... I didn't think vampires knew Lamaze. He's either having a serious freakout or trying unsuccessfully to make himself stronger. Problem being, he's not a vampire and *can't* burn energy to gain temporary strength. Not exactly sure what the crap is going on here. The poor guy's ghost is watching his body thrash, growl, and snarl. Gotta be rough on a dude. He looks a little broken, to be honest.

I glance at the spirit. "What the heck are you doing here?"

"I'd like to know that as well."

"Hmm." I shift my gaze back to the struggling cop. "Crap. Something dark and unwanted has invaded your body."

Officer Trujillo's ghost gives a weak laugh. "That's not supposed to happen outside of prison."

Sigh. "I'm talking about supernatural phenomenon."

The ghost shrugs. "Depends on who your cellmate is."

Wow. I shake my head. "Can you please try to be serious here? A dark force has evicted you out of your body."

"Happened a few times before." He nods.

I raise both eyebrows. What kind of crazy stuff has Wolent sent this guy to do? "Wow, really?"

"Yeah." The ghost of Officer Trujillo snickers. "Everyone else there called it 'tequila,' not 'a dark force.'"

"Grr."

The ghost holds his hands up in a 'hey calm down' gesture. "Sorry.

Jokes are how I deal with bad stuff, and this is the most screwed up shit I've ever seen."

"Yeah. Me, too." I ponder bonking the cop over the head to knock him out, but don't want to hurt him. "I mean 'me too' as far as cracking jokes at inappropriate moments. I've seen much stranger things than this."

"So, umm... am I dead?"

"Still working that out." I grab the physical cop's hair and lightly bonk his head on the generator a few times. "Bad tainted dark energy critter! Didn't anyone ever tell you not to possess police officers? Get out and leave him alone."

He emits a low, demonic growl. Wow. Brady's band could probably use the audio sample for one of their songs. Hmm. Let's see. Breathing. Heart rate. Body temperature. Zero supernatural strength. Yeah, the body's alive.

I look at the ghost. "Right now, you're Schrödinger's cop."

"Say what?" asks the ghost.

"You're neither alive nor dead." I tap a finger to my chin. "Or does it mean your position between life and death changes relative to the perspective of the observer?"

"Huh?" The ghost blinks.

"Schrödinger's cat? A thought experiment where a hypothetical feline is both alive and dead at the same time. Sorry, I can't explain it too well. We only went over it one night in philosophy class. It's got something to do with quantum superposition."

"I have no idea what on Earth you are talking about."

I laugh. "Good. Neither do I. Just repeating what Professor Heath said. This is all way over my head, both quantum mechanics and whatever the hell is going on with your body. Sorry, but I have to technically kidnap you."

"This is going to be difficult to explain to the department." Officer Trujillo's ghost sighs.

17

STRAIGHT INTO A NIGHTMARE

S ophia shivered from happiness.

A whole day of working with the Tome of F allowed her to successfully open a portal. She'd linked her closet door to the closet in Sarah's bedroom without a single void octopus in sight. Doing it tired her out as if she'd run up a flight of stairs, but it worked! The book also guided her along in the process to develop an enchantment for Sierra. It required a few other components like hair from the intended recipient (easy to swipe from Sierra's brush), plus hair or blood from a supernatural being in possession of abilities similar to what she wanted to give Sierra. This, too, proved easy to get. She found some hair in Sarah's brush.

The kitten assisted in obtaining a few other more difficult items.

Klepto *tried* to grab the stuff the book mentioned they'd find in Salem. However, she couldn't get into the house due to a defensive ward. Learning the creepy old house had a real spell protecting it from invasion by magical creatures simultaneously worried and excited her. More worried. Honestly, she'd probably have chickened out if not for Coralie. Not only had the spirit told her of bad stuff happening to Sierra if she kept taking vampire blood, she also *didn't* say anything about Sophia getting hurt trying to put the enchantment together.

Scary as it sounded, going to the house *had* to be safe—or at least not fatal.

She hoped.

Sophia picked Klepto up and kissed her on the head. "Will you please return this to where you found it?"

"Mew," chirped the kitten.

For the first time since being in the presence of the magical book, its emotional radiance changed from indifference to gratitude. Apparently, it quite appreciated being returned to its favorite bookstand.

She set her kitten down. Klepto promptly bit the corner of a tome ten times her size, then vanished in a violet flash along with it. She knelt on the rug, still shaking from excitement and anticipation. Discovering how to make the book work—something Darren Anderson and the mystics hadn't been able to do—would be worth serious mage cred. Unfortunately, she couldn't tell them about it without confessing to swiping it. Only her motivation to stop Sierra from getting herself killed gave her the resolve to not feel guilty about it. While rude and ostensibly unethical, borrowing a book without permission and returning it undamaged hurt no one. Her overdeveloped sense of right and wrong had to see the greater good here. The mystics lost nothing and it might save Sierra's life.

I'm so dead if they ask about it. Won't be able to lie. Gotta hope they didn't notice.

Guilt already caused a delay earlier in the afternoon. Megan and Nicole had wanted to hang out today. She couldn't even tell a minor lie to her friends. She'd been tempted to say she 'had to do some family stuff.' The lie would have been from implying her parents wanted her to do something, not *she* intended to do family stuff she could've done any time. She didn't exactly need to finish the magic for her sister before midnight to keep her alive. They did, after all, have a few years before Sierra ran into serious trouble from vampire blood. Sophia didn't want to make her friends sad, especially Megan, and knew she'd have ample time after dinner to work magic. Summer, after all, did not have school mornings and early bedtimes.

Considering she found herself presently existing in the enchanted time between dinner and bed, she prepared to do magic.

Sophia got up and made her way down the hall to the stairs.

At this hour, the 'rents took over the living room television. Sierra would be in her room on the computer playing games, possibly reading, maybe drawing. Careful not to make enough noise for Mom and Dad to hear, Sophia crept about halfway down the stairs to the landing by the front door. Two minor spells caused her and Sierra's sneakers to jump out of their cubbies and float over to her.

This isn't using magic to do what I couldn't do normally. Mom would see me and ask why we need sneakers. Are we going out? Where are we going? It's almost dark. Sophia sighed out her nose. Sneaking around *really* bothered her, but she couldn't let Sierra die. Mom barely handled Sarah turning into a vampire, and none of it had been her fault. If Sierra ended up a vamp at like fifteen by her own doing, Mom would completely freak.

Breaking rules stirred a sick feeling in the pit of her stomach. Better a guilt attack than her family disintegrate after they'd all become so close. *This is gonna work. She's not gonna die.* A moment of thinking about her happiness at getting a portal to work allowed her to set aside doubt.

Phase one complete. Sneakers obtained. A quick trip outside wouldn't have made her care about shoes, but exploring a collapsing house sounded dangerous. Getting a splinter—or worse—stuck in her foot would stink.

She crawled back upstairs. As soon as her face rose above the level of the upstairs hallway floor, Klepto—waiting at the top of the steps—licked her nose.

"Mew."

Sophia grinned, scooped the kitten up into a hug, and headed across the hall.

Her sister's bedroom, mostly dark, flickered in the glow from the computer monitor. Sierra sat on her computer chair, one leg tucked under her butt, wearing a pair of jean shorts and a grey T-shirt with a cartoon squirrel shooting a machinegun from each hand. Her giant headphones made it pointless to try talking from the door, so Sophia walked in. A bunch of tiny vehicles and little men ran back and forth on the screen building a base, some manner of strategy game. Sierra stared transfixed at it, occasionally clicking the mouse or tapping the keyboard. Though late-evening sun painted the world outside the windows orange, the room had become quite dark.

Sophia waited patiently for a few minutes until it seemed her sister hadn't noticed her. She poked her in the arm.

"Gah!" Sierra jumped so hard she fell off the chair and ended up flat on her back, legs draped over the seat cushion. The big headphones landed on the desk. "Don't *do* that!"

"Sorry." Sophia ground her toes into the rug. "I wasn't trying to scare you. Why are the lights off?"

"Wasn't dark in here when I started playing. Didn't notice." Sierra picked herself up, stretching to pause the game before standing the rest of the way. "What's up?"

"I'm gonna go get the last stuff I need for the spell. Do you wanna go with me? I'm kinda scared to go alone and Sarah's not here."

Sierra nodded. "Sure. Where's Sam?"

"Ronan's. Or Daryl's, I think." Sophia fidgeted. "Might not be a good idea to bring Sam to an old witch house. They cook and eat little boys."

"Oh, come on. That's nonsense." Sierra rolled her eyes. "The real problem would be he'd insist on bringing Ronan, too, and the boys would see some giant house and go running all over the place. We'd never be able to get them to go home before we got caught."

Sophia snickered. "True. But it's abandoned. No one is gonna be there to catch us. Sam and Ro would probably get hurt running around."

"Yeah."

They headed across the hall to Sophia's room. She handed Sierra her sneakers, then closed her closet door. Her sister backed up a step or two behind her, arms folded, a 'yeah right' expression on her face.

Sophia raised her hands at the door, following what the book said and picturing the image she'd received when attempting to 'scry' the Salem house. Her previous failure at opening gates came from three sources: doubt, overestimation, and belief. She used to doubt she had the power necessary to open gates. She overestimated the effort necessary to cover distances, expecting someone so new to casting spells couldn't possibly transport anyone more than a few hundred feet. According to the tome, opening a portal from her room to the basement didn't really take a significantly greater amount of power than going to London—or Salem. Her assumption it did—and that she lacked the experience to cast portal spells—tricked her into making herself fail. The last reason for failure had been belief. Or rather, the lack of it. She had to believe opening the gate was possible and *would* work if she tried to do it.

The test gate she pulled off right after dinner cemented her confidence. Needing to protect Sierra cemented her resolve and belief.

Light glowed from inside the closet briefly, then faded.

Sophia reached for the knob. Sierra leaned forward, preparing to tackle her out of the way of a tentacle. She grasped the door, opening it to reveal a scary, dark swath of woods. The silhouette of an enormous, partially collapsed house blackened the moonlit sky in the distance. Five or six spires rose from the third story at different angles, one of which had weak light coming from the window.

"Whoa…" Sierra grabbed Sophia from behind. "Why is it so dark? The sun's not all the way down yet."

"Salem's on the East Coast. They're like a few hours later than us."

"Oh. If we go there, are we technically up past bedtime or does bedtime remain based on West Coast time?"

Sophia blinked. "Are you serious?"

"No. I'm kinda scared."

"Really?"

Sierra blushed. "Yes, really. You can see those trees, right? It looks like a horror movie. Besides, you opened a gateway and nothing's exploded yet. I'm waiting for the giant rainbow squid to show up."

"Won't." Sophia approached the door. "Come on. The gate isn't going to last long. We have to grab the stuff and come back in about thirty minutes."

"Sec." Sierra ran out of the room.

Sophia tapped her foot on the carpet, waiting.

Her sister returned soon, carrying her sword. "Okay. Ready now."

"You're not going to need that." Sophia rolled her eyes. "We're only picking stuff up."

"Do you know for sure?"

"Umm, not really… but this place is empty."

Sierra whistled. "Wow. You even sound like the innocent blonde girl from every horror movie." She put on a fake ditzy voice. "Like no one's been there in ages. The place is abandoned. We'll be perfectly safe."

Sophia smirked. "C'mon."

They stepped into the closet. Soft carpet underfoot became damp dirt. The scent of Sophia's room—crayons, fruity shampoo, and 'kid perfume'—gave way to the fragrance of a forest with a hint of ocean. Not too odd. Depending on how the wind blew, sometimes they could smell the sea at home.

After a brief pause to pull her sneakers on, Sophia set Klepto on the ground by the gate. Anyone more than ten feet away from the opening wouldn't be able to see it. Since the kitten couldn't go into the house thanks to the defensive magic, she'd help out the most by serving as a beacon. Sophia's mental link to the kitten would let her find the gateway to home easily, even in the dark.

Jaw clenched, she started toward the house, Sierra walking beside her. It took less than five seconds for Sophia to get a serious case of the 'bad ideas.' Scraggly trees loomed over her on all sides like shadow monsters. Wavering branches looked more like long, gnarled claws. Her strides shortened until she ended up stuck in place, unable to make herself move.

Sierra paused beside her. "Are you sensing something?"

"Umm," whispered Sophia. "No. I'm just being a wimp. This is scary. I'm totally going to have nightmares about this."

"A fuzzy pom-pom gave you nightmares."

Sophia pouted at her.

"I mean…" Sierra took her hand. "This forest is legit scary. It *should* give you nightmares. You can sleep in my room tonight if you want."

Oh. Whoa. She said she's scared, she's willing to share a room tonight, and *she didn't complain about me pulling her off the game.* "Cool. Yeah. I think I will if it's okay."

Sierra nodded, then tugged her along. "Keep walking. The longer we stand here, the scarier it gets."

Sophia squeezed her sister's hand and forced herself to resume walking. *Coralie didn't say anything bad would happen.* Dead leaves and twigs crunched under her shoes. She tried not to pay attention to moving shadows, but didn't fully succeed. Whether or not the darkness genuinely watched them or her imagination ran away, she couldn't tell. It didn't matter, really. Her imagination scared her worse than real monsters, anyway.

"You know the door is gonna make this real long creeeeeak," whispered Sierra.

"Stop. You're gonna scare me too much."

Sierra gave a nervous laugh. "Trying to make a joke so it's funny instead of scary."

"It would work better if the joke was funny."

"Butt." Sierra snickered.

Sophia grinned.

"We forgot a flashlight."

"Got it covered." Sophia held her hand out. Within a second or two of her wanting it to exist, a two-inch ball of light appeared floating above her palm. It rose into the air and moved up to hover a few feet above her head.

"Nice trick."

They reached a dirt path and followed it out of the woods, then up the hill toward the house. Sophia stared at the ground, knowing if she looked up at the outside of the old building, she'd scream and run. Worse, she'd be too scared to find the gate and end up getting lost in the woods and eaten by a werewolf or some other furry monster. Probably with huge teeth.

Before she knew it, a set of ancient, crumbling wooden stairs slid into her vision. She risked looking up three steps to a porch so derelict and brittle it might collapse under someone her size. Peeling white paint flaked from the warped front door. It didn't look as if it *could* close anymore. She held her breath, gingerly climbing the three steps onto the porch. As if trying to walk across a thin layer of ice atop snow without breaking it, Sophia crept up to the door. Sierra reached out to touch the knob. A shadow in the room beyond moved. Sophia gasped, making Sierra scream, which made her scream, too.

They stared at each other.

"Sorry," whispered Sophia.

"It's okay." Sierra swallowed. "You will tell no one I screamed."

She held up one hand. "Promise."

"Okay." Sierra pushed the door open.

It did, in fact, emit a long, low creeeeeeak.

Sophia shivered. "Y-you know what they say. Whatever happens in Salem stays in Salem."

"No one says that." Sierra crept into a former living room.

The ghosts of old chairs and a sofa lurked under mildew-stained sheets in a massive living room. Yellowed wallpaper patterned in dark blue flowers sagged in spots of obvious water damage. The grandfather clock in the corner appeared so timeworn it resembled the furniture version of a zombie. Creepy shadows stretched away from everything, as if afraid of the light ball floating over her head. Ten pounds of cobweb dangled from a lightless chandelier in the middle of the room. Rather than bulbs, eight hooks hung from a ring, likely intended for small oil-burning lamps. Various creaks, groans, and soft tapping sounds came from all over the house.

"Just the wind," whispered Sierra.

"Yeah."

"What are we looking for?"

"We gotta go upstairs to the second floor. There's a bureau. Silver ring." Sophia pointed at a stairwell against the left wall on the opposite side of the room.

Sierra stared at her chest for a moment, then smiled.

"What?" Sophia peered down at herself. Nothing appeared to be wrong.

"You're wearing a pink and white dress with a unicorn on the chest." Sierra pointed at the rainbow-horned cartoon face. "It's funny to wear something like that in a house this creepy."

"I always wear stuff like this."

"Right. Trying to distract myself from feeling like a scared little kid. I sliced up a bunch of vampires trying to kill us. I shouldn't be afraid of a dusty old house."

Sophia leaned close to her. "Can I say something you'll probably hit me for?"

"Sure. I won't hit you."

"You're not afraid of the house. You're afraid of what might be *in* the house."

Sierra exhaled. "Accurate. Careful going up the stairs. They might break."

Stepping only on the very side of each step and holding the railing in both hands, Sophia pulled herself up to the second floor. Sierra put her foot through a step six away from the top and fell over sideways. The railing crunched apart under her weight, as brittle as potato chips. Sierra vanished from sight before Sophia could even scream.

Whump.

"Ow," deadpanned Sierra.

Sophia grasped the wall, stretching to peer past the edge of the stairs at the lower floor. "Sierra!"

Her sister lay in the pose of someone making a snow angel atop a white sheet and the crushed remains of a cushioned chair. A huge cloud of dust hung in the air around her, coating her in pale grey.

"I'm okay. Landed on a chair." Sierra coughed.

This is stupid. We shouldn't be in here. Gonna go home right now and wait for Sarah.

Sierra stood, looked up, then jumped vertically almost ten feet to grab the edge of the stairwell.

"Ack!" Sophia clamped a hand over her mouth.

"Still got some boost left." Sierra grunted, pulling herself over the edge onto the stairs. "It's not enough to fight a vampire, but I can do some stuff."

Sophia made a flicking gesture at her sister. All the dust burst off her and billowed away into the living room, far enough not to re-settle on her.

"Thanks."

"We should just go home. Wait for Sarah."

Sierra shrugged. "Okay. Sorry for falling."

"Not your fault. This is kinda dangerous. I didn't think the house would be this…" A weird feeling tugged at her, pulling her gaze down the hall to the left. A distant corner beckoned.

Ancient wallpaper dangled in ribbon-like strips torn from the walls. Ages ago, the carpet had been Washington blue. Dust concealed some paintings as well as the face of a small statue on a table. The odd sense seemed to beckon her.

"What?" whispered Sierra. "Why are you staring down the hall? Did you see something? Ghosts?"

"Oh, duh. I can see ghosts." Sophia smacked herself in the forehead. "Totally forgot."

"How do you forget something like that?" Sierra chuckled nervously.

Sophia gestured around. "Look at this place. I've been a scaredy cat for eleven years and only able to see ghosts for like six months. All the creepy noises and shadows people think are ghosts still scare me. If there really *are* any ghosts here, I oughta see them like they're people."

"Cool. Umm, can ghosts hide from you?"

"No."

"Good."

Sophia sighed. "I mean no, you did not just say that… now I'm scared again. I don't know if they can hide from me."

Sierra took her hand. "So, are we gonna go get Sarah or what are you looking at?"

"I dunno… We're already here. She's gonna worry too much and tell us not to do this enchant." A yawn forced its way out. "Opening gates is tiring. C'mon. I think I'm sensing the ring. Let's just get the stuff and hurry up and go home."

"Okay…"

Sophia followed the unusual pull down the hall. She didn't dare look into any doorways for fear she might see unhappy ghosts or worse. An errant raccoon erupting from an old cabinet or closet would give her nightmares for years. The floor creaked under them but didn't feel dangerously weak. Except for enough dust to choke a street cleaning truck, this hallway appeared to be in decent repair. A pervasive moldy smell grew stronger as they went deeper into the house, likely thanks to rain seeping in a roof in severe need of repair.

The unusual urge pulled her around the corner at the end of the hall, then to the fifth door on the left. She nudged it open with her sneaker, then peered in at a fancy—well *once* fancy—bedroom. Three of the bed's four posts had collapsed, dumping a canopy onto the disintegrating remains of a mattress. A small, round table, two chairs, two bookshelves, and a couple of wardrobe cabinets took up the rest of the space. The inner wall had a little fireplace nestled between two windows, neither of which offered a view of anything but darkness.

"Bureau," whispered Sophia, while looking around for ghosts. Seeing none, she entered the room.

The two tall wardrobe cabinets stood on either side of a long chest of drawers, as wide as two standard writing desks touching end to end. A frame attached to the back of the bureau held a giant, filthy mirror. All manner of little jewelry boxes and canisters littered the surface, everything covered in dust and cobwebs.

The girls rummaged the bureau. Sierra checked drawers while Sophia examined the boxes. Nothing on the surface contained anything of value or interest. The drawers had a few old bits of clothing, so rotted neither one of them could tell what the item had once been.

"This isn't right." Sophia sighed at the search turning up nothing. "It's gotta be in this room."

"If it was obvious, someone would've stolen it already." Sierra started checking drawers again. "We're not looking in the right place."

"What do you mean? This is the right place?"

Footsteps came from the hallway outside. Sharp, but not heavy. Probably a woman in boots, a woman in boots who'd likely not be too fond of a pair of young girls roaming around her house.

Sophia stopped breathing.

Sierra stepped in front of her, drawing the sword a few inches.

Sophia clung to her sister from behind.

The girls stared at the doorway, frozen in anticipation as the steady tapping of something walking grew closer. At the precise moment the sound indicated someone would barge in on them, a faint shadow flashed past the doorway, not entering the room.

Silence.

"Whoa…" Sierra exhaled. "I saw a shadow."

"Same."

"Not a ghost?"

"No. Just a black mist." Sophia bit her lip. She wanted so much to run like hell, but Sierra's life depended on her not being a wimp for another few minutes. "Hurry up. We gotta get out of here before it stops trying to scare us and starts trying to hurt us."

"You think it's going to try and hurt us?" Sierra slid the sword back into the scabbard.

"No. I'm guessing."

"Right…"

Sierra pulled out each drawer as far as it would go, looked around the opening, and replaced it. Alas, Sophia couldn't do much but keep staring at the doorway, terrified, gripped by the irrational belief something bad would get them if she dared look away. The drawers all seemed empty until Sierra got to the topmost huge one in the middle set. It also contained nothing—but the back was missing. Sierra yanked the drawer completely out of the cabinet, then climbed into the opening until only her legs stuck out.

"Be careful!" whispered Sophia.

"Aha! Found something." A dingy redwood jewelry box appeared in the drawer hole beside Sierra's right knee. "Grab that."

Sophia took the box, waiting until her sister backed out of the cabinet and dusted her hands off before opening it. A faint chill traced across the back of her shoulders. She looked behind her. No ghost. Despite not seeing anything, it certainly felt as though something or someone watched them.

Three small trays rose out of the box as she lifted the lid, lifted by a series of hinged metal struts. The tiny compartments contained an assortment of jewelry, as did the bottom chamber.

"Wow," whispered Sierra.

"We shouldn't steal this. Only the ring we're supposed to take." Sophia looked around. Still no spirits.

"No one lives here. It's an abandoned house." Sierra flapped her arms.

Sophia set the box on the bureau and carefully picked at the contents. "There's something here. It's watching us. We're not stealing anything. I need to use a ring from this box to help my sister. Only have to borrow it."

Sierra rolled her eyes.

Under a bunch of old necklaces—mostly made from agate, wooden beads, feathers, and other less-than-expensive materials, she located a plain silver band encircled in engravings. The marks appeared to be writing of some kind. Runes perhaps. Definitely not English letters.

"It's not even shiny," said Sierra.

Sophia grinned and put the ring into her little Hello Kitty purse. "It's real silver. And old. This is the first item." She closed the jewelry box before holding it out. "Would you put this back in there?"

"Fine." Sierra took it and crawled once again into the open drawer spot. "It fell by accident when the drawer broke. No one stashed it there to hide."

"How do you know a ghost didn't do it when people came to take stuff?"

"Ugh. Stop saying scary things." Sierra backed out of the cabinet. "So, what now?"

"An acanthia mushroom."

"What the heck is that?"

Sophia smiled cheesily. "A mushroom called acanthia. The drawing made it look like it had thorns on it."

"Mushrooms don't have thorns." Sierra marched across the room toward the door… and fell through the floor.

Sophia screamed.

The dust plume cleared to reveal Sierra's hands clinging to a hole in the floorboards. Her sword lay a short distance away.

"Ack!" Sophia pointed at her, concentrating on the same magic she used to help Megan jump in dance class, trying to make her weigh less without sending her floating off into the sky uncontrollably.

Sierra grunted and pulled herself up—and promptly launched out of the hole like a human cannonball. She flew, arms flailing, in an arc across the room before plunging into the destroyed bed—setting off an explosion of dust and rotten feathers. The old four-poster bed collapsed. Legs broke, the one remaining post fell inward, and the footboard tilted over to land flat, shaking the entire house.

"Oops," muttered Sophia. *Might have panicked.* "Sorry."

A faint whispery chuckle came from the direction of a tall wardrobe cabinet. Sophia whirled. Nothing there.

The bed frame wobbled. Boards clattered. As if she'd vanished into a pile of raked leaves, Sierra's head rose out from a lump of rotten bedding. The mattress had evidently once been genuine goose feather. Sophia winced at her sister's 'you will pay' narrowed eyes. However, Sierra only sorta-glared at her for a second or two.

"Are you hurt?"

"No." Sierra pulled herself out of the mess, crawling onto the floor. "I'm mad at the house, not you. I don't think it likes me."

Sophia looked around. "Anywhere else, I'd say houses can't dislike someone. But… not so sure here."

"Yeah." Sierra stood, dusting herself off. "Careful. The floor isn't safe."

"Right."

Sierra spat out a feather, picked her sword back up, and crept to the door, following the outside edge of the room so she could keep a hand on furniture. Sophia followed, torn between wanting to go slow and cautious or run like hell to get away from the scary stuff. She pictured her bed back home, a mountain of stuffed animals she could crawl into for protection. Well, they couldn't really protect her from anything, but they'd make her feel better. Bringing them to life probably wouldn't have the effect she hoped for. Besides, Mom would freak if she saw a stuffed animal running around on its own.

They made their way down the hall, pausing at every loud creak or apparent shift in the floor. The old wood squished down in places, like walking on sponge. It took them almost five minutes to go from the bedroom to the top of the stairs. When they came within a few feet of the top step, a huge oil painting leapt off the wall and slammed flat to the floor, missing them by inches.

Sophia and Sierra grabbed each other and screamed. After their lungs emptied out, they kept clinging while staring at the cloud of dust settling over the giant frame.

"I screamed because it startled me," whispered Sierra.

"Pure terror."

"Was not," muttered Sierra.

"No, I meant me." Sophia exhaled hard.

"Oh. Heh. Okay, maybe a little terror for me, too. But mostly a jump scare."

Sophia couldn't help but notice her sister hadn't let go of her yet, but didn't mind.

A minute or so later, the shock wore off. Sierra poked her sword at the frame, tapping the sheath into the wood as if prodding a dead animal with a stick.

"I don't think it's gonna move." Sophia crouched, grasped the frame, and lifted it.

The five-by-three-foot painting depicted a portrait of a woman around Mom's age, perhaps a little older. Her high-necked black dress with puffy shoulders and dour expression made her quite intimidating.

"She looks angry," whispered Sierra.

"Probably because she fell." Sophia pushed the painting upright and leaned it against the wall.

Sierra squatted, tracing her finger across a brass plaque at the bottom. "Belinda Crawford – 1813."

"Ooh, I bet she's the one haunting this place." Sophia looked at the painting taller than her, at the fixture it fell from, then back at the painting. *Not happening. This thing is too big and heavy for me.* If *she* had tripped and broke it, she might've risked attempting to use magic to fix it, even if she didn't trust how this house would react. But something threw it at them, so she preferred to ignore it and leave as fast as possible. "Sorry. We'll go away in a few minutes. Almost done."

"Let's get out of here." Sierra started down the stairs.

Sophia stepped across the rectangle of dust the fallen painting stamped into the carpet. She didn't trust the banister—or what remained of it—so she hugged the wall on the way down. All manner of strange sounds followed them across the ground floor: furniture bumps, chairs sliding, doors creaking, a noise like fingernails scratching at the walls, a lifeless chime from the grandfather clock, and footsteps upstairs.

She clutched Sierra's hand, unable to stop herself from jumping at each phantom sound. If her sister hadn't agreed to come with her, she'd be lost in the woods by now, having run in a panic from the house. She still wanted to run. It annoyed her being able to see ghosts but *still* finding them scary. How could they be *scarier* when they stayed out of sight? In an attempt to steel herself, she thought about them like annoying living people hiding and making noises to play mean games on her.

The elemental magic she'd worked on with Darren hadn't made it to the level she could throw fire at bad vampires, but she could light the heck out of a candle. Alas, using fire of any kind in this place would be *bad*. A good portion of the house smelled damp and moldy, but most of it remained extremely dry and dusty. One little spark and the whole place would erupt into an inferno.

They eventually located the way to the basement at the end of a narrow corridor between the kitchen and what had likely been servant's quarters. The black door had a weird 'lifting bar' type latch instead of a knob. Sierra grasped a pencil-sized rod sticking out of the door, raising it to disengage a metal slat from a catch mounted on the wall.

"This house is older than doorknobs," whispered Sierra. "And... why is the door metal?"

"I dunno."

Cobwebs pulled away from the wall as she dragged the slab of iron open in a series of jerky tugs. Sophia got scared, wondering if it had been used to keep people locked up—but relaxed when she noticed the latch rod sticking out the inside face. Someone could open the door from either side. The light from her floating ball illuminated a narrow, treacherous wooden stairway beneath a ceiling alive with spiders and other critters, all scurrying around the old wood in a frantic attempt to escape the glow.

"Wow, it's the tunnel to Nopeville." Sierra whistled. "I'm impressed."

Sophia looked at her.

"You okay? You aren't screaming."

"I scream at *one* spider. A hundred is so scary I can't make a sound." Sophia managed a weak smile. "Besides. Coralie didn't say we're gonna die, so..."

Sierra exhaled, shaking her head.

Trying not to think about bugs, Sophia started down the stairs. Never in her life before had she loved her sneakers so much. She preferred flip-flops, ballet flats, or going barefoot... but sneakers became armor when walking on the carcasses of 200 years' worth of dead insects. They crunched down the stairs into a vast cellar. Stacked-brick columns spanned from the floor to fancy brick archways, all mottled in dull reds, white plaster, and dark spots. A strange, unpleasant odor lurked in the dark, somewhere between rotting meat and wet, moldy wood. No doubt some unfortunate wildlife had found its way down here and died.

"Sure smells like mushrooms can grow down here." Sierra walked ahead. "I still don't think mushrooms have thorns."

"It did in the drawing."

Sierra shied away from a cobweb-covered brick column, gazing up at the arch. "This place looks like a bunker. In social studies, we watched a movie about World War II. And—eep!"

"What?" Sophia gasped and rushed to catch up.

Sierra pointed. "What the hell?"

Sophia skidded to a stop next to her, gawking at a section of the basement containing two rows of old kennel cages, five of which held the decomposed remains of large dogs. They'd definitely been here for a long time, not bought from any modern pet store. They had thick, square bars like the tines of a wrought-iron fence. The heads of several deer hung on the wall above the cages along with multiple fully taxidermized smaller animals: rabbits, two foxes, and three birds she didn't recognize.

"Eww," whispered Sophia. "I already don't like this place. People who kill animals are buttheads."

"Yeah."

"I mean… people who kill animals for fun." Sophia crept forward, shying away from the cages of remains. "If people hunt because they need to eat, that's different. I'd still rather eat vegetables but I can understand."

"Yeah. I know." Sierra chuckled. "Believe me, I know. You're turning into the vegan joke."

"Just talking to keep my mind off being in a terrifying nightmare." Sophia laughed nervously. "And I'm not vegan. Just vegetarian." She took two steps. "What vegan joke?"

"If you walk into a room with five people, how can you figure out who the vegan is?"

"I dunno."

Sierra wagged her eyebrows. "Don't worry. They'll tell you. They'll *definitely* tell you."

"How's it confusing if they'll just tell you?" Sophia nudged an open kennel door out of her way. An unexpectedly loud creak from the hinge made her jump.

"That's the joke. It's making fun of vegans for being so obnoxious. Like they never shut up about being vegan."

"Oh."

A patch of light brown at the back end of the alcove crept into range of her floating light spell. In the corner past the dog cages, a cluster of spiny mushrooms grew on a pile of earth where the brick wall had collapsed inward. They reminded her of meringue in terms of color, white in the middle, brown at the tips of the thorns. Sure enough, thistle-like spikes covered every inch of the mushrooms. They appeared sharp and painful, but for all she knew, might be soft and harmless.

"There they are!" Sophia darted forward.

A chain whipped out and wrapped around her left ankle, yanking her off her feet. Sophia flopped flat on her chest, screaming as the tether dragged her backward into a kennel—which promptly slammed closed in her face. The deafening crash of metal on metal echoed over the basement, knocking a rainstorm of dust off the ceiling.

Sierra ducked, shielding her face from the grey cloud.

Still screaming, Sierra flipped over to sit and grabbed the rusty leash coiled around her leg, struggling to unwrap it. The chain moved like a living snake, writhing in her grasp. Strong, but not so much she couldn't budge it. Rust smudges marked her skin where it grabbed. Fortunately, it hadn't cut her. She clutched the writhing leash in both hands, holding it away as the lower part thrashed side to side. If she let go, it would certainly grab her again.

"Stop!" Sophia cast a spell to cancel magic—the first thing the mystics taught her.

The leash went limp.

"Whew." She exhaled in relief—then noticed all the dog bones between her sneakers as well as the matted carpet of skin and fur she sat on.

Her brain got stuck between screaming or throwing up; she ended up doing neither, merely staring in horror.

"Soph!" Sierra grabbed the cage door, grunting.

Whispering gathered in the darkness at the edges of where her magic lantern reached. It sounded as though thirty or more spirits came to get them, held back only by some inexplicable fear of entering the light. Sophia scrambled around to stop touching dead dog. She squatted in the cage, holding the side bars for balance. Only her sneakers made contact with death.

Sierra braced a foot on the cage, pulling at the door using both hands. She'd gone red-faced already. The cage didn't have a lock or latch, merely two metal plates with aligned holes for a padlock or something. Some manner of invisible force kept the door shut. Sierra kept straining until the entire kennel slid toward her.

"Whoa..." Sierra stopped pulling, cringed, and wiped her hands on her shorts. "Ouch. That thing's seriously stuck."

Whispering in the shadows grew louder.

"Get me outta here!" yelled Sophia, at the verge of panic.

"I can't."

Whimpering, Sophia looked out at the voices. Here and there, the darkness appeared thicker, taking on almost human shapes. Shadow figures surrounded them. Watching, refusing to move into the light.

Tears rolled down Sophia's cheeks. "Sarah... help!"

"Hey," said Sierra in a soothing tone. She reached through the bars and grasped her sister's shoulders. "Relax. Remember, Coralie said we'll be fine. Or... didn't say we'd get in trouble. Same thing."

Sophia sniffled, shifting her gaze up to make eye contact. "I'm scared. They're watching us."

"Don't say creepy shit when you're trying not to be scared."

"But they *are* watching us. I can see them."

Sierra's face paled. "Try to ignore them. Look, this door is stuck. It's not locked. The hole's empty. There's no reason it shouldn't open. Be right back. Gonna go find something to pry it."

The shadow figures crept closer, testing the edge of the light. Vaporous arms stretched into view and recoiled.

"Don't leave me alone. Please." Sophia grabbed her sister's arm.

Sierra exhaled out her nose. "If you can't magic it open, you're gonna have to deal. I'm not strong enough to break whatever is holding it shut, but it feels like I'm close. If I can find something to wedge in there, I should be able to break it."

"Umm." Sophia wiped her tears on the back of her arm.

If not for being stuck in a kennel, she'd be sprinting into the forest already. Being trapped and unable to run away made the basement ten times more terrifying, but had the bizarre effect of stopping her from flying into a total screaming meltdown. She'd cried over movies not even half as scary as this basement. But, they'd also been movies. Nothing bad would happen if she refused to keep watching. Chickening out here could lead to Sierra's death.

She tried again to attack the forces holding the door closed. The shadow forms proved too distracting for her magic to work.

"Screw it," whispered Sierra, who appeared oblivious to the crowd of spirits. "Hang on, Soph. I'll be right back."

Before Sophia could even squeak, Sierra ran off into the dark. Two elongated shadow figures slipped sideways to let her pass, filling in to form a black curtain once she vanished. Light from her levitating orb shrank, compressed by the overwhelming presence of the spirits. Soon, it only illuminated an area a foot or two around the cage.

Specks of silver, eyes in the darkness, surrounded her, leaning close for a better look.

Sophia screamed.

18

A MORE THAN OCCASIONAL ADVANTAGE

I guess there comes a time in everyone's life where they find themselves in a situation they never imagined possible.

My life in particular has given me a whole bunch of those moments. A year ago, if anyone told me I'd need to figure out how best to kidnap a police officer, I'd have told them to stop smoking weed. Here I am standing over the body of Officer John Trujillo as he struggles to break the handcuffs chaining him to a generator.

The situation is somewhat more complex than merely kidnapping a law officer. For one, he tried to kill me. He's also a thrall in service of Arthur Wolent. Not sure if he's literally Wolent's thrall, but he's part of the organization. Bigger problem: he's presently been kicked out of his body by an Oblivare soul. The reliquary in the trunk of his police car objected to me taking it.

Some vampires luck into the powers of undeath. The Oblivare have to urn it.

Gah. Dad. I blame you for making me think these things.

Back to the problem at hand. As long as I stay underground in this parking garage, I'm online. Consequently, the possessed cop isn't a problem. It's still daylight out, so taking this guy out of here is impossible. Even if I handcuffed him into a human pretzel knot, the instant the sun's on me, I wouldn't be strong enough to carry a man this size. Perhaps with great effort—and assuming he did nothing to resist—I could drag him across the floor, but no way are we going up the stairs. And someone would definitely spot us. It's not unreasonable to expect the sight of someone attempting to kidnap a tied-up cop would result in badness. Best case scenario, someone calls the police. Worst, I get a Rambo wannabe jumping on me—then the possessed cop tears us both apart.

Can't take him out of here and I don't want to leave him.

He's also going to hurt himself if he keeps fighting the cuffs. Hmm. He's still alive, right?

I grab a fistful of hair and pull his head back to stare into his eyes. The purple light shining out of his irises intensifies in rage. So creepy. Peering into his head is like I've opened a door into Hell and a dozen demons stop in mid-orgy to stare at me making 'do you mind?' faces. It's a chaotic mess of random freaky images. In much the same way the average person's reaction to seeing a giant bug crawl out onto the desk in front of them is immediate smash without thinking, I hammer his brain with a compulsion to sleep.

Officer Trujillo passes out. Or at least, his body does. The actual Officer Trujillo is standing next to me as a ghost.

"What happened?" he whispers.

"Sleep. He's going to keep fighting until he tears your hands off. And someone's probably going to hear him growling and come down here to investigate who's doing what to a Norwegian heavy metal singer."

He blinks.

I back out of the generator room and shut the door.

"Why are you putting me in there?"

"Because I'd get in a ton of trouble with my parents for kidnapping a cop and bringing him home. My mom's pretty lenient, but abducting police officers is more than she's willing to tolerate. Even if you are possessed at the moment, she's a lawyer. She'd totally have a cow. Can't be near anything even remotely close to unethical or illegal."

He cackles. "You don't know many lawyers, do you?"

I smirk. "Hey, that's my mom you're talking about. And besides, it's daytime. I can't take your body anywhere. As soon as we go upstairs, he'd kick my ass."

"So, you're going to stuff me in this little room and leave?"

"No other choice right now. At least until it's dark. You have the reliquary thing in the trunk?"

"Yeah. What the freak is that thing? Gave me the creeps."

I head for the stairs. "It's basically a giant bottle of vampire mix."

"Say what?"

"You know how iced tea comes in powder form? Same thing. Only, add corpses instead of water."

He shakes his head, whistling. "Didn't think it worked that way."

"Usually doesn't. These guys are old school. They think they predate humans, but I don't believe them. Their ability to go from an energy being to a vampire requires humans. They literally could not have existed before us."

"What if they just existed as energy beings until humans came around, then realized they could take us over?" asks the ghost.

"Huh. Yeah. I suppose that's possible." And wow, since when do cops think about such abstract things?

As soon as we reach ground level, the sun nerfs me. Weird for it not to hurt anymore. Granted, it isn't too bright today. Feels more like I'm walking outside and some prankster sneaks up behind me and rips my clothes off. I go from being confident and fearless to shrinking in defensively, worried about who might be watching me. Still don't truly understand what effect it will have if I get hurt while offline. Not in a rush to find out. As much as my primary goal as a vampire is to keep living as 'normal' as possible, I'm far happier being online. Grumbling in my head, I trudge up the stairs to the fourth floor.

"And what do you mean by 'us'?" asks John. "You aren't mortal."

"No, but I'm still human. Or was. I don't get vampires who talk down about humans as if they're something so much better and hadn't once been human themselves."

"People with power often tend to forget where they came from."

"Yeah." I shove the door open to the parking garage and stop short at the sight of police cars everywhere.

Shit. Someone heard the gunfire and called the cops. They're swarming all over the place, searching around Officer Trujillo's patrol car as well. Dammit. That's gonna make it a little more difficult for me to get the reliquary. Second shit: if any of those cops opens the trunk, they might end up possessed, too. Depends on how many Oblivare souls are inside the thing and how many want to jump into a live body. Can't imagine they like doing it. Takes them out of the safety of the urn to become a creature no more fearsome than a mortal. I have a brief daydream of a bunch of glowing purple energy forms sitting in a room drawing straws to see who's the unlucky bastard.

"What now?" asks the ghost.

"Nothing." I pretend to look surprised and worried at all the cops and start making my way to where I parked. "Can't do anything about this during the day."

Officer Trujillo's ghost looks back and forth from me to his car, then decides to jog after me.

I'd complain how so many apparently simple tasks lately have exploded into long, complicated—and sometimes dangerous—messes, but my luck honestly isn't too bad. Good family, great parents, nice house, comfortable life. My first eighteen years on this planet couldn't really have been better. Sure, we *could* have been super wealthy or famous, but nah, not better. Rich families almost always seem to hate each other and rich kids usually grow up into serious douchebags. My family is—okay, Dad can be corny as hell, but I think we are—or were —at the perfect balance.

Considering what some other people have to deal with, I have no room to complain about bad luck. This is a passing annoyance. All I have to do is figure out a way to manage it. Things aren't crashing out of control yet.

My timid and nervous act works well. A few cops look at me, but only one female officer approaches.

I stop and wait.

"What's your business here?" asks the cop.

"Parked over there. Silver Sentra." I point.

"You're old enough to drive?" She blinks.

It's not difficult to act annoyed. "Yeah. I am."

"Got ID on you?"

"In the car."

"Where are you coming from?"

"The aquarium." Dammit. Hope she doesn't ask why I left my purse in the car and 'went to an aquarium.'

"You hear or see anything unusual around here?"

Oh, boy, have I. "Umm, a lot of police. Did something happen?"

"How'd you get past the officers at the entrance? We've blocked this building off for the moment."

"I just walked up the stairs." Being vague doesn't make me feel as guilty as lying, so hopefully, a technically true statement will stop my face from giving me away.

The officer frowns, seeming upset at some other cop for letting me stray into a crime scene. Maybe not a 'crime' scene as much as an investigation. No yellow tape yet. "Let me see your ID then."

"Okay." I head to my car, open it, and grab my purse.

She gives my license the same 'this is probably fake' squint every cop has done since my Transference. I don't think my appearance changed *that* much, but people look different to themselves. She asks me to wait here, then wanders over to the nearest police car, likely to run the license. Ugh. Every damn time. Fortunately, I am not too worried about them finding Officer Trujillo's body. No reasonable person would *ever* suspect a girl my size to have been able to manhandle him. Also, if they wake him up, they'll have a much bigger problem on their hands than me. Still a mess though. The PIBs will get involved. Wolent will be annoyed. Total crapstorm. However, I didn't screw up. Not like I tripped, dropped the reliquary, and let stuff out. So, I'm not afraid of getting in trouble.

Stay calm and wait.

"You really don't look like the same person on the license photo," says the ghost. "More like her younger sister. Why are you bothering with a fake ID?"

"It's not. They took the photo before I developed a mild sun allergy."

"Aha. Strange. I've met a few other vampires, but none of them did that. They all went hot."

I fold my arms. "Guess I'm just lucky. They say becoming a vampire takes five years off your face. I didn't have too many years to start with."

The live cop, Officer West, walks over and hands my license back. "Wow, kid. You won the genetic lottery. You're free to go. I told the guys at the exit to expect you and let you out. If you remember seeing anything unusual, give us a call, okay?"

"Will do, officer." I smile.

She walks back over to the group of cops by Trujillo's car.

"What are you going to do?" asks the ghost.

"Not much I can do at the moment other than to wait for dark. Anyone I might be able to get advice from isn't going to be available until sunset."

I hop in the Sentra, put my license away, and start the engine. Whew. Sometimes it really is handy to look like a harmless kid.

19

THE CRAWFORD COVEN

S ierra hurried up the basement stairs, ducking low to avoid spiders.

She clutched the handle of her sword almost painfully tight. Sophia might be afraid of everything, but her company made the house less frightening. Going off alone sucked. However, she had a mission: get Sophia out of the kennel. Freaky as it had been to watch a metal door held in place by an invisible force, she couldn't let it bother her. Nothing this house could throw at them equaled a giant multi-headed hydra-spider-wasp nope beast.

Of course, the creatures they found in the mirrorworld couldn't really exist. She believed it drew on the minds of anyone who entered to create physical nightmares. Illusions, yes, but illusions capable of hurting people. None of it could exist in the real world outside the mirror.

Exploring this house alone scared her, but not as much as school. No one ever conducted 'creepy house active shooter exercises.' Crazy people didn't travel to the middle of nowhere to find a haunted house so they could go on a rampage. Ghosts couldn't seriously hurt anyone. She had more to fear from damaged floorboards than any sort of monster.

By the time she reached the top of the stairs, Sierra decided not to be afraid of this house or anything in it. She'd entered a scary level on a video game. Creepy scenery, nothing more. She needed to find a crowbar or something like one. The force holding the kennel shut had been strong, but the door didn't act as if it had been welded. It wobbled a bit as though she fought some other being pulling against her to keep it closed. If her boost had been at full power, she could've opened it. A little leverage would make the difference.

Sierra jogged down the hallway and hooked a right into the decrepit kitchen. Enough moonlight made it past the grime on the windows for her to see the outline of cabinet doors and the counter... perhaps too clearly. At full strength, Sarah's blood let her see in the dark. Now, she basically had low-light vision. A little moonlight went a long way. She clenched her fists, trying to resist the urge demanding more blood. She hated being wrong. Drinking it had not been totally harmless. People didn't become addicted to good things. True, she'd probably have been killed without it. Sierra didn't regret insisting on it, more felt guilty for convincing Sarah it would be harmless. Not entirely her fault, though. Dalton thought it harmless, too. Maybe it would be for most people. How many thralls lived in constant fear of being killed? She *needed* to feel safe—or at least not helpless.

Her hands only shook a little bit. Nothing hurt. She probably could force herself to quit and not get sick, merely have to deal with the fear of being weak and ordinary, a victim if bad vampires attacked again. Sophia looked at her super weird earlier. When she'd come across the hallway to ask her if she'd help collect the stuff, she had this expression of desperate sorrow, almost as if she knew something bad would happen to her. Not only that, *Sophia* willingly walked into a house ten times creepier than the lame horror movies she cried at.

Yeah... Coralie definitely told her something. She's afraid I'm going to die.

Faint screaming in the distance sounded like Sophia, but she couldn't possibly be yelling so loud to be heard from the basement. The damn house had to be playing tricks on her, trying to scare her away so it could keep Sophia.

Not happening.

Sierra swallowed a lump of fear as well as saliva, then proceeded to rummage the kitchen.

One closet had some old brooms, a possible option, but the wood handles would likely break. She needed a metal crowbar or a sturdy pipe. Having zero success in the kitchen, she headed out a back door, across a small porch past some collapsing butter churns, and down four rickety steps to a rear courtyard around a small three-tiered fountain. A rusted hand-pump for water stuck up from the moss-covered cobblestones around the fountain. To the right, a garden maze. To the left, a tool shed as big as a peasant hovel. Straight ahead on the other side of the fountain stood the remains of a horse barn, already collapsed.

"Heh. Guess it's an un-stable."

This place is super dangerous. We shouldn't be here. Gotta get Soph out of the house before it falls in on her.

Sierra jogged across the courtyard to the tool shed. A rusted padlock held the door closed. She grasped the lock, braced her shoulder on the wall, and pulled. Ancient nails lost their grip on the decaying wood. The hinge plate and padlock popped off in her grip. She stared at the metal, the warped nails sticking out of it, bits of broken wood caked on, unable to tell if the shed deteriorated so much anyone could pull the lock off, or if she still had some boost left.

Fear of going back to being an ordinary kid worsened the shaking in her hands. Beyond simply being normal, she dreaded helplessness in the face of a crazy person with a gun, a bad vampire, zombie, or whatever else the hidden world might throw at her family when Sarah, her parents, or any adult wouldn't be there fast enough to make a difference. She hadn't become addicted to the blood itself, but to the chance it gave her to avoid becoming a victim.

Snarling to herself, she tossed the hinge plate and padlock aside. *I don't care what happens to me. I'm not gonna just sit there screaming if someone tries to hurt us.*

She shoved the tool shed door aside. Good chance people hadn't been on this property in a long, long time. The lawn mower—at least she assumed it to be a lawn mower—sitting in front of her had no motor, only a cylinder of twisted blades between two wheels, and a handle to push it. Nothing so given to rust would ever be useful to anyone again.

All manner of ancient hand tools hung on the walls of the shed. Trowels, shovels, spades, hoes, long wooden handles tipped with spikes. She picked one of those up, bewildered at its purpose—beyond stabbing people. The end didn't appear sharp, and it seemed too large to be one of those sticks park workers used to pick up trash. Maybe they used it to make seed holes or some such thing. She shrugged, put it back, and kept looking.

Among a pile of saws, hammers, and wrenches, she located a pry bar a few minutes later on a workbench at the back of the shed.

"Score. Hope Soph hasn't lost her mind yet."

Sierra grabbed the crowbar and dashed outside.

As soon as she ran into the kitchen, something grabbed her off her feet, swung her around, and set her seated on the dusty kitchen counter. She barely had time to process the sudden motion before a ghoulishly deformed figure appeared in front of her, dressed in a black sweater, black skirt, and tall boots. The woman—she guessed—had pale grey skin, glowing yellow eyes, a tangle of needle-like teeth jutting not quite in the same direction, and pointed ears. Not much of any hair—other than eyebrows—remained on her head. She appeared quite solid and real, definitely not a spirit. So changed had the woman's face been by undeath, she could've been anywhere from mid-twenties to sixty.

Sierra clutched the crowbar to her chest, more startled at the woman coming out of nowhere than her appearance. As the initial shock of being jump scared faded, she exhaled. "Oh... hi."

The Shadow cocked her head. "Oh, hi?"

"You were expecting a scream or something? If it'll make you feel better, I can shriek."

"Oh... I see. You know of our kind already. I sense a link to..." A note of disapproval radiated from her. "Who enthralled one so young?"

Sierra nodded. "Yes. You're a Shadow, like Glim. My older sister's a vampire. Some other ones attacked us. She had to give me a little blood so I could stay alive when we were attacked."

"Interesting." The sense of anger faded from the woman. "A most unusual situation."

"What are you doing here?" Sierra relaxed her grip on the crowbar. Despite their looks, she considered Shadows the *least* likely vampire to commit random violence. Granted, she only had Glim to base any opinions from, but she liked him.

"I used to be called Belinda."

"Crawford?" asked Sierra. "Your painting almost fell on us."

Belinda leaned back, one eyebrow slightly up. "My family has lived in this house for centuries."

"Sorry." Sierra offered a consoling smile-slash-grimace.

The woman narrowed her eyes.

"I mean for your family being gone. The house is broken. Not saying I'm sorry you're a Shadow. Glim's cool. Is this place haunted, or is my other sister seeing stuff?"

Belinda regarded her for a moment, probably looking into her mind, then relaxed. "There are spirits here, mostly family, who defend the property from outsiders. It seems they are having a little fun with your sister downstairs. They would not harm a pair of curious children, but I am certain they intend to give her enough of a scare she will never want to return. I've asked them to, as the young people say today, 'chill out.' Now, your turn."

"My turn?"

"What are you doing here?"

Sierra told her everything.

"Hmm. While I understand your situation, you cannot take the ring. It belonged to my grandmother."

"Umm, I don't think we need to keep it, just borrow it. Sophia's the mystic. She could explain it better."

"All right. Let us go speak to her." Belinda stepped back, gesturing for her to hop down.

Sierra slid off the counter. The floor crunched under her sneakers. "Umm, you should like really think about hiring someone to fix the place up a bit."

"Doing so might encourage mortals to think of trying to live here." Belinda frowned.

"Just saying." Sierra crossed the kitchen. "Sophia and I don't weigh much and the floors can barely hold us. It's not going to be much of a lair for you if it falls apart."

Belinda emitted a grunt somewhere between annoyed and acknowledging.

Sierra had enough night vision left to see her way down the stairs to the basement, jogging past piles of sheet-covered stuff to the alcove of kennels. Soft white light glowing from around a corner of jagged, crumbling bricks reassured her. If anything had happened to her sister, the light probably would've gone out.

"Soph?" called Sierra.

"Yeah," replied a teary whisper.

Sierra rushed around the corner.

The tennis-ball-sized light floated above the cage. Sophia sat cross-legged inside it, both hands over her eyes, evidently not having noticed the cage door hung open a few inches, no longer pinned shut by ghostly forces.

Sierra laughed.

"It's not funny," said Sophia.

Belinda walked up beside Sierra. "Oh, she is adorable."

At the sound of a grown woman's voice, Sophia pulled her hands away from her eyes and gawked. "You found help?"

"Door's open, dork." Sierra pointed, then tossed the crowbar aside.

The loud metal *clang* made Sophia jump. She crawled out of the kennel, dusting herself off, swatting at bits of ick stuck to the seat of her dress. Fortunately, the decomposed dog had rotted far past the point of being gooey or sticky. Furry lint fell to the ground.

Belinda appeared to react to Sophia's complete lack of fear of her by clearing her throat a few times. She sounded a bit like Mom watching a sad or mushy movie.

"We've got a little problem." Sierra helped swat funk from the dress. "The ring we found belonged to her grandmother. We can't take it."

Sophia looked up at Belinda. "I'm sorry. Didn't know anyone still owned it. Would it be okay if we borrowed it? We—"

"It's all right, child." Belinda brushed her fingers at Sophia's cheek. "I believe you. And yes, you may borrow it. I am sure my grandmother would like to see magic flowing through her ring again. Do return it as soon as you are finished."

Sierra nodded toward her. "She knows where we live."

"I do." Belinda leaned back in a humorous attempt at being intimidating.

Sophia headed over to the mushrooms, and gingerly poked one. "Soft."

"Huh?"

"The thorns. They're not really thorns." Sophia examined the cluster, then selected a four-inch-tall one, which she plucked. "This looks perfect."

"You should not eat those," said Belinda.

"What the heck are they? Mushrooms aren't supposed to have spikes." Sierra scratched her head.

"My family conducted many rituals on these grounds. The land is saturated in energies going back hundreds of years. These mushrooms occasionally develop on Earth charged with spiritual energy." Belinda rested her hands on the girls' shoulders. "They are most often used as a power source for spells as they soak up the magic."

A spinning wall of inky vapor welled up around them. When it faded a second later, they all stood outside by the front porch.

"Whoa," whispered Sophia.

Sierra blinked, too shocked at the sudden change of scenery to find words.

"The house is not safe for you two. You might fall and hurt yourselves."

"Already fell. Twice." Sierra raised a hand.

Belinda patted her on the head. "Your sister isn't as resilient as you are."

"Thank you." Sophia curtseyed. "We only need one more thing… some dirt where faeries walked. It's supposed to be under rose bushes."

"In the garden." Belinda gestured at the corner of the house. "When you return the ring, come after dark and knock on the door. I will meet you there. I'd prefer if you didn't go inside, so you don't get hurt."

The girls nodded at the same time.

Belinda vanished in a cloud of black smoke.

"So cool," whispered Sierra.

"I wanna go home." Sophia exhaled.

"Yeah."

"C'mon." Sophia darted off toward the garden.

Sierra tucked the sword under one arm and ran after her into a dead hedge maze. Sophia somehow led the way to a rectangular 'room' of hedge containing overgrown rose bushes without getting lost or finding a dead end. Sierra whistled to herself, unsure what impressed her more: Sophia seemingly knowing where to go or finding live bushes in this place.

Her sister used a small empty flowerpot to collect a quantity of soil, then promptly marched out.

Sierra turned as she passed. "Not gonna look for faeries?"

"Nope. Too scary here. Wanna go home."

"Heh." Sierra hurried after her. "But you adore faeries."

"True. Still. Too scary… and the portal's going to close soon. We have to get home before Mom or Dad notices we went anywhere."

"Think we'll get in trouble?"

Sophia wagged her head side to side while walking. "Umm, I dunno. But we won't be able to tell her where we went without telling her about the enchantment or you having vampire blood. She's probably going to freak and order me not to try enchanting you."

"It's cool. If we get interrogated, let me do the talking."

Sophia glanced over at her. "You get upset when you lie to Mom, too."

"Yes, but I don't start crying while she's still right in front of me." Sierra tossed her hair over her shoulder. "If *I* give her a story, we'll have at least a day or two to come up with a better one before she catches me."

Sophia laughed.

They followed the dirt path into the woods surrounding the house. After a few minutes, they spotted Klepto sitting patiently on the ground.

"Mew!" The kitten teleported onto Sophia's shoulder.

Three steps later, a rectangular opening shimmered into view, looking in on Sophia's closet. As soon as they stepped in, the cool dampness of Salem night air faded to the cool not-so-dampness of home.

Sophia faced the opening and made a little hand motion. The portal to the creepy forest collapsed down to a glowing spot, then faded. They removed their sneakers before entering the bedroom. Sierra slouched in relief at arriving home safely. Next time they did anything like this—if a next time happened—she'd insist Sarah be invited.

"'Kay. It's gonna take me a while to put everything together and study the magic." Sophia plopped down in the middle of the room. Klepto jumped from her shoulder to the floor beside her.

"Umm, didn't you already study? You sent the big book back."

Sophia looked up at her. "Yeah. Gonna go over my notes again." She patted a spiral notebook covered in crayon drawings. "I absolutely don't want anything to go crazy or wrong and mess with you."

"You wrote in crayons? What are you, five?" Sierra whistled.

"Wax holds power. I know it looks stupid, but it works." Sophia reached under her bed to grab a plastic tote box.

"What's in there?"

"More stuff I need for the spell. Gimme like an hour and I'll let you know if this is going to work."

Sierra tapped her sword at the floor, shaking her head. "You still don't know if it's going to work?"

"I know it will. I just wanna make triple sure." Sophia paused to take the spiky mushroom out of the flowerpot she'd carried it in before giving her an earnest stare. "Not gonna do anything if it won't be perfect. I swear."

"Okay." Sierra exhaled. "I'll be in my room."

20

BENDS RULES GIRL

A chance exists I may no longer be able to refer to myself as Follows Rules Girl.

Depends on one's interpretation of rules. It's pretty difficult to consider breaking into a police station as anything other than wrong. Technically, though, I'm not breaking into the station as much as sneaking into the parking lot to burglarize a car.

Having nothing else to do until dark, I drove back to Hunter's. Couldn't really talk much about everything with his mother in the room during dinner. He got the brief version once we retreated upstairs. As soon as the sun went down, I leapt out of his window to keep working on the issue. Owing to the idea this should have all been done *before* dark, I've got a giant blanket of anxiety wrapped around my shoulders. Wolent wanted me to grab the reliquary before sunset for a particular reason. I'm assuming said reason involves any Oblivare in the area becoming aware of the soul jar's location and likely intending to rip nonessential pieces of anatomy—perhaps essential ones too—off anyone who tries to keep them from taking it back.

The guy who originally called and gave me the job did so from a number not accepting inbound calls, so I haven't made contact with 'the boss' yet. Sure I have his direct number, but better to save it for emergencies. Not sure how happy or unhappy he's going to be about me not being able to resolve the location of the reliquary before dark. He's probably aware Ladonna is in the area. She's pretty old and is definitely going to be trying to get her hands on it. In a way, I suppose it's a good thing failure here won't lead to some kind of world-ending catastrophe. The vase isn't the key to some apocalyptic event like summoning an ancient god asleep beneath the arctic for 50,000 years who will lay waste to the Earth, the key to making SPAM a dietary staple, mind-controlling people into thinking taking cryptocurrency mainstream is a good idea, or normalizing anchovies as a pizza topping.

No end-of-the-world scenarios.

Worst that'll happen is a bunch of new Oblivare exist... which presents a certain collection of separate problems—none of which involve bitcoin farming while choking on fishy pizza. Bad, but nothing unmanageable or apocalyptic. Still, I gotta try to do what the boss wants. I am, after all, Follows Rules Girl, even if I sometimes color outside the lines. Hmm. Here's a question. If Wolent tells me to do something, but doing the thing is breaking a minor law, am I following the rules by obeying someone in authority or breaking the rules because of the law?

Argh.

Philosophy isn't as fun without Professor Heath's commentary.

The ghost of Officer Trujillo can fly. Apparently, spirits have the same sort of relationship with gravity celebrities have with the real world: they tend to ignore it whenever it gets in the way. He leads me across Seattle to where they've put his patrol car—once he gets over acting like a giant little boy going in circles, around trees, between buildings, and so forth, enamored with how it feels to fly.

Infiltrating a police station's parking area is one of those rare times where I'm almost envious of another bloodline's powers. Lost Ones—like Dalton—can hide themselves from cameras and security systems. Yanno how certain groups of people throughout history, like Roma or Pikeys, have unfairly been considered by society as being all thieves and criminals? Well, in the case of Lost Ones, it's actually true. Their vampiric abilities are all about sneaky stuff. Sure, not every Lost One actively steals or breaks into places, but they have the best tools for it, second only to Shadows.

Yeah. Here I am standing in the darkness at the edge of a police station parking lot, looking for cameras, planning to break into a police car *while it's parked at a station*. Totally normal thing for a young woman to do, right? A little low-grade felony action is the perfect end to a day of shopping at the mall, playing with my hair, talking about boys, and whining over my crappy retail job. Oh, wait. I'm not Bree Swanson.

Anyway, Follows Rules Girl is losing her damn mind.

Speaking of losing minds, Officer Trujillo's ghost has spent the past two hours ranting about how none of the cops investigating the parking garage found his body. He starts up again while I'm scoping out the police lot. Even though no one can hear him but me, having a dude shouting is super distracting when I'm trying not to be caught. Okay, to be fair he's not 'shouting' as much as talking at a somewhat raised volume. In an otherwise dead-silent parking lot, it *feels* like shouting.

Seriously, I shouldn't be on edge. If any cop sees me, they aren't going to remember it.

"Relax, okay?" I whisper-shout. "Those cops are *lucky* they didn't find you."

"I'm missing." He paces. "They should be tearing the city apart trying to find me. Makes them seem incompetent for missing me right under their noses."

Sigh. "Officer Trujillo, calm down. The entity possessing your body might be repelling them even while asleep. I don't know why it would though. Maybe it can't help but radiate creepiness and all the cops who went downstairs refused to go into the hallway."

He stops pacing. "Call me John, please. Hey, what's that thing want, anyway? Why did it attack me?"

"I think the reliquary did it as a defense mechanism. My best guess is it wanted to kill me so I couldn't bring it to a guy who can destroy it. The energy inside it can't possess me because I'm already a vampire."

"Oh." He huffs, then makes a 'well that just sucks' face at me. "Think they might have at least warned me not to go near it."

"I'm sure no one had any idea it could take over a living person." I bite my lip. Or maybe they did, hence *me* being sent to transport it.

"So, what's in that thing, anyway?"

"A bunch of vampire souls, but weird ones. Never human. They steal bodies after death."

He nods. "Oh, well, makes perfect sense."

"Why so sarcastic? You're Wolent's—or someone's—thrall. You know about us already."

"Not that. Didn't think vampires *had* souls, or could put them in jars."

"Hah. You're confusing vampires with healthcare executives. *We* have souls. The jar thing, though, isn't normal. Only one crazy bloodline. Not even sure if they count as a bloodline or they're basically Domino's."

"Those little chips people set up and knock over? You lost me. What's that gotta do with undead?"

I smile. "No, Domino's pizza."

"Still missing the relationship."

"Something that kinda looks and kinda behaves like pizza but isn't really." I wag my eyebrows. "The Oblivare are similar to vampires, but they might be an entirely separate creature people mistake for real vampires."

"Ahh." He sets his hands on his hips. "Hey, I like Domino's."

"Not saying it's bad. Just it isn't *real* pizza. Sometimes you have a craving for it, but no one craves crazy vampires who want to destroy society."

"True. I'd destroy society right now for a couple slices of pepperoni." He smacks his ethereal lips. "Damn. You made me hungry."

"It's good to see you've kept a sense of humor after possible death."

"Same to you." He winks. "Am I actually dead or is this the Domino's of death?"

"Huh?"

"Kinda looks and feels like death but isn't?"

"Oh." I smack myself in the forehead. "You turned my metaphor against me and I missed it."

"You're nervous."

"Yeah, a little."

"What are you worried about?" He gestures at me. "You're a vampire."

"You know that kid in school who breaks out in a cold sweat at the mere idea of doing something against the rules? Yeah, that used to be me. Gonna take me awhile to realize I can get away with stuff."

John chuckles. "Well, I'm a cop and I'm telling you it's okay to go get that stupid thing out of my frickin' trunk."

"Thanks. Helps. Really." I exhale.

He frowns.

"No, honestly. Helps. Here goes." I start walking into the lot. Act casual, Sare. Totally normal.

John leads me to his car, which surprisingly, is sitting in a space beside other patrol cars. I'm hardly an expert on police procedures, but it seems highly unusual for them to put it here. The cop who'd been driving it vanished without a trace—as far as they know. Shouldn't this car be in a lab somewhere? Either they think John ran off chasing a suspect he opened fire on and thus had no reason to suspect anything criminal happened around the car, or we have another thrall in the department who ran interference.

I approach the car, looking around. Doesn't look like anyone's noticed me. Doors are predictably locked. Can't get to the trunk release. Smashing a window is going to make a ton of noise, but it's easier than attempting to rip a hole in the trunk lid.

John yells, "Wait" as soon as I raise my fist.

I look at him.

He swipes a hand at the trunk.

"What are you doing?"

"I'm a ghost, right?"

"Still debating. You might be an astral projection or a momentarily displaced soul fragment."

Side eye from a ghost is kinda funny.

"Well, I feel like a ghost. I'm basically electricity right now, so I can probably make the trunk thing open. Just gotta find the right contact to touch." He reaches into the trunk lid as if fumbling around for something in a pocket.

I tap my foot, waiting.

Click.

Holy crap. Stunned, I hurry around to the back of the car. Trunk's open. "Wow… you've adjusted to being a ghost way faster than most vampires get used to the change."

John strikes a triumphant pose. "Hopefully, I'm only playing a ghost on TV for one episode."

I push the lid up the rest of the way. In among all the police stuff he's got crammed in here is a long cardboard box full of packing peanuts. Pale violet light seeps out from the Styrofoam bits.

"Either that's the world's smallest nuclear reactor or the reliquary is still here."

"Don't those things glow blue?" asks John.

"No idea." I paw at the peanuts enough to expose a blackened cylinder of dark green marble radiating a strong otherworldly energy —and more than a little bit of anger. "Yeah, this is it all right."

He nods. "Yeah. This is the thing I took out of the evidence room."

"Doesn't it bother you to remove evidence?"

"Nah. Not this. No crime happened needing to be solved. The whole thing is vampire related. Ain't as if someone's getting away with hurting innocent people."

I pick the box up. We're still breaking rules, but he's got a good way to justify it.

21

TRUE FRIENDS HELP HIDE BODIES

My phone rings.

Normally, stuffing my iPhone in a pocket isn't a big deal. However, my superhuman sense of touch makes a ringing, vibrating phone against my leg feel like a jolt from a weak stun gun when I'm already on edge. Bad enough I've broken into a cop car, but this reliquary is throwing off seriously bad vibes.

I rest the box on the trunk, yank my phone out, and prepare to ignore the call until noticing Ashley's name on the ID. It's not too common for her to call me this close to midnight. Yeah, it's almost twelve. Took me a while to get up the nerve to enter the police station lot.

"Ash?" I whisper. "What's up?"

"Sare," she whispers back. "Sorry. I know it's like real late."

"Not a problem for me. Not annoyed, just in the middle of something sensitive. This is early. 'Real late' for me is after four in the morning."

She doesn't laugh, or even chuckle. Uh oh. Something's wrong.

"I think someone's trying to kill me."

Shit! I stare at the reliquary. "Crap. Okay. What's up? This is serious? You didn't just wake up out of a nightmare after watching a scary movie?"

"I've been having an issue with a stalker for the past few months at school."

"Grr. Seriously? You didn't say anything."

"Yeah, well... I don't want to abuse our friendship. Dude has been following me around campus. Figured he'd go away when the semester ended, but he somehow found where I live. He's sitting outside my house right now watching me from his car. Or... watching the house."

I close my eyes. Dammit, Ash. Tell me about this shit as soon as it starts. Again, I stare at the reliquary. No way am I bringing this thing anywhere near Ash or she'll end up like John. Can't leave it at my house—I don't want to know what kind of unholy freakin' ridiculous nonsense mixing this thing with my family would cause—and I'd never be able to un-live with myself if anything happened to Ashley in the ten-to-fifteen minutes it would take me to deliver the reliquary to Wolent's manor house—and that's assuming I drop it like a bomb at Aziz without landing. My luck, I'd miss and it would shatter, freeing all the souls inside. Screw it. Back in the trunk you go.

Whump. I shut the lid.

"What are you doing?" asks John.

"Emergency. My friend's in trouble. Stay here and keep an eye on it. I'll be back as soon as I can."

"He's still there," whispers Ashley in a timid whine. "I'm scared."

"Hang on. I'm coming." I leap into the air. "This is gonna sound crazy, but if the guy gets out of the car before I'm there, call Sam and tell him to send the dog over."

"Uhh, you guys have a dog?"

"Kind of. Just... trust me. If that guy opens the door, either call Sam or go out the back door if you can and get to my backyard. Dog's name is Max. He understands English."

Grumbling, I aim toward home and push myself as fast as I can fly.

22

FAST BECOMING NORMAL

I cruise in over Ashley's house roughly five minutes later.

Travel in straight lines has really spoiled me for commuting purposes. Driving home from downtown would've taken about a half hour. I angle into a dive, heading for an unfamiliar dingy white Chrysler parked in front of her house. Thing's gotta be fifteen years old. I land far enough behind the car to avoid him spotting me drop out of the air. Even from this distance, dude is giving off serious creep vibes.

"Old as hell white car?" I say into the phone.

"That's him." Ashley emits a shuddering whisper. "He's just sitting there, staring at the house. So damn creepy."

"Okay. I got it."

"What are you gonna do?"

"Make him forget you exist. Maybe give him an irresistible urge to drive to Orlando."

"Uhh, why Orlando?"

I shrug. "Dunno. Florida is really damn far away from Washington and everyone uses Miami. Trying not to be so overused."

She emits a nervous laugh.

"Okay, gonna hang up now. See you in a few minutes."

"'Kay. Thanks."

Sometimes, being a higher order predator is amazingly helpful.

I sneak up to the car without him noticing me. Not in the mood for a chase scene right now. Maybe he wouldn't drive off simply from seeing me. I'm not the most intimidating critter in the world, unless anger makes my eyes glow red.

His window's open, making it easy for me to grab and pull him out of the car, then pin him against it, bracing my arm across the front of his throat. He lets off a strangled noise part scream of surprise part yell of 'WTF.' Guy's mid-twenties, pale, super-short buzzed hair like an Army recruit. Smells like cheese puffs, cheap beer, and laziness. He's either had this Hilfiger sweatshirt since he was fourteen or he got it from a thrift store.

Shock fades, flashing to anger. He grabs my shoulders, but I'm in his head before he can shove me away. The intent to erase and replace memories falls out of my proverbial hands and shatters on the floor at the sight waiting for me in between this creep's ears. Among flashes of an entire bedroom wall covered in photos of my best friend and various moments of him pleasuring himself to said photos, the overriding thought at the tip of his mind shows through, clear and horrifying. He's been sitting here for the last hour trying to get up the nerve to proceed with his plan to break into the house and kidnap her.

He hadn't been hesitating out of guilt, decency, or anything like that. No... the only reason his ass stayed in the seat as long as it did was fear of being seen by a neighbor and caught. He didn't fully trust being able to pull it off without Ashley screaming so loud someone saw him. The past fifteen minutes, he'd been beating himself up mentally for deciding against getting an out-of-state rental car. Not wanting to leave a paper trail is why he drove *his* car here. He's planning to take her to a cabin out in the forest where he's picturing Ashley becoming his 'wife.' The place is already set up to keep her captive with a lockable room, barred windows, and even a leash. He already considers her 'his' to take. The bag in the passenger seat is his 'marriage kit.' Rope, duct tape, handcuffs, his attempt at homemade chloroform, scissors to get rid of her clothes while she's tied up.

His plan: keep his wife as long as he can before 'circumstances force him to kill her.'

His reality: way, way, different.

Next thing I know, the guy's on Ashley's lawn and there's blood all over my fist. It's possible I shouted something along the lines of 'you sick freak!' but the scream might only have occurred in my mind. I'm shaking from revulsion and rage. Tears won't stop. So messed up. I'm not an angry-cry type person. What the fuck is wrong with people?

"You killed him," says John Trujillo.

I'm so freaked out by the contents of that bastard's head, I don't even jump, merely cut my gaze left at the spirit.

"I think I wanted to hit him... not kill him."

"Oh, you definitely killed him. His face exploded." John pantomimes swinging a two-handed weapon down on something. "Ever hear of Gallagher? That guy with the watermelons and the sledgehammer?"

Wince. "No, but I get the point."

"More a large blunt object than a point."

"Grr. Not helping. Crap. I didn't mean to kill him."

"You don't sound too sorry about it."

"And you don't sound too alarmed by it... *officer.*"

He chuckles. "I'm off duty right now. And you are a vampire. Trying to arrest you wouldn't work out too well for me."

I smirk. "I'm kinda not alarmed by killing him. You didn't see what he was going to do to Ash. And hey, you're not watching the reliquary."

"*Watch* is about all I'd be able to do. Ghost, remember?" He swishes his hand through me a few times.

"Ugh."

The front door opens. Ashley, still dressed in a T-shirt and jeans, runs outside and over to me, platter-eyed. "Oh, my *gawd!* You... you..."

I go to grab her by the shoulders and look her in the eye, but my right hand's a bloody mess, so I only grip her left shoulder. "Yeah. I did. And Ash, trust me. It's the best outcome. Even if I sent him to Florida, he'd have come back. This dude was gonna seriously hurt you."

She covers her face in both hands. "Not sure how to feel about you killing someone."

I pull her close, patting her back, and realize I'm still shaking from anger. "If you saw into his head what he planned to do... I don't even know what happened. Just... pure rage and horror."

"What was he going to do?" She peers between her fingers at me, tears streaming from her huge blue eyes.

Ashley looks way too innocent to hear stuff like this. It's easy to forget my sweet and wholesome best-friend-almost-sister is an adult. She surrounds herself in unicorns and girly stuff, but she's probably got the darkest sense of humor between me, her, and Michelle. She's also had sex with Aurélie, is into kinky stuff, and actually a lot more mature mentally than she appears to be.

Still, I can't help but see her as an innocent kid. Not sure if it's because we grew up together or I'm a vampire now.

"That bad?" She shivers.

I bow my head. "He was going to kidnap you tonight, keep you as long as he could as his 'wife' in some isolated cabin in the woods, then ultimately kill you once he felt it had become too difficult to avoid you escaping, him getting caught, or being separated from you."

"Jesus," whispers John. "If this dude's ghost shows up, I'm going to kick his ass again. Scrawny little bastard."

Ashley nods once, swipes her hair off her face, then forces herself to stop crying. "I didn't expect you to kill him, but I'm not complaining you did. Just wanna put it out there. Yes, I will probably freak the hell out in about an hour when it sinks in. This guy sat right behind me for weeks in class. Ugh. I'm starting to feel sick wondering what he was thinking, staring at me."

"Understood. Figured you had a garden variety creeper, not a serious wacko." I frown at the corpse. "So, umm... any idea how to get rid of a body? This is my first murder."

"Umm." Ashley blinks.

"Well, technically second. Old guy at the funeral home. But he was a killer, too. Also, didn't mean to break his neck either."

John's eyebrows go up. "What happened?"

"Guy kidnapped these two boys I know. Snuck up behind me. I meant to knock him out, but… old man. Brittle neck bones."

"Ahh."

Ashley bites her lip. "Feed him to pigs? Get a plastic kiddie pool and put acid in it? Gotta use plastic 'cause the kind of acid that'll eat a body away to nothing dissolves a normal bathtub. Or, cut it into a dozen pieces, put each one in a different bag and drop them randomly over a fifty-mile area?"

I stare at her in total shock—as does John.

"What?" She blinks.

"Damn, girl," I whisper.

"I watch a lot of crime shows." She flashes a brittle smile.

Shaking my head, I go collect the body. Leaving him sprawled out on the front lawn is a bad idea. And, ack! No wonder John knew he died. The whole front of this guy's face is mashed in like he took a header off a speeding motorcycle into a concrete post. A strip of skin about as wide as my fist—and his nose—is simply gone. Damn. Going to need to find that before some dog does. Blood and such oozes from his face as I carry him to the street and stuff him into the trunk of his Chrysler.

Ashley watches me, silent the whole time. She jumps slightly at the *whump* of the trunk closing.

"Let me make a quick call." I pull my phone out.

"Whoa." Ashley blinks. "Since when do you 'have people' to call to get rid of bodies like *Pulp Fiction*?"

"It would be hilarious if this guy's name was Marvin," says John.

I chuckle. "No, I don't 'have people'. Just looking for advice."

And sigh. I shouldn't be this casual about killing someone, even a complete piece of psycho shit like this guy. Wait. Vampire. Right.

Almost forgot.

INNOCENT AND SWEET

W hile Ashley grabs a hose to disperse the puddle of blood on her front lawn, I pace around, waiting for Aurélie to answer the phone.

"Allo, *cheri*. To what do I owe the pleasure of your voice tonight?"

"Ever see something so disturbing, so horrifying, so infuriating, you lost control and killed someone?"

"*Oui*. It 'appens more often than you might expect, though not recently. Talk to me, *cheri*. What 'appened? You sound upset."

I explain the situation. Hopefully, the PIBs pulled me off the NSA cell phone monitoring program. Or hopefully, it's only a conspiracy theory.

"Ahh. And they say *we* are the diabolical creatures." She tsks. "You did the right thing, *cheri*."

"Is it lame I feel guilty about it? Just a little, but I do."

"Yes. It is natural for you."

"Umm. For *me* or for Innocents?"

She snickers. "I suspect both, but more so you personally. You acted in defense of one you love."

"So, it doesn't mean I'm sliding away from being human and falling into darkness?"

She laughs. Like legit laughs for a good twenty seconds. "Oh, no, *cheri*. You 'ave been watching too many movies. Some of our kind may lose their minds, but there is no 'creeping darkness sneaking up on our souls.' Some merely cannot 'andle existing for so long. The gift does not change who we are, it brings our true natures forward and more vibrant, accentuating what already exists."

Great. Vampirism is MSG.

Still, good to know I'm not becoming a cold-hearted killer. Of course, this means I always had it in me to kill a bitch to protect Ash. However, non-vampire me wouldn't have splattered a guy's face from one punch. I'd probably have ended up hogtied in the trunk right next to her.

"Cool. Thanks. One more question. Any idea what I can do with the inevitable aftereffects? Don't want to leave litter on her lawn."

"Does it appear to be the obvious work of vampires?" asks Aurélie.

"It appears to be the obvious work of a sledgehammer to the nose."

John laughs.

"… and probably a broken neck," I add. "Ooh, wait. I have an idea. I can make it look like a car accident."

"That may work, *cheri*. Be careful and do not burn yourself."

"Will do. Thanks."

"Night!" chirps Aurélie, as though I called her to ask about a recipe for cake.

"Seriously?" John walks up to me. "Fake a car accident?"

"Yeah. That, I've done before."

"Truth," calls Ashley over the splatter of watering the lawn. "But the bastard deserved it."

John gawks at me. "Wow. You look so innocent and sweet."

I chuckle. "Thanks. Normally, I *am* innocent and sweet."

"Lies!" yells Ashley in a mocking tone.

This is normal Ash, but it worries me so soon after what happened. She's either in denial or showing entirely too little reaction to watching me paste a dude. I catch eye contact and peek. Yeah, denial. Plus overwhelming relief she no longer has to worry about this guy grabbing her. Plus her brain rejecting the notion she sat so close to someone who planned to kill her after months or years of horror. Good freakin' grief. She's been shitting bricks about this guy since March and never told me. Grr. This is what I get for promising not to look in her head randomly.

Oops. Broke the promise. But I claim extenuating circumstances.

Anyway, she seems to be so happy to be free of dread she's not processing the reality of death. She is a lot tougher than she looks, so maybe there's no need for me to worry about her.

"Not my first staged car fire, by the way." I wag my eyebrows. "First one was a vampire, though."

Ashley, having put the hose away, walks over. "Shame to waste the car though."

"You can't be serious." I point at a big rust hole by the left rear tire. "It's a POS. That car's probably older than we are."

"Looks like an '82 LeBaron," says John.

I exhale. "Yep. Older than us."

He quirks an eyebrow at me. "You said you're older than you look."

"I am. My real age is nineteen." I sigh into a grumble. "Not fourteen. Only been a vamp for a year."

"Yeah, but still. The car didn't do anything wrong." Ash pats it on the roof.

"Hmm. Maybe I could fly the guy up high and drop him. Make it look like he fell off a building?" I cringe. "Nah. Might hit someone, plus people would be forced to witness it—and clean up."

Ashley snaps her fingers. "Hey, why not drop him in the ocean way off where he won't drift back to shore?"

"Not a bad idea." I whistle. "Wow, this is seriously messed up. We haven't discussed doing anything this bad since that time we wanted to sneak in to see *Kick Ass* at the theater when we were eleven."

"Umm, Sare, disposing of a body is a little worse than trying to get around an R-rating on a movie."

"I know, but..." I scowl at the car. "It's not like I killed a human being."

She hugs me. "Sorry. I should've told you about him months ago, but I didn't know if he was really dangerous or just creepy. The guy followed me around school. Sometimes I thought I saw him trying to take pictures."

"Umm, yeah. He did. Speaking of…" I gotta grab the dude's wallet, find his address, and remove all traces of Ashley from his apartment. Don't need her being dragged into any investigation if the cops start looking for him.

"Speaking of what?" She tilts her head.

"Gotta delete you from his apartment or wherever he's living. His bedroom is wallpapered in your face."

"Eww." She shivers.

"If anything like this ever happens again, tell me." I exhale out my nostrils. Talk about mixed emotions. If she'd mentioned him right away and I confronted him before he had this elaborate kidnap, slave, murder plan developed, my reaction would've been to make him forget Ashley—but he'd most certainly have eventually fixated on some other woman. And the odds of his next target having a vampire BFF are minimal. It really bothers me to think this, but this situation probably worked out to the best ending possible.

"Okay." Ashley holds the hose out to rinse my hand. "I just didn't want to seem like I'm trying to take advantage of your powers or anything."

"It's fine. Take advantage. It's like everything else for the past thirteen years. My toys are your toys. I'm here for you. Friends will always help you. *True* friends help you hide the bodies."

She smirks. "Did you read that on a T-shirt?"

"No, a coffee mug." I wink.

Ashley snickers. "Dork. It's not supposed to be literal."

"I'm not asking you to help me hide the body." I pull the car door open. Might as well deal with it now.

"Can I ask you for a little favor?" whispers Ashley.

"Anything. Uhh, except maybe turn you into a vampire unless you're already about to die."

She chuckles, then clutches me by the arms. "Please make me forget seeing you mash that guy's face open—and the details of what he wanted to do to me. Let me think you chased him off, erased his memory of me, and he'll never come back."

Cool. Yeah, that I can *definitely* do. "No problem, Ash."

IT'S GOOD TO HAVE PEOPLE

Making a person disappear entirely off the face of the Earth is some CIA-level stuff over my head.

It would be a massive pain in the ass to chase down everyone who ever knew him, make his landlord forget him, erase him from the minds of co-workers, and so on. My two major concerns are eliminating any connection between him and Ashley, getting rid of the body, and doing something about the massive bloodstain in the trunk.

Creep Boy, real name Troy Allan Prince—figure I'll use all three since if he got his hands on Ashley, it would've turned into a True Crime documentary—lives in a trailer about forty-five minutes by road away from Seattle Downtown, toward Olympia. Not exactly isolated, but enough tree cover no one sees me go inside. The place is an absolute mess. Trash everywhere. Pizza boxes all over the place.

The bedroom smells like sweat, microwave dinners, and psychosis. It's a massive shrine to Ashley, literally wallpapered in color printouts of photos he's taken of her at the school. He's even Photoshopped her face on a few nude images of other women who have similar body shapes. My blood gets warm again seeing this, but he's already dead.

"Hey, you could wrap this up real easy, yanno." John points.

I follow his glowing finger to a double-barrel shotgun leaning against the wall by a collection of ninja weapons and swords.

"Leave her pictures up. Make it look like he offed himself when he couldn't have her." John pokes his ethereal foot at a laptop on the floor. "Saves you the trouble of having to go through every electronic device in here and deleting her pictures. You already made your friend forget watching him go splat, so she'll be able to talk to cops if they track her down."

"Hmm. Good idea. What about the blood in the trunk?"

"Nothing some bleach and sponges won't fix. The police won't have any reason to run lab tests on the trunk. Take less time than chasing digital cameras and phones."

"Fine."

I check the shotgun to make sure it's both real and loaded—yes to both—then go get the body from the car. Dead blood smells exceptionally foul to me. Once it's sat too long to be edible, it reeks. I'd say it smells like shit, but poop doesn't stink this bad. Probably should find a trash bag to wear so I don't have to wash blood out of my clothing. Shotguns get splattery. Especially at point-blank range.

With John's advice guiding me on how to arrange the scene, Troy Allan Prince officially committed suicide via a self-inflicted buckshot smoothie.

I took care of the car first, figuring the gunshot would disturb neighbors. Poking a hole in the bottom of the trunk with a claw so the blood could drain into a pail saved me a bunch of time. This guy didn't believe in cleaning supplies, so I had to steal some bleach from a neighbor. Did I mention vampires are really good at breaking into houses? Especially when they're trailers.

Blood from the pail poured strategically over the dead guy's head should hopefully confuse the medical examiners enough to not realize he'd already been dead before the shotgun went off. Not sure how accurate crime shows are, but they might notice something weird. Maybe they can tell if someone's been shot postmortem due to how they bleed, but there's a big difference between bullet holes and the upper half of his head disintegrating. Rigor hadn't set in nor had this other thing called 'livor mortis' John mentioned. At his suggestion, I left him on the floor in the same pose he'd been in the trunk to make it more difficult for anyone to determine the body had been moved.

Anyway, problem dealt with. If the cops don't buy the suicide angle and feel like wasting time hunting for a killer here, no big deal. I'm sure Troy has a few skeletons in his closet they'll chase down.

IT'S A LITTLE AFTER TWO IN THE MORNING WHEN I ARRIVE BACK AT THE police station.

Two cops emerge from the building on their way into the parking lot. One's a little older, like Dad's age, the other in his twenties. I swerve, aborting my original plan to land behind the car and drop into a dark spot between a police van and a K-9 SUV.

"… no kidding. The brass is practically shitting themselves over this one," says the greying cop.

"Two hundred and fifty grand… damn." Young cop whistles. "Freakin' thing must've been the size of my fist."

"Nah. Not quite as big. Maybe golf ball. Don't matter. The guy can afford to lose it. Insurance will cover it. We shouldn't be wasting our time with a stolen ruby, anyway." Older cop chuckles. "I'd rather we spent our time goin' after the sick bastards who make life hard on ordinary folks."

"You some kinda Robin Hood, pops?"

"Who you callin' pops there, rook?" The older cop laughs on his way around the nose end of a car—thankfully not the one I'm interested in.

"Eh, maybe. But it ain't like whoever stole it is going to be able to sell a rock that huge. It'll turn up. Now, if I'm gonna be your TO, the first thing you'll need to learn is how I take my coffee."

Young cop flips him the bird, then gets in the car. Both guys laugh again.

As soon as they drive off down the street, I hurry over to John's cruiser.

I'm about to ask him if he can pop the mechanism... but it's broken open.

"Dammit!" I open the lid, anyway. Sure enough, the reliquary is gone. Cardboard box and Styrofoam peanuts are still there. "Dammit."

"You said that already." John materializes next to me.

I slam the trunk. "Figures."

"If you knew it was going to walk away, why didn't you bring it?"

"Look at yourself and ask me again why I didn't want the stupid thing anywhere near Ashley." I grab two fistfuls of my hair, but stop myself from screaming, mashing my face into the trunk, or tearing the hair out of my scalp. "Even if it left her alone, it probably would've thrown a soul into the creep as soon as I killed him. I'd have had to kill him twice."

"How difficult could it possibly be to destroy a vampire when they're thirty seconds old?"

I stare at him. "No idea. But it would be annoying. Like closing a cabinet door and it pops right back open and hits you in the head."

He whistles.

"Damn. I knew it."

"Are you psychic?"

I sigh at the stars. "No. But, like, you know how if you're reading a book, and in one scene they make a really big deal about some object —like a giant book in a fancy locked case—that object is *always* going to be important later on?"

"Umm, yeah, kinda."

"Well, the instant I left the reliquary in the trunk to go help Ashley, I *knew* someone would grab it before I got back here." I pace, growling to myself. "Before, I hadn't done anything stupid or made an error. Now, it's missing and it *is* my fault. The elders aren't going to care about Ashley's life. They're gonna be on me for not prioritizing vampire stuff over 'mere mortals.' Guess this is where I finally say something stupid enough to get me killed. Ever wanna tell someone to go F themselves but you can't because the fallout will be way worse than the momentary gratification?"

"Every day. I'm a cop." John smiles. "Every. Single. Day."

"Ugh. It has to be Ladonna. Bet she's been following me. I'm seriously screwed. She's an elder."

John turns in place, glancing around. His gaze fixates on something in the distance. "Huh. I think I can sense the damn thing. Isn't far away from here."

"Huh?" I gawk at him. "Did you just say you can feel the reliquary?"

"Kinda think so, yeah. Probably because the freakin' thing that stole my body is still in my body and I'm somehow connected to the jar."

"Umm." I fidget. "There's still the problem of her being an elder. She'd tear me apart."

"Think like a cop. Call in backup. Don't matter how bad some dude thinks he is, twenty of us on him is gonna win."

I wince. "Not sure pissed off vampires scale numbers the same way mortals do, but you have a point. Let's go."

John drifts off into the air. He's not the fastest flyer, but we end up only going a few blocks down the street to a small motel. The building is a rectangular C shape, wrapped around a parking lot. Three faces of motel rooms and windows on two stories. I land in the weeds at the edge of the parking lot. John points, either at Room 11 or 12, both on the ground floor.

"Which one? The doors are kinda close together."

"Eleven. It's in there."

"Can you go look inside? She probably won't care about a ghost walking by."

John jogs across the lot, sticks his head in the window, then leans back and waves me over. As soon as I'm next to him, he whispers, "She's in there alone. Back of the room on the telephone. The thing is on the bed. You might be able to grab it and run before she notices."

Ordinarily, I'd laugh at the idea of outrunning an elder. However, Oblivare appear to lack the ability to fly. If I can make it out the door before she gets a hand on me, I'm good. Whew. Deep breaths. I nod once, then edge up to the door.

"… minimal interference with the plan," says a male voice on the other end of the phone. "The curator is on his way to claim the reliquary. He should arrive in approximately forty minutes."

"Perfect. I will be here." Ladonna emits a pleased sigh.

Hmm. Hang on. One, she's no longer distracted by a telephone call, which drastically lowers my odds of success. Two, it sounds like we have more Oblivare in the area. This might be a bigger problem than any of us think. I hurry back to my bushy hiding place and pull out my phone.

I send a text to Glim. ‹Need help plz. Important. Can you meet me where I am?› Then, I call the direct number for Wolent. It only rings twice before he picks up.

"Sarah… where are you? What's taking so long?"

"Complications," I whisper. "Will explain everything in detail soon. There are more Oblivare in Seattle. One of them—an elder a bit much for me to take on myself—got the reliquary, and she's sitting on it in a motel room waiting for someone called the curator to come get it. Sounds kinda impressive. Thought you might want to know they're going to be here in like thirty-five minutes."

"Ahh, an unexpected turn of events but perhaps in our favor," says Wolent. "Stay there and keep an eye on the situation. Call me back if anything changes. Associates will be with you soon."

"Yes, sir."

We hang up.

Hmm. Maybe I *do* 'have people' to call.

IT'S LATIN FOR DESTRUCTION

hree minutes after I stuff my iPhone back in my pocket, Glim's standing next to me.

John lets out a yelp. Most of my muscles lock in surprise, but I keep quiet.

"Are you all right?" asks Glim.

"Mostly." I take a moment to exhale and let the minor jump scare fade. "There's a dangerous object in Room 11 over there. I was supposed to bring it to Mr. Wolent, but stuff got complicated and now it's in there with a fairly old Oblivare. Wolent's sending some people to help deal with them and get the reliquary. He thinks a Shadow named Eidolon can destroy it."

Glim's eyes widen. "How do you know of him?"

"Uhh, Holden mentioned him. Why? Is he supposed to be a secret?"

"Yes."

I cringe. "Oops. No problem. I'll pretend I don't know he exists. If it makes you feel better, I don't know anything about him other than the name."

"It shouldn't be a problem. You aren't seriously considering attacking an elder alone, are you?"

"No. Mostly asked you here in hopes you might be able to make sure the reliquary gets to where it needs to go, but if you wouldn't mind helping me not get my ass kicked, I'd appreciate it. Wolent is sending some friends to take care of the ass-kicking part. It's probably going to be over my head. Only thing I'm gonna do is lurk and maybe dart in and grab the reliquary if there's an opening."

Glim nods.

"Thank you." I hug him. "Someday, you've gotta ask me to help you do something more demanding than bring beer. I owe you so much."

"It's all right, Sarah. Your friendship is more than enough."

We stand there, hidden behind Glim's ability to make people not see or hear us. No clue if he's strong enough to hide from a vampire Ladonna's age, but she hasn't come storming out of the motel yet, so maybe. To kill time, I pull my phone back out and google the American Civil War. Hmm. Started 1862. So, she's 'oh hell no' old. Not sure exactly when during the war she turned. She's at least 150 years a vampire.

An inconspicuous grey passenger van pulls over to park across the street from the motel. Clark, Virgil, Stan, Jay, and Donnie get out. Hmm. The last time I saw these guys, they'd been trying to kill my Lost One friends, Amy, Luke and Dante. Note 'trying.' Not sure these guys are going to be much of a threat to an elder.

The van rises up a few inches.

Seconds later, Aziz walks into view around the back. My brain fills in epic entrance music like from pro wrestling. Okay, things just got serious. This is like the first time he's ever gone downtown—as far as I know. Sure, it's almost three in the morning and not many people are out, but no one looking at this guy is going to think he's real. He might pass as a cosplayer in a fake muscle suit. Human beings do not have arms this big. The guy's a walking Photoshop abuse.

However, seeing him here gives me some confidence.

Glim obviously recognizes them as friends since the group sees us and walks over. Clark's the oldest—and looks it thanks to grey hair. He's a silver fox though, as they say. Prematurely grey and not bad looking. Jay's a Fury, the rest as far as I know are Old Guard. They look like a team of oddly buff corporate lawyers, except for Jay who's more of a WWE wrestler, even down to having long blond hair. I'd call him huge, but Aziz is here.

"Hey, Sarah," says Clark. "Seems you have a knack for ending up in the middle of stuff."

"Seriously." I exhale. "How much did Wolent tell you?"

"Only that there are some Oblivare here he'd like removed from the city."

I raise both eyebrows. "*Removed* removed, or just removed."

"Depends on them." Clark nods toward Aziz. "You mentioned an elder."

The big guy isn't radiating elder vibes, but Beasts are in another world. Aurélie may be 397 years old, but I couldn't say for sure she'd definitely be able to win a fight against Aziz. A fair fight, I mean. She'd totally charm the snot out of him way before anyone hit anyone.

I fill the guys in on what little I know about the situation and the telephone conversation mentioning a curator. Our plan is for me to try swiping the reliquary out of the room while the guys confront Ladonna and her friends to deliver Wolent's 'request' to leave the Seattle area. Knowing the level of contempt Oblivare hold for society, especially vampire society, we're all expecting this will end up turning into a fight. Not sure how the Portland vamps convinced them to leave. Maybe there had been a whole lot more Oblivare and only six made it out.

Regarding this curator dude, none of the guys know if it's a job title or a douchey name the guy took because he's an egomaniac, powerful, or important. Given the wild, neo-primitive aesthetic these vampires seem to like, I half expect him to be some kind of creepy 'high priest' figure like the dude in *Indiana Jones* who liked to rip hearts out of people.

Aziz suggests he may be officially responsible for handling reliquaries, sorta like the requisitions clerk at an undead sperm bank. Whenever someone wants to make a new Oblivare vampire, they have to talk to him to dispense a soul. Now I *really* don't want to know how they fill the jar.

Weirder and weirder my life gets.

Six minutes after Wolent's people arrive, a black Mercedes pulls into the motel lot and parks by Room 11. A thin, late-sixties guy gets out of the passenger side. Well-groomed white hair and a normal dark suit makes him kinda look like a doctor. The curator, I assume. Totally not what I expected. Then again, I suppose roaming around the modern world in a cultist robe and face tattoos would kinda stand out.

Wolent's guys start across the lot toward the car. The door to Room 11 opens. Ladonna takes half a step out carrying the reliquary, but pauses upon seeing the small army of men in black suits. She's not wearing the 'Xena armor' tonight, rather a short black dress, but still looks like she belongs on stage at a Eurometal show. There's no concern whatsoever in her expression, merely annoyance.

The curator sees her expression and twists to peer back at the guys, then frowns. A younger man hops out of the driver's side of the Mercedes. He's the total opposite of the curator, white shirt, biker vest, jean shorts, combat boots, bald and bearded. Right, so if Ladonna's the front woman for a symphonic metal band, the curator must be the manager and this guy's the roadie.

Ladonna leans into the room, depositing the reliquary on a small table by the window.

Glim and I stay by the sidewalk, watching. Not the most valorous moment in my unlife, but I'm not in this for glory. No one would call a soldier a coward for deciding not to challenge a tank to a fistfight. As soon as they start talking, I'm going to try making a run for the reliquary. Technically, Glim and I are going to make a run. No point for me to take it only to bring it to Wolent to hand off to someone else for transport to Eidolon. I'm hoping Glim can just bring it to him. The obvious question, of course, is why am I in the middle of this? Simple. Wolent doesn't have any Shadows on speed dial or in his circle of friends. It's kinda rare for them to associate with other vampires outside their bloodline, mostly because people are assholes and ninety-five percent of vampires who *aren't* Shadows regard them the way medieval peasants regarded lepers. Maybe too harsh. Other vampires don't burn or actively try to destroy them. I need a better analogy. Umm, they kinda treat Shadows the way people in the 1800s treated undertakers. Tried to keep distance but tolerated them when needed.

Donnie approaches the curator. "We are here on behalf of Arthur Wolent. Your ilk are not—"

Casual as anything, the curator backhand slaps Donnie, launching him almost to the sidewalk. He lands a short distance from me, jaw smashed, face in worse shape than what I did to Troy (before the shotgun).

Oh, shit. Looks like the Oblivare opted for another 'mild disagreement.'

All hell breaks loose. Aziz lunges at the curator, who wallops him in the head, sending him staggering to one side, so cross-eyed and derpy he looks like he forgot his own name. The curator raises both eyebrows, seemingly impressed by the man surviving the hit. Wolent's guys pounce, Virgil and Stan tackling the driver while Clark and Jay go after Ladonna. No surprise they're avoiding the curator after what he did, but I don't get the sense they're scared of him as much as trying to weenie smash. Not literally. 'Weenie smash' is my Dad's term —and now Sierra's—for boss fights in video games where you have to fight a powerful enemy plus a bunch of weak ones at the same time. Sometimes, the easiest way to win those fights is to initially ignore the big boss and kill the little guys first. Hence, smashing the weenies. It's not a dick joke.

It goes about as well as I expect.

The curator refuses to merely spectate. He wades in, throwing Wolent's guys around like ragdolls. Ladonna mostly keeps her distance, guarding the motel room door. My guess is the curator is old enough to see into at least one of the enforcers' heads and knows I'm out here waiting to grab the reliquary and he's told Ladonna to keep guard on it. She's not smacking Clark and Jay around anywhere near as bad as what the curator did to Donnie and is presently doing to Virgil and Stan. The old silver-haired dude is basically juggling inflatable fake vampires.

I really ought to do something more than stand here, but duh. Any one of Wolent's enforcers would break me in half, and he's laughing at them. The only reason I stood toe to toe with them last time is a sneak attack plus having a sword. A good blade and knowing how to use it makes up for a surprising amount of strength disparity. In a fist or claw fight, any of them would mop the floor with me. Wonder if the guys brought their swords and left them in the van?

Ladonna pounces at Clark, trying to grab him, but he spins around in a reversal, catching her in a headlock. She promptly melts away into a cloud of black smoke and reforms a step to his left. The driver bowls into Jay's side, picking him up into a charge before ramming him into a parked pickup truck. Jay's elbow leaves a dent in the metal. He grimaces in pain, but I don't think the bone snapped.

Oh hell. Can't just watch.

I launch myself into the air, extending claws.

Clark spins away from Ladonna and grabs the driver, attempting to ram him headfirst into the pickup. He gets his legs up in time to plant his boots on the door, knocking the truck a few inches to the right with a loud squelch of tires on paving, sparing himself a broken skull.

Ladonna rakes claws across Clark's back. He grunts in pain, losing his grip on the driver.

The curator blurs over to Jay, calmly grabs him by the back of his head, and drives him face down at the side of the pickup truck. Jay manages to get his hands up in time to catch the edge of the truck bed, but isn't strong enough to stop his forehead from pounding another dent in the steel. Blood sprays out to the side; Jay collapses to the pavement, moaning.

I dive out of the air, raking all ten of my claws down the driver's back. He lets out a shriek like someone clamped a hot waffle iron closed on his man bits. The instant my sneakers touch the ground, the world around me shifts. I'm back at the sidewalk. Driver, curator, and Ladonna all look around bewildered, evidently having no idea why Driver has claw wounds.

Glim's next to me, hand on my arm. He's also giving me a 'what the hell are you doing?' stare, as if he caught his nine-year-old kid sister playing with a gun. No, he doesn't have a kid sister. Just saying.

"Ehh, oops." I cringe. "Thanks, hard to just watch them get the crap kicked out of them."

Clark takes advantage of the driver's momentary pain paralysis, walloping a haymaker into the side of his head that throws him tumbling over the pickup truck, spinning feet over head like a thrown hatchet. Driver crashes through the side window of a parked silver Toyota six spaces away.

The curator grabs Clark by the throat. As calmly as if tossing aside an empty candy bar wrapper, he flicks his arm to the side, launching Clark into the wall of the 7-11 next door to the motel, like a hundred feet away.

Virgil howls in pain, staggering back from Ladonna, who's using him as a scratching post. She's so much faster than him, his attempts to defend himself appear more like random flailing.

Aziz, finally in control of his senses, stomps over and grabs for her. She blurs away, dodging his massive hand. Still, she's off Virgil. Stan lets out a grunt. The driver's back. He's charged linebacker style at Stan from the side, lifting the dude off his feet and carrying him into the motel wall.

We are making a crapton of noise. This has to end fast or there will be dead cops.

Ladonna backs away from Aziz, wide-eyed. Wow, something finally seems to have broken past her indifference. She looks sincerely worried. He's enough of a distraction for Virgil to land a punch to the side of her head. The physical power of it compared to her weight flings her into the Room 11 door, mostly breaking it off its hinges. However, she bounces off to her feet, giving him an irritated look way too close to how Sierra stares at Sam whenever he ambush-bonks her with a pillow.

Roaring in anger, Jay runs in, arm cocked back in an amazingly telegraphed punch—I mean this is practically a fifteen-second slow-mo close up scene from a more recent *Rocky* movie. You know, one of those overly indulgent shots where Stallone's jowls wobble on screen as he bellows out all the emotional pain and whatever angst he's going through being a boxer. Driver's too busy watching the curator slow-walk after Stan to notice Jay coming. The punch liquefies driver's jaw, flattening him to the pavement so hard his feet whip up into the air.

This buys Stan a reprieve. He takes a second to recover his balance.

Alas, the curator blurs over to Jay, backhanding him in the face. The old man's strike smashes Jay's skull like a baseball bat splattering a rotten pumpkin. Jay goes down, a third of his head missing.

"Dammit. I have to do something." I go to leap into the air again, but Glim grabs me.

He's right, but it doesn't mean I have to like it, or stop trying to stupidly involve myself in a fight I'm not high enough level for. What the hell is wrong with me? I hate fighting. Why am I struggling to rush in there knowing I'd only get one-shotted?

Aziz emits a scary deep growl and punches at the curator. The old man blurrily dodges, warping around behind the Moroccan Hulk only a little slower than teleportation. An 'I win' smile starts to form on the curator's lips—at least until Aziz swings his left arm around equally as fast, seizing the old guy by the shoulder, holding him still while spinning the rest of the way around and hammering his enormous fist into the man's face.

The curator's head simply ceases to exist.

Aziz continues rage-screaming while pounding his knuckles repeatedly into the top of the curator's torso, further tenderizing a formerly human body into a semiliquid state. Purple glowing mist seeps out of the lump of meat formerly known as the curator, but the beating continues.

Uh oh. He's upset. Beast mode activated, as they say, literally.

Oh, damn. I gawk. I didn't think it was possible to *kill* a vampire from blunt force. We're supposed to be able to come back from anything short of sunlight, fire, or acid baths. Maybe the soul inside the curator said 'screw this' and left. For all I know, they can choose to abandon a body at any time. Could be that Oblivare don't heal like us since they claim already-dead corpses to inhabit. I really don't want to believe Aziz is so strong he breaks the laws of the Universe.

Virgil, Clark, and Stan jump on the driver. It's over fairly quick and not at all in a pleasant manner—for the driver.

Ladonna gawks at Aziz continuing to mash the curator more and more into a pulp. She's got the same expression of terrified awe on her face I'd have after witnessing someone smash Aurélie. Weird, I didn't get 'elder vibes' from the curator, but he definitely had the strength and speed of one. I also never got too close to him, and maybe he's concealing his age somehow. Or was.

Aziz finally appears to realize he's making a mess hitting a lump of useless meat. He stops whomping on the remains, looks around as though he'd slipped and done something socially questionable at a fancy party, then tosses the corpse aside and faces Ladonna. Stan and Clark walk toward her, as does Virgil, though he's moving a little slower thanks to claw wounds.

Now's my chance. I fly across the parking lot to Room 11. Ladonna has zero interest in fighting four vampires herself—especially Aziz—and breaks for the motel room. We reach the door roughly at the same time. She grabs me, trying to pull me out of her way so she can get the reliquary. I cling to the doorjamb, my claws cutting trenches in the drywall. Damn, this wench is strong. Aziz pounces, grabbing her from behind. She keeps holding me. Aziz pulls on her, which pulls on me, lifting the two of us off our feet. Whee. I've always wanted to become a vampire paper doll.

Upon realizing *who* grabbed her, Ladonna gives a yelp of alarm and disintegrates into a cloud of black fog. The instant she's no longer pulling at me, my effort to cling to the motel drills my shoulder into the doorjamb. I manage to get my feet under me. She reappears a few steps away, looks rapidly back and forth between me blocking the doorway, Aziz reaching for her, and the other three guys approaching.

Her expression's about ninety percent worry, ten percent a disparaging remark about my parentage.

An instant before Aziz grabs her again, she poofs into a cloud of inky mist, which rapidly shrinks into the form of a huge blackbird. Her dress, boots, and belt fall to the ground. In seconds, the bird's gone, weaving between buildings out of sight across the street.

Son of a bitch. That damn blackbird. She *was* following me.

And... wow. *So* damn cool. A vampire turned into a freakin' blackbird. That's awesome.

I gawk. Okay, maybe even fangirl a little. Yeah, she's evil, could kill anyone without guilt, and a threat to both mortal and vampire civilizations alike, but I still gaze in awe.

"You all right, Miss Sarah?" asks Aziz.

"Yeah." I tug at my hands. "My claws are kinda stuck in the wood, but otherwise, I'm okay."

"Did she do something to your mind?" Aziz gingerly pinches each of my claws in two fingers and tugs them out. Can't say it's comfortable, but it doesn't hurt. "Heck of a grip, Miss Sarah."

"No. I'm just... wow. It *is* possible for vampires to turn into animals. Sure, she's totally crazy, but that's pretty damn cool. Is it bad I kinda wanna watch *The Crow* again now?"

Aziz chuckles.

I look down from the sky at him. A little blood trickles from his right ear. My brain attempts the math problem of comparing the curator's backhand slaps throwing people fifty, sixty feet in the air and crushing skulls to Aziz barely moving when hit. It gives up. I'll work on easier math... like calculus. Wait, no. I am done with it.

"Umm." I point at the dress on the ground. "She left her stuff behind. I thought clothes and such turned into fog with the vampire."

"No." Aziz shakes his head—someday, an intrepid team of explorers may discover he has a neck—"Mortals changed it for the stories. British imperialists and Americans cannot handle nudity."

I laugh. "Yeah, seriously. People complain more about a bare nipple popping out by accident on TV or swear words than murder or extreme gore in movies."

Aziz shrugs. "People are strange."

"They sure are. Thanks for saving our asses." I hug his left arm. "That curator guy was crazy powerful. If you weren't here..."

"Oh, yes. Speaking of which... I better get the flamethrower." Aziz starts walking off to the van.

"Uhh, you seriously have a flamethrower?"

"I do," says Aziz without slowing or looking back.

Clark and Stan drag/carry Jay and Donny's limp bodies to the van. A bashed-open skull is basically a three-Advil headache for a vampire, as long as no one burns them to permanent death before they wake up. In a way, it's less painful than claw wounds. Virgil's going to be hating unlife for a week or so.

"A flamethrower..." I shake my head in disbelief. "Don't wanna know."

I find the reliquary on the table. The three-foot-tall marble-patterned jar *looks* innocent. However, it gives off a palpable feeling of malice. This thing totally wants to kill me. I'm not even going to touch the little teapot-like lid on the top. No idea what the glowing purple runes etched on the lid say, but as far as I'm concerned, it's 'do not open.'

Glim meets me on the sidewalk outside the motel room.

"Here." I hand him the reliquary.

He takes it.

"You rock. Thanks for saving my ass."

Fwoosh.

A wave of heat washes over me as the wall lights up orange. Glim flinches as well.

The driver, draped over what's left of the curator, goes up in a bonfire. Aziz holding a flamethrower in one hand, its fuel tank in the other, looks like a normal person running around with a weed sprayer. Stan's dealing with a few curious mortals in other motel rooms, making sure they go back to sleep and remember nothing.

"Well, that's one problem solved..." I sigh.

"One problem?" Glim peers at me.

"Still have someone out there making baby vampires in large numbers."

"Ahh." He nods once.

I stare into the flames consuming the two bodies. "Oblivare, huh? Well, they found oblivion all right."

A GHOSTLY LOOSE END

Glim looks the reliquary over, gets an urgent look in his eye, and takes a step back.

"Oh, wait…" I hold up a hand. "Before you disappear…"

"Hmm?" He tilts his head.

I gesture at the ghost of John Trujillo and explain what happened to him. "Is he dead? Or can the Oblivare soul be kicked out of him? Last I saw, his body was alive."

"We will need to bring his body to Eidolon, too. If, of course, he is still alive."

"Feels like it." John nods.

"Do you know where he went?"

"Yeah. I left him in the basement of a parking garage downtown. Corner of Second Ave and Union Street."

Glim takes my hand. "Think of the place."

I close my eyes and do my best to focus on the memory.

Gravity becomes highly confused. It's as if I'm a pet mouse accidentally thrown in the washing machine, except for not drowning. I catch a fleeting glimpse of a weird, dark landscape whizzing by on all sides for only a few seconds before a bright hole seems to spring out of the ground and ambush us from the front.

Next thing I know, we're in the hallway by the generator room—and I fall over.

"Apologies," says Glim.

"It's fine. I remember. Shadow jumps are disorienting."

He smiles in a 'maybe to you' manner, making me chuckle despite wanting to throw up. It sure feels like teleportation, but we didn't. He basically pulls us into an alternate dimension where time and distance don't follow the same rules as our world. Shadows literally become shadow material there. Me? I stay somewhat solid, hence the nausea and dizziness. At least he didn't have to squeeze me through a quarter-inch gap under a door this time.

Clanking and roaring fill the hallway, coming from the generator room.

"Sounds like he's okay... and awake." I push myself upright.

Glim tucks the reliquary under his left arm, opens the door to the generator room, and gives John's body a once-over. "Should be doable. I don't understand any of the things Eidolon works with, but I do recognize this as an extreme possession."

"What makes it 'extreme?'" I tilt my head. "A viral marketing campaign?"

"Heh." Glim chuckles. "His spirit is outside the body. Ordinary possession doesn't evict the owner of the body."

"Is this like common?" I furrow my brow. "Wait, I guess it is. The mystics did the same thing to Sophia."

"Generally speaking, demons possess without displacing the soul inside the body. Other sources of possession 'steal' the bodies." Glim tries to look innocent. "I've heard of a few creatures capable of this, but none are in North America."

"Small favors." I cringe.

The possessed John glares at us. His wrists are bleeding a little, but it appears I positioned him hugging the machinery in a way he didn't have enough room to move or inflict serious damage to himself.

Glim grasps the man's shoulder, and both vanish in a whorl of blackness.

Ghost John glances at me. "What now?"

"You should probably follow your body. I'm guessing this Eidolon guy has a way to evict the dark energy so you can get back in. Might want to stay close by so you can jump in."

"Great." He exhales. "I'm gonna need to come up with one hell of a cover story to explain where I've been all day to my captain."

I blink. "Won't the vampire you're enthralled to make all awkward questions go away?"

"Yeah, she will. But… gotta put something in the logbook." John ethereally pats me on the shoulder, then vanishes.

Ugh. I look around the generator room for no particular reason. The Oblivare issue is, hopefully, done. Random baby vampires, not my problem. Well, it is… sorta. If vampires are exposed to the world and hunted, it's definitely going to be my problem. Still, I'm done for the night. It's close to four in the morning and my bed is calling for me. I want to check on Ashley, but she's going to be asleep, totally unaware of what happened. She thinks she told me about the stalker creep two months ago and I sent him away.

Might stop for a bite on the way home.

And yeah, 4:30 a.m. is a bit early for a vampire to declare a night over, but I can still enjoy lazing around in a soft bed hugging my stuffed animals before dawn knocks me out.

IT ONLY COST A CRAPTON

Sierra figured the day had gone fairly well for a summer Monday—except for all-over aches and constant dread.

Thankfully, the 'rents hadn't decided they needed to go anywhere or do anything. She did her best not to act antisocial, surly, or show any sign something happened. In truth, she didn't truly know *what* happened, only that she felt as weak as Uncle Hank looked. The soreness didn't scare her too much. It reminded her of the day after her first session of sword instruction. Going from months of sitting around playing video games and being lazy to a serious workout overnight left her sore everywhere.

All day Monday, she felt too weak to even pick up a sword. Since she still couldn't bring herself to admit anything to anyone, she imagined talking to Dad about it. She imagined him saying the boost from Sarah's blood had worn off completely, and she felt weak because she'd gotten used to being unusually strong. A few times when no one could see her—like in the bathroom—she tried doing a push-up or some other test of strength. It still worked, though her arms hurt. Maybe she hadn't become 'weak' as much as back to normal. Of course, it didn't take a lot of power for anyone in the

Wright family to do a push up. Strength didn't matter much when lifting something small.

Problem being, normal felt pathetic. If any sort of bad guy or monster showed up at the house, Sierra would have no choice but to act like a little kid and hide. So what if she happened to be a child, it still embarrassed her to act like one. Twelve shouldn't count as a child. However, she accepted it didn't count as an adult either—after all, some restaurants let 'twelve and under' eat cheap or free.

She'd gotten good at hiding her anxiety from everyone, specifically the guidance counselor and teachers. No one truly knew she regarded going to class every day as running a gauntlet she might not return from. Teachers thought her antisocial. One even said she needed to 'see someone' because she didn't talk to other kids much or seem interested in friends. What would be the point of making friends only to have them die? Sarah had only recently learned how she felt, that every unexpected loud noise at school made her jump and start shaking. She tried so hard to hide it. Sophia thought her fearless, tough, and a badass. Maybe compared to her, she was.

Sierra hated being scared. She *hated* living in constant fear. She finally found a way to escape the fear. Sure, she couldn't bring a sword to school, but being strong, fast, and 'damage resistant' enough to survive a fight with vampires would certainly let her take on a crazy person with a gun. She wouldn't have to kick anyone's ass, just get the weapon away from them. Fingers would break easy to a thrall's strength.

But now, she'd gone back to being ordinary Sierra.

She couldn't ask Sarah for blood again without being in immediate danger, or her big sis would know she'd become addicted. She couldn't talk to her about being addicted because it would guarantee Sarah never let her have blood again. She'd have to go somewhere else for it. Maybe Dalton… maybe one of the other vamps. Glim had a lot of power, but she really didn't want to end up looking like a Shadow and having to hide away from everyone.

Though, *today*, she wanted to hide from everyone.

After Nicole, Megan, and Priya went home for dinner, Sierra

considered retreating to her bedroom to play computer games, but the 'rents would know something was wrong if she didn't sit in the living room on the PlayStation. She couldn't hide under a blanket and cry like she really wanted to do in the living room, but recovery from her parents catching her in tears would not be possible, so she forced herself to sit in the usual spot blowing people up in *Call of Duty*, pretending to be unfazed by the world at large.

Sophia disappeared after dinner, probably to her bedroom to work on the spell.

With each passing hour, Sierra cared less and less how 'safe' her sister's magic would turn out to be. If it had any chance whatsoever of offering a way out of feeling weak and pathetic, she'd risk it. She suspected Sarah knew something happened. A few 'are you okay' looks had been the extent of it. Guilt crept in. She thought about the days after the cop told them Sarah had been found dead, and how blown-away thrilled she'd been when her big sis magically reappeared at the door. Their entire family dynamic had changed. She shouldn't isolate herself from Sarah. Even if admitting she'd become addicted to vampire blood—technically, she'd grown addicted to the power it gave her rather than the blood itself—embarrassed her more than getting pantsed in gym class, she ought to do it.

Her parents eventually arrived to take over the living room television. Despite wanting to rush up to her room and hide as fast as possible, she forced herself to ask for a few more minutes to finish the match so they didn't sense something wrong.

Once the game ended, she packed the PlayStation into the cabinet, hugged Mom and Dad, then hurried up to her bedroom to be alone with her fear. She flopped in her computer chair, staring at the blank screen, too sore, worried, and exhausted to bother playing anything. Her thoughts dwelled on the immediate aftermath of Sarah's near-death. Being one of the 'middle two' kids in the family sometimes made her feel invisible. However, she no longer doubted her parents and siblings would react the same way if anything happened to her as they did when they thought Sarah died.

Maybe a road paved in vampiric blood *would* lead to an inevitable bad outcome. Question being, could she trust her life and Sophia's life and Sam's life entirely to Sarah and other people until she grew up? Sierra stared into space, debating the worse of two options: wallowing in her constant fear and helplessness or her family being crushed when something happened to her. Could she let go of her armored persona and spend a few years letting everyone see how scared she was? No way could she hold it in. She'd *have* to tell her parents. The only way she'd make it to eighteen would be honesty, or she'd drive herself crazy. Telling them amounted to being forced to stand in the town square and suffer mockery from the entire village. Could she bear the shame of her bravery being exposed as a lie? Merely an excuse to hide fear. She only truly felt brave with Sarah next to her. Did that count as bravery or merely feeling protected?

Sierra bowed her head. She didn't want to make her parents go through losing her, especially younger than eighteen. Coralie had to have told Sophia something serious. No way in hell would the kid terrified of 'Fuzzydoom' willingly walk into the Salem house unless she'd been morbidly afraid of something worse—like her slightly older sister ending up dead.

She'd done that to Sophia. Tormented her innocent little sister with a scary ass house and forest. Made her walk into a scene far worse than movies she ran screaming out of the room to get away from. Yet, she *still* found herself trying to come up with excuses to give Sarah in hopes of getting another boost. She still slid down a path most likely to end with her parents devastated.

Her reflection in the computer screen looked like a blurry painting from a detective story, a murder victim slumped in a chair, legs dangling, hands hanging limp over the armrests. Every possible choice she could take from this point sucked. Multiple options all simplified down to: die or let everyone see her as a frightened little kid. Sam had demon friends. Sophia had magic—even if it didn't always do what she wanted. How could 'normal Sierra' hope to protect her family or even keep herself alive? If she kept up training, once she grew up, she could certainly use a sword to stop an ordinary bad guy, but any vampire would rip her head off. And of course, she'd have to survive long enough to grow up.

Sierra's eyes burned. A few tears leaked out.

Her door creaked open.

Ordinarily, someone walking into her room while she cried would've made her jump and try to hide as if she'd been in the middle of changing clothes. She couldn't bring herself to care. Or maybe she did. Maybe she wanted to be caught.

Sophia poked her head in. "Hey."

"Hey," mumbled Sierra.

"What's wrong?"

Sierra attempted an indifferent shrug. "Stuff."

"It's okay to say you're scared. I do it all the time." Sophia crept closer. "Great way to get hugs."

Sierra sputtered a chuckle.

"It's ready."

"Huh?" Sierra raised one leg, hooked her toes over the top of her desk, and pushed the chair around to face the door. Her sister stood two steps into the room, clutching a plastic straw and a small glass bottle from one of Mom's Starbucks Frappuccino drinks. Instead of coffee, it contained a faintly glowing blue liquid. "Whoa. How much caffeine does it take to make the stuff light up?"

"Nah." Sophia grinned. "Needed a potion bottle, so I grabbed this out of the recycle bin. Spell's done. Here it is."

Sierra sat up, her mood bursting out from the depths of fear and sadness to excitement. "Seriously? Is it gonna work?"

"Umm. It's definitely not going to hurt you. I think it will most likely work."

"Do I drink it with the straw?" Sierra slid off the chair, stood, and walked up to her, gazing at the eerily luminous blue liquid.

Sophia shook her head. "No. The straw is so you can breathe."

Sierra blinked. "Umm, what? Breathe? How crazy is this gonna be?"

"It isn't safe to drink this. There's too big a chance you could die and turn into a vampire-like monster."

"Eep!" Sierra leaned back.

"But..." Sophia held one finger up. "I know how to make sure it doesn't kill you. Water is the perfect filter to spread the enchantment out all over your body evenly and let the magic seep into you slowly. Hop in the bathtub like Sare does, completely underwater. Use the straw to breathe and I'll pour the potion into the water. Can't have any part of you above the surface or it won't be protected and the magic will get all weird since it won't be all over."

Sierra squished her toes into the carpet, blushing. Having people in the room while she tried to take a bath happened *way* too often lately. Still, Sarah got stuck outside with no clothes for two days and it didn't kill her. She could suffer a little more embarrassment if it meant she had a way to escape both her fear and the possible consequences of thralldom. Having her sister next to her in the bathroom hardly sounded as weird as the idea of drinking vampire blood. Hell, she and Sophia used to take baths together when they'd been really little. Kinda weird to do at twelve and eleven, but it's not like Sophia would be in the tub with her.

"Do you have'ta be in the room with me?"

Sophia tilted her head side to side. "Only long enough to cast the spell after pouring the potion, but I don't know what might happen to you. If you pass out, you could drown. I don't want that."

"You said drinking the potion had too big a chance to kill me." Sierra continued grinding her toes into the carpet. "What is 'too big' a chance?"

"Umm, like two percent, decimal three, repeating." Sophia flicked at the straw.

Sierra smirked. "Only two percent?"

"*Any* chance you could be hurt is too big." Sophia looked down past the line of embroidered cats on the hem of her dress at the floor. "I don't want you to get hurt."

Her cheeks warmed. *She's my sister. If it means I won't need disgusting blood anymore not to be helpless, I'll deal.* "Whatever. Okay."

Sophia headed across the hall to the bathroom. Sierra followed, leaning into the tub to turn on the water. The parents probably wouldn't think it unusual for one of them to want a bath so close to bedtime. They stood there in silence for a minute, watching the tub fill.

"So, umm... what's gonna happen?" asked Sierra.

"Are you asking what you'll experience or what the end result will be?"

Sierra blinked. "Umm, both?"

Sophia bounced nervously. "Not sure about experience. Probably tingles. It most likely won't hurt or do anything unpleasant. I didn't go cheap on materials."

"We picked a mushroom out of a basement and grabbed some dirt." Sierra folded her arms. "Hardly expensive."

"Those were the magical components. I needed a big ruby, too."

"Wait, what?"

"You know, a gemstone?" Sophia exhaled a little exasperated sigh, like an eighth-grade math teacher having to go over basic addition. "Rare crystals act as conductors to channel arcane forces between dimensions. One of the reasons magic is so rare is, stuff more than little tricks ends up being really expensive. Wasn't such a big deal back in Merlin's time, but now? Eek."

Sierra crouched to test the water temperature. Too hot, so she turned up the cold. "Where the heck did you get a ruby from? And where is it?"

"In here." Sophia held up the glowing bottle. "Dissolved. Relax. No one is ever going to find it."

Sierra gawked. "You stole a gem."

"Technically, the kitten did. But yeah, I guess since she's an extension of me, then I did." Sophia fidgeted. "But I asked her to make sure she grabbed one from someone who wouldn't be hurt by the loss and also a gem that isn't like famous or culturally significant."

"Still. My innocent little sister *stole* something... and not just like a piece of candy." Sierra whistled. "Didn't think you had it in you to be such a bad girl."

Sophia looked down. "This is your life we're talking about. I don't care what it takes to protect you."

She seemed on the verge of crying, so Sierra hugged her. "Thanks."

"Don't tell Mom, okay?" Sophia grinned past tears.

"I won't." Sierra cut off the faucet. "Okay... so what's this gonna do to me?"

Sophia exhaled. "The end result is you'll be like strong and fast and stuff, same as when Sare gave you blood. It's probably gonna let you see in the dark, too, since it's using a vampire as the focus."

"Any downsides?" Sierra fidgeted at the button on her jean shorts.

"Don't think so."

"Not too reassuring." Sierra chuckled.

"The book didn't say anything about side effects and Coralie's been quiet." Sophia smiled hopefully.

"Okay. Let's do it." Sierra blushed.

"Umm, why are you turning red?"

"Because you're in here when I'm gonna take a bath."

Sophia gestured at the door. "Go put on a swimsuit then. I never said you had to be naked, just underwater... unless you wanna take a real bath after."

"Be right back."

Sierra ran to her room, changed into a swimsuit, and returned to the bathroom. Sophia stood patiently by as she eased herself into the slightly too-warm water and sat. Part of this seemed like a really bad idea, but also like her little sister wanted to 'play magic.' It couldn't be any worse than drinking blood. Sophia stuck the straw in Sierra's mouth as she gradually lowered herself underwater to lay flat on the tub, peering up past the wavering surface at the blurry form of her blonde sister.

Sophia opened the lid on the Starbucks bottle and gradually poured the glowing concoction into the bathwater, moving it around in a big oval. Luminous fluid fell to the bottom of the tub, heavier than the water, rapidly spreading until the entire bath glowed. Strangely, the glow didn't appear diluted by the bath, keeping the same intensity.

Faint tingles prickled all over Sierra's body, static electricity crawling everywhere.

Sophia set the bottle down, then held her hands over the water, fingers spread, an expression of serious concentration narrowing her eyes. Sierra 'Mmm'-ed in surprise through the straw when a mysterious force caused her to levitate a few inches off the tub bottom. Tingling intensified. A million spiders raced across her skin. *Gotta stay underwater or it'll go wrong. Can't move. Gah!* Sierra clamped her eyes shut, trying to resist the urge to scream, squirm, or move. She clenched her hands into fists, curled her toes, and shuddered, weathering the extreme tickling.

Whud!

The entire house shook as if a giant kicked the wall outside. The lights went off. All the glowing water in the tub burst into faintly glowing fog. Sierra dropped the few inches to land on the porcelain bottom with a *thump*.

"Ow," deadpanned Sierra before spitting the straw aside.

"Are you hurt?" gasped Sophia somewhere above her, out of sight behind the dense mist.

"No. Just said 'ow' automatically because I bumped my head on the tub. It didn't hurt." Sierra gingerly patted herself down. "Weird. I'm like totally dry. My swimsuit's not even damp." She sat up, finding herself shoulder deep in chilly mist.

The bathroom appeared merely somewhat dim, despite the only source of light being the luminous fog. Soft glow cast everything an eerie—but cool looking—shade of blue. Klepto's teal eyes shone like tiny flashlights from Sophia's right shoulder.

"Weird…" Sierra swished a hand back and forth in the mist. "Looks like we're playing with dry ice."

The lights came back on.

"Did it work?" asked Sophia.

Sierra looked at her hands. She didn't feel sore anywhere, at least. Her swimsuit hadn't melted into her skin. Nothing hurt, nor did she feel much different at all. "Not sure."

"What happened?" yelled Sam out in the hall.

Heavy footsteps came up the stairs. Sierra guessed Mom since Dad tromped more forcefully. Mom went past the door.

"Uh oh," whispered Sophia.

After exchanging a 'what was that / I dunno' with Sam and a pause long enough to suggest she looked into each bedroom, Mom stepped into the bathroom. Whatever she had planned to say stalled as she regarded the fog rolling out of the tub. Her expression gave off an 'oh, what now?' vibe.

Sophia managed a cheesy smile.

"Girls? What are you doing in here? The whole downstairs filled with a blue glow, and a lightning bolt jumped out of the microwave and lit your father's hair on fire."

"Eep!" Sophia clamped her hands over her mouth.

"Sorry." Sierra cringed. "Soph tried to enchant my bath with lavender and kinda overdid it. Is Dad okay?"

"Yes." Mom pressed a hand to her chest. "Only a small mark. Not much worse than static shock from the carpet. He was more annoyed having to go downstairs to flip the breaker. Sierra?"

"Yeah?"

"Why are you wearing a swimsuit in the bathtub?"

She nodded at Sophia. "Just until she's out of the room."

Mom sighed, nodding, then looked at Sophia. "Young lady, you need to be a little more careful with magic or I might have to suspend those tutoring sessions."

Sophia looked down. "Yes, Mom."

"She was really careful." Sierra reached over to squeeze her sister's hand. "Just never did this before."

"All right, then. No harm done. Try to be more aware of what else your spells might do." Mom kissed Sophia on the head, then left, closing the door behind her.

Sierra exhaled in relief.

Mom poked her head back in. "Oh, girls. Please clean the eerie glowing mist out of the bathtub before you leave the room. That better not stain the porcelain."

"Yes, Mom," said Sierra and Sophia together.

Mom smiled.

Once the door closed again, Sierra grasped her sister's hand. "Hey.

It's just Mom being Mom. I know you've never been so careful about doing magic before this. You weren't careless at all."

"I know," said Sophia in a soft voice. "I just don't like lying to Mom."

"Would you rather tell her you took an expensive ruby and melted it? If she knew, it might get her fired from being a lawyer."

"Ugh." Sophia sniffled. "I don't like that lying to her is the best choice."

Sierra chuckled. "Depends if you mean 'best' as in life continues normally or best as in moral."

"If this worked and you aren't gonna die and turn into a vampire, it's definitely the best." She picked up the empty Frappuccino bottle. "I should put this back in the recycle bin. Did it work?"

Sierra stood in the tub, stomach-deep in fog. "I don't feel any different. Let me try something."

"What?"

She reached out to grasp Sophia under the armpits and lifted her off her feet. Her younger sister felt as light as a hollow plastic mannequin. She set her down, then threw a few punches as fast as she could past Sophia's face—intentionally missing.

"Eek!" Sophia jumped away a second or two after Sierra stopped moving.

"Ooh! I think it worked." Sierra bounced on her toes. "It's just like when Sarah first boosted me. Umm, you're sure there aren't going to be any bad effects?"

"Yeah. I mega-tuple checked." She held up the bottle. "Might've been some side effects if you drank it, but the water made it safe. Gave up some power for safety."

"How much power?" Sierra climbed out of the tub and stuck her face in the mirror to check herself. No fangs. Win.

"Umm, if you drank it, you would've been like *Terminator* strong… but the magic wouldn't have lasted long and might've killed you. Moderating it with water traded power for permanence."

Sierra did a few push-ups, feeling weightless. A good shove threw her up to her feet. "This is about perfect. I don't need to be stupid strong. Especially if it could kill me. Just enough to have a chance. Wow. So, no death."

"Nope. This has nothing to do with vampires. I basically enchanted you to boost strength and agility."

"Hah." Sierra snickered. "We're not D&D characters."

Sophia shrugged. "It's the easiest way to explain it in a way you'll understand without talking for two hours. According to my calculations, factoring in the water, you should now be about as strong as an adult man. Once you grow up, you'll probably be a teeny bit superhuman. Umm, speed's already kinda superhuman, so you'll have to be careful and not show off."

"Cool." Sierra choked up. "Thank you."

"Why are you crying?"

"Because you saved me from having to be scared." Sierra hugged her.

"You're welcome. I can be scared enough for both of us."

Sierra laughed.

"Oh... I also asked the book about the blood."

"Uh oh." Sierra leaned back from the hug to make eye contact. "You're about to tell me there is a side effect."

"Umm, I'm talking about what would've happened if you kept drinking blood. Being a thrall stops you from aging. It's not a big deal if a person doesn't particularly care about power, but since you're so worried about someone hurting you, or us, eventually, you'd get like addicted and stuff and go crazy if you didn't have it."

"Yeah." Sierra looked down, then resumed the hug. "I noticed. Thanks."

UNSTABLE FIENDS

Ever get that weird feeling something just isn't right, but you can't tell what?

I'm regretting my promise to not eavesdrop on my family's minds. So, I wake up Tuesday, right? No big deal. The Oblivare are most likely no longer a problem anymore. Ladonna's still out there, but after witnessing Aziz mash the curator into pudding, it's unlikely she is going to come back for revenge, at least not soon. Still have the babymaker vampire—wow, that totally sounds bad, doesn't it? Whatever, he or she is out there and it's a problem, but hardly a scary one.

Ordinary innocent Tuesday in late June. So why does it feel wrong?

Mostly due to my sisters. Sierra is visibly happy. Nothing, as far as I know, has happened to cheer her up so much. Maybe Dad promised to buy her a PlayStation 5 when it comes out next year. Sophia's totally acting like she did something slightly wrong and is waiting to get caught and in trouble. Then again, to her, 'doing something wrong' is like arriving at class five minutes late without being noticed. She probably forgot to do some chore Mom assigned her or maybe got into an argument with Nicole. Soph keeps looking at me like she wants to say something, but doesn't.

Ugh. So tempting to look, but I gave them my word.

I don't have an obvious imminent emergency to justify breaking the promise. If whatever's going on is bad enough, they will eventually come clean. Sophia can't hold in a lie forever.

Maybe it's the sheer mundanity of the day bothering me. One doesn't go from cops having their bodies stolen by dark soul energy and getting into a giant vampire claw fight one day, then spend the next playing board games with the family on a rainy summer Tuesday. Oh, yeah. Another thing bothering me. Sierra hugged me *three times*. Randomly. Like just walking past me to go to the bathroom or get snacks, she gave me a brief hug. Completely out of character for her. She's like a cat who won't let you pick her up, but sometimes sits next to you and leans against you.

So… so… tempting to see what's going on in that devious little brain of hers.

Really don't know what vampires did with themselves before video games, television, and movies became a thing. Summer break has freed me from homework for a few months, so unless Wolent throws random jobs at me, I'm left to myself. My goal hasn't changed. I still want to be as normal as possible and pretend—insofar as I am able to—none of the crazy vampire stuff ever happened. It's a little difficult to keep up the illusion when unnatural biology keeps me awake to sunrise every day. I'm merely a night owl. Really. Umm, not buying it? Okay, fine. An extreme night owl.

T'was the night after Monday and all through the house, not a Little was stirring, not even the kitten. The parents were snug in their bed with care, in hopes no one to mischief would dare. Blix on Sam's PlayStation, Max in the yard, I've nothing else to rhyme here, so I'll say bard.

Seriously though, everything's quiet. The hellhound is snoring outside. Or maybe breathing. Hard to tell.

"Hey, Siri, do I have a scheduled attempt on my life today?"

"I don't understand," replies my phone.

Heh.

Oh, hey, in better news, the last bits of phantom stinging from the claw marks are gone. And on that note, I'm hungry. It's kinda difficult to enjoy a bowl of blood while watching a movie. Vampire society really needs to put some resources into developing portable movie-friendly snacks. For now, I'm stuck doing it the traditional way. On the upside, it's an excuse to fly.

EVER SINCE I STUMBLED ON THE ONE BASTARD WHO ABUSED HIS LITTLE stepdaughter, feeding has made me nervous.

I dread the sort of nonsense I'm going to see inside people's minds. Got lucky tonight. The dude I picked for a snack had to be the single most wholesome man on all of the West Coast. Usually, someone roving at night in a white cargo van is up to no good. This guy's driving around a portable shower for homeless people and giving out free meals. I almost felt guilty for feeding on him. Also been a really long time since I had a cheese steak. Or at least the flavor of one.

No weird, disgusting creeps, no vampires trying to rip my head off, nothing odd at all.

A feeding trip going so smoothly only tells me *something* is about to go wrong. Do I qualify as a pessimist or a realist?

On the way home, I notice an odd scene playing out on the ground at a small gas station. It's not 'Fuzzydoom escaped from the mirrorworld' odd or even 'Sierra wearing a dress' odd, merely ordinary odd. The sort of odd people watch on TV shows like *COPS*. A small crowd has formed on the side of the convenience store attached to the gas station, near the bathrooms. They're horseshoed around a young guy—early twenties—in a wool hat and grunge couture. Someone needs to tell him the Nirvana era is over. I can practically smell those jeans from up here.

Curious, I glide to the right and descend for a better look.

"Go look if you don't believe me," says the guy in a manic, freaked out voice. "I'm telling you, some dude jumped me. Soon as I started kicking *his* ass, he totally exploded into dust and bones."

Ack!

I'm intending to do mind surgery on the guy anyway, so I swoop in to land behind the crowd, not caring if he can see me flying. Grunge Boy promptly gawks. No one pays little ol' me any attention as I round the edge of the group and walk up to the guy. Two seconds of eye contact and he's cruising to Derptown. With him on pause, I look over the crowd, one by one giving everyone a light mental nudge to think this guy's high and rambling nonsense. Doesn't take much. His story sounded pretty wild. Most of them already thought the dude got a hold of some tainted weed.

The crowd disperses back to their cars, about a third going into the convenience store.

I take the dude by the hand and lead him around behind the convenience store. An entire human skeleton's worth of bones lays atop a spread of pale grey ash not far from a pair of dumpsters. Still towing Grunge Boy, I approach the bones and crouch to examine the skull. Obvious fangs.

Crap.

Great. Now what? Is this a case of SVC? Spontaneous vampiric combustion? The bones show no signs of charring or fire. Ground's concrete, so any blackening from a burn would be obvious. Okay, here's the weird moment I'd been expecting. Right. First things first.

I stand back up, go nose to nose with Grunge Boy, and plunge into his head. In his memory, he'd come back here in search of an air pump for his tire. Someone pounced on him from behind, shoving him into the wall. This guy fought back, believing he'd been targeted for a garden variety mugging. It took him only a few seconds to get the upper hand and start beating the snot out of a slightly smaller guy. The attacker definitely fits the profile of the 'baby vamp' problem, looking about eighteen or so. He makes a 'think you can kick *my* ass?' face… then bursts apart into a cloud of ash and bones.

Something tells me he hadn't intended to do that.

All his meaty bits dried out and became dust in two seconds. The bones simply fell to the ground. Either someone's given the Transference to Ashton Kutcher and there's now a vampire version of *Pranked*, or something entirely weird and messed up is going on.

I alter Grunge Boy's memory to having a drunk guy bump into him and walk off. Plausible alterations take less effort to make permanent than straight up deleting stuff. I also insert knowledge: this gas station's air pump is out front. No clue how the guy missed it.

Problem one dealt with.

I tow Grunge Boy with me around the building again and leave him standing in the well-lit area before going into the convenience store to buy a small box of trash bags. Humming innocently to myself, I open it and pull a bag out while heading around behind the building again. Even at vampire speed, it takes me a while to gather all the little individual bones into the Hefty bag. I pause, holding the fanged skull up, making eye-to-socket contact. Yeah, I can't let anyone find this. Hmm… what to do.

Having no better ideas, I finish bagging the bones and take off into the night sky.

The idea of bringing these home for the moment doesn't bother me like the reliquary. Beyond the simple morbidity of keeping someone's bones around, they're not going to hurt anyone. Spontaneously disintegrating vampires sounds like an issue the powers that be might want to know about. However, I'm also kinda curious. I generally trust Wolent, but he might not always give me every scrap of information about a situation. Also, the more I know going into a meeting with him, the better. He's also not the first guy I think of in terms of having vast obscure knowledge. He's way more Godfather than Einstein.

Idea…

I swing around and head for Seattle Central College.

THE BUILDING'S CLOSED FOR THE NIGHT, BUT I USE MY ALTERNATE ID badge to get in.

My *very* alternate ID badge. It's so alternate, in fact, it belongs to a security guard.

I didn't hurt him. Merely 'asked' him to let me in. He also didn't question the clattering plastic bag. This is, after all, a college. People bring bizarre things here all the time. Most people looking at a partially yellowed skeleton with a fanged skull would assume it to be fake. Amazing how easy it is to hide the truth right in the open sometimes. I go straight to the building where my philosophy class was, down to the basement, and to the cabinet containing the secret button.

Professor Heath is pulling a Laszlo from *Real Genius*. He lives in a secret area under the school. He doesn't have a long train car to get to his place, merely a disused elevator shaft. The man also lacks a doorbell, so I've no choice but to barge in. He is, of course, waiting for me in his 'living room.' To a vampire's hearing, opening this door is louder than dropping a bucket of forks down three flights of stairs.

"Oh, hello, Sarah. Wasn't expecting to see you again so soon." Professor Heath offers a warm 'young grandfatherly' smile that masterfully hides the elder vampire lurking beneath.

He's basically the grown man version of me: looks totally harmless on the outside, but reality is way different. Imagine a vampire story where the king of all undead is like a British version of Mr. Rogers with bushy eyebrows, played by an actor somewhere between Michael Caine and John Cleese. To be fair, I'm more harmless on the inside than he is. Not only am I a baby by comparison age wise, I'm also generally too nice for my own good. Heath's an awesome dude, but I doubt he'd feel any guilt whatsoever for killing someone who tried to destroy him.

"Sorry to bother you, but you're like the smartest person I know with fangs. Can you look at this?" I hold up the bag. "Need to understand what happened."

"It appears to be a trash bag."

"Hah. Everyone's a comedian. It's bones. Vampire bones." I hand him the bag.

He takes it over to a table mostly covered in stacks of books. One by one, he removes some of the larger bones from the bag, glances at them, then sets them on the table. I wait patiently until all the major arm and leg bones, skull, and pelvis are on the table. He left all the little stuff in the bag. Don't blame him. Picking that crap up was tedious as hell.

"So… what do you think?"

He continues examining a femur. "I've never seen anything like this before. These bones don't appear to have been chemically treated to strip the flesh, nor have they disintegrated. Typically, if a vampire is consumed by fire, our bones turn to ash except for the largest pieces. Vampirism does make certain changes to the structure. You see here the whiter parts… still mortal. Yet there is yellowing, too. Some of the bone surface resembles an ancient skeleton one might find in an archeological tomb. The blending is quite bizarre."

"Any idea what it means?"

"Somewhat, yes. The man had only been a vampire for a few days. Not enough time for his bones to fully change."

I fidget. No doubt my bones have 'fully changed,' whatever it means. Yeah, I am happy being a vampire, but still not fond of reminders about death. "I kinda figured he was pretty new. You're out of the loop, so…" I explain the situation of someone running around imparting the Transference to multiple people, then leaving them to fend for themselves. "Any idea why he disintegrated? He tried to attack some rando at a gas station. They got into a fight and the mortal turned out to be a much bigger threat than he expected. The vamp made this 'I got you now' face, then *poof!*"

"Hmm." Professor Heath picked up the skull, turning it over in his hands.

"Any ideas?"

"One theory, although I have never seen it in action." He presses a thumb at the cranium. "The weakness here—and I'm referring to his inability to easily defeat a mortal in fisticuffs, not the bones being flimsy—makes me suspect it."

"Suspect what?" I lean closer, peering at the skull.

"When we give the Transference to a mortal, it weakens us. Not permanently, mind you, merely a severe exertion. The older we are, the less we notice this exertion. If a young vampire gives the Transference, it hurts. Too young, they may incapacitate themselves for some time. Our general rule of thumb is not to risk attempting a Transference until one's fiftieth year as a vampire. Earlier than that, it may leave the sire in a greatly weakened state for an extended time. If a vampire is *too* weak when giving the Transference, the progeny they create can be unstable. I do not mean that in terms of mental stability. More like mixing volatile chemicals." He glances over at me. "You mentioned this one started a fight with a mortal and found himself losing?"

"Yeah."

"Mmm." Heath sets the skull on the table, leaving his hand on it. "He likely attempted to temporarily increase his physical strength, and in doing so, entirely consumed all of his power, destroying himself."

I gasp.

"This is my theory, mind you. I've never seen it actually occur."

"Eek... so he literally got so angry he blew up? Wow. We can really flame out like that?"

Professor Heath pats me on the arm. "Relax, child. Healthy vampires cannot overexert themselves to the point of destruction. Attempting to draw power when there is nothing in the battery simply fails to work. A situation like this could only occur from an incredibly unstable vampire who"—he taps the mottled femur—"has not yet fully developed into a vampire at all."

"This has to be related to the baby vamp issue. Someone is making a ton of newbies."

"Whatever for?" Professor Heath makes the sort of face one might make when watching a person spread mustard on a chocolate cupcake.

"I have no idea. No one does. Well, except for the idiot doing it." I glance at the bones. The separation between pure white and old, yellowed bone looks kinda like a zipper with peanut-shaped teeth, slightly fat and rounded at the ends. "Thanks for giving me a plausible theory. Umm, what should I do with these bones?"

"Ideally, burn them. We cannot leave such things around for mortals to discover." He starts putting them back in the trash bag. "I can toss them in the boiler here if you like."

"Cool. Works. Thank you."

He offers me a femur. "Unless you need one to show the society people."

"Nah. They know what's going on already. Not sure randomly disintegrating vampires makes much difference. It's basically a self-fixing problem… unless the wrong person finds the bones." I take the femur. "On second thought, maybe I should show this to Mr. Wolent."

29

SORRY, MY BAD

Sam cheated slightly at Nerf war.

He'd gone to Daryl's place for the afternoon to hang out because Mr. Linton chose today, Wednesday the 27th of June, to open the pool. A spontaneous nerf battle developed, pitting Sam and Daryl against Ronan and Jordan. Not only did Ronan and Jordan both have blonde hair, they both wore blue swim trunks, defaulting them to being in uniform on the same team. Except for the battery operated nerf dart guns—one of which Sam used—the 'fighting' migrated in and out of the water.

Daryl's older sister Miranda sunned herself on a lounge chair in the middle of the warzone, occasionally yelling at them whenever a Nerf projectile or ball bounced off her. She'd turned fifteen a few weeks ago on the eighth and operated on the mistaken belief she'd become an adult with authority to order the boys around.

As far as cheating came into it, Blix did something to cause all the nerf darts Sam fired to reappear inside the gun a second after they came to rest on the ground, effectively giving him unlimited ammunition—until the batteries died. They didn't play any sort of organized game. No rules. No points. No winning or losing, so he didn't mind 'cheating.' Somehow, Daryl and Jordan didn't notice he'd been firing continuously without reloading once for fifteen minutes.

Jordan darted out from behind cover—an overturned picnic table —and ran sideways toward the diving board while lobbing a hand grenade (Nerf football) at Sam. By most conventional rules of boyhood, Sam was obligated to scream and dive for cover. He would have, if not for a most unusual sight.

Miranda's bikini top had disappeared.

Whoa. That's... not right.

An odd feeling made him shift his gaze left at a scrap of black fabric floating in the middle of the pool. None of his friends had gone anywhere near her, and she certainly hadn't thrown half her suit into the water. Daryl wouldn't dare prank his sister like that. Blix, as far as Sam knew, hadn't done it. He perched on the fake grass turf behind Sam, occasionally throwing Nerf balls at Jordan and Ronan.

Miranda had been a complete pain to the boys all day, screaming at them, trying to get the parents to kick them out so she could have the pool all to herself, and generally acting like a brat. He could possibly see Blix playing a trick on her as revenge for a selfish attitude, but knew he hadn't done it. Imps also *adored* embarrassing people. Disappearing clothing ranked high on their list of go-to pranks, below property destruction, serious bodily injury, and overflowing toilets.

Another reason Sam failed to follow the code and pretend to dodge a 'dangerous' hand grenade: he sensed a demonic presence in the air worse than Miranda. It seemed strongest by the end of the pool. Exactly where he sensed the presence, a three-foot-tall potbellied creature emerged from the bushes and scampered onto the diving board behind Jordan, rushing up behind him.

The Nerf football bounced off Sam's forehead the same moment the boy leapt for the water. Jordan's cheer of victory at a direct hit turned into a pitiful squeal as his swim trunks snagged on the corner of the board, pinned under the little demon's foot. All of Jordan's weight came down on his crotch when the springy diving board arrested his fall, then catapulted him back up into the air a short distance. Cackling, the demon ran away into the bushes at the back of the yard. Jordan hit the water in a fetal position and went under.

Sympathetic pain made Sam wilt on his feet. Ronan and Daryl both groaned and grabbed themselves.

Miranda sat up, screaming due to being splashed... and noticed her missing top. She screamed even louder, clamped her arms over her chest and shouted, "You little shits!"

"Blix," whispered Sam. "Fix that, please!"

"On it!" chirped the imp.

Evidently blaming Daryl for... reasons, Miranda jumped to her feet and chased him, murder in her eyes. He soon slipped on the wet 'AstroTurf' like stuff around the pool and went skidding into the fence. Miranda, shrieking in anger, began walloping him with one flip-flop, calling him every name she knew—until she noticed her swimsuit mysteriously back where it belonged. She stopped swinging, staring at herself, making the same face most people did the first time they witnessed something supernatural and couldn't come up with a way to explain it.

"What are you talking about, Ran?" Daryl lowered his arms away from his face. "No one ripped your top off. Eww. Like seriously. Who'd want to see that?"

She whacked him over the head again.

Sam dropped the Nerf gun and jumped into the water, swimming down to grab Jordan's arm. The boy had sunk to the bottom, still in a fetal position. Sam towed his friend to the surface and helped him to the side. Jordan clung to the pool's edge as Sam climbed out of the water, offering him a hand up.

"Not yet. I'm gonna just float here for now. My nuts are somewhere up behind my stomach."

Crack!

A sudden, sharp noise like a tiny pistol firing made Sam spin to the right.

Miranda teetered up on her toes, her mouth open wide as if screaming, though no sound came from her. Another little demon stood behind her, holding the wet towel it had just snapped her in the backside with. Ronan, who'd been innocently walking along the edge of the pool, stopped short, gawking at the floating towel. Except for Blix, who allowed the boy to see him, Ronan couldn't see supernatural beings. The demon tossed the wet towel at Ronan before scurrying off.

Miranda grabbed her butt, seemingly at the verge of tears from pain. A second later, she screamed and whirled—staring straight at Ronan, who hadn't moved. The boy was easily the smallest of Sam's friends. He wouldn't be ten until August, but he could pass for an eight-year-old. In that moment, he looked like a terrified field mouse staring up at the eagle diving for him. Despite not having had anything at all to do with the giant red mark on Miranda's posterior, he shrieked and ran like a guilty brat.

Fuming, Miranda chased him.

Motion at the corner of the pool caught Sam's eye. Another demon lurked behind a lounge chair, holding a long-handled pool net. In the span of a half second, Sam looked at Miranda, the net, and the metal handrail of the ladder going into the water. He knew without a doubt the demon intended to trip her and she'd hit her head on the steel curve, breaking her neck.

Crap!

He panicked for a split second, then randomly grabbed the Nerf gun and opened fire on the demon, hoping to distract it. Demons didn't react well to being seen by humans. His first nerf dart hit the small demon in the face, ripping a three-inch-wide hole all the way through its head. The second and third darts left equally huge wounds in its fat chest. Wailing, the demon fell over backward and melted into a cloud of orangey-red smoke.

Miranda chased Ronan past the pool net without tripping over it, mostly because no demon lifted it to tangle her feet.

"I didn't do it!" shouted Ronan.

Sam's swim trunks yanked downward to his ankles.

Faint growls came from behind. He calmly pulled his bathing suit back up, no one appearing to have noticed the depantsing amid the chaos. Blix and another, darker grey, imp wrestled and bit each other, rolling back and forth.

Sam pointed the Nerf gun at the bad imp.

Scrape.

A folding lounge chair slid on its own into Ronan's path. He tripped over it and went sliding on his chest across the AstroTurf. As soon as he stopped moving, he curled on his side, grabbed his pectorals, and wailed in agony.

"Hah!" Miranda held her nose in the air. "Serves you right, you little turd."

Another demon near the house picked up one of Mrs. Linton's lawn gnomes and threw it. The porcelain figure shattered over Miranda's head, knocking her senseless. She collapsed, falling sideways into the water.

"What the hell!" Daryl dove after her.

Sam narrowed his eyes, stepped on the imp's wing to pin it down, and shot it in the face, point blank. The imp's entire head exploded like a water balloon. Blix scrambled backward, then offered a nod of approval.

"Guys," yelled Daryl. "Help!" He struggled to keep his sister's head above water so she didn't drown.

Jordan still appeared to be in too much pain to pull himself out of the water. Ronan sobbed like a small child, his chest red from fake grass burns. Sam again dropped the Nerf gun and jumped in, swimming over to Miranda.

Blix flew over and helped, pulling Miranda by the hair. Between the three of them, they got her to the stairs at the shallow end where she couldn't slip underwater.

"What the hell is going on?" whispered Daryl, out of breath.

Sam figured immediate need outweighed long term secrecy. Sarah could clean it up later. "Demons are attacking us."

"Will you stop calling my sister a demon?" Daryl grumbled.

"I'm not. I mean real demons."

Ronan screamed.

Sam and Daryl twisted to look.

The skinny blonde boy floated in the air, half mummified in a garden hose doing a spot-on impression of an angry anaconda. A taller, barrel-shaped demon held the hose, apparently trying to get it around Ronan's neck.

"Okay, maybe you're right," deadpanned Daryl. "That hose is alive..."

Sam hurried over to the Nerf gun and unloaded five shots into the demon trying to kill Ronan. The instant the fiend evaporated into a smoke cloud, the hose went limp, dumping the boy to the ground.

"What did you do, Sam?" wheezed Ronan.

"Shot it."

"No, I mean, why is stuff messing with us?" Ronan detangled himself from the hose and looked at the spot where the demon had been. "I didn't know demons followed Nerf war rules."

"No idea and umm, neither did I." Sam looked over the bright orange plastic gun. "One tried to hurt Miranda. I just wanted to distract it, hoping it would freak out at someone seeing it... didn't expect to blow a big hole in it. This thing hits them like a real gun."

Grunting, Daryl dragged Miranda up to lay on the ground at the top of the pool steps. She bled a little from a cut over one eye, but didn't appear seriously hurt.

Blix ambled over to them. "The dart isn't kill. Sam kill."

"Umm, sorry." Sam glanced at the giant toy gun.

"No sorry." Blix shook his head rapidly, making his floppy ears slap back and forth. "Bad demons. Good kill."

Another demon raced out from under the deck, scurried over the small lawn, and jumped on Miranda's chest, grabbing her neck in both hands.

Sam swung the Nerf gun up, sighted, and fired three times, blasting the demon into a splatter of beige slime. The darts bounced off Miranda's chest harmlessly, hit the ground, and disappeared back into the magazine.

"Dude..." Daryl gestured at her. "She's hurt. Why are you shooting her?"

"I'm not. I'm shooting the demon trying to make her stop

breathing."

Yet another pudgy, short demon emerged from the bushes around the deck, holding a garden gnome over its head in both hands, poised to smash over Daryl's head.

"Look out!" Sam pointed.

Daryl spun in time to see the gnome fly. He got his arms up to block, sparing his skull. The force of the hit against his crossed arms made him trip over Miranda and fall into the water.

"Whoa," whispered Jordan. "Did that lawn gnome just fly?"

"Sorta." Sam chased the demon around the pool with Nerf darts. Hitting a sprinting three-foot-tall demon proved challenging. The eighteenth shot finally clipped it in the knee, blasting the leg off. Once it fell, he had little trouble shooting it twice more, destroying it. Considering the magazine only held ten darts, he wouldn't have nailed the annoying critter without the trick enchantment. "Thanks, Blix."

The imp gave a thumbs up.

Three faint pops accompanied a few more darts reappearing in the magazine.

"Hey, is your ammo trick why it's killing them?"

Blix shook his head again. "You kill. Have magic like Sophia, but linked demons. Nerf, real bullet, knife, ping pong ball, same." The imp cleared his throat. "The foam darts are a physical representation of you wanting to send the demons back to their home plane, so it works."

Sam chuckled. "You sound weird when you talk in full sentences."

Blix flashed a cheesy grin. "Make fun humans."

Sam glanced at the Nerf rifle. "So even though this is a toy, if I want to smash a demon, it works?"

Blix gave a thumb-up.

"Who are you talking to?" asked Daryl.

"Not funny," said Jordan.

Everyone looked at him. The boy still clung to the edge of the pool, only visible from the chin up.

"What's not funny?" asked Daryl.

"Which one of you buttheads stole my swimsuit?"

"I got it," chirped Blix before leaping into the air and retrieving a pair of bright yellow shorts from the roof.

"Dude. Seriously uncool," muttered Sam to no demon in particular. He sighed, shaking his head. "Guys if an imp pantses you, act like you don't care. They'll stop doing it if they don't think it bothers you."

Daryl gawked at the swim trunks seemingly flying on their own, then disappearing.

"Thanks." Sam saluted Blix.

"What is wrong with you?" Daryl nudged him. "Who are you talking to?"

"A friendly demon," said Sam before raising his voice. "Jord, look down."

Jordan peered down at himself. "What the crap? I swear they were missing a second ago." Still blushing a little, he pulled himself up out of the water and limped over to Sam, Ronan, and Daryl. "Something seriously weird is going on."

"Yeah, really. Miranda's been quiet for ten whole minutes," mumbled Sam.

"Duuuuude!" Daryl bumped his arm. "She's knocked out. We gotta call 911."

"Your sister is *not* a knockout," muttered Jordan.

Ronan shrugged. "I think she's pretty."

"Speaking completely objectively here," said Sam, "your sister is physically pretty but her personality makes her unattractive."

"Guys!" yelled Daryl, "You are—"

Clank.

A shovel bounced off his head.

Daryl collapsed to the ground, both hands clamped to the back of his skull. He whimpered, "Ow. Shit."

"Where is it?" Sam spun in a circle, Nerf gun up.

"Why are you asking us?" Ronan ducked the swinging Nerf weapon. "You're the only one who can see them."

Blix went wild-eyed, reared back, and bit Ronan on the left wrist.

"Yaaaaah!" He screamed, yanking his arm up with such force Blix flew in an arc to the pool. "Ow!"

Two little puncture wounds dribbled blood.

Sam smiled. "He did magic on you so you can see demons."

"How do you know that?" Ronan clamped his mouth over the wound.

"I dunno. I just know. Same way I just knew the demon was gonna try to kill Miranda by tripping her so she broke her neck." Sam pivoted and fired two Nerf darts into a moving bush. Something went splat. "Hah! Got one."

"Wait, so if some Blix thing bites us, we can see demons?" asked Daryl, still rubbing his head.

"Yeah." Sam scanned the yard. "It's too dangerous out here. We need to get inside and set up a defensive fortification in the living room."

"What about Miranda?" asked Daryl.

"I got her." Blix scampered over to the unconscious teen. At a snap of his fingers, the girl floated a few inches off the ground. He grasped her arm and towed her up the stairs to the deck.

Daryl and Jordan gawked at her seemingly floating off by herself.

Sam helped Daryl up. "You okay?"

"Yeah. This is seriously happening?"

"It is." Sam shrugged. "Unless we're all asleep and sharing the same crazy dream."

"Why do you always say weird stuff?" Daryl chuckled.

"I dunno." Sam grinned. "C'mon. It's too dangerous out here."

They hurried across the yard, onto the deck, and into the kitchen.

Mrs. Linton stood by the fridge, staring into space.

"Crap. Your mom's catatonic." Sam poked her. "I don't know how to fix it."

"Mom?" Daryl nudged her. "Mom?"

"She'll be fine." Sam headed to the living room. "The demons wanted parents out of the way so they could get us. You know the rules."

"What rules?" Daryl followed, Ronan and Jordan close behind.

"Haven't you seen any Eighties movies?" Sam pushed two recliners around against the couch to form a bunker. "The parents are *never* around when all the crazy stuff happens."

"We're not in an Eighties movie, though," said Jordan.

Sam folded his arms. "Four boys our age in a house with no functional parents, being watched by the annoying older sister and then something supernatural happens. We go crazy for like an hour or two trying to survive the weird stuff, then it all stops. There's a giant mess, the parents come back, and we get in a bunch of trouble because they don't believe us about the monsters."

His friends stared at him.

"Whatever is wrong with you isn't something small." Daryl patted him on the arm. "Where's my sister?"

"Behind the couch, safe." Sam climbed over the sofa.

Miranda lay on the rug behind it, now wearing a T-shirt and jeans. The other boys also pulled themselves over the sofa back into the space between it and the wall.

Daryl gawked. "What the hell? Is she messing with us? How did she change clothes?"

"Blix," said Sam, matter-of-factly.

"Oh, come on. Who's doing creepy shit to my sister?" asked Daryl.

Blix appeared on the sofa back. He snapped his fingers. Daryl's swim trunks shifted in an instant to a T-shirt and jeans. One by one, the imp put the boys back in the stuff they had on before changing to go swimming.

Daryl merely stared at himself, too stunned to speak.

"Whoa," whispered Jordan.

"Knife!" yelled Ronan.

The four boys looked up. A tall, skinny, crimson demon shaped like a stretched ferret running on its hind legs came charging in from the kitchen holding a steak knife. Sam shot it, blowing it in half at the middle.

Another one rushed down from the second floor carrying a bowling ball. Sam waited for it to reach the bottom of the steps before blowing it away so the ball didn't bounce down the stairs and make a giant hole in the wall. Ronan risked leaving the safety of the bunker long enough to grab an iron poker from the fireplace. Being able to see them, he could help defend the fort.

An increasingly frenetic army of small demons tried their damndest to inflict injury on the boys. Thanks to Blix's 'infinite ammo' magic, Sam felt like a machine-gunner in a nest, defending the front lines from an invading horde. Fortunately, the Nerf darts didn't consume themselves on contact, merely passing through the demons as if he blew holes in monsters made from bath suds.

Every so often, a sharp or hard object slipped past his onslaught of Nerf doom and hit someone in the shoulder, arm, or forehead.

Miranda gave a moan and sat up. "Where am I?"

"Ran, you okay?" asked Daryl.

"What the hell are you little shitheels doing?" She noticed her outfit changed, and turned scarlet.

"Chill." Daryl shook his head. "None of the guys did that. We're being attacked by demons. A friendly one helped protect you and changed your clothes with magic."

"Daryl, you need serious, serious help." Miranda sat up—and stared at chaos.

At least a dozen demons ran or flew around carrying anything they could find in the house heavy or sharp enough to possibly inflict injury.

"We have a freakin' poltergeist," whispered Miranda. "Holy shit. Where's my phone? I gotta put this on Insta."

"No." Sam fired Nerf darts into a flying demon trying to dive bomb at them with an electric iron. The creature exploded into smoke; the iron sailed over his head and hit the wall behind him. "No Instagram. You can't tell anyone about this."

"That's Mom's new iron." Miranda gasped. "She's gonna freak."

Something smashed in another room.

Miranda grabbed Daryl and shook him. "We are going to be in so much trouble. What did you do?"

"Nothing," yelled Daryl, Jordan, and Ronan at once.

"Sam?" asked Miranda in an accusing tone. "Is this your fault?"

"I don't know. If it is, it's because something's mad at me for unrelated reasons. Not because I did something wrong."

"Why would anything be mad at you if you didn't do anything wrong?" A tiny plate shattered over Miranda's head. She fell to the floor, clutching the spot. "Ow!"

Sam fired as fast as the Nerf gun could unload darts. Billiard balls, books, plates, golf clubs, and all sorts of dangerous junk continued flying at them. Ronan swung the fire poker back and forth, trying to swat incoming projectiles away.

"Blix, do I need the nerf gun or can I just do it?"

The imp murmured an inconclusive noise.

Sam glared at a demon, trying to make it go back to wherever it belonged. Nothing happened. "Guess not." He shot it, blasting it apart into a puddle of beige goo—for a second. At least the demons evaporated to smoke and didn't make a mess.

Jordan stayed down, holding a serving tray over his head as a shield. "Should we try taking out a Oujia board?"

Sam felt like a character in *Call of Duty*, blowing enemies away as they mindlessly charged their defensive fortification. The whiny electric motor in the toy gun started to sound labored. "Crap. Batteries are going."

"Ouija boards not work," said Blix. "Sometimes, spirits or demons prank people when they Ouija, but it not board work. Game made by toy factory."

"The heck did he say?" asked Ronan.

Sam translated while continuing to shoot. "Dar, need more batteries. This thing's gonna crap out soon."

"Uhh, my dad keeps batteries in the kitchen. There's a thing on the wall."

Ronan stood, making a face like a soldier volunteering for a suicide mission. "I'll go. If I don't come back, tell my mom and bro I love them."

Daryl and Jordan chuckled.

Ronan scrambled over the couch, swatting the fire poker at a few demons on the way to the kitchen. Sam kept shooting.

"So, Oujia boards are worthless?" asked Jordan. "Really?"

Blix held up a finger. "Witchwood board. Letters and numbers engraved bones of a murderer. Planchette made from skull of murder or sacrifice victim, contains a small amount of deconsecrated blood, then work."

"Uhh, eww," muttered Sam. "I don't think my parents would allow me to have that. Besides, yuck. I don't want it. Way too evil."

Blix nodded. "Agree. Definitely not good idea. Any human who use real Ouija go insane, possessed, and then die. You no touch real one. No witchwood with bones of killer."

"Promise. Won't happen." Sam pulled the trigger. The Nerf gun struggled to spit out a dart.

Ronan screamed in fear.

"Ro!" shouted Sam.

"Imps!" yelled Ronan, before giving a pained wail. "I'm okay! Just a nuclear wedgie."

Two short, fat demons leapt off the top of the stairs carrying giant plastic totes. They flew on stubby wings to the floor near the hall leading to the kitchen and dumped out a massive quantity of Lego bricks.

Sam gasped, realizing none of them had shoes on. "Minefield! Ro! Be careful." He gunned down the vicious little fiends, both of which burst into a shower of red slime before fading to smoke.

Ronan limped into view, saw the field of Legos, and made a 'Well, this is it. This is where I die' face. "There's no way I'm getting past that alive, but I gotta try."

Sam gave his best melodramatic, "Nooooo!" as his friend forged ahead into the deadly hazard.

Flailing his arms and gasping, Ronan braved a twenty-foot-swath of Lego while barefoot. He did his best to avoid stepping on them, but his attempt at care only slowed him down and made him an easy target for demons throwing books, knives, tennis balls, and whatever else they could get their hands on.

Sam concentrated fire on demons using the most dangerous weapons. Ronan collapsed to all fours, feet curled in pain with multiple Legos stuck to his soles. He dragged himself the rest of the way to the bunker sofa. Jordan and Daryl reached over the top, grabbed his arms, and hauled him in to safety. Ronan rolled on his back, his body limp, and shakily held up two C-cell batteries.

"I… got 'em," rasped Ronan, before pretending to die.

Sam took the batteries and 'reloaded' the nerf gun.

Daryl nudged Ronan. "Don't make me give you mouth-to-mouth."

Ronan sat up, laughing. Then cringed, and plucked a few Lego bricks off his feet. "Ow."

"Un-be-leeev-able." Miranda shook her head. "You guys are weird."

A steak knife stuck into the wall beside her head.

She screamed and ducked, curling up on the floor behind the sofa.

Sam translated what Blix said about Ouija boards to the guys as he resumed shooting the endless army of demons, starting with knife thrower. "I don't know why anyone would make one if they're so bad."

"People don't make." Blix smiled sheepishly. "Bad demons make. Trick humans to use."

"Bad demons… who are these losers, anyway?" Sam grumbled.

A stronger presence manifested at the center of the living room. All the demons skidded to a stop, dropped their 'weapons,' and ran, disappearing into cabinets, drawers, closets, and up the stairs.

Olmaz stepped out from a column of grey smoke, ducking to keep his tall, straight horns from punching holes in the ceiling. "Human dwellings are so annoyingly short."

"Olmaz." Sam stood up, grinning.

Ronan waved at him, also smiling.

"Sorry, Samuel. My bad." Olmaz gestured at the chaos. "These cockroaches were summoned by the entity responsible for Mel being trapped in a jar. He is somewhat annoyed at you for freeing her. My fault entirely. I shall go deal with the problem."

"Oh." Sam stood, letting the Nerf gun hang at his side. "No problem."

"Least I can do is clean up around here so you don't get in trouble." Olmaz smiled.

"Awesome. Thanks. Umm, question."

The tall demon paused. "Hmm?"

"Why did this guy send imps and daemons? Stealing our bathing suits and snapping towels isn't gonna seriously hurt anyone. Is he trying to kill us for revenge or just be a butthead?"

Olmaz pulled his clawed fingers down his beard, contemplating. "I believe the expectation for the apparel pilfering was twofold: one, humans panic and stop thinking when highly embarrassed. Sudden exposure in public is only slightly less effective than being lit on fire for causing people to run around randomly into hazardous situations. Two, they likely expected you would jump in the water for cover, where you would be easier to drown."

"Oh, I understand that stuff. I mean, why send little daemons and imps instead of full demons or something seriously dangerous?" Sam held his arms out to either side. "I'm not complaining. Just curious. Doesn't seem like he really wanted to kill anyone."

Olmaz chuckled. "Budget cutbacks."

In an instant, Sam found himself treading water in the pool, once more in swim trunks. Ronan floated next to him, giving him a 'did that just happen' eyebrow. Daryl ran to the back corner of the yard to retrieve a stray Frisbee while Jordan appeared clueless anything unusual happened. Miranda lay on the folding lounge chair as before, still frowning over the boys 'messing up' her sunbathing time. The cut above her eye had vanished.

Blix did a backstroke past Sam and Jordan, paddling his tail for extra propulsion.

"Yeah," whispered Sam. "We didn't imagine that."

"Okay. So, I'm not nuts." Ronan fake wiped sweat from his forehead.

"Nope. Not nuts."

"Nerf war!" shouted Jordan—exactly as he'd done about ten minutes before the chaos erupted.

Ronan leaned closer to Sam, whispering, "Did Olmaz send us back in time?"

"Looks like it. Don't ask questions. Just run with it." Sam swam for the edge. "Dibs on the orange rifle!"

30

FAREWELL TO THE SUN

Wednesday makes two normal days in a row.

The girls went over Nicole's for most of the day. I did Mom a favor and ran Sophia to dance class, then back home for dinner. She's still acting a little off. Don't want to make her feel worse, so I bide my time. When she's ready, she'll tell me what's bothering her. She can't not. It's part of who she is.

Sam spent the day at Daryl's. Apparently, they opened their pool today. If you ask me, it's still a touch chilly for swimming but, boys… right? I said normal, didn't I. Sam had a heck of a story about what happened at Daryl's. Turns out, Olmaz didn't rewind time, merely set everyone up back as they'd been earlier and altered memories. Sam and Ronan remembered everything, while the other boys and one bossy older sister remained clueless. Fortunately, demon magic un-broke all the smashed objects and fixed various gouges and holes in the wall. It's probably kinda weird for demons to *undo* chaos. It's like imagining Sophia getting violent or breaking the law.

Anyway, it doesn't sound like it's going to be much of a problem. Whatever entity is upset at Sam for letting Mel out sounds pretty lame if he sent weak daemons after my brother. I'm starting to wonder if demons really did get something of a distorted reputation from humans. They don't sound so evil and fearsome as much as a bunch of beered-up frat brothers with magical powers, poor impulse control, and a limited ability to comprehend the consequences of their actions beforehand. Oh, I've just described boys in general, except for the magic powers.

As for me, I had a nice afternoon hanging out with Ashley and Michelle. Well, not really afternoon as much as evening. My friends both had to work until six. We went out for food, hit the mall, and basically tried to act like high school kids again. Hey, we only have four more years where summer break is even remotely a thing. Gotta enjoy it while possible. My friends will soon be part of the real world and have to work all year round, no longer getting a vacation for three months. 'Course, ever since sophomore year in high school, we had summer jobs so it really didn't feel like a total break. Michelle's putting in serious time at the law firm this summer and Ashley's gone up to full time hours at the vet clinic until school starts again. My friends are impersonating adults if not in salary or responsibility, but time being drained by work. Me? I'm still the lazy ass. No job for me.

Unless being part of Wolent's organization counts as a job. Maybe it does.

We retreat to Ash's place and throw on a movie. Sadly, my friends are both unconscious before midnight. So much for 'let's stay up late and watch a movie, even though we all know it's a bad idea.' I lay on the sofa between them, watching the last twenty minutes of *Vampire Academy*. Yeah, my friends have a sense of humor.

Soon after the credits start rolling, Michelle stirs. She realizes the movie's over and it's almost midnight, and drags herself up. "I really gotta get going. Need to be at the firm tomorrow morning."

"Okay." I sit up. "You look exhausted. I'll drive you."

"I can dri—nah. You're right. I'm half awake and the room's spinning." Michelle fumbles around for her shoes.

Ash is out cold, so I pat her on the head and whisper, "Night."

Michelle's so yawny and wobbly on her feet, I have to help her stay upright on the way out to her car. I steer her to the passenger side, help her in, and give her a mental poke to sleep. Doesn't take me long to drive to her house, park the car, and carry her up to her bed. Mere seconds after I go out her window to fly home, my phone rings.

Oh, it's Amy. I hover to a stop and answer. "Hey, what's up?"

"Girl, this dude you left here is *seriously* depressing. He thinks he's evil and shouldn't exist. Keeps moping around talking about how he misses the sun."

I chuckle. "Sounds exactly the same as he was in high school, only he hadn't been a real vampire then."

She whistles. "I'm serious. The guy didn't even want to feed. We had to tell him if he didn't do it, he'd end up losing control and hurting people."

"I already explained that to him." I rake a hand up through my hair. Argh.

"Since he kinda knows you from before, think you could try talking to him? He's not gonna last long if he keeps going like this."

Hmm. My thoughts drift to the exploding vampire at the gas station. Brady might not last long regardless of what he does or doesn't do… He might only still exist because he's never tried to use any powers. The gas station exploder attempted to make himself stronger and the power drain consumed him. Death is one thing when it's a total stranger. Granted, I don't really know Brady beyond seeing him every day for four years—summer break not included. He's somewhere between stranger and a person I know. It would freak me out if someone I kinda-sorta knew (of) explodes.

"Yeah, sure. Be right there."

"Cool. Hope I'm not interrupting."

"Nah, my plans were kind of up in the air."

"Hah. Great. Okay. See you soon."

I gaze down past my sneakers at a nice lawn. Flying really is cool.

THE LOCAL LOST ONES, OR AT LEAST THE THREE I KNOW, ARE IN MID conversation when I arrive.

Dante thinks they should 'just go out' and let Brady stay here if he doesn't want to join them. Luke's uncomfortable leaving him alone for fear he'll do something stupid to himself. Amy's torn. She's referring to Dante as 'Mike,' which means she's annoyed. The guy's real name *is* Mike. He changed it post-vampirism since he thought his birth name sounded 'lame' for a creature of the night. Luke sometimes calls him 'Count Mike-u-la' to get a rise out of him if he's being moody.

As soon as I walk in, Dante grabs me by the shoulders and 'gently shoves' me toward Amy. "There. Problem solved. Babysitter's here."

Amy catches me in a brief hug.

"I don't need a damn babysitter," drones Brady from the couch.

"Dude." Amy sighs. "You've been talking about being an abomination that shouldn't be allowed to exist for the past three days. Sorry if you're upset we're actually concerned about you."

"Hey, if you guys wanna go party somewhere, I can hang with Brady. It's cool. Least I can do." I fist-bump Luke and Dante, then sit on the armrest of the sofa. Brady's crashed there looking hung over.

"He needs to get out there and do stuff." Luke nods at the door. "See if you can talk some sense into him."

Brady gives me this 'sorry they dragged you into it' eyeroll. "Hey."

"Hey. So, what's up?"

"Nothing's 'up.' I'm dead."

"Is that the problem? Little guy won't listen?"

Amy, Dante, and Luke snicker.

Brady groans. "Really? I thought only guys made stupid dick jokes."

"To be fair," says Dante, "you did kinda emphasize the word 'up.' Anyone'd take it the way she took it."

"Come on..." Brady exhales. "There's more to life than hanging out, partying, going to concerts, and having sex."

"Maybe so." Luke chuckles. "But ain't none of that other shit worth worryin' about."

"What's wrong?" I ask.

"What's wrong? Seriously?" Brady pushes himself up to sit. "Everything is wrong. I'm dead. I can't tolerate sunlight. I'll never see the sky again during the day. Everyone who knows me thinks I'm missing."

"Those are all valid things to be upset about." I flick a lint ball off the leg of my jeans. "Have you spent any time thinking about the good parts?"

"Being a killer?" Brady scoffs.

"Nah. Vampires aren't killers. Sure, we're predators, but we don't need to kill our food. How many people out there would give anything to stop getting old? We'll never get sick. No cancer. No diabetes, no—"

"We *can't* get diabetes because we can't eat any freakin' real food," yells Brady. "I'm seriously fiending for a goddamned Hostess cupcake right now. I love those things. They're little bundles of awesomeness."

"And an express train to the beetus," mutters Dante.

"Not in moderation." Brady sighs. "I didn't eat tons of them."

I squirm, a tad guilty since I can eat real food and fly. Can't say for sure if the inability to consume food would bother me. Since doing so for fun is still an option for me, it's difficult for me to sympathize. Closest I've come to violently throwing up everything I try to eat was a bad stomach virus at fourteen. And yeah, those two weeks *sucked*. If normal vampirism reacts like that to standard food, then yeah, he deserves to be upset. He doesn't look like he's suffering the cold sweats though. Hmm. He's probably a Scion, so... not really sure what they're known for. They evolved from Old Guard, so perhaps similar.

"You're strong, fast, tough... you'll eventually develop some other cool powers totally out of my reach."

Brady shrugs. "I don't want powers. What I want is not to be an evil monster."

"You're not. Stop thinking you're defined by your physical existence. Being a vampire doesn't mean you have to act a certain way or do certain things."

"I have to drink freakin' blood from people. That's kinda required."

Dante makes a silent 'ooh, bitchy' gesture.

"Yeah, but so what. They don't remember anything and it doesn't hurt them unless *you* decide to do it wrong." I tell him about my first feeding and how awkward it had been to get close to a total stranger and bite, only to taste pizza. "You really do get used to it. Doesn't bother me at all anymore to give hickeys to people I've never seen before."

Amy laughs.

"Do you think of people like walking cupcakes?" asks Brady.

"Only if they're in a giant foam cupcake costume."

"You know what I mean." He does the epic goth-emo eye roll. "Are they still people to you or merely food?"

"Still people. You're being melodramatic. Being a vampire is really awesome. I'm serious."

Brady smirks. "Easy for you to say. You went home to your family."

"She's one in a million," says Amy. "Almost none of us ever do that."

"It opens you up for a ton of problems." Luke shakes his head. "Sarah wouldn't have done it if she knew then what she knows now."

I point at him. "No way. I might do a few little things differently, but I'd still absolutely go home. Knowing what I know now also includes the knowledge my family would have basically imploded if I'd let them believe me dead. Yeah, shit's crazy as hell now, but it's good crazy. And we're really close."

Brady buries his face in his hands. "I used to be so angry at my parents for wanting me to stop dressing Goth, act normal, try to get into a big-name college, get a fancy job. They hated everything I liked: music, fashion, girls."

"They hate girls?" asked Luke. "Weird."

"No, man." Brady sighs. "No girl I dated was ever good enough for them. They'd always find something to complain about and tell me being with her would be wasting my life."

"A lot of parents can be like that." Luke takes a joint out of his coat pocket and sniffs it. "Uptight rich folks."

"We aren't rich. Middle class. Maybe upper middle class. I dunno." Brady grinds his face into his palms. "Now, I don't care how much they complained. All I want to do is go home. I never even got a chance to tell them what happened or say goodbye. I can't be this evil creature."

I put a hand on his shoulder. "You're thinking about it all wrong. This is like the most awesome thing ever. C'mon, man. I used to think those 'oh, poor me, I'll never see the sun again' emo vamps were just a Hollywood thing."

Dante barks a laugh. "Easy for you to say, girl."

I chuckle. "Fair, but I still love being a vampire. This is seriously cool. Never asked for it, but shiz happened and here I am."

"Heh." Dante shakes his head. "Nah, girl. 'Shiz' don' work for you. You're way too 'suburban white girl.'"

"Ouch. Okay." I fake roll my eyes. "Fair point. I cringe whenever my dad quotes rap songs."

Everyone except Brady chuckles.

I glance over at them. "Do you guys ever miss the sun?"

"Kinda." Amy shrugs. "But I'm over it. At first, it bothered me since I'd always been such an ordinary 'good girl,' but I'm used to it now."

"Never gave it much thought." Dante shrugs.

"What is, is." Luke sniffs the joint again. "Don't much care about the sun, but I damn sure wouldn't mind bein' able to smoke up again. Damn pain in the ass having to give this wonderfulness to a mortal, get them baked as hell, then feed on them. An' even then, it don't last near long enough."

"You poor, deprived man." Dante claps him on the shoulder. "Takes a half a trunk load to get him high these days, plus about ten people smoking it."

Amy mouths 'nowhere near that much' at me.

"Yeah. Only good thing is, I don't gotta pay for none of it." Luke again takes a long sniff, dragging the joint under his nose. "Ain't never smelled so good when I's alive, neither. Damn, talk about unfair."

Blink. "Hey, wait a second."

Everyone stares at me.

"Waiting," says Luke, pausing in mid sniff.

Heh. "Everyone's going nuts looking for the source of the noob invasion. I might be able to cheat and find it."

Amy, Luke, and Dante shrug, roll their eyes, and murmur. They couldn't care less if anyone finds the guy or girl doing this.

"You guys don't care this could cause a crapstorm for us all if our existence gets out?" I ask.

"Nah." Dante waves dismissively. "No one will ever believe it because it's true. People out there only believe dumb shit some idiot makes up in their mother's basement. Like vaccines causing autism or being some kinda secret government plan to track people. Say some shit like that, some people believe it. Say something true, they laugh and ignore it."

Amy snort-laughs. "If someone tries to put video or pictures of a 'real' vampire on the internet, it's gonna get shredded. In between comments telling the person who posted it to do random sexual things to farm animals, everyone's gonna be saying 'fake' or 'special effects' or 'video editing.' People don't want to believe in the supernatural."

"She's right." Luke tucks the joint back in the breast pocket of his Army jacket. "Post vids about ghosts, light orbs, aliens, any of that stuff, it's gonna get laughed at. Won't take the information ministry long at all to make it go away."

"Uhh, what?" I scrunch my nose. "The information ministry?"

Luke waves his hand around at random. "Whatever vamps are out there working to keep us secret."

"Tinfoil hat stuff isn't limited to mortals." Dante winks. "Luke here thinks there's a secret order of vampires who go around like dudes from that *Men in Black* movie. Next time you're on YouTube search for 'real men in black' and so forth."

"Most of those sightings are during the day, though." Amy smirks. "They're not vampires, whatever they are."

I take Brady's hand. "Forget about Men in Black. I need you to go somewhere with me."

"I don't even really know you." Brady shrugs. "Is this a date?"

"No. You'd be helping possibly stop a giant poop storm and maybe help stop a bunch of other random people from being turned into vampires against their will."

He looks down, most of his face hidden behind an unruly mop of black. "If it will stop anyone else from having to go through this, sure."

The Lost Ones all shake their heads in unison. Dante mouths 'lost cause.'

I tug Brady to his feet. "C'mon. It'll be fun."

31

OUTSIDE THE SYSTEM

One could say it's a bit presumptuous of me to think I have a chance to solve a problem all the vampires of Seattle have thus far been unable to. Maybe so. But I have two possible advantages the rest of the vampires don't.

We exit the apartment building and walk to the curb. I pull my phone out and open the Uber app. Brady chuckles.

"What?"

"Just find it funny a vampire's using Uber. No horse and carriage?"

"Are you serious?"

"No." He sorta smiles. "Still weird you don't have a car. If being a vampire is so awesome, why not use your mind powers to steal one?"

"There's no way to tell you the truth without making you more depressed, so can I stay quiet?"

"You couldn't make me more depressed."

"Are you really depressed or just playing a Goth on TV?"

He shrugs. "Sometimes I lose track. Not really sure... I do want to go home, though. How much trouble would it really cause if I did?"

"A lot of it depends on how your parents react. Mine took it well. Not every parent would. My friend Michelle? Her parents are so religious they'd probably try to kill her if she revealed herself to be a vampire."

He whistles. "Wow. She lives with them and they'd kill her if they knew?"

"No. She's mortal."

"Whoa. You have mortal friends?"

"Yeah. As I said, my life is complicated. How do you think your parents would react?"

"Heh. Dad would accuse me of doing it on purpose as the 'next phase of Goth.'"

I shake from silent laughter while finishing up summoning the Uber. "Wow. Well... once we're done, if you want to go talk to them, I'll tag along to erase their minds if they freak out. Won't know how they'll react until you try."

"So, what were you gonna say that would depress me?"

"I *do* have a car. It's old and I didn't need to use mind control to get it. Also, the reason my car isn't here is because I usually fly."

"Fly..." He blinks.

I float up off the ground briefly. "Yes, fly. Not every vamp can. I've heard it's pretty lucky for me to have considering my bloodline. I'm like the slowest possible flyer in the vampire kingdom. Glim makes me feel like an old lady with a walker trying to chase a speeding car."

"Seriously? Flying. That's so... out there."

"And vampires aren't?" I snap my fingers. "Oh, hey, another plus. We can see and talk to ghosts. Didn't you and your friends start a paranormal club or something?"

"Yeah. Got some EVPs. Nothing real decent though. Mostly, we went to creepy places late at night and freaked each other out."

We get to talking about high school and how it felt completely different to each of us. A blue Honda pulls up—our Uber—so we transplant the conversation to the backseat. I had a tiny group of friends and mostly got ignored by the school as a whole. Brady hung out with a larger group of friends, but they usually suffered stares, ridicule, avoidance, or occasionally ended up in trouble with the administration for simply being goths. Once, they even had the cops called on them for wearing long coats. Someone thought they might be hiding guns.

"I think I remember that…" I whistle. "Locked down the school, but never told us why."

"Such bullshit." Brady scowls. "We didn't do anything wrong, but they grilled us for like an hour over where the guns were. Searched our lockers, dragged us home, searched the house. My dad was pissed. Almost sued the school."

"Damn. I'm sorry." I nibble on my lip.

Hearing this, it somewhat makes sense why he's so emo over becoming a vampire. He's used to being ostracized for being different. One could say he always had the choice to dress like everyone else and stop being goth, but why the hell does society think it has the right to force people to act a certain way? Now, he's stuck as a vampire and probably thinking it's going to be more of the same.

Can't talk about vamp stuff until we're out of the car.

"Not your fault. People are dicks."

Brady and I keep talking about random crap for the fortyish minutes it takes the driver to reach my house. We'd never work as a dating couple. For example, I've never heard of any of the bands he likes and he's never watched anime. Upon arriving home, I pay the driver via the app, thank him for the ride, and drag Brady inside.

"Don't get any ideas, but you're only the second boy to see my bedroom."

He laughs. "So, wow. Seriously. You went home. This is the place you grew up?"

"Yeah." I lead him across to the kitchen and downstairs. "My bedroom used to be upstairs. Had to move it for sun reasons."

"Makes sense."

As soon as he walks into my room, he stares at the stuffed animals on the bed. "You are kidding."

"Huh?"

He points. "You're a vampire with an army of cute stuffed animals on your bed."

"So? Remember how I said being a vampire doesn't make you a

killer? It also doesn't make anyone into a black-clothing-obsessed doom queen."

"Sarah, how does going to your bedroom help us stop other people from being vamped?"

"Working on it." Time to test possible advantage number one. "Coralie? Are you around? It'd be super amazing if you could pop in for a bit."

Cue fifteen seconds of Brady and me awkwardly standing there staring at each other, not talking.

Coralie sinks into view out of the ceiling. "Hello, Sarah. I was already here."

"Holy shit." Brady jumps back. "A ghost."

She laughs.

"He's new. Don't mind him." I pat him on the back. "Can you tell who his sire is?"

"Hmm." Coralie regards him for a long moment. "Alas. This is not something possible for me to discern. My suggestion would be to try divination."

"The heck is divination?" asks Brady.

I fold my arms. Drat. "Crystal balls, reading tea leaves, tarot, that sort of thing."

He snickers. "So, totally scientific."

"Says the vampire," I mutter.

"Ugh. True." He gazes at the ceiling. "Crap. This is really real."

"It is," says Coralie.

Well, I still have my second possible advantage. Figured it might come down to magic. "Sec."

Coralie and Brady get into a conversation, mostly about the early 1800s and her being a former mystic while I send Darren Anderson a text.

‹Hi. Are you awake and do you have time for a question?›

‹U caught me preparing for bed. If it's short, ask away.›

‹Can you divine a V to determine the sire?›

‹Possibly, but it involves blood magic we have neither tried nor are willing to risk. I strongly advise you not to involve Sophia. Blood magic goes dark extremely quickly, especially with impressionable minds. It is tapdancing on the edge of an abyss while wearing roller skates.›

Argh. Dammit. ‹Okay. Thanks. Def will not bother Soph.›

"Drat."

Coralie and Brady look at me.

"Mystics can't help. They say finding a sire requires blood magic. Is it true using blood magic is a dangerous, dark path?"

Coralie nods. "Yes. Even my husband refused to touch it."

"I didn't realize your husband was dark."

"*You* would call him so. Back then, he would have been considered average. In those days, most mystics dabbled in whatever, unconcerned at consequences. My husband's problem involved wanting power by any means necessary, but he did have lines he wouldn't cross. Pity one of those lines wasn't killing me."

Brady makes an 'oh, daaaaamn' face.

"Hmm." I tap my foot. Aww, hell. So much for my advantages. Hang on. I look up at the ceiling. "One more idea. Wait here a sec."

I fly up to the second floor and hover—not literally—outside Sam's room.

"Blix?" I whisper. "Are you awake?"

The imp opens the door a moment later, PlayStation headphones hanging loose around his neck. Behind him, Sam's room flickers in various shades of blue from the monitor. My brother is thoroughly asleep. Aww. He looks so innocent when his eyes are closed.

"*Eieboo?*" asks Blix in a high-pitched voice like a thoroughly baked Gremlin.

"Might be a long shot, but do you have any way to tell who sired a vampire?"

Blix rubs his chin, one eye huge, the other narrow. His eyes switch sizes twice as he thinks. "*Nerble marfat.*"

"Uhh, right."

Blix nods once, then gives me a weaselly look before pointing at the PlayStation.

"You can do it, but it will require a tribute of a new game?"

He nods again.

"Sure. No problem."

Blix tilts his head, holds his fingers up to mimic fangs, then shrugs.

"Down in my room. I need to find the vampire who turned Brady."

"*Neeb nobu.*" Blix zooms off down the hall. The headphones snap back into Sam's room due to being on a wire, and land on the rug.

I gingerly shut Sam's door and hurry after the imp.

When I walk into my room, it's damn hard not to laugh. Brady's standing on my desk like a 1950s housewife freaked out by a mouse, pointing at Blix.

He looks at me. "What the heck is that?"

"Please don't call Blix an it. He's an imp. A minor demon. If you want to get technical, he's a daemon."

"What the freakin' heck is going on in this house?" Brady stares at me.

"Remember when I said going home to live with my family created certain issues and complications? I wasn't talking about vampire politics. Shiz has been weird."

Blix looks up at me and makes a throat-cutting gesture.

Ugh, everyone's a critic. Guess he agrees with Dante.

"He can help find the vampire who turned you. If we can find them, we can stop them from ambushing anyone else."

Blix flies up to Brady, who whimpers but holds totally still as though a highly venomous snake sniffed at him. After a few minutes of looking, some additional sniffing, and one brief taste, Blix walks out of the room, waving for me to follow.

Brady wipes his cheek. "He licked me."

"Imps do that sometimes. It's a sign of affection. Come on."

Blix pauses to give me a 'really?' look, then resumes gliding across the basement. He leads us upstairs to Sam's room, heads over to the closet, and opens it. Not sure how many boys have a full-length mirror on the inside of their closets, but the house came with it. The imp runs his claws down the glass, not scratching it. Reflection changes to a view of another place, a dark black-and-white hallway like something straight out of a haunted mental asylum movie.

"Oh crap. He's taking us *to* the sire. Hang on. Be right back. Gonna go get my sword."

"You have a sword?" asks Brady. "And whoa. There's a little kid in the bed."

"My brother."

Blix babbles.

"The heck did he say?" whispers Brady.

"He said you're just like Sierra," mumbles Sam from the bed in a half-awake voice.

"Huh?" I ask. "How so?"

Blix rambles.

"Wanting to go get a sword before going into a portal," says Sam.

"Sierra went into a portal?" I blink.

"Uh oh," mutters Blix, then babbles rapidly at Sam.

"He says it's nothing bad. She and Soph were just testing something."

I cringe. "Yeah, that usually doesn't go very well. And why are you awake at this hour?"

"Gotta pee. Was gonna wait for you to leave first but…" Sam sits up. "Since you know I'm up, it doesn't matter."

Brady stares at Sam. "Wow. You really *did* go home, didn't you?"

"Yeah."

"Why does he smell like chocolate cupcakes?" whispers Brady.

I rest my hand on his shoulder. "Unless you're one of the weirdoes who enjoys the flavor of blood, kids typically smell and taste like stuff we consider desserts or candy. Also, if your fangs make contact with any of my siblings, your head will end up in your colon."

Brady leans back, hands up. "Chill. I hate the idea of biting adults. No way am I gonna hurt a kid."

"Who's this guy?" Sam slides out of bed to stand. "He doesn't look like your type."

"He's not. We're working together to stop an idiot."

Sam nods, yawns, then walks past us out to the hallway.

"Your family is like cool with you being a vampire?" Brady gazes around the room. "Wow."

"Considering what the alternative would have been, yeah."

"Beyond cool," says Sam from the hallway. "Sarah is awesome."

"Give me one sec." I walk out. "Just gonna grab my sword real quick."

ONE HORROR MOVIE SET AFTER ANOTHER

ll things considered, Brady tolerates crossing mirrors in
stride.

As much as becoming a vampire messed with his head,
it's kinda bizarre for him to brush off proof of alternate dimensions
like no big deal. Hey, if nothing else, it seems to have distracted him
from feeling all emo about himself. Blix leads us across the
mirrorverse, most of which takes on the appearance of abandoned
medical buildings. Some bits of furniture or windows look like they're
from the 1940s. Others are more modern, but highly creepy.
Generally, it's fairly ordinary except for the six-foot-long pillbugs
crawling by on the ceiling and a handful of partially molten bodies
fused into the walls.

By ordinary, I mean there aren't any gravity-defying stairwells
straight out of an MC Escher drawing this time. No shattering sky
raining broken glass, and no large anthropomorphic mice who want
to eat us. The giant pillbugs are pretty trippy, though.

I think having Blix here makes the mirrorworld much tamer.

We roam various creepy hallways, operating rooms, patient wards,
and a giant dark chamber full of industrial boilers. I'm sure hospital
boiler rooms often have thousands of long ass chains randomly

hanging from the ceiling. The clinking as we move among them is pretty damn eerie. If I wasn't a vampire, I'd be scared.

At the end of the boiler room from hell, we enter a massive bathroom. It's stark white, like a dream sequence from a tech noir movie. A long shelf sink on the left stretches to a ridiculous distance with over thirty individual basins and faucets. The wall above it is all mirror. Gotta hand it to Blix, he's making it easy. No need to squeeze through any tiny spaces.

Naturally, the giant mirror is not reflecting the overly white room. It's dark and grungy on the other side, but still looks like a commercial bathroom of some kind. Blix jumps into the mirror, or rather, open hole. I follow, as does Brady.

As soon as I experience a faint sense of passing a squishy membrane, a horrible smell blasts me in the face. It's a combination of rotting trash, mold, dead animals, and urine. The room we enter is also a large bathroom, and this one is definitely not white. Might have once been, but it's long since decayed past saving. The shelf sink on this side is much more reasonable, only six faucets. None of it looks operable. It's a men's room, obvious from the wall urinals. Spray paint graffiti on the walls offers more proof we're no longer in the mirror universe but back in reality. Can't tell if it's English, but since we only spent about fifteen minutes inside the mirror, I'm sure we couldn't have gone *too* far.

Blix heads out of the bathroom.

I follow into a large hallway. Out here, the smell improves. It's merely mold, wetness, and some odd antiseptic chemical. Hundreds of doors on both sides look like patient rooms in a hospital. Gurneys, wheelchairs, IV stands, and pushcarts litter the area. This place has clearly been abandoned for at least twenty years, but it doesn't feel like we're alone. I'm starting to get the impression the mirrorverse takes on aspects of the intended destination—if there is one. Maybe the craziness we experienced last time happened due to us not having any particular endpoint in mind.

"What is this place?" I whisper. "Damn, this might be a bad idea. We've walked into a horror movie too scary for me to watch."

Blix babbles, grinning at me.

"He says you sound like Sophia," says my little brother from behind us.

I spin to stare at Sam. He's leaning out from the bathroom, one hand gripping the doorjamb. The boy is still wearing his Iron Man pajamas... and he's barefoot. "What the hell are you doing following us into a place like this?"

"You need me to translate Blix."

"This place is filthy. You don't have any shoes on."

Sam holds up his sneakers, which he'd been concealing behind his back. "Didn't have a chance to put them on. Had to hurry to stay close enough to Blix to follow you guys."

"This is dangerous. Go back to bed."

"You want me to go into the mirror alone?" Sam raises an eyebrow. "Really dangerous to go alone. Having no one to talk to makes it way easier for the place to get into your head and make you go crazy. It's safer here. Besides, if it gets serious, I can ask Mel for help. She's really nice. And she's super happy we let her out of the jar."

"Huh? Who's Mel, and are you being literal about a jar?" asks Brady.

"No time to explain." I facepalm. "Okay, fine. I can't send you to the mirrorverse alone, but you are to stay close to me. If this vampire isn't in a talking mood, you run before anything gets dangerous."

Sam nods.

"Wait. You're seriously bringing a little kid into a place like this?" asks Brady.

Blix rambles.

Sam laughs. "He said you did, too. On a ghost hunt. Ariana?"

Blix chirps and chatters, talking to my brother.

"Kid sister of the girl you dated at the time." Sam grins. "That kid was younger than me."

"A ghost hunt is way different than going into a place where a vampire lives." Brady exhales.

"It's not fine, but it's fine." I rub the bridge of my nose. "Sam's been in the middle of vampire BS before."

Blix points ahead and mutters to Sam, who says, "The guy who turned Brady is in here. Oh, please don't tell Mom I snuck after you."

"Are you crazy? She'd totally ground me for bringing my nine—I mean ten-year-old brother into a creepy abandoned hospital after midnight."

Sam grins. "You have my silence. I won't tell her."

Sigh.

Blix salutes, warbling, "*Eem oo.*"

"He said 'mine, too'." Sam pulls his sneakers on.

"Brady, how are you at fighting?" I start down the hallway in the direction Blix pointed.

"Umm, okay I guess. Haven't really gotten into too many fights. I mean, I got my ass kicked a lot in school. Wouldn't call any of them fights. Four, five, six on one isn't really a fight." He eyes the katana. "You know how to use that?"

"Yeah."

"Seriously?"

"Yes. I'd be better off using a single-edged blade balanced slightly tip-heavy, like a falchion or cutlass. Maybe even a longsword—but those are double-edged. Katana's a little light for my style. Requires different techniques. But I can fake it enough treating it as a light saber."

"Like from Star Wars?" Brady chuckles.

"No, dork. Light as in the opposite of heavy." I swing the sheathed blade around in a few basic movements.

"Ooo kay." Brady golf claps. "Guess you do know what you're doing."

"You've got claws," I say.

He stares at me. "I do?"

"Yes, you do. You had them out the night I saw you chasing the security guard."

Brady looks down at his hands. "How do they work?"

"Wow. This guy's really new, isn't he?" asks Sam.

"It's super difficult. Think about having claws and wanting them to grow long and sharp."

Brady's fingernails creak slightly, and elongate to three-inch talons. "Whoa. Umm, okay. Doesn't work on toenails does it?"

"Eww." I shiver. "Never tried. Not going to. Okay. Gotta admit it feels weird being the oldest. Let me worry about the fighting part if it comes to that. Your job is to play goalie and watch Sam."

"Okay."

A hollow metallic clatter comes from a patient room ahead of us along with a zombie moan. Oh, good grief. Not more of these things. Is the 'baby maker' one of Anselme Ernoul's associates trying to get revenge by deliberately attracting hunters here? Sam stops at the sound, not scared, but cautious. I reach across myself and grasp the handle of the katana, ready to draw the blade.

The door opens inward. A young man clumsily shoves it aside as he stumbles out into the corridor. He feels like a vampire, almost. Doesn't appear to be hostile. He staggers one step closer, raising a hand in a 'help me' reaching gesture. We don't get much of a chance to look at him before he disintegrates into ashes and loose bones.

"Uhh." Brady looks at me. "I think that was Manuel."

"You knew him?"

"Not totally sure. He kinda looked like him. You don't remember Manuel Cordero?"

"Name sounds familiar, but no."

Blix picks up one of the arm bones, sniffs it, then babbles.

Sam nods. "Blix says you're right. Manuel Cordero. He was too weak to survive."

The imp tosses the bone to the ground, chattering away.

"He said the sire keeps making himself weaker each time he creates a new vampire." Sam pauses to listen to Blix speak, then looks back at me. "The guy's probably too weak to even walk right now."

"Which guy?" I ask. "The sire?"

Blix nods.

Hmm. Professor Heath told me giving the Transference is draining, especially to a new vampire. What Blix is saying matches. Is it possible this guy is so stupid he's destroying himself to make tons of unstable vampires? If so, it rules out the idea of a survivor from

Anselme's group. What kind of moron is he? If it's true he's too weak to stand, I won't feel quite so stupid and reckless for allowing Sam to tag along with us. Honestly, sending him back across the mirror alone would be more dangerous. The mirrorverse is unpredictable and freaky. Sam's been near vampire fights before. I don't like it at all, but I trust him to not be an idiot. Also, leaving him alone in the bathroom long enough for Blix to lead us to this sire then go back to help Sam get home is equally scary. Anything could be in this place. I'd rather keep my li'l bro close so I can watch over him.

I continue going down the hall. Another baby vampire drags himself out of a room. He's early twenties, dressed like a street punk. Skinny, white, bald, and drained to being a skeleton in a skin bag. Looks like what would happen if they left someone hooked up to that machine in *The Princess Bride* too long. He snarls, pulling himself toward us.

"*Meem, woo, un.*" Blix ticks his fingers in a countdown from three to one.

The vampire convulses, then bursts into ash and bones.

"Umm… am I going to die like that?" asks Brady in a shaky voice.

"Mmm…" Blix ambles over to him and sniffs at his leg, then shrugs, making a hand tilt while muttering.

"He says maybe, but you've got more energy than the ones who popped, so you might be one of the first ones he made," says Sam.

"Which means you might not be unstable." I lightly kick the skull back into the room he came from. "Any vampires he tries to make now aren't viable."

We make our way down the hallway to an intersection, follow Blix to the right past an empty nurse's station, and along another corridor to a stairwell. Down three stories, we're in the basement. Oh, goody. More horror movie ambiance. Yay. What's scarier than an abandoned hospital at night? The *basement* of an abandoned hospital at night.

Sigh.

Tons of trash, broken small appliances, old oxygen tanks, and other junk lay scattered everywhere. Naked cinder block walls make it clear we are in a part of the building patients or the public aren't meant to see. Employees only. Bare cinder blocks have the unfortunate side effect of reminding me of a spooky documentary about an old tuberculosis sanatorium somewhere where they used an underground tunnel to transport the dead unobtrusively out of the building. The place is supposedly haunted.

I really shouldn't be afraid of ghosts, or abandoned hospitals, or tunnels, but the hairs on the back of my neck still stand on end. Luckily, this basement corridor doesn't appear dark to me. All the weird moaning and random noises aren't making me feel any less on edge. The sounds are probably coming from a bunch of half-conscious wretches littered around the building who can barely stand, couldn't give their own name if asked, and have no idea where they are or what they're even doing here.

How'd you end up in the House of Parliament? asks Dalton over our mental link.

Being nervous makes me highly susceptible to inappropriate laughter. Sam and Brady stare at me like I'm going insane... until I explain what made me laugh. Sam snickers while Brady appears clueless.

Near the end of the basement corridor, Blix stops by a pair of dark brown double doors decorated with a spray-painted goat—I think—skull above the words 'Hose of Satin.' Dayum. Those words lead to multiple different destinations on the highway of mockery humor. Seems a fitting palace for the kind of mental midget who'd burn himself out making an army of vampires less functional than mannequins.

Blix gestures both hands at it like a game show hostess indicating a prize.

"Okay. This could still be dangerous." I examine the doors. They appear to push open. "Sam, stay back and watch the hallway."

"Got it."

Brady moves a half step to his left. Not sure if he's hiding behind me or shielding Sam. Maybe both.

I give the doors a shove and step into a big rectangular room. Stacks of long cafeteria style tables stand on a bunch of large pushcarts the left. The right near corner is packed full of similar pushcarts holding tons of folding chairs. Dozens of loose mattresses litter the floor in the middle of the room, most likely dragged here by vampires or maybe homeless squatters. Human bones litter the area around the mattresses. I stop counting at twenty-two skulls. There's so much ash and dust everywhere, I think Pablo Escobar used this place as a packaging facility.

Three sofas are lined up along the innermost wall, probably relocated from waiting areas upstairs. A guy sits on the dark blue one in the center, leaned back in an extreme slouch, almost as if he's been shot in the head and left here. He's in full goth regalia, bushy black hair, pale white face and hands, black lipstick, big ass boots, leather bracers, trench coat. This dude is a portrait of heroin withdrawal at its most bleak. Or at least, what I imagine heroin withdrawal might look like. Don't take my word for it. I've never been around the stuff.

It takes the guy a second or three to realize we're here. He struggles to lift his head from the sofa back.

Feels like a vampire. He's so new no one's peeled the plastic off him yet.

"Connor?" asks Brady, stepping out from behind me. "Are you serious?"

"You know this guy?" I gesture my katana at him.

"Yeah. Connor Landry." Brady walks toward him, stepping over bones and mattresses. "We've been best friends since high school. Two months ago, he stopped showing up for band rehearsals. Never called. Never answered email. Just disappeared. None of us had any damn idea what happened to him."

"Kinda makes sense why," I say in a soft voice. "He got turned."

"And he bites me without a damn word or asking me if I wanted it?" Arms out to the sides, Brady shouts, "Dude, what the hell?"

I hurry after him, glancing back at Sam. Since there's only the one guy in here and he looks wasted as hell, I wave for my li'l bro to follow us inside so nothing sneaks up on him from the hallway.

"Hey, Bray," says Connor in a dazed voice. "What's up, man? Who's the chick?"

33

A SERIOUS CASE OF BURNOUT

Brady grabs Connor by the collar of his trench coat, drags him to his feet, and shakes him.

Connor dangles, lifeless as a full-size rag doll. It takes him a second to react, at which point, he waves his arms around, his glazed eyes seemingly unable to find the reason the world is rocking back and forth.

"Dude!" yells Brady. "You turned me into a fuckin' vampire? Why?"

I rush forward and sorta-gently separate the two. Connor sways to one side, staggering a few steps before finding his balance. His physical balance. Not talking about any sort of Buddhist stuff.

Blix warbles, making Sam chuckle.

"Yeah, you're right," whispers my brother. "He can barely stand."

This close to the guy, I *do* recognize him from school. One of the goth kids Brady used to hang out with, the guy who often wore plastic vampire teeth. I vaguely remember him being the 'weird, scary kid' no one picked on, afraid he carried a knife or would burn their house down days later. He's probably the one they called the cops on for 'having a gun,' whether or not whoever called sincerely believed he had one. I don't know much about him other than he dressed in black and acted creepy and distant. Connor starts laughing for no particular reason, a dry, whispery sort of noise one might expect from the mad scientist right before they tell someone we're too late to stop their plan.

"The hell's so funny, man?" Brady shoves him.

Conner stumbles away, swinging his arms like a broken marionette to keep from falling over. "Life is funny."

"Hey." I step up on him. "What the heck are you doing? Do you even realize what's happening?"

"Yeah. I'm sharing the most awesome thing in the world." Connor holds his arms out, teeters to his left, and almost falls again.

"He's drunk," mutters Brady.

"No, he's delirious. We can't get drunk... unless we feed from a mortal who's so ripped they can't even stand." I look back at Connor. "You're maybe a month into undeath. You're way too young to make any new vampires at all."

"Chill, bitch." Connor sways to the other side. "Being a vampire is perfection. It is beneath us to hide ourselves. We should be out there. Proud. Kings and queens of the night."

"You should try being king of standing unassisted first," mutters Sam.

Ugh. He can't be an Oblivare, but he sure sounds like one. I wonder if they can pass the Transference on in the usual way? Hate to think it might be like some of the folkloric stories about a simple bite transmitting the curse, though it could explain why the Oblivare tend to be kill feeders. A person can't gradually slide into vampirism over the course of a week after being bitten if they're dead from the feeding. Also, the whole 'three bites turns you into a vampire' thing as you gradually get 'sicker' is a total fabrication of medieval peasant folklore.

Obviously, I'm guessing here. No clue if Connor's sire is an Oblivare or merely an idiot for leaving him unattended.

"Listen to me." I snap my fingers in his face a few times. "Setting all these wild, new vampires loose on the city is going to make it dangerous for everyone else. We keep it secret because there are billions of mortals. If they took vampires seriously, we would be in *big* trouble."

"You sound just like them." Connor throws a wave at me. "Go away. You don't understand."

I point at him. "King of the night? At the moment, you're not even king of a nursing home. You can barely walk. Giving someone the Transference drains you, making you weaker. You're not allowing any recovery time before you do it again. You are new and weak. The vampires you make are even weaker. And now, everyone you try to turn into a vampire is so unstable they randomly die. Do you even see all the bones in here? You aren't 'sharing awesomeness' with anyone. You're killing them. You have to stop, if only so you don't destroy yourself."

He squints at me.

"Is that true or are you just making it up to scare him?" asks Brady.

"*Look* at him." I prod Connor in the shoulder with the sheathed katana. "The Transference takes a lot out of the sire. The older they are at the time, the faster they recover from it. It's a seriously bad idea to make a progeny at all before spending fifty years as a vampire—or so. Some people are tougher than others. He's what, maybe two months? I mean seriously. He smells new. And if *I* can smell someone's newness, they're really damn new."

Blix rambles.

"He said the guy is definitely killing himself making so many vamps," says Sam, a little closer than I'd like him to be.

I glance back. He's about a quarter of the way across the room, partially hiding behind a column. Okay, good Sam. Got some cover.

"Don't you see?" yells Connor, raising his hands. "This is *amazing.* It's all the stuff we pretended about in school. This shit is *real*? I never imagined. But I found it, Bray! I *found* it."

"Dude, listen to her." Brady grabs his arm. "You're gonna destroy yourself."

"Bray. Screw the band. Screw those dickhead parents of yours. This is the real thing. I had to share it with you first."

I grab Connor's arm to steady him and also make sure he doesn't try anything sudden. "How long have you been a vampire?"

He dazedly looks at me. "Uhh, I dunno. It's been like three or four weeks. Hooked up online with this chick who said she was the real deal. Went down to Cali to meet her." His head lolls back.

"Let me guess. She lives in Ventura," I mutter.

"Whoa." Connor stares in awe at me.

"Figures. They don't give a crap down there."

Brady glances at me. "What does that mean?"

"Lawless. Don't care about anything. Going to Ventura to get the Transference is the vampire equivalent of a Las Vegas wedding. Fast, easy, cheap, no questions... and a ton of regrets the next day." I shake my head. "She probably knew he'd go freakin' batshit and did it anyway for laughs."

"Bray, man. Who is this chick? She kinda looks like that girl in our class who got stabbed." Connor lifts his head to look at me again. "Didn't know she had a younger sister. Nice LL Bean sweater, kid." He chuckles. "Dude, since when do you date squares?"

I push Connor back a step. "One, we're not dating. Two, *dude!* Listen to what we're saying here. You are gonna kill yourself. Stop making vampires. Two of them exploded right in front of us as we walked in here. You aren't giving anyone 'awesome vampire powers,' you're turning them into macabre floor artwork."

Blix babbles.

"Sare, what does 'feng shui' mean?" asks Sam.

I furrow my brows. "I'll explain tomorrow."

"Okay. Whatever it is, Blix says this guy doesn't have any."

Connor swings his right arm up, pointing at me. He's leaning so far back he's going to fall at any second. "You have no idea what power means." He lurches forward, nearly falling. The stomp of his boot slamming concrete reports like a gunshot off the cinder block walls. "Bray, you bring this chick here to get the gift? She knows a lot of shit, man. We gotta keep her."

"Listen to me, you infuriating dumbass." I jab the tip of the katana scabbard into his chest. "I'm not saying vampires are bad. I'm saying you are too young to make more and you are making them so fast you are going to destroy yourself. You have to stop."

Connor staggers forward, falling into me like a drunk and grabbing my arms a little above my elbows. His slightly manic expression tells me he's about to escalate things.

"This doesn't need to turn into a fight," I say. "You're not in your right mind."

"Get off my sister or else," yells Sam.

"Heh." Connor leans left, peering past me. "Cute kid."

"He's adorable, but he's got a demon of a temper."

Sam blinks at me. "Okay, bad. Worse than one of Dad's jokes. No points."

"Ouch." I pretend to gasp, hurt. "How can you say that, Sam?"

"With my lips."

Connor squeezes my arms. "I'm not gonna fight. I'm only gonna throw you out of my domicile."

"Uhh, dude. 'Domicile?' Who talks like that?"

He grunts, trying unsuccessfully to pick me up.

I plant my right hand on his shoulder, holding him down. "Look, you're so weak you can barely stand. I'm not as harmless as I look." I extend my fangs. "Stop. Making. More. Vampires. I'm telling you this so you don't die. Don't force me to drag you out of here. There are quite a few other vampires in Seattle who'd really like to take their time explaining to you why what you're doing is a seriously bad idea."

Connor pauses, giving me an 'oh shit' look. "You're one of them."

"You're only figuring it out now? How many mortals do you know talk about stuff like the Transference?"

He points a shaky finger at me. "Like, you're one of *them,* trying to keep all the power for yourselves in the secret little vampire society. Don't want to share."

"It's totally not about that." I sigh. "You're not listening."

"It's a class reunion, Bray." Connor teeters back.

"Duuuude." Brady rubs his forehead. "I can't believe you freakin' killed me."

This guy has to be delirious from his condition. No one is this oblivious to reality. Not even people who think coal has a future. "Relax. And freakin' listen to what I'm trying to tell you."

"You won't stop me from…" Connor grabs my arms again, grunting. "Sharing. Awesome. Everyone." He grunts louder.

"Don't!" I shout. "You're gonna des—"

Connor bursts into a cloud of ash and flying bones, a hint of fire at the center of where his torso used to be. I raise my arms to shield my face from the heat. Brady screams, falling over backward to the ground—and passes out. Uhh, did he like faint at the sight of his best friend blowing up? No one usually screams *that* loud unless they're having their first Brazilian wax.

"I didn't do it!" yells Sam.

Blix chatters.

"He burned himself out." Sam jogs over to examine the bones. "Can I keep the skull? It has fangs."

"You want a fanged skull in your room?" I wince. "Not sure Mom would allow it in the house."

"She let you have Coralie's mummy in your room."

"Different situation entirely."

"How?" He sticks his arms out to the sides. "Dead bodies are dead bodies and this is only a skull."

"The difference between letting a friend sleep over for a few nights and taking a trophy that used to be a person." I exhale out my nose.

He gets this 'ohhhh' expression. "Okay. You're right. Forget it."

Agonized screams erupt from all over the hospital.

"Uh oh." Sam peers around. "We woke up the nest."

"Crap." I grab Brady and throw him over one shoulder. "Time to go, Sam. Run."

"Blix! Closest mirror!" yells my brother.

"*Aoba oda!*" chirps Blix before flying out the door.

Sam races after the imp. "He said 'on it'"

34

HERE COMES THE SUN

Y ou know those funny YouTube videos where some guy in an underdeveloped country loads up a tiny pickup truck or bicycle with a giant mound of cargo three times the size of the vehicle and it can barely move? Yeah, I feel like one of those little trucks flying while carrying Brady.

The dude isn't terribly big. I mean, as guys go, he's lanky. Still, he's heavier than Ashley and way heavier than any of the Littles. Giving my little brother rides around the lake had been fun. Lugging this dude across Seattle is the exact opposite of fun. Flying him is a constant state of straining myself to gain altitude, pausing to take a proverbial breath—which causes me to start plummeting—then straining again to recover lost altitude. There's a reason people use the phrase 'dead weight' to describe something burdensome.

I dragged Brady out a window of the abandoned hospital after making sure Sam got into a mirror. Blix is leading him home, so I'm not worried. The boy is almost *more* comfortable in the mirrorworld than Sophia—probably because it's way harder to scare him. Pretty sure the world on the other side feeds off our fears and nightmares. People who are timid or easily scared generally have a more dangerous time there. The mirrorverse really is a literal representation of a person potentially getting lost inside their own fears and insecurities, never to emerge.

So. My little brother is safe. I don't feel like *too* much of a dumbass for not sending him home immediately. The 'big bad monster' we went looking for ended up being a pretty useless moron. Given Connor's state when we found him, Sophia probably could have kicked his ass without using magic. Her magic really isn't terribly helpful in a fight. Except for moments of extreme emotion, it takes her anywhere from five minutes to several hours to cast any spells. Though, a localized change from day to night in a pinch is super handy, at least for me.

Right. Brady.

The unstable ones simply disintegrated, but Connor had some kind of fiery nonsense going on inside his core at the moment of destruction. When he exploded, Brady faceplanted. Seems there is some sort of effect if a sire is destroyed in front of the progeny. Maybe some kind of psychic feedback wave went off when their mind link broke that bought Brady a ticket for the express train to Derptown. Hopefully, it's round-trip passage.

I didn't want to leave Brady behind, mostly because he's not in a great emotional place right now. He needs to learn how to vampire properly, too. Also, from the sound of it, like twenty or more angry vampires had a serious need to find an ass to kick. I couldn't take the chance they recognized him as a 'brother' and didn't hurt him.

Fair bet all are Connor's progeny and probably would've been weak enough for me to cut down. But... this sweater is new. It's actually from Nordstrom, not LL Bean. Don't want to get blood all over it, and vampire blood is a total pain to wash out of fabric. Not quite as bad as demon blood, but still bad. They don't teach this stuff in home ec. Well, they don't really teach home ec at all anymore. Bleh.

I decided to take Brady to Aurelie's apartment for a few reasons. We're already close. Her balcony is high up, so no one will see me lugging a body around. This is also around the time Dad often wanders down to the kitchen for his nocturnal feeding. Not sure he'd approve of me dragging strange unconscious boys into the house this late. Mostly, I don't want to fly all the damn way home lugging this guy. I'm going to run out of steam halfway there and crash. Those movies where they have vampires swoop down out of the night sky, grab some random victim and carry them off like hawks taking gophers out of a field? Yeah. I have no damn idea where anyone got the idea. Adults are damn heavy. We don't have wings. Vampire flight is pure desire, magic, and giving the middle finger to physics.

Hmm. Okay, maybe Shadows are strong enough flyers to do it.

Eventually, Aurélie's building comes into view ahead. The promise of the chance to drop Brady somewhere safe gives me the energy to power ahead and stop bobbing up and down like a moth on LSD. I aim for the patio. For a high-rise, she's got a nicely sized porch area recessed into one wall. It's a pleasant spot for a cocktail party—I'd say barbecue but she's not the sort of person to host such things—also great for an emergency crash landing. My attempt to avoid shredding my new sweater results in a rather ungraceful belly flop by the door. Brady's kind enough to knock for me, using his head.

He's only burdensomely heavy to my flight ability. On the ground, I'm strong enough to maneuver him around like a six-foot pillow. Aurélie, her expression curious, comes gliding across the large living room toward the door. Her voluminous ball gown conceals the motion of her legs, making her look like a life-sized chess piece sliding at the push of an invisible hand.

She opens the door.

I carry Brady inside and lay him on the floor. Best to ask permission first before depositing strange, grungy vampires on expensive furniture.

Aurélie emits a soft giggle. "Oh, *cheri*, you do not need to bring snacks when you come to visit."

Wow, he must be seriously new if she can't tell he's a vampire. Say what? I raise an eyebrow at her. "He's not a snack. He's one of the new vampires from the idiot running around."

"This boy is no vampire." Aurélie puts a hand to my forehead as if checking for a fever.

"Umm." I shift my gaze to Brady, then crouch, pressing the back of my hand to his neck. Oh, wow. He's warm—sorta—and has a pulse. Sniff. "Holy crap. He smells like a mortal."

"Mortals typically do smell like mortals." Aurélie titters again. "Are you feeling all right, child?'

"*Putain de merde*," I mutter—sending her into full on laughter. I think the phrase is basically the same as WTF. She finds it cute when I try to use French, even if it is only a few phrases. "This guy was a vampire like twenty minutes ago."

"Are you sure?" She lowers a hand from her mouth, humor giving way to curiosity and a piercing stare, surely looking into my memory.

"A baby vampire, yeah, but still a vampire. He's been staying with a couple Lost Ones I sorta know for the past few days." I explain when I first spotted him out of his mind from hunger, chasing a poor security guard across a cargo lot like a starving feral barn cat pursuing the first mouse he's seen in a week.

Aurélie crouches—a true feat of agility in that gown—and lifts Brady's face by a palm under one cheek. "This boy was so weak and so new when his sire suffered permanent destruction, the Transference broke." She pushes his lip up as if examining the teeth of a horse. "*Pas de crocs.*"

"Umm."

"No fangs." She lowers his head to rest on the carpet, then stands. "There exists a small window of opportunity wherein a newly made vampire may be deprived of the gift if the sire is destroyed."

I blink. "Whoa. Professor Heath said something about the bones not fully changing. This other vamp blew up at a gas station. Fell apart into ash and bones." I describe how the bones appeared partially white and partially yellowed and ancient.

"Perhaps. I am no doctor. It may be related. Years ago, some mortals considered it a chance to 'save someone from the curse.'" She mutes a giggle. "Curse, indeed."

"Yeah, well." I shrug. "People are usually afraid of what they don't understand. Like this guy. He kept moping about missing the sun. Guess it's not a problem for him anymore."

"*Oui.*"

"Hmm. Oh, wow. Do you think all the vampires Connor made went back to being mortal?"

Aurélie snaps her fan open and waves it at herself. "It is difficult to say without more information. Those who are too unstable likely fell to pieces from the spiritual shockwave. It is as likely they exist no more as became mortal."

Maybe all the screaming we heard came from non-viable vampires writhing in agony before disintegrating. Brady reverted to mortal and kissed the floor so fast he had no time to do much more than scream. He's also the first one Connor turned. Best friends indeed. Hell, I think vampire life is amazing and you don't see me rushing to bite Ashley and Michelle. Either one of them would be super pissed at me if I did it to them out of the blue without even asking first. Can't fault Brady being angry with Connor, and more than a little hurt.

Okay, now I feel like Sophia. A big chicken. We didn't need to panic run out of the hospital.

"Do not feel sorrow, *cheri*." Aurélie puts an arm around me. "The Transference only breaks if the progeny loses their mortality to exsanguination. In your case, you would 'ave been alive again for only a few seconds before succumbing to your wound."

"Oh, yeah, well." I smile at her. "Not going there. I wasn't even thinking about being jealous or anything. I'm happy as is. Besides, the idea of getting my mortality back would require killing Dalton, which isn't cool. Kinda think I'm past my sell-by date, anyway."

Aurélie laughs. "*Oui*, it 'as to 'appen before a month passes... give or take a week or two depending on bloodline. Another reason you should not feel sorrow. It is impossible for you to become mortal again."

"Honestly. I'm cool. Happy as is." I stretch my arms, working out a few sore spots from flying Brady around. "So, what do we do with him?"

"'E should go to the 'ospital. Preferably one which is not abandoned. The boy is low on blood." Aurélie glances off across the room, staring at the wall.

She's summoning one of her employees. Neat trick using telepathy on someone not in line of sight. No idea if it's a 'standard' vampire ability I'll get with age or if it's an Old Guard thing, but whatever. Any new abilities I develop are simply icing on an already awesome cake. Won't bother me either way. Turning into a raven would be pretty damn cool, but it's not something I *need*. Ladonna can't fly otherwise. As cool as shapeshifting into a bird is, having to get naked every time I wanted to fly would totally stink. Probably not as big a deal living out in the wilderness like pagans, but in a city? Yeah, no thanks.

A large, bodyguard type guy in a black suit walks in. He nods respectfully at Aurélie before collecting Brady from the floor and holding him upright so she can stare into his eyes. Yeah, Brady is not going to remember anything about vampires. Expected that. Better for everyone involved. Maybe she'll let him recall some manner of near-death experience so he still wants to mend bridges with his parents. Got a feeling he's likely to develop an aversion to all things morbid or creepy.

Poor guy wanted to see the sun again real bad. Seems he got his wish after all. Maybe Aurélie will let him quasi-remember the vampire stuff but turn it into a nightmare... and do the whole 'the names and faces of the Innocent have been changed' deal so he doesn't remember me being a vampire. Doesn't matter if he thinks he dreamed Connor becoming an undead. The guy is genuinely gone for good. As far as the real world is concerned, he's a missing person who will never be found. Easy for Brady to think his mind reacted to the trauma of his best friend disappearing by having a nightmare about vampires. I mean, these guys pretended to be vampires all four years of high school.

Aurélie gives me side eye and a sly smile. Yeah, she's totally doing that.

Weird. I wonder if his regret for being turned had anything to do with him becoming mortal again? Like, if he loved being a vampire, would the gift have been stolen from him upon Connor's death? Bleh. I don't really want to waste time thinking about pointless what-ifs.

I'm done with philosophy class.

35

DUST TO... SPARKLES?

The flight home is awesome.

Primarily because I'm not carrying a dude. Another reason is, I don't see a giant raven following me. She might be a psycho bitch trying to destroy society, but Ladonna was kinda cool. Like, a villain from a book or movie you can't help but respect. It wouldn't really have bothered me if Aziz squished her, but I'm also not upset she escaped. She's evil in a way other vampires aren't, so it probably *should* bother me she's still out there. We, at least, have human souls. Oblivare are made from purple glowing goop in a jar. A spectral hijacker stealing a corpse. Wonder what the woman whose body she stole had been like?

It's maybe an hour and a half before sunrise at this point. Time for a nice, relaxing bath.

A debate about which scent of bath bomb to use consumes the last few minutes of the flight home. I land on the back deck, slip inside to the kitchen, and pause at the smell of burnt hair. What the heck? It's strongest near the microwave. Probably happened a couple days ago... but my nose is extremely sensitive while online. Worried, I open the door. Thankfully, the microwave does not contain the charred corpse of a small furry animal. Strange something hairy burned in the micro and no one said anything. I'm about to dismiss it as a weird Blix-ism when I notice the faint outline of bare feet burned into the floor. Based on size, they can only be Dad's. Their position indicates the microwave oven probably expressed its discontent about something in an electrical manner. Eep!

I hurry upstairs to the parents' room. The same smell of burning hair is present. It's fairly weak, again suggesting it's more in the pillow than my father's hair. The 'rents are asleep and don't look hurt. Dad's hair's standing on end, doing an impression of a koosh, the world's absolute worst case of static electricity. I creep over to take a closer look. Don't see a burn. No blood. No damage. An ozone smell hangs in the air near his head. Hmm. Safe to say something weird happened. If it occurred days ago and his hair is *still* standing up, it sounds like Sophia lost control of a spell again.

Oh well. They don't appear upset, so it must not have been bad. I head out to the hall and poke my head into Sam's room to check on him. He's in bed, safe and sound. Blix is sprawled out on the bed next to him, asleep as well. Good. Just to be thorough, I check on the girls. Sierra and Sophia are not exactly where they're supposed to be. Sierra's in Sophia's bed with her. Based on the way Soph is clinging to her, she probably had a nightmare.

Wow. Sierra willingly sharing the bed? Something happened. I will need to talk to them tomorrow.

Klepto perks up to look at me. I wave at her.

"Mew," says the kitten in her best try at whispering.

The noise is so tiny and cute I almost fail to resist the urge to go over and squeeze her.

Satisfied the kids are okay, I head downstairs to stash the katana in my closet and get undressed. A big towel wrap is enough for a stealthy trip back upstairs to the bathroom. Oh, and I grab a blueberry dream bath bomb. Change of pace.

Once in the bathroom, I close and lock the door, then pull the shower curtain aside.

The tub glimmers and sparkles from a coating of... red glitter? What the hell? Okay, either the world's most *fabulous* vampire spontaneously self-destructed in our bathtub, or Sophia's up to something. I swipe a finger at the stuff. Feels gritty rubbed between my fingertips. Up close, it looks like red salt. Tiny crystals, like rubies.

I recall overhearing two cops talking about a $250,000 ruby stolen from somewhere in the area.

Oh em gee.

Seriously?

Nah. Can't be.

Swipe. Yeah. Definitely ruby dust all over the inside of our bathtub. What the hell happened here? This certainly explains what's been bothering Sophia lately. It's mildly worrisome she's been acting only as guilty as she'd have been if she forgot to do some minor chore. Deliberate theft? The girl would never... she'd freak out if she accidentally stole a candy bar. How on Earth did she mentally handle theft this major. Maybe the kitten thought it pretty and she merely destroyed the evidence? No... she'd have asked Klepto to put it back. Gonna go out on a limb here and make a wild assumption my kid sister doesn't have a giant gem smashing machine under her bed. This reeks of magic. It's almost impossible for me to believe, but it sure looks like Sophia intentionally had some role in the theft of a serious gemstone.

Suppose I could feel guilty for corrupting my family. I could ignore this. Or... find it hilarious a kitten stole a giant ruby from a guy with more money than some entire countries. Hmm. How about a little of everything?

Screw it.

I rinse the ruby residue down the drain and run myself a bath.

36

SIERRA'S GONE EXTRA

Once I'm out of bed the next afternoon, I throw on a shirt and shorts, then head upstairs.

As the guy on that old-ass television show says, Sophia, you got some 'splainin' ta do. I find the girls, plus Nicole, Megan, and Priya, hanging out in the living room. Mom used to often complain at the Littles for not being more like me. Meaning, at their age, Ashley and I tended to hang out at her house about sixty to seventy percent of the time, or be quiet in my room. Sophia and Sam adore inviting their friends here. Ever since I 'died,' Mom's never once complained about the kids always being here.

No surprise they're indoors today. It's so damn rainy and gloomy outside, I'm nearly online at three in the afternoon standing in the living room. Not *quite* online. It's like a switch one millimeter from contact where a spark occasionally jumps across.

"Soph? Sierra? Can I borrow you two for a minute?" I keep going past the living room to the dining room. It's darker in there already. Once I close the curtains, I'm online as long as I stay tucked back at the end behind the table, away from the alcove leading to the kitchen or living room.

The girls trail in. Sierra's still smiling. Sophia stares at the floor, trudging like a convict making her way to the gallows.

"Relax, Soph," I say. "No one's in trouble."

It occurs to me Sierra is giving off noticeable energy. The same way I can sense a vampire or felt an unusual presence around that werewolf I met in London, Ron Haddon, something else is all over her. I lean close to sniff at her. Still mortal. She has an obvious pulse in the side of her neck.

"If you bite me, I am gonna kick your ass." Sierra grins.

Normally, two plus two equals four, but this is my family. Weird ruby residue in the bathtub plus crazy microwave activity plus Sierra radiating energy should point to the logical conclusion something magic happened. I don't trust anything in my life to be so straightforward.

"Why is Sierra radioactive?" I ask.

"Umm, what?" She shoots a look at Sophia. "You didn't say anything about radioactivity."

Sophia gasps.

"Not literal radioactivity," I say, lowering my voice. "She feels paranormal. Not a vampire, not a werewolf… something weird."

"She's always been weird." Sophia puts on a totally unconvincing smile. "She reached critical mass of weird so now you can smell it."

In my family, only one person has the capability of lying with a straight face: Mom. No, this isn't a lawyer joke. Also no, my mother doesn't lie for her job. She tells selective truths. Sierra sorta inherited Mom's ability to play truth games. She can lie about as well as any average person. My Dad's horrible at deceit. He struggles to even surprise us with gifts, gets this 'aww shucks' face every time he's not being truthful. He also loves seeing us happy and can't bear the wait of keeping a surprise hidden for more than a day, so usually reveals it early. Sophia and I can't lie to save our lives. My brother *could* lie. He's so deadpan all the time it would be easy for him. The boy simply doesn't bother. Somewhere in his brain, he calculates the net effort required to create and maintain a lie exceeds the cost of being immediately truthful. In fact, the only untruths I've ever seen from him are due to needing to keep vampires and demons secret.

Which goes back to the cost/reward comparison.

Now what Sophia did here isn't even her attempt to sincerely lie. The smile, the misdirection to Sierra's weirdness—which is a well-documented phenomenon—comes off entirely as a joke hoping to lessen the impact of whatever badness she expects to follow. It's the cute defense. It's really hard to be angry at her sometimes. And I'm far from angry at her. Merely confused.

Sierra does not call her a butthead. Red flag.

"You two conspired to do something together."

"Yeah." Sierra doesn't look down. White flag. Uh oh. Serious. "She saved my life."

Blink.

Sophia glances at the living room where the friends wait. "Sare, just look in my head. It's faster and no one can overhear."

"Okay."

"It's light out, duh," whispers Sierra.

"Her eyes went red for a sec. It's dark enough in here." Sophia looks up, allowing me easy eye contact.

And wow. She enchanted Sierra to not need vampire blood. Dead at fifteen because future me said no more blood. Well, undead at fifteen. Sophia did send the cat to get a ruby, but at least she made sure to take it from someone who wouldn't even notice the loss of the money. She feels guilty about stealing but no more so than she'd be upset by taking a handful of M&Ms from Sierra without asking. Honestly, the comparison's about the same. Whoever owned the ruby could replace it as easily as most people could obtain a pack of M&Ms. She didn't personally benefit from the theft beyond getting to keep her sister alive and safe.

And holy crap! She got a portal to work. Mom's going to freak. Good thing Sophia's usually a total angel. How does a parent ground a kid by taking their car keys away when they can go anywhere on Earth via their closet? Another good thing: Sophia's not likely to go randomly roaming strange places alone. She scares easy and she's the sort of person who could spend all day every day at home and not mind. If wanderlust could exist as a negative value, she has it. Also, the bed sharing last night makes sense. Soph's been having nightmares every night since they went to the freaky forest and terrifying house. Oh, wow... another Shadow. But yeah, ugh. The blood driving her crazy.

"I was afraid of that." I pull the girls into a squish hug. "It becoming addictive, I mean."

Sierra bounces on her toes. "It worked. So awesome!" Her enthusiasm fades to seriousness. "I was scared. Like, really scared. She fixed it."

"Hey, nothing wrong with being scared. Everyone gets scared." I pat her on the back, then relax the hug.

"I was super, super careful. Coralie said nothing bad would happen to her because of the magic." Sophia slouches, relieved she no longer has to keep what she did a secret.

"You haven't told Sierra the rest of what she said." I wink at her.

Sierra stares at her. "Spill."

Sophia lets out a long, slow breath. "Coralie said because I used Sarah's hair in the spell and based the effect on a boost from a vampire, it, umm... might take you a little longer to grow up."

Sierra's eyebrows become a flat line. "Uhh, what?"

"Sorry." Sophia winces. "It's from the protection part. Apparently, the spell considers growing up an 'attack' on your body. There's a chance you might grow up slow. You're not stuck like a vampire at twelve... but you might take like five years to turn thirteen."

Sierra gives me this 'help' look.

"It's also just a chance. Might not even do it." Sophia bites her lip. "We won't really know for a while until it's obvious you should be taller and aren't."

"Hey, not the end of the world." I press my knuckles into Sierra's shoulder and give a little shove. "Every class has a runt. This kid Lee I graduated with was eighteen but looked younger than you are. He was really small. You could pass for a short high school student, except for the obvious."

"What obvious?" Sierra resumes glaring.

"No curves. You have the shape of a tween. Nothing baggy clothes can't fix if you're stuck like this in high school."

Sierra's expression goes mixed. "Does it mean I'm gonna live longer than I ought to?"

"Maybe." Sophia shrugs. "Coralie didn't say you're *definitely* aging slow. Just a chance. But, yeah if you are, you'll live a long time."

Sierra fidgets at her shirt. "Whatever. Boys can wait. Easy trade for getting a couple more decades to live."

"Umm, if it worked, it's like a five to one thing." Sophia whistles innocently. "You might live to 400."

Sierra grabs Sophia by the collar in both hands. "No way. If that's gonna happen, you better enchant yourself, too. Don't wanna watch you die and still have over 300 years left to miss you."

Aww. I tear up.

"Working on it," rasps Sophia. "Need air."

Sierra lets go. "What about Sam?"

"Oh, he's already gonna live as long as he wants. I dunno the details, but he made a deal with Olmaz because he didn't want Sarah to be lonely."

Sierra and I gawk at her.

"He's going to grow up." Sophia shrugs. "Like I said, I don't know all the details."

"Umm." Sierra looks at me. "So, if this really happens, how am I going to deal with it at school?"

I pat her on the shoulder. "Nothing will be noticeable until at least mid to late high school. Just be the short kid. If anyone gives you grief, I'll mind-zap them to leave you alone."

Sierra folds her arms. "You won't have to. No one's going to bully me."

"At least be diplomatic, okay? Mom will be mad if you get expelled for breaking too many arms."

She laughs.

The doorbell rings.

"Okay. Good meeting. Just…" I poke Sophia in the side. "Mind the grand larceny, okay?"

"Totally." She traces an X over her chest. "Only did it 'cause Sierra's life."

I nod.

The girls return to their friends. I get the door. It's Hunter. Ooh, yeah. Date time.

THE LAST BOYFRIEND

W e're in Hunter's old Buick, driving to our backup date plan, a haunted mansion tour.

It's freakin' pouring, so going for a nature hike is off the table. Talk about ambiance, taking a tour of a giant haunted house out in the countryside during a gloomy monsoon of a rainstorm. Maybe I could get a 'job' as a spirit medium or a debunker of supposedly-but-not-really haunted places. Nah. Who would pay for that?

There's something about driving in a pounding rainstorm. It's not at all soothing, but at least I'm not terrified. It's dark enough for me to temporarily redirect power from my sun resistance to general vampire toughness in the event of a crash and not burn. My only worry is Hunter getting hurt. Fortunately, he's driving like my Dad. Then again, this is a twelve-year-old Buick. Even if he wanted to drive like a typical guy his age, he couldn't. Most gas pedals tell the car to go. This gas pedal asks nicely.

"I've been trying to figure out if I should do something for our dating anniversary," says Hunter.

"It's fine. I'm not one of those neurotic girls who makes a big deal out of one-month, three-month, and six-month dating anniversaries.

If you ask me, girls who do that are deeply insecure... or shocked a relationship lasted that long."

He laughs.

"It's sweet if you want to do something special. Not going to complain, but don't worry about me being upset if you don't."

"Okay. Figured I'd take you somewhere like a ballet or theater production, but you're not really into either one of those."

"Neither are you."

"True. What I'm into doesn't matter when trying to do something nice for you. If you like something, I'll like it—or at least tolerate it."

My turn to laugh. "If you do something for me, I adore it no matter what day of the year it is."

He takes my hand.

"I love holding hands with you, but we're driving in a downpour. Might want to keep it on the wheel."

"We're at a red light."

I blink. "Oh. So we are."

He chuckles. "You are so cute when you're confused."

"I'm not confused. I'm in deep thought."

"Oh?" He leans over to kiss me. The light goes green the instant our lips touch. He keeps kissing me for a few seconds until the people behind us honk. "What are you thinking about?"

I stay quiet for a moment as we start driving again. It's been on my mind for a while. Never quite got around to saying it to him. Probably should. "No matter what happened, you were going to be my last boyfriend, anyway."

"Uhh, what do you mean?"

"Well, after Scott, I wasn't sure I ever wanted to take the chance again."

Hunter nods. "Understandable."

"Stupid right? Not like I could be murdered a second time." I puff at a strand of hair over my face.

He emits a forced chuckle. My being a vampire doesn't bother him at all. The idea of me almost dying is what bothers him.

"I mean, after we met in the admissions office, I pretty much made up my mind you'd be the last boyfriend. It would either work or not. If things with you went bad, I'd probably never bother with boys again. Things with you are *not* bad, so we probably would've ended up spending the rest of our lives together, which also means no more boyfriends for me."

"But… you're gonna live longer than me. Like, forever."

"Yep." I lean against him. "When I lose you, I'm not going to want to go through it all again. Not sure I will ever get over the loss. I'm never going to have with anyone else what I have with you."

He's quiet for a while. The drumming of rain on the car feels like a military march at a state funeral. The moment's gone from romantic to maudlin. My head fills with images of me pretending to be a surprise granddaughter at Hunter's funeral, surrounded by… well, no one. We wouldn't have kids. Maybe an old man version of Ronan would be there. The Littles, too. My brain turns Sophia and Sierra into a pair of eternal twelve-year-olds, creepy like those kids in *The Shining*. Sam's a dapper twenty-something with Blix perched on his shoulder. Heh. Ugh, my life.

"Do you think I should become a vampire?" asks Hunter.

I shrug one shoulder. "Can't make that decision for you. It's all you."

"But how do you feel about it?"

"Umm. Both options suck in their own way. Either you get old and die, or you die and don't get old."

"Hah." He wags his eyebrows attempting to drive faster, but the car kinda shrugs in response. "What's that thing about live fast, die young, leave a good-looking corpse?"

"Ugh. Pretentious douchebaggery. Besides, haven't you seen vampire movies? If a vampire falls in love with a mortal, the one who isn't a vampire *always* gets turned into a vampire, too. Feels cliché."

"Oh. Well, that's it then. I'd so hate to be a cliché." He snickers. "Gotta avoid *that* at all costs."

I flash a sly grin. "Do you really want to put your mother and Ronan through the wringer?"

"Would they have to know? Who says we need to tell them anything or fake a public death?"

"You want to do the same thing I did." I cringe. "It's pretty hard to hide. Don't you want kids?"

"I dunno. Ronan could carry on the family. And honestly… if our dad is any judge of who we are genetically, maybe it's not the worst thing in the world for our line to stop."

"Hunter, you are nothing like him. And neither is Ronan."

"Sorry." He looks down.

"Hey. Eyes on the road. And what are you apologizing for?"

"Heh." He leans back, clicking the wipers up a notch to go faster. "Sorry for making you think about this stuff. It's obviously upsetting you."

"Eh. It's okay. Both choices, like I said, suck."

Hunter wags his eyebrows at me. "Vampirism sucks more."

I groan. "You have been spending entirely too much time around my dad."

He laughs.

I point at the road ahead. "Drive."

"Yes, ma'am."

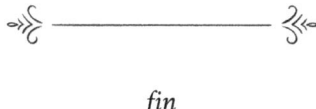

fin

ACKNOWLEDGMENTS

Thank you for reading Vampire Innocent book 12! Sarah and the Littles will return in book 13.

Additional thanks to Lee Sheridan for editing and Alexandria Thompson for the cover and interior art.

ABOUT THE AUTHOR

Originally from South Amboy NJ, Matthew has been creating science fiction and fantasy worlds for most of his reasoning life. Since 1996, he has developed the "Divergent Fates" world, in which *Division Zero, Virtual Immortality, The Awakened Series, The Harmony Paradox, and the Daughter of Mars series* take place. Along with being an editor at Curiosity Quills press, he has worked in IT and technical support.

Matthew is an avid gamer, a recovered WoW addict, Gamemaster for two custom RPG systems, and a fan of anime, British humour, and intellectual science fiction that questions the nature of reality, life, and what happens after it.

He is also fond of cats.

Visit me online at:
    Facebook: https://www.facebook.com/MatthewSCoxAuthor
    Pinterest: https://www.pinterest.com/matthewcox10420/
    Goodreads: https://www.goodreads.com/author/show/7712730.
Matthew_S_Cox
    Email: mcox2112@gmail.com

OTHER BOOKS BY MATTHEW S. COX

Divergent Fates Universe Novels

Division Zero series

- Division Zero
- Lex De Mortuis
- Thrall
- Guardian
- Harbinger
- The Shadow Fixer
- Neuroshock

The Awakened series

- Prophet of the Badlands
- Archon's Queen
- Grey Ronin
- Daughter of Ash
- Zero Rogue
- Angel Descended

Daughter of Mars series

- The Hand of Raziel
- Araphel
- Ghost Black

Virtual Immortality series

- Virtual Immortality
- The Harmony Paradox

Prophet of the Badlands Series

- Prophet's Journey
- Prophet's Mercy

Divergent Fates Anthology

(Fiction Novels - Adult)
The Roadhouse Chronicles Series

- One More Run
- The Redeemed
- Dead Man's Number

Faded Skies series

- Heir Ascendant
- Ascendant Unrest
- Ascendant Revolution

Temporal Armistice Series

- Nascent Shadow
- The Shadow Collector
- The Gate to Oblivion
- The Queen of Discord
- The Burning Alchemist

Vampire Innocent series

- A Nighttime of Forever
- A Beginner's Guide to Fangs
- The Artist of Ruin

- The Last Family Road Trip
- The Phantom Oracle
- How Not to Summon Demons
- Ordinary Problems of a College Vampire
- A Vampire's Guide to Surviving Holidays
- An Introduction to Paranormal Diplomacy
- A Vampire's Guide to Adulting
- How to Stop a Vampire War in Six Easy Steps
- Ancient Vampire Death Cults and Other Annoyances
- Hunting Vampires for Fun and Profit
- A String of Seriously Unlucky Events
- The Summer of Completely Usual Strangeness
- Demonic Crisis Management for the Modern Vampire

Standalones

- Wayfarer: AV494
- Axillon99
- Chiaroscuro: The Mouse and the Candle
- The Spirits of Six Minstrel Run
- Sophie's Light
- The Far Side of Promise anthology
- Operation: Chimera (with Tony Healey)
- The Dysfunctional Conspiracy (with Christopher Veltmann)
- Of Myth and Shadow
- The Girl Who Found the Sun

Winter Solstice series (with J.R. Rain)

- Convergence
- Containment
- Catalyst
- Catacombs

Alexis Silver series (with J.R. Rain)

- Silver Light
- Deep Silver
- Silver Quarrel
- Silver Crucible
- Silver Heart

Samantha Moon Origins series (with J.R. Rain)

- New Moon Rising
- Moon Mourning
- Haunted Moon

Vampire For Hire series (with J.R. Rain)

- Moon Master
- Dead Moon
- Lost Moon
- Vampire Destiny
- Infinite Moon
- Vampire Empress
- Moon Elder
- Wicked Moon
- Moon Blade

Maddy Wimsey series (with J.R. Rain)

- The Devil's Eye
- The Drifting Gloom
- Dark Mercy
- Primal Wrath

Samantha Moon Case Files series (with J.R. Rain)

- Blood Moon

Immortal Operative (with J.R. Rain)

- Broken Ice
- Broken Wing

Four Elements series (with J.R. Rain)

- The Elementalist
- The Black Rose
- The Wakefield Curse

Witches series (with J.R. Rain)

- The Witch and the Hangman

Zeb Clemens series (with J.R. Rain)

- The Beast of Devil's Creek
- Wanted: Undead or Alive

Young Adult Novels

The Eldritch Heart Series

- The Eldritch Heart
- The Cursed Crown
- The Sapphire Soul

Evergreen Series

- Evergreen
- The World That Remains

- The Lucky Ones
- Nuclear Summer
- The Nuclear Frontier
- The World We Make
- The Threat Unseen

Progenitor Series

- Out of Sight
- Out of Mind

Diary of a Teenage Fey

(Short story series)

- Elder Horror
- The Hag of Barrow Falls
- Babysitter's Nightmare
- Lharakki
- Bauble for a Soul
- Simulacrum
- Amorphous
- Manticore

Standalones

- Caller 107
- The Summer the World Ended
- Nine Candles of Deepest Black
- The Forest Beyond the Earth

Middle Grade Novels

The Adventures of Ubergirl series

- My Dad is a Mad Scientist
- Aliens Ate My Homework
- The End of all Halloweens
- Dr. Infinity and the Soul Smasher

Tales of Widowswood series

- Emma and the Banderwigh
- Emma and the Silk Thieves
- Emma and the Silverbell Faeries
- Emma and the Elixir of Madness
- Emma and the Weeping Spirit

Standalones

- Citadel: The Concordant Sequence
- The Cursed Codex
- The Menagerie of Jenkins Bailey